P9-AZX-047

THE BEST AMERICAN

NONREQUIRED
READING
2005

THE BEST AMERICAN

NONREQUIRED
READING
2005

EDITED BY

DAVE EGGERS

INTRODUCTION BY

BECK

HOUGHTON MIFFLIN COMPANY

BOSTON ▪ NEW YORK

2005

Visit our Web site: www.houghtonmifflinbooks.com.

ISSN: 1539-316x
ISBN-13: 978-0-618-57047-8   ISBN-10: 0-618-57047-0
ISBN-13: 978-0-618-57048-5 (pbk.)   ISBN-10: 0-618-57048-9 (pbk.)

Printed in the United States of America

VB 10 9 8 7 6 5 4 3 2 1

CONTENTS

Contents / ix

FOREWORD

THIS COLLECTION, as has been the case in past years, was selected in large part by a group of high school students from the
Bay Area, which is in California and near San Francisco. As always, the committee — this year comprising twelve members, including one named Todd — met once a week over the course of a
year. During those meetings and on their own time, they pored
over pretty much every weekly, monthly, and quarterly magazine,
every self-published chapbook, every comic book and poorly sta-
pled zine published and findable in the United States. In these periodicals, the students looked for things they liked, and their pa-
rameters were, as always, wide; this collection, unlike the other
Best Americans — which Todd insists are never as Best as this
one — can draw from any medium or genre: fiction, journalism,
essay, cartoon, or any combination thereof. The only requirements
are that the selections be engaging, somewhat direct in approach,
have something to say about the world at the moment, and that
they not be too long or about the relationship problems of wealthy
people in Manhattan. With that in mind, we try to focus on lesser-
known writers and periodicals, and mix them with some of the
better-known examples in each category. The process, such as it is,
usually works out very well.

But this year we had some problems. We had, actually, one
problem, which was that a few things everyone liked a great deal,
and which we felt added something very good to the mix, did
not look right in alphabetical order amid all the other works of
prose. We felt that we were dressing up certain pieces in clothes
they would not normally wear. We were sending the Andorra to
the G-8.

Case in point: There is a man named Joe Sayers who self-publishes chapbooks of his cartoons. One day Felicia, one of the committee members, brought in one of these booklets, called "Passing Periods." It was one of the funniest things we'd ever seen, we thought. We chose a bunch of the cartoons for the collection, and then, when we saw them all laid out — two three-panel cartoons per page! — they were no longer funny. The pressure put on these cartoons, which we'd seen in a booklet the size of a thumb, was too great.

It's a strange thing. Context always, always plays a part in how something is read, and until we find a solution to this problem — and we have some top people working on it — we have to deal with it in sneaky ways. One such sneaky way is by slipping such things in unexpectedly, and without great fanfare.

See? You loved that cartoon more than your mother, and why? Because we snuck up on you with it. Here's another:

You are in love with Joe Sayers. You are Googling Joe Sayers. But if you had seen these cartoons in the body of this book, you might have been very angry with Joe Sayers and with the makers of this book. There was another such cartoon, by Anders Nilsen:

the mediocrity principle

See? We got you again. We caught you unawares, and now you are nominating Mr. Nilsen for NEA grants, which, if you are reading this after 2005, do not, effectively, exist.

For the rest of these introductory pages, let's follow this plan:

— We'll have some more Joe Sayers

— Then we'll have some of the short-short stories I've been adding to these introductions as space-fillers and to satisfy the Republicans and the Swedes

— After that, we'll have some information about 826 Valencia, followed by six pages about Captain Rick, who is a menace and we'll explain why

— Finally, we'll have bios of the students who selected the works in this book and bear no responsibility for this introduction. When it was written, they were on summer vacation.

Very Short Story No. 1: *Also He Was Wearing a Fila Sweatsuit*

"I'll say goodbye before I leave," Jim said. "No need," said Marcus. "Let's just say goodbye now. You're leaving so early, and I'll be asleep." "That's OK," Jim said. "I'll just nudge you awake for a second and say bye. No big deal." "Well," said Marcus, "I'll be sad to see you leave, but really, I'd rather not be woken up. It's midnight now, and I gotta get to sleep, so I'll just say bye now. It was great having you here, and I'll see you next time I'm in town. Hope the couch wasn't too uncomfortable." "No, no, buster-boy. I'll see you in the morning. I'll just give you a quick goodbye punch on the shoulder. It's something I like doing, so I'll see you then. Afterward, you can go back to sleep if you want to." "Oh boy, Jim," Marcus said. "It really sounds great, that goodbye punch you're talking about, but you know, I really love my sleep to be sorta of the uninterrupted kind, and besides, I just had a booster shot, and man, it'd hurt like a mother to have you punching my shoulder there, especially in the cruel light of morning. So anyway, I guess we'll say farewell here, while we're both lucid and all. Farewell, goodbye, et cetera. It's been good." "No-no-no. No! No. No. I can't let you off that easy; you mean too much to me. What is this, Russia? No, I insist, as a good guest, on thanking you properly. I'll just whisper —" "Listen, shitwipe. If you dare to even turn the knob on my door, I'm gonna hack you to death with an ax made from your own tibia and fragments of your skull. I'm gonna —" "Well then. Good night, Dad." "Yeah. Good night. Come back soon, son. Any time at all."

Very Short Story No. 2: *Accident*

You all get out of your cars. You are alone in yours, and there are three teenagers in theirs, an older Camaro in new condition. The accident was your fault and you go over to tell them this. Walking to their car, which you have ruined, it occurs to you that if the three teenagers are angry teenagers, this encounter could be very unpleasant. You pulled into an intersection, obstructing them, and their car hit yours. They have every right to be upset, or livid, or even contemplating violence. As you approach, you see that their driver's-side door won't open. The driver pushes against it, and you are reminded of scenes where drivers are stuck in submerged cars. Soon they all exit through the passenger-side door and walk around the Camaro, inspecting the damage. "Just bought this today," the driver says. He is eighteen, blond, average in all ways. "Today?" you ask. You are a bad person, you think. You also think: What a strange car for a teenager to buy in 2005. "Yeah, today," he says, then sighs. You tell him that you are sorry. That you are so, so sorry. That it was your fault and you will cover all costs. You exchange insurance information, and you find yourself, minute by minute, evermore thankful that none of these teenagers has punched you, or even made a remark about your being drunk or blind, which you are not. You become more friendly with all of them, and you realize that you are much more connected to them, particularly to the driver, than possible in perhaps any other way. You have done him and his friends harm, you jeopardized their health, and now you are so close you feel like you share a heart. The driver knows your name and you know his, and you almost killed him and because you got so close but didn't, you want to fall on him, weeping, because you are so lonely, so lonely always, and all contact is contact, and all contact makes us so grateful we want to cry and dance and cry and cry. In a moment of clarity you finally understand why boxers, who want so badly to hurt each other, can rest their heads on the shoulders of their opponent, can lean against one another like tired lovers, so thankful for a moment of rest.

Very Short Story No. 3: *Georgia Is Lost*

Rodney is looking for his daughter. He's looking desperately for his daughter, Georgia, who is tiny, only two, and has run off from the bowling alley and is presumed lost. Today is her uncle Beau's birthday party; he insisted on a bowling theme because he must always be offbeat and clever. Georgia loves her uncle Beau (Rodney's brother-in-law) but somewhere between the second and third frames, she disappeared and now everyone is looking for her. Rodney's wife, Pollyanna, is losing her mind. People are desperate. Someone has called the police. The partygoer-bowlers are running around the alley, the parking lot, the streets surrounding; all are calling Georgia's name. Pollyanna, after joining the search for ten minutes, has now collapsed into a puddle by the vending machines, weeping. "Someone took my daughter!" she moans. Rodney has searched the bar, the snack area, and the bathrooms. He has sent two of the party's attendees to their cars, to comb the neighborhood, and while Rodney is looking for Georgia, he can't help hoping — he is so, so ashamed the thought has entered his mind — that Beau doesn't find her first. It would be just like Beau. Beau the Beautard. Beau the pisswad, who has, since Georgia was born, made sure that everyone — especially Georgia — thinks he, and not Rodney, is the girl's primary male presence or focus or role model, or whatever the hell the term is. His Christmas gifts have to be bigger, more obscenely clever. His weekend outings have to be more spectacular and unforgettable and well-thought-out. Archery! Whale watching! Glass blowing! Beau is a putz. He makes his own clothes, wears clogs at home, and insisted last year on defacing poor Georgia's room with a floor-to-ceiling mural of the signing of the Magna Carta. "Uncle Beau!" Georgia could say that before she could say "Daddy" or "food" or even "no." And now Beau is running around, his fanny pack bouncing off his bloated backside, calling out Georgia's name. Rodney is running, too, thinking *Please God, let it be me, let it be anyone but Beau — let anyone but Beau find my daughter.* And his hair! Did he really wear barrettes that one day at the beach? Does he really color his graying hair with brown shampoo? Why can't Georgia see through that kind of narcissism? Oh, Georgia, where are you? And why doesn't he have a real job? He's a "life coach"? If he had a real job he wouldn't be around every goddamned day when Rodney got home from work. He wouldn't be chasing Georgia through the house, both of them shrieking like pigs, Georgia passing by her own father like he was a hat rack. Uncle Beau with the ankle tattoo, the legs of a satyr, and the ass of an ass. Well, for once Rodney will not come second when it comes to his own daughter. Not this time. No chance. For once — Oh no. Oh lord. Please no. Here he comes. Yes, I see who you found, Beau. Hello, honey. Thanks, Beau. Yes, I was scared, too. Yep, she's lucky to have her uncle Beau. Aren't you, Georgia? I just don't know how to repay you, Beau. I guess I'll have to start thinking about that. I'm gonna get started right away, about just how best to repay you, our good Uncle Beau.

Now, about 826 Valencia and this Captain Rick problem: 826 Valencia started in 2002 as a nonprofit writing and publishing and tutoring center for San Francisco youth. It now has affiliated locations in Brooklyn, Los Angeles, Seattle, Ann Arbor, and Chicago. In all of these places, we offer free tutoring after school, and we send tutors into schools all over the city to help students and teachers with writing-related projects. In addition, classes are held at 826 every evening, ranging from rock music reviewing for the radio (wherein the students actually read their record reviews on the local station) to writing persuasive essays in dealing with your parents (wherein students learn terrible Machiavellian tricks that will bring them trouble and great success). We also have a very busy publishing schedule, which allows San Francisco students to bring about fifty new books, journals, newspapers, zines, and comic books into the world each year. If you have read the BANR before, you know all this. You know, too, that if you would like more information, you can look at Google us and visit our Web sites. You also know that all the proceeds from this and previous BANR editions go directly to the San Francisco center.

And perhaps you even know that in the storefront of the San Francisco tutoring center, we sell supplies to buccaneers. Yes, you know this. We sell eyepatches, peg legs, lard, planks (by the foot), hand replacements, puffy shirts, and red and white striped socks. This is true. We run the Bay Area's only *independent* pirate-supply store, but this is not easy. As you know, we have competition.

There is a chain pirate-supply store, and every week, it seems, they open a new franchise, encroaching evermore closely on our territory, such as it is. Can we survive the tidal wave that is known as Captain Rick's Booty Cove? We are not sure, but we intend to fight to the end.

Who is Captain Rick? you ask. That is what many people want to know. He claims to be a seafarer of some renown, who, after many decades on the ocean, decided to hang up his parrot and perpetual tan, and open a few humble supply shops. Sounds like a nice story — if it were true. In the interest of informing you, the buying public, about Captain Rick, we're enclosing in these pages six of our ongoing informational posters about Captain Rick. Once a week or so, 826 Valencia publishes its newest findings about our competitor, and though this may not be the most appropriate venue, the truth must be heard. One thing not mentioned in these announcements is that Captain Rick's planks are made of balsa. Balsa is no good for planks.

BASIC QUESTION: IS CAPTAIN RICK AN AUTHENTIC CAPTAIN?

	RICK SAYS	BUT THE TRUTH IS
LEADERSHIP	He commanded over eighty men	He commanded one man, who was over eighty
COURAGE	He throttled a great serpentine beast of the deep	Declined to battle serpentine beast
SEAFARING EXPERTISE	Seven Seas, blah blah blah	Took the ferry once, to Sausalito
GARB	His are brine-soaked, wind-torn	His are in fact from Ross, Dress-for-Less, and artificially tattered. Tore holes in jeans himself.
PUBLIC SPEAKING	He's like some big expert	He gets all nervous and sweaty. Thinks Power-Point means to point at something very forcefully.
SCURVY PREVENTION	He's real good at scurvy prevention	Was not aware that limes were good to have around

826 VALENCIA: WE JUST WANT YOU TO KNOW ALL THE FACTS BEFORE YOU DECIDE WHERE TO BUY OCEAN MAPS AND LARD

HAS CAPTAIN RICK EVER EATEN A TURTLE? THERE'S ALMOST NO CHANCE

As we all know, when you are out to sea for months or years at a time, often you need to find and eat whatever you can find in the sea. Sometimes this means eating fish. Fish are pretty common in the sea, and thus make a practical meal. But when you can find some turtles, then you eat the turtles. Why? Let us count the reasons:

1. You can keep the turtles in the ship, in buckets or chests, and with just a little water and food, you can keep them fresh for a long time.
2. They are tasty. 3. They are very big, and thus feed many people.
4. They don't talk or complain.

For all these reasons, turtles are eaten by seafarers everywhere. They're favored by northern seafarers and southern seafarers and seafarers who go both ways. But does Captain Rick eat turtles? Pretty unlikely. We had a spy call Captain Rick one morning, and this is how it went down:

Spy: Ring, ring.
Captain Rick: Hello?
Spy: Hey, Captain Rick. Have you eaten turtles before?
Captain Rick: Excuse me? Who is this?
Spy: No one. [Hangs up.]

This spy was not one of our best people; she panicked. But she insisted that before she hung up, Captain Rick seemed scared by the question, which proves to any reasonable person that he's never eaten turtles, and thus is a fraud, and thus should not be selling pirate supplies.

826 VALENCIA: WE EAT THEM WITH GUSTO

SHOULDN'T A CAPTAIN KNOW A CANNONBALL FROM A ROCK?

Anne Frontere-Mammon writes us from Portland, which is either
in Oregon or Washington, and is either next to Seattle or is actually
the same city as Seattle:

"I used to see Captain Rick at the beach. He was always very afraid
to go near the water. He came to the beach, even on the hottest days,
wearing plaid slacks and sandals with socks. People would
just stare at him and laugh.

"Anyway, I remember one day he came down to the beach and he got all
excited. He ran down to the shore and he started picking something up.
'I can't believe I found a cannonball here on the beach!' he said. 'I can't
wait to give this a ludicrous mark-up and sell it at my store!'

"So then he started trying to lift the object, which was a rock. It wasn't a
cannonball; I could tell that from about 200 feet away.
It was just a black rock, and it wasn't even round.

"But he went at it for 45 minutes, digging around it, trying to roll it,
sweating profusely all the time, in his plaid pants. He never got the rock
out to his car, which was a Ford Explorer, by the way. A big white one
with some kind of custom detailing. Pretty lame."

826 VALENCIA: WE DRIVE A PASSAT AND WE ORDER OUR CANNONBALLS FROM SPAIN

CAPTAIN RICK WEARS SOCKS WITH SANDALS

Listen: It's not our place to say if it's wrong or right. We only report the information that might be relevant to your lives. And in this case, friends, the information at hand concerns the fact that many witnesses have noted that Captain Rick wears, under his sandals, socks. They are usually socks of the gold-toe variety. They are not official Gold Toe™ socks. Rather, they seem to be a sort of Gold Toe™ knockoff sort of sock. Again, we make no judgments; we only report the facts. Given the current political climate and the outcome of the Nov. 5 elections, we just felt it was our responsibility—our duty even, perhaps—to let you, the concerned shopping citizens of this city, know that this man, who owns a chain of 1,500 pirate-supply stores, wears sandals—and not even Birkenstocks—and under those, he wears thin brown socks with faux golden toes. Use this information any way you wish.

826 VALENCIA: WE WEAR TASTEFUL AND SOMETIMES AWESOME SHOES

CAPTAIN RICK ONLY KNOWS HOW TO TIE TWO KNOTS, AND ONE OF THEM IS THE WINDSOR

Seafarers should be able to tie knots. Are we crazy to say that? We don't think we're crazy at all in saying that. We just plain think that someone who has supposedly sailed a lot should know how to tie some rope into some knots.

All of the employees at 826 Valencia are sent to Halifax to study knot-tying with some of the world's foremost experts, including Dr. Marcus Sigurdsson and this one other guy named Gary. But has Captain Rick ever studied knots? It's pretty doubtful. While he was supposed to be studying knot-tying, he was probably out getting his hair done, or maybe he was shopping for fake Gold Toe socks. Your guess is as good as ours.

What we are sure about is that Captain Rick only knows two knots, and that one of these knots is the Windsor, which is only used in tying neckties. If you tried to use a Windsor knot on a ship or boat of any kind, you would drown really quickly, and then you'd be eaten by fish with huge fangs.

It's incredible that anyone would buy supplies from a guy like that, who's just waiting to be eaten by fish like that.

826 VALENCIA: WE KNOW ALL 112 KNOTS AND HAVE A FRAMED CERTIFICATE TO PROVE IT

CAPTAIN RICK MISUSES THE WORD "OSTENSIBLY"

READ THESE TESTIMONIES FROM RECENT BOOTY COVE CUSTOMERS:

"I was in there recently, just looking around, and all of a sudden Captain Rick comes out of the back room, wearing a robe, and misusing the word 'ostensibly' like crazy. It was really bad. I felt dirty and betrayed and will never shop there again." — *Helen, age 25*

"I had already had a hard day, and I went into Captain Rick's Booty Cove, just to do some browsing. The last thing in the world I needed to hear was someone misusing the word 'ostensibly.' But lo and behold, within five minutes, some guy came out in a robe, and did it. Twice." — *Ronald, age 40*

"I thought people stopped misusing that word years ago, but I guess that tells you a lot about Captain Rick. He's so out of it. And his beard doesn't even match his eyebrows." — *Susie, age 15*

826 VALENCIA: WE ONLY MISUSE GERMAN WORDS

Now that we have that illuminated, we should and will introduce the Best American Nonrequired committee members. About the students specifically, we have these bios, written by the students themselves, which perhaps wasn't a good idea, to give them freedom like that.

Rachel Bolten has dedicated her life to the study of linguistics. Her revolutionary 1957 book *Syntactic Structures* changed forever the field of transformational generative grammar. Currently a professor at MIT, her most recent works have included *Manufacturing Consent* and *Propaganda and the Public Mind*. Actually, that's Noam Chomsky. Rachel Bolten is really a seventeen-year-old junior at Castilleja School in Palo Alto, where she is the leader of the celebrated Sumerian Philosophy and Cheese-Tasting Club and is occasionally forced to wear a dress uniform that looks like a sailor suit. Not so much proud as self-satisfied, she also recently cowrote her first play, an "absurdist farce" featuring the poet Mary Oliver, a man who looks like Sigmund Freud, writing implements that talk, and a mail-order bride.

Alison Cagle is dedicated to the worship of one Harry J. Potter and is a longtime member of the Brute Squad. Resident student of the S.F. Bay Area and agonizingly aware of young America's desperate need to learn our history, she is widely known for frequent bursts into song at local bus stops: *Melting in the noonday sun / I think the last bus came at 1 / Other buses come that aren't mine / Happy people getting home on time / Oh, sittin' on the hottest day / Waiting for the bus to roll my way / Just sittin' at the stop all day, counting tiiime.*

Meilani Clay is a seventeen-year-old Oakland native who currently finds herself away from her hometown living in a city known to some as "the Haystack." She enjoys *naan* and *horchata* and hopes one day to be fluent in a minimum of five languages. Meilani has a record of making it from 826 Valencia to the Sixteenth Street BART station in eight minutes, which is quite a feat. [*Editor's note: That is very fast. It's about seven long blocks. People are impressed when you can do this walk that quickly.*]

Teresa Cotsirilos is a junior at the College Preparatory School in Oakland, and has been late to class every day for the past three years. She laughs too loud in movies, inevitably at moments no one else finds funny. Her friends took her to *Kill Bill Vol. 2* just to watch her watch the movie. The management refunded her money and asked her to leave.

Jennifer Florin — known in the BANR world as "Florin" — is originally from San Francisco but will be relocating this fall to attend Eugene Lang College of the New School University in New York City. The BANR committee will miss her frequent random outbursts, her chocolate chip cookies, and her over-the-top usage of the dreaded word *cute*.

Adrienne Formentos has not yet reached the height of five feet but will never give up hope. She is proud to attend Thurgood Marshall Academic High School, despite bloodsucking media coverage that paints her school as a dangerous place. Adrienne tries to learn something every day and is forever thankful for all the blessings in her life.

Melanie Glass is a young lass who resides in San Francisco. A graduate of San Francisco University High School, she will be moving to New York City (or, as she sees it, the land of UGGs and sub-par burritos) to study photography. Melanie likes cryptozoology, Segway human transporters, not-socks, Leonard Nimoy's former singing career, live-action role-playing games, and various other things that are awesome. Melanie works in the 826 Valencia Pirate-Supply Store under the alias "Shutter-Eye." No glass-eye jokes, please. She sorely misses Karl, and wishes there were some sort of bimonthly support group for the bereaved. KARL! [*Editor's note: Karl was a puffer fish, originally from Prague, who served as the unofficial mascot of 826 Valencia. Karl's life was cut short by forces of darkness/Czech loyalists, but he shall not be forgotten, chiefly because he was a very strange fish who scared everyone who saw him.*]

Camila-Dolores Osorio was born and raised in San Francisco's sunny Mission District. She graduated from John O'Connell High School of Technology, and in the fall of 2005 will attend the University of San Francisco in the foggy Anza Vista, outer-Haight District. She enjoys playing soccer, writing, reading, and average-length walks on the beach. Camila is also a member of SPOKES, the youth advisory board of Youth Speaks, the legendary San Francisco poetry and spoken-word organization. She aspires to enjoy her life. [*Editor's note: Camila will be mayor of San Francisco some day.*]

Evangelina Thomas-Guevara is a sixteen-year-old student at the School of the Arts in San Francisco. She likes roller blading, metal, chapbook making, journalism, and poetry. She plans to finish her new chapbook on the insights of being a queer teenager and soon hopes to launch a website for LGBTQQ youth.

Kerry Tiedeman attends Burlingame High School and resides in Burlingame. Kerry enjoys long walks on the beach (seriously!), volunteering at the local thrift shop, and listening to music in her spare time. Above all, Kerry's number-one priority is to have fun. [*Editor's note: It is evident that Kerry makes this priority a priority. Not in a bad way; in a good way.*]

Todd von Ammon is the last living male von Ammon, and, as such, is expected to continue his family's grand narrative by 1) giving birth to at least one healthy son, and 2) simply surviving (in no particular order). An aspiring big-in-Japan romance novelist, Todd will be attending a tree-dominated college next year to hone his craft.

A good majority of this year's committee members are, by the time you read this, doing all the things one does in college, including eating food and walking. And we miss them already. I feel like I say this every year, but it will be very hard to come to 826 Valencia on Wednesday nights knowing so many of these spectacular human beings will not be walking through the door each week, ready to gossip loudly and with unbelievable speed for fifteen or twenty or thirty minutes — before finally getting down to the work of reading and discussing, and then discussing more intensely, everything that was written in North America in a given year. We wish the departing members success and happiness and no hummus whatsoever.

The editors would like to acknowledge the intrepid assistance of Christopher Ying and Allison Athens in preparing this book.

DAVE EGGERS

INTRODUCTION

BURLY TOMES bulge from shelves and barely know I'm there.

Someday I plan to read the classics. Someday I plan to traverse their pages and see for myself what raw weight they wield. Actually, I have read a handful of them — Dickens, Dostoevsky, Twain, Fitzgerald, Voltaire — but in a haphazard, zigzagging fashion. No chronology, historical context, or classroom guidance.

I dropped out of school early and started work at a young age, but I spent a lot of time hanging around LACC, an inner-city community college a few miles from my mother's house. I made friends with some of the professors. One of them lived with the poet Wanda Coleman, and I was invited to hang out at their place behind the campus. I got to sit in and hear their discussions on writers and writing. That was where I first realized that there were myriad subtexts to a given piece of writing, and that writers seemed to be able to tap into the profundities of daily existence.

I kind of knew these themes and patterns were always there in books and stories, but these people seemed to have some key, some tool to unlock the densest texts or find some illuminating insight into a mundane occurrence. It was mysterious to me how they pulled these observations out of their hats. Was it education, experience, divination — an innate sense of the world?

I started picking up books from thrift stores and spent a lot of time hanging out at the library. The books I came upon were pretty random, a patchwork more than a definitive list. James Baldwin, H. G. Wells's history of the world, Sam Shepard's plays. The library became my other home. I didn't have a bedroom in my mom's house, so the library was one of the only places I could go and be alone. When that downtown library burned down, it was a big blow to me. I remember watching the five o'clock news — big black plumes billowing out of the windows, and all those books burning.

Later, I tried some of the smaller neighborhood libraries, but they were disappointing. A bunch of romance novels, ancient how-to intructionals, and some worn-out kids' books.

I made friends with this kid from Laos who worked in a cool little bookshop in the then-uncool East Hollywood neighborhood of Los Feliz. Books were not always available and became somewhat of a commodity, so I'd go up there and we'd hang around, talk about writers, and he'd show me the new books they'd gotten in. He was into obscure stuff, like a German poet named Georg Trakl or St.-John Perse. We'd sit around on long summer afternoons reading magazines and bits from various books. In a way, it was kind of our own nonrequired reading. We were picking up various writings and mashing them up into some kind of piecemeal perspective. Not having any academic structure about us, everything we gravitated to probably had the weight of something discovered on one's own, like we'd uncovered some secret thing nobody else knew. Which is kind of an adolescent thrill, or pomposity, but I'm still guilty of it.

There was an old art house movie theater next door. We were friendly with the assistant manager, and he would let us in for free. The Wim Wenders film *Wings of Desire* played for six or seven months and we must have seen it thirty times. We'd hang out in the projection booth sometimes, already having memorized all the scenes. I remember that it started out in a library, with an angel listening in on people's thoughts. We knew there was something going on in this movie and we'd learned what that was from reading.

We were also listening to Sonic Youth's *Evol,* Einstürzende

Neubauten, and old Delta blues. It seemed like we'd found what was relevant to us. The required world seemed a little gray and uninspired maybe. We were digging into the nonrequired past (which I think was the thing to do at the time). I remember Georges Bataille being very cool at the time. Also an old hobo account from the 1930s by Jack Black (the hobo, not the movie star) called *You Can't Win* had recently been rediscovered and reissued. Even quasi-sci-fi writers like Philip K. Dick were being reassessed and held in high regard. There wasn't much talk of the classics. It was more about the stuff that had gotten missed in between the major "important" works. It was like there was a questioning and a mistrust that were manifested in this stream of curiosities forming a new forgotten canon. But trends change and perspective shifts. Works sometimes speak to a moment or fill a need at the time. And the classics still stand unmoved.

When I came upon this series a few years back, it immediately made sense to me. It was what I was always doing: reading things here and there in airports, in waiting rooms, and on tour buses. There are always those bits from some article — a weird fact, an anecdote, an image even — you pick up somewhere that become lodged in your brain, just as deeply as anything would from a great novel or film. Sometimes those things crop up outside of the great canon of literature and only breathe into our awareness for a minute. If literature moves slow and we live in dog years, this book may come in handy. I've found the mix-tape aesthetic works for me. The humor and the humane, the hugeness and the miniature. It coheres into some other kind of implied story or novel that we're still living out. This is something we're figuring out together and apart, like it or not.

And if you want some advice you'll get only in this book: don't fall asleep riding a bicycle like my friend Brian did. You might wake up bleeding in a rent-a-cop car.

BECK
Los Angeles, 2005

THE BEST AMERICAN

NONREQUIRED
READING
2005

DANIEL ALARCÓN

■

Florida

FROM *Swink*

BENNY'S LAUGHING now, he's got that turning red look, a New-
port to his lips, but it's not lit yet. We're all sunshine smiles, beautiful day uptown, just clean and bright and blue, no clouds. We're
talking to Joey, one of those cats that knew Benny from back then,
back when niggas used to call him Bingo. Joey just came in from
Florida. He's dressed in turquoise to match the sky. Dolphins cap,
Dan Marino jersey, black pants, and he says, "I hate the fucking
Bronx," laughing a little so we laugh too, waving his arms around
like a helicopter, not pointing at any one thing, but at all of it.
"Look at this shit," he says. I don't see much except the sameness
of it, the buildings that lean against one another, ashy and brick. I
grew up around the corner. I work at the shop right here on Southern. We lean back against the wall. One step toward the center of
the street and the sunlight is cloudy and cut by the shadows of the
tracks above. A five train runs over and it's quiet, noise swallowing
noise. For a moment, Benny doesn't talk and Joey doesn't talk and
I don't either. We stare at each other and step toward the wall,
catching clear sun like we're gasping for air.

　　Joey touches the cross on his gold chain, rubbing it softly. He
has stubby blackish fingers, oil ground into the skin. The train
passes, life begins again. "Shit, Bingo, how ya been?" he says for
the hundredth time.

　　I'm on the outside of this one, I can tell. These two have stories that go back forever, lives and memories woven and inseparable. They've seen blood together, got laid together. Shit they won't admit to themselves, the other knows. They look at each other deep, for someone else lurking in the black behind their eyes. I'm not even here for them. They haven't seen each other in ten years.

"Same shit, Jojo, you know how it is. Working. Making do." He lights his cigarette. Blue smoke disappears into the sky.

Joey has a recycling thing going on down there in Florida. Car parts and metals and shit. He smells of aluminum, he says, so at nights he goes swimming to wash off the stench. "The condo's got a pool, you know."

Benny nods and looks away.

"So when you moving down? I heard your son was in Orlando," Joey says.

At the mention of his son, Benny breaks into a smile. "Been down there two years. Got married and everything."

"Yeah?"

"Yeah." Benny grins. "Flying," he says, the word slipping out like a prayer. It's one of those words that means something. "He's a pilot. Makes good money."

He says nothing about himself.

Joey is bronzed and tan, looking like he eats mangoes by the poolside. His belly pushes at the seams of his football jersey. He pats it with his left hand now and again to remind us that life is good. They play catch up: who got caught doing what, who got divorced, who had a kid, who died, whose moms moved back to San Juan. Old-timer shit. Who died. They keep coming back to it. It's a long list. My people haven't started dying yet, not really. Benny's have been dying for years. He's fifty-three.

"I'm sorry about Marco, Bing. That shit was terrible."

"You heard about it?"

"He deserved better than that," Joey says. Benny sighs.

A mother calls out a grocery list to her son on the street. Her voice is ragged and tired. It sounds like a train. Then another one comes, and in the thick quiet of it, Benny and Joey hug and exchange promises. Joey jots his phone number down on the back of a receipt. Benny looks at it for a second and slides it into his pocket. "Yeah," he shouts, yelling against the train, "and you know where to find me."

Be safe, they say, and say hi to your mom for me. Their smiles are banners and they grip each other at the biceps, warmly. They don't talk to their moms though. At least Benny doesn't, hasn't since Marco died. And the smile he wears is hurtful, like the sun when you stare. Jojo walks up Southern, turns on Prospect, and is gone.

Then the train leaves and the street is loud again. Benny squints against the bright blue of the sky. We step back into the shop, just the two of us, and it feels empty. It's like Joey was never here.

I've been working with Benny since high school. That's four years.

We're overflow mostly. Work that other shops can't handle, they send us. We copy it, bind it, fold it, whatever. We work late or come in early, depending on what other people need. Sometimes it's busy and other times there isn't shit to do for days. I get paid either way, so in that sense it's good. We make thousands of copies a day, but don't come in asking for two impressions of a single sheet. We lose money on the small shit. These machines are expensive to run. We don't get walk-ins. Twice a month, Gary comes in with a skid of paper, a big mountain of the shit, and we spend the whole morning unloading it. We put on those bra-looking things for our backs and carry the boxes two at a time. They're heavy as a bitch. Then we finish and Benny sits up on top of the pile like it was his throne and smokes a cigarette or two. That's about it. Not friends, not family. Deliveries, documents, paper. Moises, the owner, drops by every couple of weeks, make sure we're there. Cuban guy. He reminds us to keep the bathroom light off. *Es-pen-seef,* he says in his thick-ass accent. Then there's the water cooler guy. The repair people if a machine breaks down.

What I mean to say is that Benny wasn't expecting Joey to show up.

He's bothered by it, I can tell, in one of those moods where the work can't come fast enough. He tapes Joey's number on the wall by the phone. Walking back, he almost trips on the cord, which is so long it curls in circles on the floor. We joke you could talk at the bodega across the street. Moises got long distance blocked ages ago, so I sort of look at Benny sideways, but then just let it be. He won't call Joey. I go back to reading. My machine spits out copies, one by one, and asks nothing of me. An hour later, Benny is back at the phone, shaking his head, peeling the number nervously off the wall. Then he balls the paper up in his hand and runs back to his machines. He's manic, running two jobs at once even though there's no rush. Benny gets this way sometimes, and the shop gets unbearable with him in it: a pot slow-boiling until we just can't work. I heard it in his voice, talking to Joey, the way he said *flying*, the way the sun lit his face. Moving to Florida has been the idea for two years now, this dream that keeps getting postponed. "When I get the money, man . . ." he says, his voice rising as it fades.

Benny is his own weather system. Sometimes, when he gets like this, we close up early, or he just kicks me out. Other times, we work late in silence, just the hum of the machines and their green light kissing the walls and vanishing. Even now, he's caught between talking and not talking. You can tell when he's got something to say. His face changes, a little tighter, a little smaller. He tries to catch your eye and then turns away. Now we each take care of our machines, lose ourselves in the mindlessness of it. He's a kid really, in the way we all are, trying to understand why we act a certain way but unable. Forgetting to reason.

He'll forget about this too, or remember it, but speak of something else. You don't get too far with Benny. You learn not to expect much. He's got two, maybe three stories. There's the Yankees story: how he told them he was eighteen when he was really twenty-four. How the coaches were really checking him out. How his tryout ended when he stole second and jammed his finger against the bag. The glove wouldn't come on the next day and Benny says he cried like a baby. I don't know if I buy that one, but Benny never tires of telling it. He gets emotional thinking of all the championship rings he doesn't have.

But the other one is about a girl. He keeps her folded in his wallet. Yanice. Twenty-five years later, but she's still smiling in the picture. She was studying at Hostos and he was back from the army. He rented a room from her. I've heard this before so I know when Benny asks, "You ever stalk somebody?" he means it, and the strange shape of that question has lost its edge for me. It wasn't Yanice he was stalking though.

"Naw, Benny," I say now, like I always say. "I never stalked nobody."

"I was sleeping during the day and at night I stayed on the roof across from my ex-girl's place, trying to catch a nigga going up to see her. Renting a room from a homegirl, but I was never there." He nods at the picture. "Out all night, looking to see if my ex's light came on, what time, who she was with. The army made me lose my shit. I was crazy. I'd come home when Yanice was getting ready for class and she'd see me all tired and broke and dirty, looking fucked up."

He shakes his head at this part. The touching part: how Yanice saw past that, and wasn't disgusted by him or his actions, but how she wanted to help — which is great, I guess, if you want to sleep with your mother, but I don't respect women like that. I feel sorry for them. Benny idealizes them. The story goes that eventually, his ex's old man found out, came up to the roof with two of his boys, and kicked Benny's ass island-style. Family honor and shit. Benny shows the scars at this point, knife-edge on his stomach, a deeper one, white and fleshy, across his leg. "I stumbled home, don't know how. Yanice took me in. She cleaned me up. First time I ever cried in front of a woman." He pauses, then adds smiling, "We made love."

He lost her, of course. Probably fucked some other girl and broke her heart. He doesn't tell that part. Yanice wising up. Lost a year of her life to him and was no better for it. The story doesn't end so much as float away. *So what happened* you ask and the only answer you get is *well, you know* . . . His stories always come undone like this, cycles of hurt, betraying everyone but yourself because you're the only one who expects nothing. He can't be someone he isn't. He smiles too much and whistles: He likes strong brown thighs wrapped tight around him like any man does. Even now we get calls at the shop sometimes, women with insistent voices: *Is Benny there? Benny in?* And I just hand the phone off to him with a nod. "Is it Carla?" he mouths, but it's not, never is. His wife doesn't call. She's tired of trying to mother him.

The picture is from the boardwalk at Coney Island. Classic. They're seated on a bench, both smiling. Yanice is cocoa-colored with long wavy brown hair. Benny looks young and healthy, happy in ways he isn't now. Maybe she made him believe. Maybe he could have been someone else. He's wearing an orange wife-beater and green shorts. He has a full head of black hair. His naked arm loops around her neck, and he sort of leans out to catch the camera's glance. His smile is crooked, almost goofy. It's a playful moment. Yanice has her hand on his thigh, just lightly, and her smile is hopeful. Benny considers the picture for a moment, admiring her, admiring the memory. Like an asshole, I break the spell. "So what happened, Benny?" I ask. I always ask. Seems like she was a nice girl. She wanted to be a lawyer or some shit.

Now Benny folds her up neatly and buries her in his wallet again.

"Damn. I liked that girl," he says.

We all think about leaving. Some nights I stay out in Queens with Bianca, then in the morning ride the train into the city and imagine it's headed somewhere else. Coming into Manhattan the train goes underground. Everything is suddenly louder but the city is gone and the tracks could lead you anywhere. At least you try to imagine they could. I wouldn't go to Florida the way Benny would, but maybe somewhere similar, with sun and beaches and soft breezes. Thailand sounds nice, or Belize, or anywhere.

Queens is different: built different, smells different, feels different. Not better, not necessarily, just a little off, enough so you know you've crossed some border, passed into another place and that change is good. Bianca lives in Jackson Heights, in a building full of Colombians and Indians and Ecuadorians. There's a Croatian couple with twins and a Chinese man that nods when he sees me in the elevator. Bianca's building is about the loudest place on earth, but when we close the door to her room, the world ends, and we say almost nothing, but know exactly what to do. An orange light slants in from the window. I undress her, slowly, take time with each button, slip the clothes off her until she's bare and perfect before me. I won't even kiss her until she's naked.

I tell her she's beautiful.

Afterward, we lie in bed and she tells me about work, about her family, what's happened or hasn't since we last spoke. She has a sister in juvie who's always good for a laugh. The little fuck-up robbed her neighbor and got sent down to this boot camp out in Huntington. Then there's her job, one of these travel agencies on Roosevelt that does everything — money wire, immigration, real estate, international calls. She answers questions, mostly about courier tickets and visas to people either eager to go home or anxious to stay away. On Friday afternoons, working men come in with grimy bills to send money home to the thousand places where home is: Pakistan, Ghana, Peru. On Saturdays, couples holding hands leaf through photos of a dozen identical white sand beaches. Bianca recites the brochures from memory. They fill in the blanks themselves with scenes from movies and beer commercials. Their fingers curl into a knot, she says, and when they're in love, they're an easy sell. It's the most beautiful island, she always tells them, wherever they decide to go. That's where my boyfriend and I went last January.

The happy ones come back and thank her. They bring pictures. If it rained the whole time, they come back angry. They blame her.

Bianca has never been anywhere but here.

We talk about traveling, about leaving. Not together and not in any concrete way, but just possibilities, things that could happen. I've learned geography because of her, her stories. Because of her, I keep lists of countries in my wallet, the way Benny keeps photographs of old girlfriends: the corners of the earth, with no logic or scheme. *This Filipino man came in today* Bianca says, and I close my eyes and try to imagine what shade of green that earth is. *This Kazak couple was asking about* she says, and I climb out of bed and go straight to the map she has tacked on her wall. It's something we do. "It's cold! Come back!" she groans, but I want to know. I pull the covers off her and she's suddenly modest and covers herself. I grab her by the ankle and pull her. She laughs and screams and pulls the pillows down with her. Then Bianca stands by me. It's October, but the heat hasn't come on yet, and so we lace our bodies together for warmth. Naked, we examine the world. She guides my hand, my index finger running flat over oceans and deserts and mountain ranges until we find it: a green- or pink- or orange-shaded country, usually a small one, and usually far from us. How did they get here, I wonder, but my parents came, and hers too. And Benny's and everyone's.

Here.

Then the map starts to scare me, the world seems monstrous, too big and misshapen for me to comprehend. The map is fiction. New York is not a dot. Bianca holds me and tries to make me laugh. I crawl back in bed. I start worrying that all the things I meant to do will go undone not for a while, but forever. College. Family. Success. I finished high school and thought I'd work for a year, save some money. Four years later, I still make copies and listen to the same stories that Benny has been telling since the day I first walked in. The radio still plays the same songs. Benny still sits on the skid of paper and blows blue smoke in clouds above his head. I bring in library books and copy them so I can read them slow or twice and write in the margins without reservation, and Benny still asks what the fuck I'm doing. The routines are so solid they're brick walls and then Bianca's map seems too immense to be real. I'm not as fucked up as Benny, but I reason that I'm young yet, that my years too will add up. The sum of my disappointments. Black thoughts build on each other. "Mexico, what about Mexico?" she says, pulling me back from the darkness. She would do anything to make me smile. I'm lying on my back and she's on top of me. When she leans in, her hair tickles my face, but I don't give in. "We could go to Mexico!" she says again and she means it, and we could, but we won't and we both know this. From the shaft, a man's voice calls out. The world interrupts us. Bianca kisses me, frantically.

In the morning, I am a man again. I leave before she wakes. I buy the paper and check the scores and skim the nothing that happened overnight. The world seems small again.

I won't call her for weeks.

"We used to call Joey *Knuckles,* you know?"

Benny is running the binding machine the way he knows how, unconscious, books coming in and out blurred and quick. The machine is louder than you'd think it would be, just a big hole punch really, but the little motor whirls and revs. If you slip up, it'll cut you good. Benny is a pro. His fingers know exactly what to do. "Joey was bad," Benny says, not even looking at his hands. "Real bad. Used to fuck kids up."

I nod, expecting Benny to go on, but he pauses, pays attention to the machine for a second. We're finishing a report from some university. They need four hundred sets. The machine collates and everything, so I just sit there, waiting. A set comes out every thirty seconds, the paper a touch warm. I pull the copy from the machine, a hundred pages or so, and stack it on the tray, at a right angle. When the tray is full, I roll it over to Benny, who binds them. When he's done, he rolls it back.

Today is slow. One person could do what we do.

"I knew a kid named Knuckles too."

Benny looks up. "That's a good nickname, right?" He laughs. "What'd he do?"

What *did* he do? It's buried in my memory somewhere. We must have talked about it, when it went down. We must have laughed and felt something, enough to change his name. Knuckles came into existence because he *did* something. It's always that way. Before that, he was nobody. Afterward, he was Knuckles. What was it? A scene flickers and I grin.

"He smacked this other kid, this fat kid we called Meatball. Meatball liked Knuckles's sister. This was fourth grade. He touched her ass in the cafeteria. Knuckles wasn't having that. He got him right in the grill, laid him out."

Benny has seen this before. He loves it. "Big crowd?"

"Oh yeah," I say, and the whole incident is so clear to me now. I can see the bright faces, the balled fists, the painted lines on the asphalt schoolyard. "Meatball was older, so you know how that is."

"Knuckles was the man?"

"Knuckles was the man," I say, nodding.

And what I can't remember is who Knuckles was before. I can remember his face, his close-set eyes, his stupid surprised grin when he realized Meatball was down, but his name? Who you are is a question of space and time: the way Benny was Bingo, the way he sometimes still is. I was crazy, Benny says at least twice a week, but when he says *I*, what he really means is *he*. That *he* is someone else. And Bingo had a street and a neighborhood and a crew and a history so specific that now, *he* is gone. Benny never left. The people who knew Bingo have died or moved away. Now Bingo only reappears when the past comes in from Florida on holiday.

Which means you can be someone else.

The machines hum and whir. I picture Knuckles in the moment, his victory lap around the schoolyard; earning a name, as true and as beautiful as being born.

"You ever have a nickname, D?" Benny asks.

I roll him the tray full of warm reports. "Sure," I say, but the truth is I never did.

In the late afternoon, after Joey comes by, after Yanice has been put away, after the reports are bound, there is nothing left to do. Joey made us frantic and we finished early. I'm reading or trying to, but Benny won't let me. It's like something has been lifted off him and he can't stay quiet. The settlement, the settlement. The money that's going to fall into his lap.

"You know the lawyer called me the other day, right?" He raps his knuckles against the counter. "It's coming, kid! It's coming!"

"For real?" I barely look up from my book. I've heard this before. Benny is eyes, only eyes, roving everywhere and not settling. He's spent five thousand days in this shop.

"The judge set a date for a hearing and things are finally moving is what the lawyer said . . ." His words tumble over each other. He turns to face me and smiles. "When I get all this money, I'm going to give you the shop . . ." Benny nods as he says it.

Inside it's plasticky hot. The sweat sticks to your pores. We were laminating invitations all morning and the chemical heat has clung to us. I laugh. "It's yours to give, B?" I say sarcastically. "What about Moises?" It makes me laugh, the whole thing.

"Fuck you," he says, frowning. "You know what I mean."

I do. He's still waiting for that cash.

It all goes back to a car accident seven years ago. It's his other story, the unfinished one. The one about his brother. The details aren't there like they used to be. Even Benny doesn't remember just how it happened. His brother Marco was driving at the time. They got rear-ended. I'm not sure if Benny really got hurt, I mean in the medical sense, but at this point it's immaterial. I know his brother was in the hospital for a minute, bad enough to sue. Plus the guy that hit them worked for the city, Parks Department or something, and was driving a city truck. Any lawyer knows that's money. But six months later, Marco was murdered at the 174th Street station. With his brother dead, Benny took the case and has run with it since. Always about to collect, always just one more hurdle to get over; but he talks about that money like it was the real thing, like it's going to change everything.

I was in high school when Benny's brother got killed. I remember because it was all in the papers. It was in broad daylight that they got him. The why of it was never clear. Boredom probably. They have a cop up there now all the time. Marco wasn't rich or flashy. He had a little business, a wife, and three little daughters who got their teary faces on the evening news. Some politicians came to the funeral. The kids wanted to take his leather bag and his chain from him, but Marco wouldn't give it up. Like a dumbass. I'll give a nigga anything he wants; the truth is I just want to live. Benny is proud of it though. He'll tell you: "My brother was no joke. Those kids that stepped to him should have known better. He wasn't the kind to give in without a fight."

Cold comfort. They were swinging on him, Marco swinging back. The papers said people from the street could hear what was happening but they didn't do a thing. 174th Street Station: If you stand on the platform you can feel Southern Boulevard below, barber shops and bodegas, hubcaps and hot dog stands, and two blocks down, our shop. I remember walking past the scene, the crowd of people craning their necks to get a look, wondering if it was someone they knew. I was fifteen, I think. I ran into this kid from my school who told me they'd moved the body already. He said you could see it from the street, sprawled on the tracks, a shadow draped over the third rail. I remember being sick to my stomach, thinking it was fucked up, even for around here.

Months after I got hired, it came up in conversation, "You remember that shit that went down at 174th?"

"That was my brother," was all he said.

Suddenly I saw Benny in a different light: the grieving family, the weeping faces flush behind cupped hands, Benny dressed all in black, holding onto his mother so tight you couldn't tell who was supporting who.

The lawsuit is from that same era, but we never speak about the details. The murder erases it all. Even though they're completely unrelated, Benny goes after that money like it was sweet revenge.

It's been a couple of weeks since Joey came by. For three or four days, all Benny could speak of was Florida and the money. How the money was going to get him there. The palm trees and the condo and the pool. Health and happiness. The gilded sun floating in the blue-green sky. He had the radio up extra loud and was singing a lot. He was energized. But it passed and there were some black days in here too. Something happened with the lawyer, but Benny didn't tell me what exactly. The talk dried up and the money is still far away, as far away as the Everglades or the white sand beaches. Joey was never mentioned again, his number probably lost intentionally, dropped onto the street, or onto the train tracks to be run over and buried. And then it got cold, haggard winter sunlight not warming the city, and I called Bianca, wondering if she had heat yet. She was happy to hear from me, I know, but she played like she wasn't. She had exams, she said, but maybe I could come by next week.

Sure, I said, but it's her maps I wanted, not her.

Things have been good at the shop, quiet, uneventful. I've been reading a lot. Books on flight. On the conquest of the world. On empires that crumbled, and the details of each fall. Benny jokes Moises should deduct all my book copies from my check, but I know Moises doesn't give a shit. We make him good money. And from Benny, no outbursts, no drama. Yesterday he spilled a bag of toner over these reports we'd just about finished, fucked them all up, but he laughed it off. He's back to not caring, and this is the Benny I like, the one I can deal with.

We're still running the same jobs, the same random reports, the same nothing.

Benny is late. The shop is just me and the machines. From my wallet, I pull out my list of lovers. If we still had long distance, I'd call all those places, all those blue and green and red-pink countries. *Is this Malaysia?* I'd say. *Cape Verde? Paraguay?* And I'd ask them, as if I could speak to the whole of a nation, politely, in my steadiest voice, if there was room enough for one more within those borders. I'd tell them my name, my age, and hope for the best.

I'm quitting today.

I've made a million copies on these machines. Duplication is a sad line of work. And an even sadder way of life. I know what'll happen today, only because I was here yesterday, and the day before that. Benny will walk in an hour late, no hurry, with a cup of coffee in one hand and a newspaper in the other. He'll be all happy about last night's game, how we stuck it to the A's again. He'll call out, "I'll take any bets against the Yankees, twenty'll get ya forty! Any bets against the Yankees, motherfucker! Ha ha!" He'll open the door and the shop will fill with crisp October air. Winter is threatening. "Twenty'll get ya forty!"

He'll be sitting in the back, reading the paper, skimming it really, not even thinking about work. I'll come up to him and say, "Benny, can I talk to you for a minute?"

"My man! What's happening? What you need?"

I'll tell him I'm quitting, just like that. No hello, no small talk, straight.

"Aw shit . . . All right . . . Damn . . ."

He'll be surprised, but he'll be happy for me, outwardly at least. "That's good, D. Do your thing, kid." He won't ask me what my thing is, but he'll wonder. I'll wonder too. He'll ask where I'm going, and I'll pull my list out and read it like a poem, and he'll laugh, a booming, don't-give-a-fuck laugh, and say I need to get my head out of the books and get laid. And then on the last day, Friday, maybe we'll even get drunk up in the shop. He'll buy a twelve-pack of Presidente. We'll drink toasts to our health, to good luck, to the Yankees, to Florida. To my stupid poem. He'll put on his old tape of El Gran Combo and invite me to dance to my future, brassy melodies filling the shop. He'll be all nostalgic, all the laughs we had back here, all the stupid shit we copied, the hundreds of ways we invented to keep ourselves entertained while we slept-walked through the day. And at five o'clock this Friday, I'll step out onto Southern Boulevard and have the whole world new, days of my own design. That's the idea at least. I'll walk, I'll run. Crawl, swim, flee.

You won't see me around here anymore.

Now the door swings open, the little bell ringing brightly. Benny walks in smiling broadly. A quarter to ten. He's early. He tosses the paper on the counter, shaking the cold off. The steam rises from his coffee cup. "What's happening?" he says, to the walls, to the air, but not to me. Outside, a train barrels by, unsteady on its tracks. There is no sound more hopeful.

JESSICA ANTHONY

■

The Death of Mustango Salvaje

FROM *McSweeney's*

L'amour est un oiseau rebelle
Que nul ne peut apprivoiser.
Et c'est bien en vain qu'on l'appelle
S'il lui convient de refuser.
— Carmen

Uno. They say that it's amazing: I am not only a woman bull-fighter, but the best bullfighter that ever lived. No one can believe it. Reporters stand packed around me, arms waving like flags. They're asking the usual questions. Where did I come from? How was I trained? Blah, blah, blah?

"Cristina," they say. "Tell us how it feels to fight in the ring."

I say, "As soon as I enter the ring, I only concentrate on the bull. I appraise its agility, intelligence, sight, and, most importantly, whether it favors one horn or the other."

Now they're getting excited.

Papers rustle. A microphone becomes unplugged.

"How large are the bulls you fight?" they ask.

"Not less than four years old," I say, "with a weight somewhere between five and eight hundred kilos. The same as any fighting bull."

A woman steps forward. She asks me if — because of my female sensibilities — I ever feel sympathy for the bull.

I say, "If I have made a clean, quick kill, I will be applauded. I will do a lap of honor, and be showered with flowers, hats, and cushions. If the bull has put up a good fight, its carcass will also receive a lap of honor."

"*Mustango Salvaje,*" they beg. "Strike a pose!"

They, the conduits to the people, call me "Wild Mustang." And it isn't long before they start getting impatient. They would prefer it if Wild Mustang didn't answer the questions in the traditional way. They would prefer it if she tossed her brown ponytail over her shoulder and pinched her cheeks to make them blush and maybe did a little *Olé!* on the pavement. If she pretended to twirl her cape.

They are frequently disappointed.

When Wild Mustang doesn't strike a pose, they turn away glum, microphones swinging at their hips. This makes her feel bad for them, so she holds her fist in the air and shouts *Toro!* so they get to cheer and scribble on their writing tablets. I do this now and there is the sound of a thousand popping bulbs. Their cameras flash, illuminating the parking lot. Two men yell, "Love me, Cristina! Love me!" They clap to my name: "Bar-re-ra! Bar-re-ra!" Little children who do not understand names go, "Oo! Oo! Oo!" The boys hold their fingers to their heads and play bull. The girls toss petals at my feet. The air smells like coal and perfume.

"The people are calling your name, Cristina," cries my father, Eugenio. "They're calling your name over and over!"

We're making our way to our sport utility vehicle. Eugenio is red-faced with joy. He waves at the reporters, his grin stretching tight as rubber. "Barrera!" he shouts, half to the crowd, half to himself. He's tickled by the sound of his own name.

"Bah-ra-ra," I mumble. "*Maw-maw-maw.*"

Eugenio shoots me a scathing look. What's important to Eugenio is not important to his daughter. What's important is that today I, Cristina Barrera, stabbed and killed a bull more cleanly and swiftly than any bullfighter in the history of the Real Maestranza, the largest bullfighting ring with the largest bullfighting crowd in Seville, the largest bullfighting city in Andalusia.

For my final maneuver, I employed a dramatic *farol*, kneeling, with the cape spread out in front of me. When the bull charged, I swung the cape over my head, around to my back, and he barreled past. I rose slowly and positioned my sword forward and held him low. Entranced. Then I stabbed him. I thrust my sword deep between his thick-boned shoulders and pushed and threw back my hands, gasping from the feel of it. A wave of sound rose from the stadium. The bull's knees buckled. He tipped forward and then fell to his stomach. A breeze kissed my neck, tilting me forward with the bull. The spectators — the twelve thousand five hundred — took this as my bow. Flowers began to pour: roses, chrysanthemums, zinnias, roses, violets, roses, begonias. And more roses. Roses full stem, and just the simple heads, soared. The sweet of the bull-blood and the torrent of the floralia overwhelmed me. I dropped to my knees. The people who were closest, the ones standing in the *callejon,* the first row of the *plaza de toros,* threw their hands in the air and wept.

The people love their Wild Mustang. Their cape-swinging, bull-puncturing she-matador. Their Madonna. But there are some men that are less in love. These men see Wild Mustang and they want to possess her; they want to watch her and at the same time possess her. She wants to tell them that possession is not love: owning talent is not like owning a pretty vase: this is not the first time she has killed.

Nor will it be the last.

Then people rushed the ring. In seconds, I was lifted high in the air and paraded like a trophy around the perimeter. I caught a rose as I was carried from the ring to the waiting room, where Eugenio was waiting to greet me.

The people dropped me to the floor. I handed the rose to my father.

"Cristina," Eugenio said, beaming. He glowed from head to toe. "Do you realize how much money we made tonight?" He clasped his hands together, and ushered me to the changing room. "Everyone will pay to see you fight now. Even if you are a woman."

(This is my father.)

I changed out of my Suit of Lights — the *Traje de Luces* — and into my street clothing: blue jeans and cowboy boots and a T-shirt tucked into the jeans. Eugenio thinks I should wear more elegant streetwear, but Eugenio thinks a lot of things. Since my mother left us, I am his only concern. He's concerned for our finances. He's concerned for my image. He's concerned that since I am a bullfighter, I will never find a man and settle down and live in the country. Hence, my father's paradox: to reap the benefit of his daughter's success or to stay true to the traditions of our Andalusian geography. We have mountains. We are embraced by oceans.

Lately he's been enjoying the success.

"Let us walk out together," he said. "So the reporters can see that you belong to a family. That you are not a woman out of no-where."

"Yes, Eugenio," I said.

"It will be less awkward that way," he explained.

Eugenio is frequently in awkward positions because Wild Mustang does not have *cojones,* what the men call "cushions of courage." It's common knowledge that cojones allow a bullfighter to fight and fight well — beyond that — survive. Wild Mustang does not believe cojones are something a bullfighter needs to survive. In fact, she believes that the tight pants she must wear in the ring are less tight because she does not have to maneuver around a bagful of coins. So there's that. And there's the litany of *fatalidades,* the cojones-bearing bullfighters whose tiny cushions did absolutely nothing for them in the ring when they took a horn someplace crucial and died. There have been forty-eight fatalidades in Andalusia: ten were named Jose, nine, Manuel.

None were named Cristina Barrera.

Eugenio and I walked outside arm in arm. (In this way, we were less awkward.) As soon as they saw us, reporters rushed forward and hurried toward the parking lot, which is where we are now. The Traje de Luces, which only moments ago sparkled in the center of a dusty ring, is now wrapped in a black plastic bag. It hangs lifelessly over my arm.

There have been the usual questions. We're about to load in

when one reporter shouts, "Cristina, show us the *oreja!*" So I re-move the bull's ear from beneath the smothered Traje de Luces. But as I do, the same reporter asks, "Cristina, are you in love?"

I turn to look at this reporter. He's very short, wearing a jacket much too large for him. The sleeves are rolled.

I look at Eugenio. "I have no *time* for love," I say.

Eugenio grabs my hand tight. "Say yes," he seethes. "If you are in love they will treat you like a human being and not a cold idol."

So Wild Mustang faces the reporter. She lifts one eyebrow. "OK," she says, "I *am* in love," and holds up the ear.

A dozen bulbs flash.

"With who!" the short reporter screams. "What's his name?"

"What's your name?" she says.

The reporter laughs. "Jaime Ostos."

"Then I am in love with Jaime Ostos," she says, and closes the door to the sport utility vehicle.

Dos. The following week I'm fighting in the Baena ring, in the Córdoba Province. It is close to my hometown, Hinojosa el Duque, so Eugenio and I don't have far to travel. We wake at first light. Eugenio dresses and makes the coffee and rolls and slices or-anges. I yawn and lean on my elbows at the windowsill to watch our neighbor, Victor Liria, dig up potatoes that do not exist out of the earth in his backyard with bare hands.

Victor will hold a clump of dirt in his thick paws and smell it as if it were salted and fried and served hot with tomatoes. Then he will grin, wide, like a madman. There are, of course, no potatoes in his yard, but several dozen lines of lemon trees that are never har-vested. I fall asleep listening to the whump of lemons dropping in the night. During the day they rot in the sun, stinking with sweet and sour. The smell carries easily on the breeze from his house to our house. I've gotten used to the smell of rotten lemons. When I travel, it reminds me of home. Eugenio is not as understanding. He'll hear them drop and shake his fist out the window and shout, "Curses to you and your lemons, you madman!"

This morning is like any other morning. Victor holds the imaginary potato in both hands above his head and shakes it at the sky that at this very moment is breaking into a thousand yellows. He cries, "Once again, God has given me great pleasures!" then drops the ball of dirt onto the ground.

I shout, "Victor, got a big one?"

Victor is short, but wearing those brown trousers that only reach midcalf he looks even shorter. Around his thick arms he wears a loosely assembled boar pelt. Victor likes pretending he's a shepherd. An imaginary flock of ewes follows him everywhere, even to the toilet. Sometimes he gets so fed up with the ewes he curses and spits, and has to slam the door. Then he feels bad about this treatment, and has to make up with each and every one of them.

This can take all week.

For a false shepherd, Victor is very serious-looking. The boar pelt is supported with leather straps that cross his stomach, and underneath the pelt he wears a blue-and-white-striped sailor shirt that he says he got in Irkutsk. We all know that he's never been anywhere, but Victor says he was in a war with Russians and the Russians gave him the shirt and a small crown of flowers when he saved the lives of their village people.

Some days Victor is a soldier. Other days, a shepherd.

Wild Mustang likes Victor immensely.

Victor stands up and squints. His face is heart-shaped and rough, like the backside of good leather, and his eyes perpetually squint, even in our darker, Andalusian winters. Today he holds his hand over his eyes to block the sun. When he sees me, he clasps his hands together. *"Matadora!"* he cries, and runs to my windowsill.

Victor knows more about bullfighting than any man alive. It was not Eugenio who trained Wild Mustang to flick her wrists in a hard left when performing swirling *mariposas,* making the cape look like a butterfly; nor was it Eugenio who sat with her in the lemon trees telling her stories of famous matadors, like José Cándido, who in 1771 jumped over the bull's forehead and was the first to die in the ring; or "Fortuna" Diego Mazquiarán, who in 1928 slaughtered a bull that had escaped from the corrals; or Luis

Freg, who was gored fifty-seven times; or "Gafe" Marcial Lalanda, the "Bad Luck Sign" who fought alongside four other matadors on the day they were killed; or Wild Mustang's favorite matador, "Manolete."

Manuel Rodriguez y Sánchez, the highest-paid *torero* for eight years in the 1940s, only ever employed one single maneuver with the bull: a simple *verónica*, or pass of the cape, that beckoned the bull to a ninety-degree angle, which, the newspapers noted, he had mastered with "an elegant, cold perfection."

Victor arrives at the windowsill, breathless. "How big was the *toro bravo?*" he asks. "Half a ton?"

"Bigger," I say.

"A large one," he says, rubbing his palms. "And the kill?"

"Swift," I say. "Clean."

His eyes shine. "And the men," he says. "They love you now?"

"The people love me," I say.

"The people will always love you, *Mi Batata,*" says Victor. My Sweet Potato, he calls me, and puts his rough hand on mine. He looks at me. "You're not happy?"

"I'm fighting today," I say. "At the Baena."

"So soon?" he says.

"We need the money."

Victor leans in, very close. "Tell Eugenio that a famous bull-fighter needs her rest," he says.

I shrug.

"Tell Eugenio," he says, "that there is more to life than money."

Victor spits on the ground, then resumes digging. So I turn on the television set to watch the morning episode of *Yolanda!*

Hinojosa el Duque: the apex of modernism. We have female bullfighters. We have television. The only television station we get in this area is Channel Two, which alternates *El Lobo*, the news-source, and the Spanish-American program out of New York City called *Yolanda!*

This morning there are two Spanish-American women fighting on *Yolanda!* Both of them are wearing suits with silver breastpins in the shapes of dung beetles. The Spanish caption tells me they are sisters. They are extremely fast-talking sisters. I'm impressed; my English is only acceptable, and they spit out the syllables like a machine gun.

Yolanda! herself is named Yolanda Thomas. Yolanda Thomas is an incredibly fit woman with large breasts. She wears only pink suits with padded shoulders. Yolanda Thomas tells us that *Yolanda!* is designed to aid the plight of the Spanish-American people. She interrupts the discussion with extreme gestures, alternating faces of perplexity and disgust. One woman says she's sick and tired of all this crazy American life and misses Spain. The other responds that the Spanish people who live in America must work through the craziness to achieve their goals. Yolanda Thomas agrees with the second woman and then points menacingly at the camera with a long white fingernail and then they go to commercial. *Yolanda!* is the number-one program in Andalusia.

In America, it is number three hundred and fifty-seven.

Sometimes Victor will leave his potato-digging to join me at the window and we will watch together. Victor is very puzzled by *Yolanda!* He doesn't understand what kind of a show it is.

"It's not drama," he says, wringing his hands.

"No," I say.

"It's not comedy," he says, "and it's not news."

"No."

Victor shakes his head. "Then what is it?"

"It's just people talking," I say. "It's American."

This always makes him laugh. But not now. Now Victor's far too absorbed in his potato-collecting to watch television. So I gather together my fighting garments, my Traje de Luces and my white shirt, black tie, green sash, black slippers, and my black *astra-khan* — the two-sided hat — in boxes and long plastic bags and go downstairs to greet my father.

"*Buenos dias,* Eugenio," I say, and peck him on the cheek.

He coughs. "Good morning, Cristina."

My father is sitting at the breakfast table in the middle of his morning ritual of sucking oranges. It takes a half-hour. He wakes up early to do it. He slices the oranges in eight pieces and puts an entire slice in his mouth — rind and all — and sucks so hard his normally round cheeks draw inward. He holds them in for a good twenty seconds or so, until his cheekbones begin to show, and his chin and his eyes bulge from their sockets. Once the rind is dry, he picks it out of his mouth with his thumb and middle finger, and drops it into a blue bowl. The rind, rounded. The flesh, emaciated. Eugenio eats the oranges so he can take his anti-anxiety pills. He's always taking the little white pills because he says that I give him anxiety.

We're quiet at the table. I nibble on a roll.

"What's the matter," Eugenio says, his mouth full of orange.

"Nothing, Eugenio," I say.

"Nothing, Eugenio," he says, as if I exhaust him.

He flicks the newspaper.

My father is nearly sixty. His eyebrows arch in points off-center from each other. His cheeks, I imagine, were once full, but age has pulled them and now they sag low around his mouth. His nose presses flat against his face, and rises up thick to a pair of eyes so rounded they barely have visible lids. The eyes are startling; people who don't know him think Eugenio is staring wide-eyed at them. As though glaring.

After breakfast, Eugenio and I pile into the sport utility vehicle with my garments and sword. There's a tense moment when I accidentally slam the door on my Traje de Luces, but after a long inspection and a few harsh words, Eugenio sees that no damage has been done and I'm forgiven.

The Barreras arrive at the Baena. I'm tired today. The sun is too bright. I'm too hot. Eugenio dresses me in the light of a small white room. A plastic cross of Jesus the Savior hangs on the wall above a cluster of red silk flowers. Outside we can hear the people stir, and the smell of the fried pancakes they sell to the spectators on paper plates seeps in through the open window. There is a noticeable absence of a breeze.

Wordlessly, I pull on the tight satin pants. Eugenio designed the whole thing. He chose deep pink, with hand-stitched panels of gold that rise up each leg and divide my waist, just below the breasts. The suit was made ten years ago, after I took my *alterna- tiva* and graduated to matadora. It took six people a month to cre- ate and cost Eugenio over a million pesetas, the sum of which Wild Mustang made in three fights, and promptly returned to his bank account. Ten years later, the Traje de Luces still fits like a glove. My body is firm anyway, but wearing the bottoms of the suit, I am invincibly so.

"Victor was pulling potatoes again," I say, "because —"

"Hmpf," says Eugenio. There's a pin in his mouth. He holds onto it with his mouth, his lips pinched as tight as an asshole. He removes the pin and his pointed brows furrow. "Victor's an idiot. If we're lucky, he'll be dead in two years like the doctors say." He pulls my hair back tightly into a single ponytail and brushes until the tail shines. He tugs the small coat of the Traje de Luces tightly over my shoulders so the gold frames my neck. "Then," he says, "we can buy out his property. Then we won't have to listen to those infernal lemons."

(Eugenio Barrera: humanitarian.)

He sighs, and pulls the coat rough and tight. "There is tension today, Cristina," he says. "You need to be focused."

"Yes, Eugenio," I say.

"You are fighting with Pepin Romero and Antonio Mondejar."

"Yes, Eugenio."

"They have both won the Real Maestranza, and the women love them."

"There are men in the audience too, Father."

"Yes, but a man only watches the bullfight to pretend that he is the matador. How can a man pretend to be a matadora?"

Wild Mustang! The children go, Oo! Oo! Oo!

Eugenio pulls the tie close to my neck and exhales loudly from his nose. It's an annoying habit that started only recently. With it he looks and sounds a decade older than he really is. He holds me firm at the shoulders, then reaches down to tie the strings that hang from the pants. These are my *machas*.

"Cristina," he says, "this is serious business. There are reputa- ble men out there that want to roast you on a spit. You are a rarity:

not all women are beautiful. Not all women have talent. To them, you are spitting in the face of tradition."

"Talent," I tell him, "isn't something you have, it's something you use."

"Serious business," he repeats, and stands up to give me the once-over. "You look tired," he says. "Take this." In his hand is a small white pill. He places the pill in my hand. "For your nerves," he says.

"I don't have any nerves," I say, and hand back the pill.

He starts to say something but changes his mind. He replaces the pill in a bag he keeps in the small pocket of his vestcoat. Together, we enter the Doma Crucifixione, the small church that has been a part of the Baena for years. Together, the old man and I kneel before the wooden altar of Jesus the Savior. Eugenio's eyes are closed very tight, and he whispers with an impassioned urgency. Eugenio never looks at me while reciting his mantras, but always says them loud enough so I can hear him.

"Please," he begs, "first let the girl fight well. Then let her marry well and live in the country."

But that isn't even my favorite part. My favorite part comes right —

"Above all, let her recognize You and thank You for bringing her to this moment of stardom."

Stardom? Wild Mustang didn't earn her stardom. One day, when she was just a girl, a stranger passing her by on the street gave her a piece of cloth and said it was a cape. He said if she learned to use the cape a certain way, she would be able to talk to the animals. And since she grew up in the country without a mother, animals were Cristina Barrera's only friends. "How marvelous," she marveled, "to talk to animals." And she flicked the cape right. Clouds swung together, and the birds shut up. The cape flicked left. Whisper: *toro*. And she lay in bed that night holding the cape in her fists, listening across the countryside; listening to the collective sigh of the souls of a thousand bulls.

I sigh. I do the North/South/West/East and silently thank my father's God.

The old man stirs. He snuffles out of penitence for mistakes he never made, and rises. "Now," he growls at his only child, his daughter, *"lucha."*

I look him in the eye and say, "Of course, Eugenio."

There will always be a fight.

Tres. Eugenio and I walk down a narrow corridor with a cement floor that smells of steel and mold. The Baena's not in the best of shape. The water that runs through the drainage pipes gurgles overhead, and if we're not careful, pellets will drip onto the Traje de Luces. Eugenio has brought along a sliced plastic bag that he places over my head and shoulders until we get to the waiting area, where Pepin Romero and Antonio Mondejar are waiting on the waiting couch sporting their Trajes de Luces. They're watching *Yolanda!* on a small TV that hangs from a ceiling in the corner of the room.

I've seen this one. It's about mothers and prostitutes, and prostitutes that are mothers and the mothers of the prostitutes. There's a lot of crossed arms, loud voices. General hooting.

Pepin has his girlfriend, Lola Baroja, with him. Lola is wearing a traditional white dress with a red rose over the breast, and is quite beautiful. Her black hair falls loose around her shoulders. She's a dancer in the *romeria,* the dance that leads a pilgrimage to the shrine of a saint. She's half-gypsy, and also a dancer in the gypsy caves of the Sacro Monte in Granada, which used to be only for the real gypsies who lived there, but now has been taken over by half-gypsies like her who make a bundle from the tourists as a marketable attraction. I see her and think of one word only: plucked. Lola is extremely tan and extremely fleshy and can't be older than nineteen. She eyes me as though terribly bored by my presence, but behind the boredom is a flicker of curiosity that she is too inexperienced in life to hide.

Pepin and Antonio used to stand up to greet me — like all men in Andalusia rise to greet a woman — but now when they see me, they just go back to watching *Yolanda!* Perhaps I'm too pale, too wan. (I'm a skeleton compared to Lola Baroja.) Perhaps I am just Cristina Barrera. But mostly I think it's because Antonio Mondejar and Pepin Romero are both very handsome men, and I would imagine that if you are handsome, there is nothing more irritating than someone else soaking up what should be your God-given attention.

"Pepin," I nod. "Antonio."

Pepin waves, absently. "You remember Lola," he says.

The fleshy thing bats her lashes, long as handheld fans.

Eugénio pulls me aside and whispers, "They're only competing for your attention." Then he holds my head tight, like a vise, and kisses me dry on both cheeks. He bows to the boys on the couch and departs for the entrance of the ring to watch.

I stare at the matadors. We're all sweaty, and pushing thirty. Pepin has been performing wonderfully. Audiences love him. He invented a move called the *adalia* after his last girlfriend who became pregnant with his baby. Both died in childbirth. They had never married, but Pepin named the move after her, which seemed to suffice for him. The adalia is a swift move, where he slides the cape over the bull's head while holding a posture like a statue, making it look like the cape is more human than he is. Pepin would be the top moneymaking matador if I were not around. About this, I have no doubt.

Antonio is married, has two children, and has not been getting good reviews. During his last fight he stumbled and the bull charged. Antonio, possessed by an irrational fear, jumped over the fence into the *callejon*. Audiences are skeptical of his talent, but enjoy his fights for nothing if not their unpredictability. His wife is not as understanding. Antonio and I have fought together a dozen times before; I have always received top billing.

Now he watches both me and the television, simultaneously. There's a mother on *Yolanda!* with four children who are about to be taken away from her. The caption says she's a prostitute. I'm skeptical of this, because she's largely overweight, wearing nothing but a bra and a miniskirt. Her thighs roll out onto the chair like dough, and she's screaming like a large, wronged bird. I've heard that Americans hire actors to go on television and pretend they have problems in real life.

Quietly, I admire her chaos.

"Whore," seethes Antonio, and dry-spits at the TV. He stands up and stares at me and fluffs his cape, sending a wave of heat rippling in my direction. His Traje de Luces is dark purple with gold beading. "I have never *seen* such a whore."

Antonio looks at Pepin, and then they both look at me.

Lola smiles, and nuzzles her head against Pepin. They murmur at each other. Sweat glistens along the crown of her head like tiny diamonds. Pepin kisses them off one by one and runs his tongue over his lips to taste her salt. Then Pepin and Lola rise and leave the room. Lola walks with her head against Pepin's shoulders and he lowers his hand to her ass. They close the door behind them.

What people won't do, Wild Mustang always marvels, for something as commonplace as sodium.

Antonio parades to the other end of the room to groom himself in front of the long mirror. "They're going to fuck, don't you think?" He looks at me.

I shrug.

"Are you offended?" he says. "Have I offended you?"

Antonio is a large, square presence. He should have been an actor. He picks at his dark hair and runs his tongue across his teeth. He stands up as tall as he can with his feet together, arms swung across his chest as though assuming the first position we take with the bull. His toes are too close together for the proper stance, but I don't say a word. He breathes in deeply through his nostrils. Above us, the Baena roars and then dies down.

"I'm not offended," I say.

Antonio laughs like he didn't hear me. "You behave like a man. Why shouldn't I treat you like a man?" He makes a vulgar gesture with his tongue and two fingers. Staring at him, I'm suddenly curious as his head begins to grow. His chin extends outward. The round of his head rises up like a back. Then his ears point, becoming two sharp horns. The horns grow sideways for a few thick inches, then take a sharp turn north and sprout up toward the ceiling. Antonio is an extremely silly-looking bull. His horns are imbalanced. His eyes, cocked.

The children go, Oo! Oo! Oo!

I look up. The ceiling is threatening to drip condensation from the cold water pipes, just centimeters from the bull's satin jacket. One large drip hangs like a plum then falls in slow motion, staining a dark crescent onto a flank of the glittering, purple material.

"Shit!" shouts Antonio, a full octave above his normal register.

Pepin returns from the room without Lola. "What happened?" he says.

"My jacket," Antonio cries. He is red-faced and shakes his fist at the ceiling. "Shit!" he cries again. He stomps his foot.

Pepin ignores him and goes right for the floor-length mirror. He adjusts his coat and turns to look at his butt. He changes position, alternately standing on one leg and then the other, trying to get a glimpse of how his butt might look from any angle. He alternates back and forth for a while, then opens a crack in the small window above the mirror. The pancake smell pours in with the sun. It's bright out there, and it's hot. It's hot and bright.

Our Trajes de Luces blaze.

Rafael Camino comes in with the papers. He's the manager for the Baena and always likes to give us a copy of the papers with the announcement of the fight. We all rise and look at the papers. Wild Mustang has once again received top billing. Today Antonio has received third billing, in the smallest print. He will be paid the least out of all of us, even though he will fight the same fight. Usually when Antonio sees that I have received top billing, he throws a fit. He will glare at me and say something like, "This is fucking ridiculous," and slam the paper on the couch. But today there is no fit. Instead, he calmly strides over to the couch, reaches in his bag and opens a Diet Coke. He's careful to hold it away from his suit, though now with the stain it hardly matters.

"It's too hot to fight," Pepin says to Rafael, and shakes his head. His face is bright red. He shifts his tie, uncomfortably. "Look at Cristina. She looks like hell."

I look at Pepin.

Rafael beams. "Wild Mustang," he says, lovingly, like he never gets to say it.

Rafael Camino is a squat man with arms like rolled sausage.

He smells of chicken, the only thing he ever eats. His fingernails are stained bright orange from paprika. He approaches me and reaches out to touch the sash on my Traje de Luces with one hand. From the other, he holds a burning cigar. An inch of ash slips to the floor.

"Cristina," he warbles. "*Bella.*"

"Get away from her," Pepin says, crossly. "You'll burn the suit."

Rafael backs away but keeps staring at me. His eyes well up. "Cristina," he gushes, "I can't believe that you would come to my little Baena after your incredible win at the Real. I thought you'd be touring around Europe and America by now. I can't tell you how much it means to me. It's — unthinkable. I don't have enough room for all the spectators!" He clasps his hands together and kisses air.

(In his eyes, he's counting the pesetas.)

"You've ruined my suit," cries Antonio, and rushes up to show him. "Look what your broken ceiling has done to my suit! This place is a dump!" He dry-spits. "I'm never fighting here again!"

Rafael gestures with pinched fingers like an Italian. "It's an old place, Antonio. The bones of your ancestors are buried in the cemetery next door. Why don't you keep yelling and disturb their peaceful slumber?" He turns to me. "Now," he says, "are we ready to fight?"

"What about the *sorteo*?" I say.

We usually draw lots on which bulls we fight, numbers written on cigarette papers.

"There's no time for lots," says Antonio.

"No time," says Rafael.

Pepin fusses with his tie. "It's too hot to fight," he says again. "Dammit."

I'm about to complain to Rafael that this is not professional, not professional at all, but then the trumpet sings for the entrance of the bullfighters.

There's no time.

We line up. Our friends and close family are gathered at the entrance. As we pass, they stare nervously at our frail bodies.

Eugenio rests his back against the wall with one foot propped up. He sees me and his brow drops. He holds his hands together, tight. *"Lucha,"* he whispers.

The Baena chants above us. We step forth to the berth of the ring. The crowd sees us, and the noise breaks. The sand of the ring is smooth. Six bulls in the cage to our right swallow thickly.

Cuatro. The bullfight, like any bullfight, begins with a *paseo*, the parade of all of us involved: the matadors, the picadors, the banderillos, the peones, the mulillas. We enter into the ring, the open desert, in three long lines, dressed in our costumes, waving. It's dusty out there, and hot as fire. The sun makes us blink, it's so white. The contestants and bailiffs salute the president, the man who controls the fight. This president is a small man seated in the president's box, in mid-bleachers. He's wearing tan slacks and a cool-looking hat for shade, and sunglasses and a red scarf tied around his neck.

Immediately, I don't recognize this president, which is strange because I have fought here so many times and could recognize one of them on the street if I had to. I look over and see Pepin salute the president in the traditional way and I place my feet together to ready myself. But Antonio, to my left, has not saluted the president properly. Instead of raising only one hand to his brow, he has raised both hands, a gesture that any normal president would find self-serving and offensive. But this president does not seem to mind. He acknowledges Antonio's gesture and even brings his fingers to his mouth and kisses them.

I look at Pepin.

"It's his uncle," Pepin says, and shrugs.

We retreat to our waiting space. The next three stages take place to weaken and tire the bull, and prepare him for killing. In the meantime, I watch my bull. All bulls must be between the ages of four and six, and my bull looks an even five. The horns are distinctly *playero;* the two points lay wide across the top of his head. I don't envy my peon, Manuel, who works very hard to exhaust the bull. Manuel is a boy from the outskirts of Hinojosa el Duque.

He's grown up on a farm, working with cattle and horses, and is an excellent peon. Antonio's peon is his cousin, Luis. Luis grew up in the city, is very fat, and uses the cape like he's bored with it. It's a disgrace. Such sloppy performance is an insult to the animal, the spectators, and, most important, the matador.

"Antonio," I want to say, "look at your peon. He's a mess!" But I never do, because Antonio is a man driven by private inner rages that, like dangerous fish, are disturbed by the slightest tremor in their waters. And at this particular moment, the dangerous fish is not even watching; he's lying with his back against the wall, examining his fingernails.

Then Pepin says, "Cristina." He points at my bull.

We are in the third stage, the *Tercio de Varas*. A circle is drawn in the sand. The picadors ride blinded horses, holding a long lance with a spike at the end. They prick the bull's neck to lower the head for the kill, but always keeping at the circle's distance. The problem is that my bull isn't responding to the taunts of the horse or the picador. He's just standing still, leaning slightly to the right. Then he shifts his weight to the left. It looks like he's waiting in a grocery line. Because of the bull's reluctance to go to the picador, the president gives permission to cross the circle and go to the bull.

The picador gallops past and pricks the neck.

From the unexpected puncture, the bull lifts his head and quickly looks left and right for the picador but cannot seem to find him. The picador goes by again, closer, and gives the bull a second prick, this time deeper. The bull growls, his head lashing north.

The final time the picador rides by, he rides as close as a picador can ride next to a bull. It's an extremely dangerous maneuver, and I sense that given this bull's unpredictable behavior, it's a bad idea.

Pepin has noticed this too. "Don't do it!" he shouts.

The picador gallops right up to the bull, at which point the bull kneels down and lifts his head sharply skyward, forking the horse straight up the gut. The horse collapses, bucking the picador, who crashes hard on his head.

"*Tumbos!*" shouts the audience.

The bull disengages his horns from the body of the horse and makes for the picador, who rushes over the fence that lines the entire ring, and into the callejon. The bull trots to the place where the picador suffered his fall, pulls his hooves together, sniffs, and continues standing completely, and oddly, still.

Usually if a bull does not appear to want a fight, the president will raise a green flag and the bull will be removed. But this president, Antonio's uncle, is flagless.

Pepin looks at me. "I'm going to tell the president to pull it," he says. He motions for Rafael. They argue about the bull. Pepin accuses Rafael of accepting bulls from poor breeders. Rafael accuses Pepin of snobbish perfection.

"Just back out," Pepin says to me.

But Wild Mustang cannot back out. She will be seen as a coward if she backs out now. Worse, a woman. No: she will own the bull. She will make him fight. She will dazzle him with her elegant, cold *verónicas* until he can't help but bow his head and walk headlong into her sword.

"I'm fighting," I say, and that's the end of it. I look to the president who, at the moment, is enjoying a faceful of pancake. Is there a green flag?

There is not.

So I remove my hat and salute him, asking permission to perform. He waves his hand, absently. I begin matadora-ing. I use a series of passes with my red cape, none of which succeed in bringing the bull closer. I'm hot and constricted in my Traje de Luces. A bead of sweat travels from my neck down to the small of my back in one long ride. I take a deep breath and hold it. I stride closer to the bull. The banderillas hang across his back as though yoked; I hold my cape forth and flick it quickly to the right. Now he sees it, and charges madly. He even froths at the mouth. But once he gets a few meters beyond me, he stops and looks quickly around the perimeter of the Baena, licking his lips.

My bull, my *toro*, can't see beyond a few feet in front of him.

I glance at Antonio, who sees me seeing him, and smirks. No *sorteo*? Somehow Antonio has arranged with his uncle for Wild

Mustang to be ridiculed. It's a good one: she could kill this bad bull, she could run up from behind him and slam her sword into his back, but an improper death is worse than no death at all. Lesser violations have killed whole careers of some matadors. For a matadora, they barely even need a reason.

I motion for Rafael, who scuttles into the ring.

"This bull," I say, "is blind."

"That's impossible," he says.

"I'm not going to kill a blind bull," I say.

Rafael puts his hands out. He reeks of sour chicken. "This is your bull. You must kill him. Besides, the fight has already begun. Look at him! He's suffering. It would be less humane to let him live."

"Get me another bull," I say, "or I'm never fighting here again."

Rafael goes to the president. The president gestures angrily toward Rafael and then angrily toward me. The crowd's restless. Even the people not sitting in the sun-side of the stands look hot. I know how they feel: my neck sweats, my toes burn. I'm having trouble breathing. The president decides to remove my bull from the ring while they make their decision. They send in Pepin's bull instead.

Pepin has a good wrangle with his bull. He executes several veronicas and adalias close enough to warrant an *Ole!* from the audience. Soon the bull is charmed. Pepin holds his sword high and thrusts it neatly into the back. The bull rises on his hind legs, cries out in a terrifying song, and then collapses.

The audience thunders appreciatively.

When Antonio's bull is ready, he kisses his hands and bows to the crowd. It doesn't take long to win. This bull, thick with fat, is lulled to the cape like a drunk. So Antonio begins performing all sorts of ridiculous adornos with his spotted Traje de Luces to garner attention from the crowd. First he touches the bull's horn with his finger, then he kisses the bull's forehead, then he does *telefono*, resting his elbow on the bull's forehead with his hands to his head as though speaking on the telephone. There's moderate applause. He gets so carried away that he performs what with a regular bull is the most dangerous adorno there is: he lines himself up in front of the bull and tips his head forward, so the edge of his chin rests on the spike of the horn. He lingers there for a moment, perched on the horn, then rises slowly, as though it were dramatic, as though there was anything *remotely* dangerous about what he'd just done, and drives the sword in. The bull buckles forward, hissing like a deflated balloon.

The president applauds, wildly. But the people always know a cheap performance when they see one. A few flowers are scattered, then Rafael returns with the message: I am to kill the bull that was allotted to me. But if I'm afraid, the president will understand, and I may withdraw.

If I withdraw, I'm a coward. If I fight, it will be an improper fight. I look to Eugenio, standing by the entrance of the ring. He glares at me and slowly slices a finger across his throat.

So I enter the ring. I salute the president with a smile. The people roar with pleasure. They cheer, "Mus-tan-go! Sal-va-je!" They stomp their feet.

My bull reenters the ring. He tears in lopsided. The froth at his mouth has thickened. His eyes look glazed and confused. This bull cannot be charmed. It could turn at any moment. I keep my distance, but examine him as closely as possible. There's a marking on his rear of a circle with another smaller circle inside it.

This is the marking of the Félix de la Corte ranch in Córdoba. It's a small ranch, but dates from 1845, specializing in the Saltillo breed of bull, the foundation stock of most Mexican ranches, which are highly regarded in Spain. These bulls are extremely bright, and extremely dangerous. But the Félix de la Corte ranch also produced the famous Civilón, the bull that was tame as a cow. It's a story Victor told Wild Mustang when she was only eight years old.

"It was the early 1930s," Victor said. "A magical time for the *corrida*."

The small girl sat next to him, listening. Her knees at her chin.

"Civilón was owned by a man named Isidoro Tirado," he continued, "a matador-turned-farmhand. Isidoro observed that Civilón seemed calmer than the other bulls on his ranch. He didn't have the same inner rage. So Isidoro fed him tender branches to eat from horseback. He kept a safe distance until eventually he felt comfortable enough to dismount from the horse and feed him like a regular farm animal. He was so tame, children were allowed in to pet him."

The girl smiled.

"But when Civilón was five years old," he said, "it was decided that his time to fight had come. He was sent into the ring. When the cape danced in front of him, nature took over. Civilón's instincts ignited. He charged, wildly! And then Isidoro was dared to enter the ring and pet the bull, to see if it truly had been domesticated."

"What happened?" said the girl.

"He entered."

"And?"

"Civilón saw his old master and headed right for him."

The girl gasped.

"But instead of attacking," he said, "the bull nuzzled Isidoro's coat, and followed him out of the ring."

"Then what happened?" said the girl.

"Then the audience rose," said Victor, "demanding that the bull be discharged and his life spared. Everyone agreed. It was decided that Civilón would be a stud for future fighting bulls, but would remain at the arena until he had recovered from the fight."

"That's good," said the girl.

"I'm not finished," said Victor. "A few nights later, rebel soldiers entered Barcelona. Desperate and hungry, they went to the ring in search of beef. There was Civilón. He was shot to death, and butchered."

"Civilón!" whispered the girl.

"So you see," said Victor, "there are many different uses for a life."

I move in closer, standing just a few feet in front of the bull. I look at him, at the odd way his feet turn inward. I drop my cape. A murmur floats through the crowd. No one understands why Wild Mustang has dropped the *capa*. From the stands, the spectators block their eyes, but not from the sun: it's the glow of my Traje de Luces.

"Civilón," I whisper.

The bull turns his head, fast.

"No, Cristina," Pepin yells. "It's suicide!"

I look again at my father. He glares back. *"Lucha,"* he whispers. But next to my father, a little further on down the wall, is a short, shadowy figure with cropped trousers. It's Victor. He leans against the wall by the entrance, smoking a cigarette. He sees me seeing him and smiles.

"Mi Batata," he whispers.

I gesture for Manuel to bring me my sword. He hurries back with it. I take the sword and place it on the ground next to the cape.

"Civilón," I say, this time louder.

The bull snorts, disagreeably.

A shout goes out: "Someone rescue the woman!"

There's commotion in the stands. The president doesn't like what he is seeing. The kill is always performed with a sword thrusting through the back of the bull. There are even certain classicists who believe the bullfighter should keep one foot on the ground as the sword is placed. It does not appear that Wild Mustang plans to do either. "This fight will not be counted," the president announces. "This is not skill! This is not talent! She is breaking all the rules."

But Wild Mustang cannot hear him. Capeless, swordless, I drop my hands into fists. "God has given me great pleasures!" I shout, as the bull rushes blindly forward.

I'm well aware of my surroundings:

Antonio has fallen to his knees in shock. He doesn't know it, but this is his last fight and no one will remember him. His wife will leave him. He will die only a dozen years from now, poor and alone, from a messy and uncomfortable digestive disorder. And Pepin? Who stands nearby, ready with his own sword? He doesn't know it, but he's about to become the best matador in the world. He'll step into the shoe like it was his all along, garnishing many accolades from many respected bullfighting officials. He will retire, rich and respected, to a large house with many mirrors from which he can view his butt from any angle. Someplace lovely.

Italy, perhaps.

Then there's Eugenio. Eugenio sees the bull charge and grabs his chest so hard he crushes the anti-anxiety pills into powder. He's having a mild heart attack. Oh, he'll live. Only after today, there will be no more bullfighting. No more money. What will he do? He will continue listening to the lemons. He will continue to be an average man, which will make him angry. Angrier than he's ever been. Because from now on he will have to live with what happened to his daughter.

And there are simply not enough pills in the world for that.

Then there are the rescuers. The brave, brave men. They make their way down from their seats and, in a spectacular display, tumble over themselves to jump over the callejon and be the first one into the ring to save me.

There is no need.

In a flicker, I slide to the ground, reach for my sword with both hands, and lie flat on my back. I angle the blade up, holding steady with both hands. When a bullfighter places a sword into the back of the bull, the blade slices not the heart itself, but only an aorta. It is a slower death, designed purely for the drama of the kill. So when this bull gallops over me, I catch him underneath; the sword slides deep into the center of his heart, and he dies instantly. It is illegal, but the quickest way, with the least pain.

In this way, Wild Mustang dies too.

I suffer only a few cuts and bruises.

AIMEE BENDER

■

Tiger Mending

FROM *BlackBook*

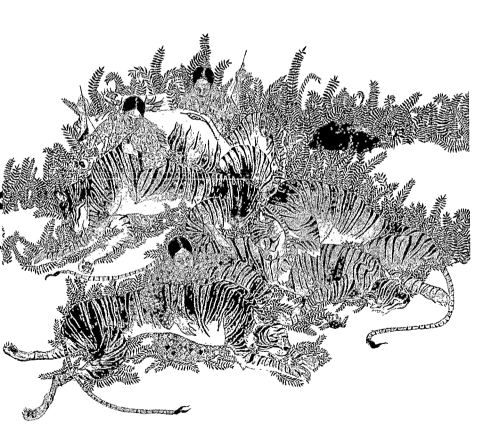

MY SISTER GOT the job. She's the overachiever, and she went to med school for two years before she decided she wanted to be a gifted seamstress. (What? they said, on the day she left. A surgeon! they told her. You could be a tremendous surgeon! But she said she didn't like the late hours, she got too tired around midnight.) She has small-motor skills better than a machine; she'll fix your handkerchief so well you can't even see the stitches, like she became one with the handkerchief. I once split my lip, jumping from the tree, and she sewed it up, with ice and a needle she'd run through the fire. I never even had a scar, just the thinnest white line.

So of course, when the two women came through the sewing school, they spotted her first. She was working on her final exam, a lime-colored ball gown with tiny diamonds sewn into the collar, and she was fully absorbed in it, constructing infinitesimal loops, while they hovered with their severe hair and heady tree smell — like bamboo, my sister said — watching her work. My sister's so steady she didn't even flinch, but everyone else in class seized upon the distraction, staring at the two Amazonian women, both six feet tall and strikingly beautiful. When I met them later I felt like I'd landed straight inside a magazine ad. At the time, I was working at Burger King, as a block manager (there were two on the block), and I took any distraction offered me and used it to the hilt. Once, a guy came in and ordered a Big Mac, and for two days I told that story to every customer, and it's not a good story. There's so rarely any intrigue in this shabberdash world of burger warming, you take what you can get.

But my sister was born with supernatural focus, and the two women watched her and her alone. Who can compete? My sister's won all the contests she's ever been in, not because she's such an outrageous competitor, but because she's so focused in this gentle way. Why not win? Sometimes it's all you need to run the fastest, or to play the clearest piano, or to ace the standardized test, pausing at each question until it has slid through your mind to exit as a penciled-in circle.

In low, sweet voices, the women asked my sister if she'd like to see Asia. She finally looked up from her work. Is there a sewing job there? They nodded. She said she'd love to see Asia, she'd never left America. They said, Well, it's a highly unusual job. May I bring my sister? she asked. She's never traveled either.

The two women glanced at each other. What does your sister do?

She's the manager of the Burger King down on Fourth.

Their disapproval was faint but palpable, especially in the upper lip.

She would simply keep you company?

What we are offering you is a position of tremendous privilege. Aren't you interested in hearing about it first?

My sister nodded lightly. It sounds very interesting, she said. But I cannot travel without my sister.

This is true. My sister, the one with that incredible focus, has a terrible fear of airplanes. Terrible. Incapacitating. The only way she can relax on a flight is if I am there, because I am always, always having some kind of crisis, and she focuses in and fixes me and forgets her own concerns. I become her ripped hemline. In general, I call her every night, and we talk for an hour, which is forty-five minutes of me, and fifteen minutes of her stirring her tea, which she steeps with the kind of Zen patience that would make Buddhists sit up in envy, and then breathe through their envy, and then move past their envy. I'm really really lucky she's my sister. Otherwise, no one like her would give someone like me the time of day.

The two Amazonian women, lousy with confidence, with their ridiculous cheekbones, in these long yellow print dresses, said OK. They observed my sister's hands quiet in her lap.

Do you get along with animals? they asked and she said, Yes. She loved every animal. Do you have allergies to cats? they asked, and she said, No. She was allergic only to pine nuts. The slightly taller one reached into her dress pocket, a pocket so well hidden inside the fabric it was like she was reaching into the ether of space, and from it her hand returned with an airplane ticket.

We are very happy to have found you, they said. The additional ticket will arrive tomorrow.

My sister smiled. I know her; she was probably terrified to see that ticket, and also she really wanted to return to the diamond loops. She probably wasn't even that curious about the new job yet. She was and is stubbornly, mind-numbingly, interested in the present moment.

When we were kids, I used to come home and she'd be at the living room window. It was the best window in the apartment, looking out, in the far distance, on the tip of a mountain. For years I tried to get her to play with me, but she was unplayable. She'd stare out that window, never moving, for hours. By night, when she'd returned, I'd usually injured myself in some way or other, and I'd ask her about it as she tended to me; she said the reason she could pay acute attention was because of the window. It empties me out, she'd said, which scared me. No, she'd said, to my frightened face, and she'd sat on the edge of my bed and ran a washcloth over my forehead. It's good, she'd said. It makes room for other things.

Me? I'd asked, with hope, and she'd nodded. You.

We had no parents, by that point. They'd died at the hands of surgeons, which is the real reason my sister stopped medical school.

That night, after she took the job, she called me up and told me to quit my job, which was what I'd been praying for for months — that somehow I'd get a magical phone call telling me to quit my job because I was going on an exciting vacation. I threw down my BK apron, packed, and prepared as long an account of my life complaints as I could. On the plane, I asked my sister what we were doing, what her job was, but she refolded her tray table and said nothing. Asia, I said. What country? She stared out the porthole. It was the pilot who told us, as we buckled our seat belts; we were heading to Kuala Lumpur, straight into the heart of Malaysia.

Wait, where's Malaysia again? I whispered, and my sister drew a map on the napkin beneath her ginger ale.

During the flight, I drank Bloody Marys while my sister embroidered a doily. Even the other passengers seemed soothed by watching her work. I whispered all my problems into her ear and she returned them back to me in slow sentences that did the work of a lullaby. My eyes grew heavy. During the descent, she gave the doily to the man across the aisle, worried about his ailing son, and the needlework was so elegant it made him feel better just holding it. That's the thing with handmade items. They still have the person's mark on them, and when you hold them, you feel less alone. This is why everyone who eats a Whopper leaves a little more depressed than they were when they came in. Nobody cooked that burger.

When we arrived, a friendly driver took us to a cheerful green hotel, where we found a note on the bed telling my sister to be ready at 6 A.M. sharp. It didn't say I could come, but bright and early the next morning, scrubbed and fed, we faced the two Amazons in the lobby, who looked scornfully at me and my unsteady hands — I sort of pick at my hair a lot — and asked my sister why I was there. Can't she watch? she asked, and they said they weren't sure. She, they said, might be too anxious.

I swear I won't touch anything, I said.

This is a private operation, they said.

My sister breathed. I work best when she's nearby, she said. Please.

And like usual, it was the way she said it. In that gentle voice that had a back to it. They opened the car door.

Thank you, my sister said.

They blindfolded us, for reasons of security, and we drove for more than an hour, down winding, screeching roads, parking finally in a place that smelled like garlic and fruit. In front of a stone mansion, two more women dressed in printed robes waved as we removed our blindfolds. These two were short. Delicate. Calm. They led us into the living room, and we hadn't been there for ten minutes when we heard the moaning.

A bad moaning sound. A real bad, real mournful moaning, coming from the north, outside, that reminded me of the worst loneliness, the worst long lonely night. The Amazonian with the short shining cap of hair nodded.

Those are the tigers, she said.

What tigers? I said.

Shh, she said. I will call her Sloane, for no other reason than it's a good name for an intimidating person.

Sloane said, Shh. Quiet now. She took my sister by the shoulders and led her to a wide window that looked out on the land. As if she knew, instinctively, how wise it was to place my sister at a window.

Watch, Sloane whispered.

I stood behind. The two women from the front walked into view and settled on the ground near some clumps of ferns. They waited. They were very still-minded, like my sister, that stillness of mind. That ability I will never have, to sit still. That ability to have the hands forget they are hands. They closed their eyes, and the moaning I'd heard before got louder, and then in the distance, I mean waaaay off, the moaning grew even louder, almost unbearable to hear, and limping from the side lumbered two enormous tigers. Wailing, as if they were dying. As they got closer, you could see that their backs were split open, sort of peeled, as if someone had torn them in two. The fur was matted, and the stripes hung loose, like packing tape, ripped off their bodies. The women did not seem to move, but two glittering needles worked their way out of their knuckles, climbing up out of their hands, and one of the tigers stepped closer. I thought I'd lose it; he was easily four times her size, and she was small, a tiger's snack, but he limped over, in his giantness, and fell into her lap. Let his heavy striped head sink to the ground. She smoothed the stripe back over, and the moment she pierced his fur with the needle, those big cat eyes dripped over with tears.

It was very powerful. It brought me to tears, too. Those expert hands, as steady as if they were holding a pair of pants, while the tiger's enormous head hung to the ground. My sister didn't move, but I cried and cried, seeing those giant broken animals resting in the laps of the small precise women. It is so often surprising, who rescues you at your lowest moment. When our parents died in surgery, the jerk at the liquor store suddenly became the nicest man alive, and gave us free cranberry juice for a year.

What happened to them? I asked Sloane. Why are they like that?

She lifted her chin slightly. We do not know, but they emerge from the forests, peeling. More and more of them. Always torn at the central stripe.

Do they ever eat people?

Not so far, she said. But they do not respond well to fidgeting, she said, watching me clear out my thumbnail with my other thumbnail.

Well, I'm not doing it.

You have not been asked.

They are so sad, said my sister.

Well, wouldn't you be? If you were a tiger, peeling? Sloane put a hand on my sister's shoulder. When mending was done, all four — women and beasts — sat in the sun for at least half an hour, tigers' chests heaving, women's hands clutched in their fur. The day grew warm. In the distance, the moaning began again, and two more tigers limped up while the first two stretched out and slept. The women sewed the next two, and the next. One had a bloody rip across its white belly.

After a few hours of work, the women put their needles away, the tigers raised themselves up, and without any lick or acknowledgment, walked off, deep into that place where tigers live. The women returned to the house. Inside, they smelled so deeply and earthily of cat that they were almost unrecognizable. They also seemed lighter, nearly giddy. It was lunchtime. They joined us at the table, where Sloane served an amazing soup of curry and prawns.

It is an honor, said Sloane, to mend the tigers.

I see, said my sister.

You will need very little training, since your skill level is already so high.

But my sister seemed frightened, in a way I hadn't seen before. She didn't eat much of her soup, and she returned her eyes to the window, to the tangles of fluttering leaves.

I would have to go find out, she said finally, when the chef entered with a tray of mango tartlets.

Find out what?

Why they peel, she said. She hung her head, as if she was ashamed of her interest.

You are a mender, said Sloane, gently. Not a zoologist.

I support my sister's interest in the source, I said.

Sloane flinched every time I opened my mouth.

The source, my sister echoed.

The world has changed, said Sloane, passing a mango tartlet to me, reluctantly, which I ate, pronto.

It was unlike my sister, to need the cause. She was fine, usually, with just how things were. But she whispered to me, as we roamed outside looking for clues, of which we found none; she whispered that she felt something dangerous in the peeling, and she felt she would have to know about it in order to sew the tigers suitably. I am not worried about the sewing, she said. I am worried about the gesture I place inside the thread.

I nodded. I am a good fighter, is all. I don't care about thread gestures, but I am willing to throw a punch at some tiger asshole if need be.

We spent the rest of the day outside, but there were no tigers to be seen — where they lived was somewhere far, far off, and the journey they took to arrive here must have been the worst time of their lives, ripped open like that, suddenly prey to vultures and other predators, when they were usually the ones to instill fear.

We spent that night at the mansion, in feather beds so soft I found them impossible to sleep in. Come morning, Sloane had my sister join the two women outside, and I cried again, watching the big tiger head at her feet while she sewed with her usual still-ness. The three together were unusually productive, and sewn tigers piled up around them. But instead of that giddiness that showed up in the other women, my sister grew heavier that after-noon, and said she was sure she was doing something wrong. Oh no, said Sloane, serving us tea. You were remarkable.

I am missing something, said my sister. I am missing some-thing important.

Sloane retired for a nap, but I snuck out. I had been warned, but really, they were treating me like shit anyway. I walked a long distance, but I'm a sturdy walker, and I trusted where my feet went, and I did not like the sight of my sister staring into her teacup. I did not like the feeling it gave me, of worrying. Before I left, I sat her in front of the window and told her to empty herself, and her eyes were grateful in a way I was used to feeling in my own face but was not accustomed to seeing in hers.

I walked for hours, and the wet air clung to my shirt and hair. I took a nap inside some ferns. The sun was setting, and I would've walked all night, but when I reached a cluster of trees something felt different. There was no wailing yet, but I could feel the stirring before the wailing, which is almost worse. I swear I could hear the dread. I climbed up a tree and waited.

I don't know what I expected — people, I guess. People with knives, cutting in. I did not expect to see the tigers themselves, jumpy, agitated, yawning their mouths beyond wide, the wildness in their eyes, and finally the yawning so large and insistent that they split their own back in two. They all did it, one after the other — as if they wanted to peel the fur off their backs, and then, amazed at what they'd done, the wailing began.

One by one, they left the trees and began their slow journey to be mended. It left me with the oddest, most unsettled feeling.

I walked back when it was night, under a half-moon, and found my sister still at the window.

They do it to themselves, I whispered to her, and she took my hand. Her face lightened. Thank you, she said. She tried to hug me, but I pulled away. No, I said, and in the morning, I left for the airport.

RYAN BOUDINOT

■

Free Burgers for Life

FROM *Monkeybicycle*

A FEW MONTHS AGO I won a free deluxe cheeseburger, fries, and twelve-ounce fountain drink every day for the rest of my life from Big Dave's drive-thru burgers. I often ate there on my lunch breaks when I worked at the print shop next door. The print shop had been surviving on industrial-safety manuals and church bulletins for years, but had recently begun branching out into digital photography and Web design. Mr. Meyer, my boss, had sunk what was supposed to be his retirement fund into new technology and a series of consultants who fed him contradictory information he didn't understand anyway. He ended up with a scanner that wasn't compatible with his PC, a printer that continually jammed, and a bunch of software that was way over our heads. Harlan Meyer got suckered into any offer that involved free promotional merchandise, so all we had to show for our efforts was a storage box full of glare guards, a couple lumbar supports, and mouse pads. Even during the times Mr. Meyer couldn't pay me, I still showed up for work, mostly to mess around on the computer. Being laid off and having a place to hang out like the print shop combined the best aspects of being unemployed and having a job. I could take breaks whenever I wanted and any work I actually performed made Mr. Meyer guilty enough to buy me lunch. So naturally, when Big Dave's announced its Free Burgers for Life contest, I was one of the first to enter. I was even there when they drew the winner one

Sunday morning. They had billed it as a big media event, but the only journalist who showed up was Josh Bland, an ex–rock star who wrote a column for the alternative weekly, the one that ran the ads for escort services that I masturbated to when I was drunk.

During the ceremony, Josh Bland sat in the "barnyard," the kids' section furnished with saddles instead of booths, scribbling notes, sipping his complimentary mocha shake, and mumbling cryptically into a tape recorder. He basically made fun of everybody in the article.

All the parents and siblings of Big Dave's employees had shown up to receive their free "Family Appreciation Day" meals, even though it was ten in the morning. Dennis, the manager and son of the joint's deceased founder (Dave), passed out kazoos and silly hats and encouraged everyone to wear their Twentieth Anniversary T-shirt. Dennis's wife, Theresa, remained in the back manning the fry station and telling would-be customers coming through the drive-thru that the place was closed. She had a physical deformity, a harelip, and was shy around anyone outside Big Dave's circle of employees and suppliers. For a long time I thought she was deaf. She refused to speak to me as a customer. Whenever I said hello she'd do a little pinky-wave and go back to restocking napkins.

I usually took my extended lunches at Big Dave's whenever Mr. Meyer's wife, Rita, showed up unannounced to provoke Mr. Meyer into vicious arguments about money and software. Rita would try to flatter me and belittle her husband in a single sentence. "If you'd just hire more geniuses like Elliott around here, Harlan, then maybe you wouldn't have to subcontract out for Internet whatever-it-is." She was stubbornly Luddite and acted as though she weren't so much uninterested in computers as above them. Maybe this attitude was her way of expressing resentment at Mr. Meyer for squandering their money on what she considered toys. The Meyers had mentioned they were going to show up for the Free Burgers for Life ceremony, but never did.

Dennis had officially invited the public, but there were few of us among the crowd of teenagers and their parents. Somebody called us all over to the condiment bar, where Dennis drew my name from a cardboard box covered in aluminum foil and masking tape. For a second his mouth went slack then pulled itself back up into a wrinkly grin while everyone clapped. I later found out that Dennis and Theresa suspected me of rigging the contest. That evening after closing they opened the ballot box and read all the entries. I had submitted only one. There was no way they could stop me from claiming my prize. Later still, I found out that Big Dave's employees had been encouraged to enter the drawing as many times as they wanted, encouraged, in fact, to fill out stacks of ballots in the break room. Dennis hoped to give the prize to one of the teenagers who worked for him. I was so elated I didn't even notice how disappointed everyone else was.

I'm not usually an extravagant kind of guy. At wedding receptions and bar mitzvahs I'm not known as the kind of dancer who hogs the floor and gets serious for three hours straight. I'm more the kind of dancer who, when called upon, can bust a particular move that shows everyone I am the shit. I have one discernible talent on the dance floor, one maneuver I retained from my grade school gymnastics class. First, I kick my right leg forward and my left leg back, dropping to a full split. Then, *without using my hands,* I rise back up to a standing position. I then drop to the floor with my left leg forward and my right leg back, and finally rise again to continue dancing like it's no big deal. It's not the move itself that impresses people, but the nonchalance with which I execute it. But that day, after I performed it on Big Dave's freshly waxed brown tile floor, I had a hard time containing myself and kind of hurt my groin.

I was entitled to any combination of menu items up to a five-dollar value every day for the rest of my life. If I wanted to substitute a chicken sandwich or a French dip for the burger or a soft-serve cone for the fries, I was welcome to do so. If I wanted four orders of fries, that was no problem. Or five Cokes. If I missed a day, it didn't mean I got two meals the next day. All I had to do was show them my little laminated card, which, incidentally, I had laminated personally, as Big Dave's did all their copy work through the print shop. Mostly coupons and fliers. Big Dave's offered forty-seven different flavors of shake and I was determined to try every one of them at least once. All they did to make a new flavor was dump different syrups from the espresso bar into vanilla ice cream and stir it up. Never trust espresso from a burger place, I have found.

About a month after I won the drawing, my brother Steve visited me so I took him out for a complimentary burger, fry, and fountain drink. He's twenty years old and goes to a liberal arts college nobody has ever heard of. He's an art major and once sent me, as a Christmas gift, a green mannequin head with a light bulb inside it. He said it was a lamp but there was no way for the light to get out. Steve is the kind of person who watches TV for hours just so he can make fun of it. He has a withering comment for any advertisement, popular band, movie, or book that he perceives as pandering to mainstream tastes. Maybe I'm being too harsh. No, not really. I was always the responsible one, he was always the screwup. He had dreadlocks for a while, I have always had short hair, etc. There are times, though, when I've wondered if he is a genius and I'm a thirty-year-old loser making paper clip chains at a string of boring gigs. He has his own Web site, a mess of penis enlargement ads scanned from porno mags and links that lead you in circles, which I had been checking out at work and finding pretty amusing. We e-mailed each other every couple weeks and when he dropped me a note to say he was coming into town, I held off telling him about my prize because I wanted to see his reaction. He arrived at my apartment in his van, where he lives. Our parents don't approve of it, but I think it's pretty cool actually. He's got a little refrigerator in there, curtains on the windows, and a foldout bed.

On our way to Big Dave's, Steve couldn't stop laughing about my free burgers for life. I hadn't been in his van for a while and the whole thing smelled like cat pee.

"Did you get a cat?" I said.

"Not that I'm aware of," Steve said.

"Has there been a cat in here recently?"

"What are you saying?"

"What is this, old Pink Floyd we're listening to?"

"Velvet. What? Velvet Underground."

"You still got my Creedence CD?"

"You think it smells bad in here or something?"

I could fill the rest of this tale with our back and forth, but we had burgers to eat. It was raining hard when we pulled up to the Big D. A teenage guy named Benjamin with a really thin head stood in the landscaping, wearing a sandwich board advertising $1.99 double cheeseburgers, waving at traffic hissing past him on the arterial.

"Hey, Elliott! How's it going!" Don, Sandra, Dennis, Carlo, Marie, Thomas, and Paula greeted me as we entered the building. Theresa, the fake-out deaf-mute, didn't say anything.

"Hi, everybody. I brought my brother along with me today."

"Hi, Elliott's brother!"

Steve stood beside me trembling with laughter while I surveyed the menu as though for the first time.

"So what does your heart desire?" I said.

"Elliott, man, I can't believe this. This is so fuckin great," Steve said.

Steve ordered a garden burger, fries, and a kiwi-almond shake. I paid for a deluxe baked potato, side salad with Thousand Island, and a small pop. We sat in a booth across from some high school girls who had all ordered large Cokes and were busy dabbing droplets of pop on their scrunched-up straw wrappers to make them expand.

"See this?" I said, pointing to the specials menu in its plastic standee frame. "I printed this."

"Wow, impressive," Steve said, flipping it around. "Oops. Spotted a typo."

"You're kidding me. Where?"

"Here. Says 'bruger' instead of 'burger.'"

"*Damn.* How come I didn't catch that?"

Sandra slid our tray onto the table and asked if I had gotten sick of eating here yet. She was one of those proud, overweight black girls you see with the elaborate hairstyles. Her hair today was diagonally cantilevered out over her forehead. I liked her a lot. We'd gotten to talking a few days before about desktop publishing. She was going to a community college, studying graphic arts. I told her that if she wanted to apply at the print shop she could put me down as a reference, even though I knew there was no way Mr. Meyer was ever going to hire more than one employee at a time.

"Whatever you do, *stay away from the fishwich*," Sandra said.

"Why's that?"

"I'm not at liberty to say. Nondisclosure agreement. We take an oath, raise our right hand, and all that shit."

I had sensed a lot of tension in Big Dave's that day, as if everybody was wearing his or her required smile despite some horrible drama that had played out just before we arrived. Steve sat across from me eating his fries in that retarded way he always has, dipping each individual fry into a carefully opened ketchup packet. Every few seconds he'd snort, look around, and shake his head or roll his eyes. It was starting to piss me off. If I was going to share my free food with the guy, I expected a little gratitude.

"You still seeing that one chick, what's-her-face?" Steve said.

"You talking about Katy?"

"That must be the one."

"No, I'm not. I mean yeah, in a way."

"What the hell is that supposed to mean? Yea or nay?"

"We broke up a while ago. But we still see each other once in a while."

"Ah, nostalgia fucking."

"I didn't say that," I said.

"Well, do you call meeting each other for coffee 'still seeing each other'? Still seeing each other means —"

"What about you? Still going out with that girl from Arizona or wherever?"

"Colorado. Dude, I had my first three-way with her and her roommate last week."

Which goes to show how my younger brother's sex life had always been more exotic and fulfilling than my own. I both wanted to hear about it and didn't want to hear about it. Steve recounted the entire incident — the scented oils, the hot wax on nipples — in a perhaps louder-than-necessary voice, causing a booth of elderly women whom I had seen holding hands and praying over their side salads to pick up their trays and move to the other side of the restaurant. The high school girls, on the other hand, expended a great deal of energy pretending not to listen. I knew that if I said anything Steve would make an even bigger show of it, so I decided instead to suffer through the story, stirring chives and bacon bits into my cold potato. Outside, the rain dumped on Benjamin, who looked increasingly pathetic the more enthusiastically he tried to wave. I felt bad for the guy. Perhaps this was punishment for something he had done to the fishwiches.

I scribbled some numbers on a napkin, figuring out how much my free meals were costing Big Dave's. Five dollars times 365 days was $1,825. Granted, there were days when I didn't reach my five-dollar limit and a couple days when I didn't get anything at all, but my prize was costing them at least $1,500 a year. Take away the markup, which I guessed to be about fifty percent, and my free burgers, fries, and pops were setting them back about $750. Which is probably about as much as Big Dave's made on a good day.

"You think this place can really afford to give me a free meal every day for the rest of my life?" I said.

Steve shook his head. "The whole thing has the vibe of a last-gasp promotional deal to me. I wouldn't be surprised if this place went out of business soon."

Most of the time after work I got my food from the drive-thru, then went home and ate it alone in my apartment. I have never had a weight problem, owing to my high metabolism, but after a few weeks I started noticing a ring around my belly like a slowly inflating inner tube. For breakfast I usually ate toast and for lunch a couple of those instant soups you just pour hot water into. On a couple occasions I threw up after eating my barbecue burger or chicken fillet. My body was telling me it was tired of Big Dave's but I couldn't resist my free meal. I enjoyed getting something for free, whether or not I really wanted it. Once I even took a single bite out of a double bacon cheeseburger and stuffed the rest down the garbage disposal with a spatula.

I decided one night to shop for a birthday card for Katy, who hadn't returned my calls for a month. I thought she would budge a little if I got her something sweet, one of those cards with a poem in it or a funny cartoon. I was in Hallmark when Sandra snuck up behind me and pinched me on the neck.

"You don't work at Big Dave's anymore," I said. "Where did you go?"

"I got a new job! Last week, at the Nickel and Dime Want-Ads. I'm gonna be doing layout and paste-up. You still getting those free burgers? *Damn*, Elliott. I thought you would have gotten mad cow disease by now."

"Free food is free food, I guess. Who's the lucky person?"

Sandra was holding a teddy bear crammed into a coffee mug.

"It's for my nephew James. He turns three this weekend."

"Your nephew drinks coffee?"

"Oh, say, Elliott. I'm glad I ran into you. You still showing up on Benjamin's shift?"

"Yeah, once in a while."

Sandra looked concerned. It took her a while to communicate through euphemisms and gestures what Benjamin had done that I should be aware of. Not only had he been spitting into my burgers, but he had once put a pube in one of them.

I felt it was my responsibility to report Benjamin to Dennis. We sat in the booth farthest from the counter and I recounted what I had been told. Dennis shook his head and breathed a lot through his nose and rubbed his mustache. He still wore his drive-thru headset and microphone.

"Did you find some, uh, *evidence* in one of your burgers?" Dennis said.

"An inside source told me."

"It was Sandra, wasn't it?"

"Well, yeah."

Dennis rolled his eyes. "Sandra got fired last week. She had some bone to pick with Benjamin. I'm sure she just lied to get him in trouble. We caught her on surveillance cam stealing chicken patties from the walk-in. She's been diagnosed as a pathological liar and now she's in therapy for it."

"You're kidding. She seems so cool."

"Oh, she's a great kid. No question. She's just a kleptomaniac and has some problems comprehending the truth. She was stealing from the *tampon* machine for Christsakes. When we confronted her with the chicken patty thing, she denied it, even when we played her footage from the cam. She said it was doctored, that we had this big conspiracy against her because she's black. Really severe pathological liars like Sandra believe their own lies, even when the facts are staring them straight in the face. I've been doing a little research about this stuff on-line. I'm sure Sandra believes in her heart that what she told you was true. She probably thinks you're a nice guy and wants you to like her. But basically she has this self-esteem problem. She loves attention. People listen to her when she makes up some big story. She probably told you she's going to community college, right?"

I nodded, sadly.

"Well, it isn't true. She picks up things from talk shows and goes with them, steals other people's psychodramas and reenacts them for your sympathy. It's really pretty sad. At any rate, I'm sorry she upset you. Tell you what. I have to get back to the drive-thru. Want a couple burgers?"

I drove around the parking lot of the grocery store where Katy worked, trying to watch her through the windows. There were signs advertising two-for-one maple bars and 99-cent canned peaches in the way, but I could see her at the express lane checking people out. If I drove by the front of the store at about three miles an hour I could see her for maybe five seconds. She had her hair up in a ponytail and was wearing the red vest the store illegally made their employees pay for. I used to pick her up when she was working swing shift and she'd give me free day-old doughnuts from the bakery. I wanted to marry Katy and move to Alaska. I've never actually been to Alaska, but Steve has and I've seen pictures of the place. The sun shines 24/7 up there during the summer. But there's a downside, the winter, when all you can do is drink and plot your suicide. Then everything gets better again. Katy hadn't written or called me since I sent her that card. I had even added a couple lines to the poem myself.

I watched another checker walk up to Katy and say something, gesturing out the window. Katy turned and saw me. I gunned it and stared straight ahead, as if I was on my way someplace else.

Some of the print jobs Mr. Meyer took on were just bizarre. End-of-the-world propaganda and UPC symbol = 666 type stuff. I'd seen a lot of right-wing literature come through that I didn't particularly agree with, but when you're in the print business you have to leave your political views at the door. Besides, he was paying me $6.50 an hour and I didn't particularly care where it was coming from.

I came to work one Monday to find Mr. Meyer sitting at my desk, dividing all my papers into little piles. His stringy hair was combed over his bald spot, except for a few strands that stuck straight up off the side of his head like a flag on a mailbox. I could tell he'd been here a while, working himself up for something.

"Mr. Meyer. You're sitting in my chair."

"I think we have to talk, Elliott."

"OK."

"I'd like to know the meaning of this," he said, sliding some printouts across the desk.

"They're my brother's Web site."

"Your brother is quite an artist."

"I think so."

"Besides the fact there's a rule here about using the equipment and supplies for personal use, I don't approve of my computer being used to download pornography."

"Pornography?"

"Take a look."

I flipped through the pile of paper. Reviews of shows, angry commentary about oil companies, poorly drawn pothead comix. Then I found what Mr. Meyer must have been talking about.

"You're kidding. It's just a drawing. It's not even a photo."

"Smut is smut, whether it is drawn or not."

"But it's not like he's *advocating* bestiality."

It was hopeless. Mr. Meyer was the boss and I was the employee. He would have laid me off again sooner or later anyway. Truthfully, I had been walking the edge for months now. Typos weren't the half of it. Steve's Web site was just the reason he found for finally getting around to firing me.

A double cheeseburger with no tomatoes, a large curly fry, and a small chocolate peanut-butter shake. Side of ranch for the fries, please. Yes, I'm aware that's twenty-five cents extra.

That night Tony, Miguel, and Lissa visited me at my apartment. They're high school kids I occasionally buy beer for. Once in a while they give me a free CD. Miguel works at a music store and gets to take home the promos. That's how I've kept up with current music. They let me keep the change whenever I buy for them. Usually it's just a couple half-racks. When they came over I was in rough shape, watching *Taxi* reruns in my sweatpants, smoking some cigarettes Steve accidentally left at my place. Miguel put a new disc on the stereo. Lissa lay on the couch with her head in Tony's lap, groaning, "I'm so tired," while Tony provided a running commentary on kids dropping acid in a shop class and science-fiction movies. Tony had grown a mustache before it was actually thick enough to look like he wasn't trying so hard to grow one. Truth is, I saw something of myself in Tony and perhaps that's why I kept agreeing to buy for them. I was amused by their company. Plus, free CDs.

"Then this really fat chick was fuckin all like . . ."

"What kind of beer do you guys want?" I finally said.

"You all right, Elliott? You seem kinda burnt," Lissa said. If only I was ten years younger, as they say. She was making me horny the way she was draped all over Tony, who seemed not to notice or care. High school sex. In playgrounds at night, in parents' bedrooms. Katy had still been in high school when we had begun dating the year before, but she had been a senior. Lissa was a sophomore. She could have passed for a senior, though.

"I got fired today."

"Sounds like we need to treat *you* tonight, my friend," Tony said, though I knew he didn't really consider me a friend.

"Whatever you guys want. Let's just get it over with. What'll it be?"

Tony slid a couple twenties across the coffee table with the toe of his elaborate basketball shoe. "We'll go for a couple racks of the fancier shit tonight. You pick it out. Plus a couple forties."

"I'll be right back, then," I said, putting on my jacket. The apartment complex is next door to a mini mart. Within five minutes I had returned with their beer and some change.

"You guys can drink it here if you want," I said. The stereo was playing something I didn't understand, something that didn't sound like music but like a bunch of photocopiers and barking dogs with a woman saying the same thing over and over again. Tony commandeered the remote and cracked the first beer. I used to have cable but forgot to pay the bill for a few months so now all I had left were the local channels.

"Can I use your bathroom?" Lissa said.

"Yeah, sure," I said, trying to visualize the sorry state of my toilet bowl. I shivered, thinking of what Benjamin had done to my burger. I felt embarrassed but also a little aroused by the idea that Lissa was using my bathroom. I used to watch Katy pee after we had sex. I tried to pass it off as just curiosity, but I think toward the end she suspected it was more than that. Once I even told her to pee on me in the shower, but then pretended I'd been joking when she flipped out about it. Katy wasn't what you'd call sexually adventurous. She had three things she did and that was about it. Not like I imagined Lissa to be. Damn, if only I was in high school. She was one of those slightly plump girls I find so attractive for whatever reason. And if only Tony wasn't in the picture. I hoped he'd leave or pass out so I could mess around with her. Then there was Miguel to think about. No matter how much he drank, he never seemed to get drunk. He just sat in a corner with his hat pulled over his eyes, pretending to scratch records on an imaginary turntable.

"Still getting them free burgers?" Tony said.

"Still going strong," I said, cracking another beer.

"Dude, maybe we should rent a movie," Tony said.

"I've got a lot of movies here. They're in that milk crate under the T-shirt."

While Tony dug through my DVDs I pretended to look for something in my bedroom so I could "accidentally" run into Lissa. I heard her washing her hands and arranged to be coming out of the bedroom as she was leaving the bathroom. She gave a little embarrassed smile, and said, "Hi," then turned toward the living room.

"Hey, hold on," I said. "I wanted to ask you something. I wanted to know if you guys knew where I could get some pot."

"Tony's the one to ask."

"I just thought you might know."

"We could probably get some for you. Tony knows these guys." Lissa started toward the other room and shouted to Tony over the music, "Hey, Tony, know where Elliott can score some bud?"

"Elliott! The man!" Tony laughed.

They made a big show out of it but I wasn't really after pot at all. I just wanted to get high with Lissa alone in my bedroom. I drank two more beers and put on the director's cut of *Blade Runner.* Miguel mumbled something about a Spanish exchange student who had a lot of bud on him and was willing to give it away to make friends with Americans. We all crammed into my car, with Tony and Lissa groping in the back and Miguel manipulating the EQ on my crappy stereo in the front. We drove past the bowling alley and the espresso huts and all those places where you can get an oil change and I thought about Katy in her red vest running cans of vegetables over the scanner, except in my daydream the scanner didn't pick up the bar code and she had to run the same can over the laser again and again, stubbornly refusing to manually type in the code. She never wanted to see the movies I wanted to see, never wanted to go to a new restaurant or try a new menu item at Denny's, where we usually went on our dates. She refused to give me head. She threw a shit fit if she missed *Everybody Loves Raymond* because she hadn't missed an episode since the series began. Why couldn't I stop thinking about her? Every time I called, her parents erased my messages, I was sure. Her dad even answered a couple times and told me to stop calling and even though I was respectful of him he still wouldn't let me talk to her. On our way to get the pot we drove past the grocery store where she worked, but I didn't see her car in the parking lot, which was strange because her shift was right now. Maybe she had gone home sick. I wondered if I should call her to make sure she was all right.

Ferdinand, the guy we were going to get the pot from, lived with the Andersons, his host family, in one of the yuppier neighborhoods in the hills above where I lived. Tony said it would probably look bad if I came along, so I parked a block away and sat in the car while he and Miguel went to see if he was home. Lissa lay down in the back seat.

"You can sit in the front, you know. You don't have to make me feel like a chauffeur."

Lissa sat up and rested her chin on the back of my seat and started blowing on my neck to annoy me but you know what it really did. I couldn't believe it. Knowing I was supposed to tell her to knock it off, I gave her hand a slap. I also knew this would get her to do it more and she did. She laughed and fell back in her seat and said, "I think I just got my period."

"Did you need something right away?" I said, trying to sound sensitive to her womanly needs. "I think I have some old Dunkin Donuts napkins in the glove box."

"Um, let me see," she said. I could hear her sticking her hand down the front of her pants, the actual scratchiness of her pubic hair. She checked her fingers. I tried to look in the rearview mirror but it was too dark and she was lying down. I think she saw me looking. "Yeah, I think that would be a good idea," she said.

I opened the glove compartment and grabbed a handful of thin little pink and orange napkins. I heard her unzip her jeans and shove them into her underwear.

"You're not going to tell Tony about this, are you? He'll make fun of me," she said.

"No, of course not," I said. "Why are you going out with a guy like Tony, anyway? You could do so much better than him."

"What, you think he's a dick?"

"I didn't say that."

"Yeah, you did. You think he's a loser. Well, guess what, Mr. Elliott. He's talented. You should see the sculptures he does in woodshop. He's not half the loser you are."

That really hurt. I cranked the radio, which was playing the kind of music I listened to in high school, *good* music, none of this electronic crap. Boston, Grand Funk, Bachman Turner Overdrive. I wanted to turn around and slap Lissa but Miguel, Tony, and Ferdinand had already returned.

"Pleased to meet you," Ferdinand said as he squeezed into the back. "You want pot? I get you the kind of pot that gets you so stoned."

Ferdinand didn't know his way around town very well, and if he did, he wasn't giving very good directions. Besides, Tony kept messing him up, asking how to say certain obscenities in Spanish, which struck me as odd because Miguel spoke Spanish and Tony could have asked him. With Miguel translating Ferdinand's directions, we ended up in the parking lot at the mall. Ferdinand disappeared into a Starbucks and started talking to one of the baristas. This suddenly felt volatile to me, entrusting a drug deal to a high school student who had lived here only a month and didn't speak any English. I put the car in gear and got out of there.

"Hey! What are you doing! Stop, you fuckin prick!"

As soon as I got to the first light, Tony, Miguel, and Lissa all bailed out of the car. Tony flipped me off and spit on my windshield, called me something he'd just learned. I hated those kids anyway. We'd see next week when they came back begging me to buy for them again.

I was still feeling hungry and decided to get some more food at Big Dave's. I pulled up to the drive-thru, where Dennis was working.

"Didn't you already get your free meal today?" Dennis said, leaning out of the window.

"Yeah, but I thought maybe I could get tomorrow's meal in advance," I said, "I promise not to come back tomorrow."

"That's not the way it works. Have you been drinking?"

"Come on, man. It's just a burger, fries, and soft drink. OK, forget the fries. It's not like I'm going to rip you off. What difference does it make whether I get tomorrow's free burger today?"

"You're putting me in an uncomfortable position, Elliott."

"You mean you're not going to give it to me? Come on."

"Sorry."

"Asshole," I said, and drove away.

Back at home I did up a packet of beef-flavored Ramen and started crying. There was a message from Judy in the rental office saying I was behind on rent. I called Katy again but no answer. Now I really did want some pot and felt bad that I had left those kids all the way out at the strip mall without a car. I was pissed off at Steve for no good reason so I called him but he wasn't home or wasn't answering. I left three messages on his voicemail, the first one angry, the second one apologetic, the third one crying, asking him to come over because I was in really bad shape. I overcooked the Ramen and tried to breathe as I ate the noodles while the TV played episodes of shows I liked when I was in grade school. The kids had left their beer and I decided I was going to drink all fifteen that were left, plus the lone forty that sat perspiring on the kitchen counter. I decided to watch the entire *Star Wars* trilogy with headphones on. I fell asleep before Luke and Obi-Wan even made it to Mos Eisley.

I wasn't going to take this avoidance from Katy anymore, was my first thought when I woke up. I needed some orange juice and a good meal, I decided, but I had left the bread bag open and there were only two stale heels left. In order to conserve orange juice, I made a glass at a time, taking a spoonful of concentrate from a can in the freezer and mixing it in a glass of water. I decided to not overly dilute my OJ this morning and treated myself to three glasses, after which I threw up. I ate a couple Oreos, put my clothes on, and drove to the grocery store. I saw Katy's car in the parking lot and entered through the deli entrance so she wouldn't see me. She was working the express again. I pretended I was shopping, picking out a couple things — a potato, some Cream of Wheat, a bottle of soy sauce. She must have seen me because suddenly another checker was working her lane. I asked her where Katy was. She said she didn't know, that Katy had just gone on break. I could tell the checker was covering for her and besides, the morning shift had just started so it wasn't time for Katy's break yet. My head felt like it was being repeatedly slammed in a pair of automatic doors. I went back to the employee bathrooms, knowing that's where she went when she didn't want to see me, and waited for her to come out. When she did, she jumped and gave me this awful look.

"What's going on? Why don't you return my calls?" I said. "Didn't you get the card I sent you? With the — the poem I added to?" I followed her through the store. Shoppers were looking but I didn't care.

"Leave. I want you to leave."

"I'm shopping just like everyone else. I have a right to shop here," I said, holding up my potato.

"I can get a restraining order, you know."

"You think I'm some kind of stalker? What is this? You didn't even congratulate me on winning the contest. Free burgers for life. *For life.* You know what that means? I can take you out any time you want. You can even get something over the five-dollar value and I'll pay the difference."

Somebody tapped me on the shoulder. Why do all white, male, middle-aged grocers look the same? He asked me to get out. I told him I had some things to buy. He let me pay at checkstand 8, where a woman I had never seen before scanned my items and put them in a plastic bag. I had forgotten my checkbook and I'd left the change from the beer on the coffee table, so I tried to use my debit card but found I had insufficient funds. Katy had disappeared again, probably to go cry somewhere. I didn't want that food anyway.

By the time my hangover disappeared, I decided I needed to get a new job. I had only a few hundred in savings and that was all going to get sucked up in rent. I decided to place a "Help Available!" ad in the Nickel and Dime, because that's how I got my job at the print shop. I drove out to the little office complex and was surprised when I walked into the suite to find Sandra sitting behind the reception desk. I think she was surprised to see me, too, or maybe I just looked like crap. I stammered a little and finally told her everything Dennis had said about her. She shook her head and fumed.

"That asshole had it out for me ever since I started working there. He treats all his employees of color like that. *He's* the pathological liar. Benjamin really did do that to your burger."

I was so angry I forgot why I was there to begin with. Finally I calmed down enough to dictate an ad to her and pay the twenty-dollar fee with a check. I could transfer money later to cover it, but I would end up forgetting and the check would bounce anyway.

I drove to Big Dave's to find both Benjamin and Dennis working. I was starving, so I ordered first and just stewed until my order came up.

"I didn't appreciate what you pulled last night," Dennis said as he handed me my bag.

"And I didn't appreciate being lied to, prick."

"Whoa. Whoa there," Dennis said.

"I saw Sandra today at the Nickel and Dime Want-Ads. She works there, like she said. She didn't fucking lie about it. I don't understand how you can make such a big deal about your fucking contest, the we-love-our-customers bit, and then turn around and treat the winner with such disrespect. You!" I pointed to Benjamin, who stood nervously with a mop in his hand next to the fry baskets. "You're gonna get sued, you twisted son of a bitch."

There were people looking. I was so tired of people looking. A table full of little girls having a birthday party started to cry. Some big guy with ketchup on his chin helped Dennis push me out the door, but I didn't budge until I noticed the strip of tape running alongside the door marking off increments of feet. Remembering the security cam, I bolted.

On my way home I ran out of gas and had to park in the bowling alley parking lot. It was only a block from my apartment, so I just walked. What made me most irate was that I had left my free food on the counter; I hadn't grabbed it while being forcibly removed. Now they were sure to revoke my free burgers for life, I just knew it, and I started to cry again.

At home I finally yanked my picture of Katy out of its frame, tore it into pieces, and flushed them down the toilet. It was the portrait she had posed for at Glamour Shots, where they spend two hours coordinating your outfit and doing your makeup for you. I got her that for Christmas. When my toaster burned my bread heels even on its lowest setting, I yanked it out of the wall and threw it on the floor. I would have destroyed a lot more stuff if Steve hadn't showed up.

"What the fuck is this?" he said from the doorway. My free burger days were over, I realized. If only I had known that a month later Dennis and Theresa would torch the place in a sad attempt at insurance fraud, I would have been happier. I told Steve that I didn't really blame him for getting me fired, that I'd had it coming. I had accidentally exposed four hundred dollars' worth of photographic paper, had shown up for work late on several occasions, and had misplaced some negatives for an important client, so we had to schedule a reshoot. I had inadvertently erased files from the computer, left the coffee maker on overnight, and spilled toner on the masters of the Rotary Club Annual Report. Steve put his arm around me and asked if I was hungry, which made me cry harder. He'd take me out to lunch, he said.

"I have no friends in this town anymore," I said. "How come it's so hard to get people to like me?"

Steve took me to Royal Fork Buffet. I piled my tray with tacos, pizza, salad, and four different kinds of dessert. The pizza was too hot to eat but I was starving and I burned the roof of my mouth. Outside, a tour bus parked and disgorged a group of twenty or so pairs of elderly identical twins. Each pair wore matching hats and windbreakers with nametags. When they took their places in line the whole restaurant stopped eating to gawk at them, but after the novelty wore off and the twins had sat down to eat, nobody seemed to notice them anymore except Steve and me. We watched two old ladies take turns devouring a sundae with a single pair of dentures between them. The one on the left took a bite, removed the dentures, licked them off, then handed them to her sister, who stuck them in her mouth and repeated the process. Steve and I were laughing so hard soda was dribbling out our noses. I tried to imagine what it must be like to grow up knowing someone else that intimately, to wear matching outfits, to finish their sentences for them, to sense their presence across great distances.

DAN CHAON

■

Five Forgotten Instincts

I.

I LIKE FOR PEOPLE to look at my scars. I watch their eyes settle
and a small bright spot opens up inside me, because for a minute
it is as if they are at my mercy. They see the thick, furrowed line
along my cheek, another cutting through my eyebrow, a jagged
nick of missing ear. *Jesus Christ,* they think, *what happened to him?*
They should see me naked.

Sometimes they ask, though mostly they don't. I've developed a
certain frank, expectant look, and their curiosity turns awkward
and uncomfortable. Most of them think: *A car accident?* They wonder about plastic surgery, but I don't offer any explanations. If you
don't like it, don't look, motherfucker! But they can't help it. They
wonder.

It's not as interesting as they imagine. I was six years old, teasing my grandfather's Doberman. The dog just snapped, just tore
me apart, and in a lot of ways I deserved it. I was a clueless little
kid, willfully cruel and relentless. I pushed the bitch over the edge.

It was a miracle that I didn't die. I imagine that people might
think — *poor little boy, what horror he must have experienced!* But
most of it is outside my memory. I recall pressing a flap of my skin
against my face, as if it were a puzzle piece I was trying to fit. I remember being hunched in the corner of the bathtub and striking
the dog on the head with the toilet plunger as she lunged forward.

There was a lot of blood, but very little pain. That didn't come until afterward.

People sometimes ask: Who was supposed to be watching you? Where was your primary caretaker? This was my grandfather, but I don't mean to implicate him in what happened. He was an old man, almost seventy, and he didn't deserve to be saddled with the day to day care of a young child. He was a drinker, a morning sipper of Jack Daniel's. It is a human urge to blame him, since no doubt he was in a state near sleep when I was attacked. It would also be common for people to blame my mother for leaving me with such a person, knowing as she did that he was a drunkard and a lazeabout. But what should she have done? She was a young woman with a child out of wedlock. She had to go to work. She had to earn a living.

When I tell the story, people imagine that my grandfather must have been in a state of stupor to allow such a thing to happen, and it's true that he must have been on the couch, dozing in front of a game show. But I don't remember if I cried out. I don't think I called for help, or screamed, and I feel certain that if I had he would have awakened; he would have saved me. But the truth is, I don't remember uttering a sound. Here was the dog, the sharp teeth, the heavy weight of her paws. I don't think that most people understand what it means to be an animal — to be prey, being eaten. A quiet peacefulness settles over you. Your body relaxes; you accept everything.

II.

Of course I was ugly afterward, but I've found that it doesn't matter. There is something about me that people are attracted to nevertheless, though I was taunted in the schoolyard (Frankenstein! Scarface! Zipper Head!), though people stare — yes, you gapers, I *did* have plastic surgery. You should've seen me before.

But some people are different, as we know. Playing nurse makes them horny, and I can't tell you the number of times a lover has touched my bare chest and drawn in that little intake of breath. Oh! As if desire is a little pinprick, a static shock. Oh! Tracing their fingers along the lines a dog's teeth left in me. And these aren't just the homely ones, not just the desperate, or the twisted. I've slept with a lot of very nice folks.

So why should I be angry or bitter? The world bestows its beautiful mysteries upon me, I tell some of my lovers. To other people I am more blunt: I can get it seven nights a week, I tell them. Look: I walk into a bar, and I know someone will come home with me. I can't understand it, but I certainly accept it as my due.

I don't mean for that to come across as crassly as it sounds. I'm not just some scar-boy Don Juan, some endlessly seducing appetite. And no, I don't want to hurt you, or help you explore your darker side. I'm not going to tie you up and tattoo you, or let you wear a dog collar and nip — "very lightly!" one lady once assured me — on my skin. And I'm not the saintly type either, some Jesus-eyed frail flower, waiting for you to worship my scars. I am not interested in the secret desires of your warped and damaged psyches.

What we would do together, you and me, would be something else entirely. But I'd have to show it to you for you to understand.

The other day it was a college girl, Karissa — I think she made up the name for herself, but she was a round-faced, honest-looking girl, with generous hips and black and blond hair she said she dyed herself. I watched her in the morning, padding barefoot around my apartment with dirty, red-soled feet, and I was paying attention because I sometimes wonder myself why they come home with me. I observed as she gathered pills from her purse — allergy medication, a Prozac, a multivitamin — and swallowed them down with a little milk she'd poured into a coffee mug. She looked up, awkwardly, but I was wearing my T-shirt and jeans, politely covered.

"Hey," I said, and she smiled sheepishly down at the kitchen table, her eyes widening and unwidening with some secret thought.

"What?" I said. "What are you thinking?"

She shook her head. "Nothing," she said, and then shrugged. "I was just wondering about your mom," she said shyly. "I mean, what did she do when she — saw you?"

"She screamed," I said. And Karissa looked at me before nodding solemnly.

"Oh," she said.

In movies, there are generally two types of mothers for handicapped kids. There are the good ones — the brave, determined ones, the ones that tell you you can "be whatever you want to be" and "you're the same as everyone else underneath the skin," and do a lot of supporting and nourishing, maybe giving up whatever dreams they might have had to support and nourish round the clock. And then there are the bad ones — the smothering ones who don't push you toward your full potential, who keep you down with their own guilt, sometimes even making you a prisoner until some light, free-spirited girl comes along and steals you away, teaching you to love yourself.

I think Karissa held one or both of these types in her mind as she looked at me, but in fact my mother wasn't either one. She wasn't much older than Karissa when I had my "accident," and she didn't know what to do. She was a poor, superstitious woman, vaguely a hippie, believing in astrology and some misguided notions of Celtic myth, and mostly ignored my scars once they healed. Sometimes she would tell me I was beautiful — "like a rugged tree," she said — and sometimes she thought that I might have special powers. In any case, her many boyfriends never bothered me.

"She wasn't a bad woman," I told Karissa. "She used to tell me that I was psychic. Or that now I'd be able to communicate with animals if I concentrated really hard."

Karissa looked at me credulously, her big eyes interested in magic, and suffering. "That makes sense, I guess," she said.

I smiled, pouring myself some coffee. "Actually," I said, "I hate animals. Any kind of animal just gives me the creeps. If I could talk to them, I'd tell them to go screw themselves."

She smiled, a bit uncomfortable with my jokiness. "Ha," she said politely, and sipped her milk.

But somehow it reminded me of the man, Dr. B, who I'd been with a few weeks before Karissa. He didn't like my jokes either, said there was something "passive-aggressive" about my tone. He had recently left his wife and four children, and was heavy with

the significance of it. We rested there in my bed and he traced the
thick line that divided my nipple in half, into two brown half-
moons.

"You can see shapes there, you know," Dr. B. said, and I knew
that. People saw rivers, and road maps, and constellations. "It's
like a Rorschach," he said, and ran his finger over the center of my
chest. He said the one that ran along my shoulder blade looked
like the zodiac symbol for Leo. "The lion," he said.

I shifted. "I'm actually a Cancer," I said. "Which I think is more
appropriate."

He looked at me grimly, and I could see his fatherly eyes growing sad. "You sleep with a lot of people, do you not?" Dr. B. said.

"I don't know," I said. "I suppose."

"Men and women?"

"Yes."

"And you're not worried," he said.

"Well," I said, "Really, I'm very careful."

"I'm not talking about disease, necessarily," he said, and smiled
thinly, since I was smiling. "I was just thinking that if you keep
bringing desperate people home with you, sooner or later one is
going to kill you."

"You're not desperate," I said. And for the first time, he laughed
at something I said.

III.

I like the idea of kindness. I don't know whether kindness appears
in nature, whether it evolves out of some necessity or whether it is
a human anomaly, but it seems to me that most people I have met
have a secret need for it. Maybe my gift, if I have one, is the ability
to spot this, to smell it out among the staring people I pass. I suppose the need to be kind is not much different than something
like lust, though it might be rarer.

My mother used to fall in love with the most hateful of men —
drunks, druggies, liars, bullies with short tempers who would hit
her, smack her up against the wall, their tightened fingers on her
throat.

But unbelievably, none of them ever hit me. None of them ever laughed at my mess of scars or teased me, and in fact the man who was worst for my mother, the one she had to get a restraining order against, Nat, was the one who I remembered most fondly. We used to go to drive-ins together, Nat and me, to see scary movies, and he would put his arms around my shoulder when he startled, tightening his grip when the killer popped out to slay a teenager; when I was eight, I sat in his lap and drove his car down the interstate, my hands on the steering wheel, his behind his head. The two of us sang along with the radio, and he was almost like another kid until we pulled into the driveway. We both looked to the door where my mother was standing, and then he wasn't a kid anymore. He was gearing up for the inevitable fight, his hand already tightening with anger at what she was going to say — whatever she was going to say.

I used to think of Nat. He eventually went to prison, not for hurting my mother but for something else, like killing someone in a bar fight — and I would wonder if I should look him up, should visit him maybe. On TV, prison men met their visitors in small booths, separated by thick Plexiglas. The prisoner pressed his hand to the clear plastic, and the visitor responded in kind, lining up fingers and thumbs as if touching, though in fact we never did this, never met again.

I once slept with a guy who looked like Nat, and I thought, *OK, this makes sense, maybe there's a pattern here.* His fingers ran along the ridges of my face as I sucked his cock. And for a short time I thought I had a handle on things, because the next one was a lady in her mid-fifties, about my mother's age. She was wiry and athletic of body, and planted her fingers firmly into the skin of my unscarred back like stakes as I pushed inside her. I was pretty happy.

The lady was happy, too, at first. She told me that I would have been beautiful — she liked my eyes, which are a very light blue, and my hair, which is black and curly, and my face, which she said would have been sleepy and gentle, like a surfer boy. "But now it's something different altogether," she said, and leaned toward me. "I can't put my finger on it," she said, and reached out and touched my lips with her index finger.

But then, afterward, in the dark of my bedroom, she seemed sad and upset. She drew her knees up under the covers, and put her chin on them. "Uff," she said, by which I guess that she meant "What am I doing here?" Or: "What have I done?"

"Are you OK?" I said. I was thinking of my mother, who used to sit like this, naked under the covers, drinking wine from a plastic tumbler and reading her books on unexplained mysteries. It occurred to me that this woman had a son who was gravely injured — killed perhaps — and that she was thinking of him now. "Hey," I said. "Don't be sad. It's OK."

"No," she said, with bitterness. "It's not 'OK.' It's actually something very different than 'OK.'"

OK, I thought. What she was saying was probably true, and I waited for her to continue, but she didn't. "You can tell me if you want," I said at last, but she shook her head. "Sometimes it helps to talk about it," I said. "Is it about your son?"

"I don't have a *son!*" she said venomously, and when she looked at me a film of tear-water was thickening over her eyes and lashes.

"Jesus," she said. "What are you?"

I was silent for a moment, not really understanding her question. "I'm just a person," I said. "I'm not anything specific." It made me feel weird. I think that sometimes, because of my scars, people expect an experience that goes beyond fucking. I have come to believe that I am a pretty decent lay, but sometimes that isn't enough.

"Why do you think I have a son?" said this lady, who looked so much like my mom. Her eyes were wide and suspicious now, and she flinched out of bed when I tried to talk, leaning over the floor to pick up her clothes and press them against her breasts and crotch as if I had sneaked into her house while she was naked. She cradled her clothes as she backed into the bathroom and shut the door.

"What's wrong?" I called to her, and I could hear her beyond the door, grunting and struggling into her clothes. "Are you all right?" I called. But she wouldn't answer.

IV.

I am nothing. Just a guy. I work in a restaurant as a cook, mostly cutting vegetables, chopping: I'm good at my job. I can slice a mushroom into paper-thin pieces, can reduce a head of broccoli into tiny flowerettes in minutes. The cuts on my fingers I barely notice, and people sometimes think this is funny, maybe because I am so scarred up. I think something is probably wrong with my nerves, because most of the time I don't even notice pain, and I've sliced the ends off my fingers and it was only the blood that told me that I'd made a mistake. "*Primo*," they call me. "*Primo*, you are bleeding." Most of the men I work with are Mexican, or from Latin America or something, and they are always talking in Spanish and then looking at me brightly and laughing. I pick up a few things. I know words like *cebolla* and *cuchillo* and *cabron*, and sometimes they will teach me phrases — like once they got me to say, "*muchas panochas en America*," and when I repeated it there was an uproar of hilarity, and I knew it was probably obscene. But when I asked the line cook, Alfonso, what *panocha* meant, he was solemn. "It means 'sugar,' *Primo*," he said. "Brown sugar."

Are we friends, myself and these men? I suppose, since I spend so much time with them, that we are close in a way, but most of the time I don't really know what they are saying. I have thought about trying to learn Spanish, but I actually think that if I could speak their language they wouldn't like me as much anymore.

None of them seem curious about my scars, though once a little dishwasher, a wiry, high-cheekboned Mayan-looking boy named Ernesto had pointed to them. He balled up his fists and made a soft "tok" with his tongue, miming fighting. I shook my head. "No," I said.

I showed him my teeth, tapping them.

"*Dientes*," he said.

"Woof," I said, imitating a dog. "Arf, arf."

"*Perro*," he said.

He nodded solemnly, apparently understanding, though also wary. He reached out and ran his finger along the thick, pale raised skin that ran along my forearm. "*Perro?*" he said again, uncertainly, and I nodded. I unbuttoned my shirt and showed him a little of my chest. "*Ay,*" he said, and I smiled at him, shrugging. I waited, not breathing, while he touched my skin. "*El Lobo,*" I said, which I knew was the Spanish word for wolf, and he chuckled, drawing away a little. "It's OK," I told him, and he smiled back at me. He puffed out his chest and drew an *X* over my bared skin with his finger, *swip, swip*, like Zorro. "S'OK," he said, repeating, imitating me as if I were full of bravado. I figured it was the beginning of something.

But a few days later he was gone, and I learned from Alfonso that he had been killed — stabbed in a fight outside some bar in the Mexican area of town.

"Jesus," I said. "He was just a kid, wasn't he? How old was he?"

"I don't know," Alfonso said, and looked at me heavily. "Old enough to die, I guess," he said, and showed me the palms of his hands. It wasn't my fault, of course, that Ernesto was dead, but the way that Alfonso looked at me left a film of guilt over me for the rest of the day. I thought of that woman, backing away from me. "What *are* you," she said.

V.

I ride the bus home from work, and it takes about a half hour, so I read the newspaper. People will sit next to me, or they won't. Sometimes they will start to talk to me but when they see my face their voice will trail away. Sometimes I fall asleep and let people see me there, in my seat, my eyes closed, and it is as if I am naked because they can look for as long as they want and I will not know. I get off the bus at my stop and walk about three blocks to my apartment. I have my keys ready. I unlock the door and then lock it again. I am not happy, but I am not necessarily sad, either.

My grandfather died, he killed himself about a year after I was hurt. By that time it was clear that I'd be OK, and I guess he was waiting to hear, to be certain that I was out of the woods. His dog, the Doberman, whose name was Elizabeth, had already been put to death for her crimes.

In the bathtub, he cut his own throat with his razor. Then he sank down into the warm water and bled, letting his jugular pump pink curlicues, eddies, into the water. When my mother found him, I was still in the hospital, watching educational puppets on television. Their mouths moved like a thumb and forefinger in a sock.

I was happy then, adrift in my hospital bed, just as I am perhaps happiest now, in my bed, with the television running, silent like a hibernating creature. I am quiet, and sometimes I think that all I know is instinct — all the instincts we are born with, that most people forget about. I can hear him in there sometimes, the bath water running, the soft echo of his body sluicing against the porcelain.

My grandfather used to tease me all the time. It wasn't mean-spirited, I don't think. Just something to amuse himself with. I remember on the day that I got torn up, not long after my mom left for work, he called me to the window. He lived in a house near the railroad tracks, and he pointed out to where some boxcars were parked. "I see the carnival came through here last night," he said. "Look at that! They left an elephant here!"
"Where?" I said, and tried to follow his finger.
"There! Don't you see it?"
"No."
"It's right there — where I'm pointing. You don't see it?"
"No. . . ." I said doubtfully — but I craned my neck.
"You mean to tell me that you don't see an elephant standing there?" he demanded.
"Well . . ." I said. This was only hours before the dog, Elizabeth, would tear me apart.
"Well . . ." I said. I scoped along the lines and shapes outside the window again. I didn't see the elephant, but then, after a time, it seemed that I did. In my memory, there is still the figure of an elephant, standing at the edge of the train tracks. It curls its trunk languidly, thoughtfully, and brings a piece of hay to its mouth.

∎

Lyndon

FROM *Zoetrope*

MY FATHER DIED because our house was infested with ladybugs. Our French neighbors, the Herouxs, had imported a hearty species of the insect to combat aphids in their garden. The ladybugs bred and migrated. Hundreds upon hundreds were living in our curtains, our cabinets, the ventilation system. At first, we thought it was hilarious and fitting for us to be plagued by something so cute and benign. But these weren't nursery-rhyme ladybugs. Not the adorable, shiny, red-and-black beetles. These ladybugs were orange. They had uneven brown splotches. When I squished their shells between my thumb and forefinger, they left a rust-colored stain on my skin and an acrid smell that wouldn't wash off. Dad used a vacuum hose to suck up the little arched creatures, but they quickly replaced themselves. The numbers never dwindled. Dad must have smoked a lot of pot before he climbed the ladder to our roof. My guess is that he wanted to cover the opening in the chimney. He'd suspected that the flue wasn't closed all the way. Our house was three stories high. When he fell, he landed on the Herouxs' cement patio, his skull fractured, his neck broken.

For months after his death, I kept finding the ladybugs everywhere. When I stripped my bed, I'd find them in the sheets. When I did laundry, I'd find their dead carapaces in the dryer. When I woke up in the morning, I'd find a pair scuffling along my freshly laundered pillowcases. Then just like that, they were gone.

*

Long after the last ladybug's departure, I pulled a pair of sunglasses from Mom's purse on the car seat, fogged the lenses with my breath, rubbed the plastic eyes against my chest, and said to her, "You missed the scenic overlook."

Mom swiped her sunglasses away from me. "There will be other stops, Elise," she said.

We were driving through the Texas Hill Country in an upgraded rental car, cruising a roadway called the Devil's Backbone. Our destination: LBJ. His ranch. His reconstructed birth site. The rental-car guy had flashed a brilliant smile when he bumped us up from a white Taurus to a monster green SUV. Mom couldn't resist bullying the skinny clerk. "No one screws me on gas mileage. I'm not paying extra to fuel that obscenity. Knock ten dollars off the daily fee." As the car clerk hammered his keyboard and readjusted the price, Mom winked at me.

My mother the investment banker. Every morning, well before dawn, she would maneuver her own Ford Explorer across the George Washington Bridge into Manhattan, cell-phoning her underlings while cutting off other commuters. Mom called her first-year analysts "Meat" and bragged that she, in turn, was known as "The Lion." Mom always wore her long, straightened red hair loose and down her back. She'd sport short skirts and sleeveless dresses, showing off her sculpted calves and biceps. Mom specialized in M&As, corporate restructuring, and bankruptcy. She traveled a lot. Dad had brainstormed our presidential sightseeing tours as a way for him to keep me entertained while Mom flew off to Chicago and Denver, dismantling pharmaceutical corporations along the way.

"I really think we were supposed to stop at that overlook." We coasted past juniper trees, live oaks, limestone cliffs. As far as I could tell, the whole point of driving the Devil's Backbone was to stop at that particular overlook and view the span of gently sloping hills from the highest vantage point. "Dad would have turned back," I said.

Mom just kept driving. I passed the time by reading snippets from the *Lonely Planet Guide to Texas* and rattling off the names of local towns: Wimberley, Comfort, and Boerne. I flipped down the

sun visor, replaited my French braids in the vanity mirror. I'd
worn my favorite outfit: red high-top sneakers, baggy khaki shorts,
and a T-shirt I'd special-ordered at a mall in Teaneck. For twenty-
eight dollars, a man from Weehawken had ironed black velvet letters onto the front of a tiny green jersey. The letters spelled out
VICTIM. When my mother asked how I got off being so self-pity-
ing, I told her it was the name of my favorite underground band.

The Devil's Backbone reminded me of the shingles sore tor-
menting my lower torso. The giant scab resembled a hard red
shell. The family doctor had explained how sometimes the
chicken pox virus would remain dormant in a nerve ending, waiting for the immune system to weaken before reemerging. He was
concerned because he'd never seen shingles in anyone my age.
Usually he treated it in older patients, or in cases occurring with
cancer or AIDS. People closing in on death. I told Mom the shingles were proof I was special. The agony wasn't limited to the blis-
ters on my back. My whole body felt inflamed, as if a rabid wolf
were hunting rabid squirrels inside my chest. The doctor recom-
mended ibuprofen for the pain. He gave me pamphlets describing
stress-reducing breathing exercises. The first few nights Mom
slipped me half a Vicodin and a nip of Benedictine brandy. As I
tried to sleep, I heard her roaming from living room to bedroom to
family room. I listened. My mother the widow did not weep, did
not cry out for her dead husband.

A year after my father died, my mother's breasts began to grow.
She developed a deep, embarrassing plunge of cleavage, a pendu-
lous swinging bosom that attacked my own flat body each time
she hugged me good night. Mom's belly had pouted. Ballooned. I
could detect the domed button of her navel pressing out against
the soft silk of her blouses. Her ankles swelled and I became suspicious. Mom was maybe six months into her pregnancy. I did
the math. Dad had been pushing dead too long to be the father. I
was about to enter my sophomore year at the Academy of Holy
Angels. Before school started, I wanted the shingles on my back to
disappear, I wanted to tour the reconstructed birthplace of Lyndon

Baines Johnson, and I wanted my mother to admit to me that she was pregnant.

With Dad gone, I'd insisted on upholding our family's tradition of visiting presidential landmarks. Dad and I had been doing them in chronological order. We'd seen the big ones: Mount Vernon, Monticello, The Hermitage, Sagamore Hill. Weeks before Dad broke his neck, we'd spent a lively afternoon in the gift shop of the John Fitzgerald Kennedy Library, rubbing our faces in the soft velour of JFK commemorative golf towels. The less popular the sites, the more obscure the leader of our country, the more Dad got excited: "Elise, can you imagine? John Tyler actually sat in this breakfast nook and ate soft-boiled eggs from those egg cups." In Columbia, Tennessee, I tore white azalea petals from James K. Polk's ancestral garden while Dad rambled on about the Mexican War, the "dark horse," and "Fifty-four Forty or Fight." At the Albany Rural Cemetery, Dad and I knelt solemnly before the grave of Chester Alan Arthur. A giant marble angel with voluminous wings towered over us. We prayed to our favorite forgotten leader, the father of civil service reform. One year, we spent Christmas on Cape Cod at a beachside inn that had been a secret getaway for Grover Cleveland and his mistress. Mom couldn't make that trip, so Dad and I tramped by ourselves on the snow-covered sand dunes, plotting my own future run for the presidency. "You need a catchphrase. And a trademark hairdo so the cartoonists can immortalize you."

All day we'd been driving in various stages of silence and radio static. Mom asked whether I'd like to stop for sundaes. I considered patting her belly and making a joke about cravings for ice cream and pickles. I had expected Mom to nix my travel plans for us, but really, I just wanted her to be honest and say to me, "Elise, I can't fly. Not in my condition." Instead, when I said, "Johnson," Mom folded her arms against her burgeoning chest. She swung her hair over her shoulders, and said, "Texas in August? Why can't it be Hawaii? I'm certain Lyndon Johnson loved the hula."

The day before, we'd visited the Sixth Floor Museum in Dallas. Mom and I took the elevator up to the top of the Texas School Book Depository. We slowly worked our way through the permanent exhibit dedicated to the Kennedy assassination. Though a glass wall surrounded the actual Oswald window, Mom and I got close enough to size up the short distance between the building and the X on the street below. The X marked the spot where Kennedy was first hit. I'd always imagined Dealey Plaza as an enormous expanse of traffic and park, but here it was in front of me, tiny and green, more like a miniature replica made by a film crew. One SUV after another covered the X as the cars drove over the site in perpetual reenactment of Kennedy's last ride. This was the bona fide scene of the infamous crime. Mom whispered, "Even I could make that shot." She hugged me from behind and I felt the baby's heartbeat vibrate through her belly. In anticipation of our trip, I'd begun calling my secret sibling "Lyndon." I asked, "Is Lyndon kicking?" Mom ignored me. Weeks ago, when I'd asked her point-blank if she was pregnant and quizzed her on what she intended to do with the baby, instead of answering the question she told me that her new goal in life was to get me away from "the fucking Holy Angels."

Dad was the Catholic. Mom's family had come over on the *Mayflower*. "Elise, a lot of Yankees brag about tracing their roots back. Always be conscious of your place in history. Most of the people on that ship were poor. Your relatives were the lucky ones with money." Before her parents divorced and squandered everything, my mother grew up rich in Manhattan. Her childhood bedroom had a view of the Sheep Meadow and the Central Park Reservoir. Both of Mom's doormen were named Fritz. When she turned six, her folks hired Richard Avedon to take the snapshots at her birthday party. At sixteen, she'd curtsied before Princess Grace at a charity fundraiser for retired racehorses. I often felt as though Dad and I were descended from one class of people, while Mom hailed from another class entirely.

My father sold pies for a living. Nominally, he was the vice president of "The Pie Piper," his parents' international bakery corporation, but mostly what Dad chose to do was drive his pie truck around the Tri-State area. Checking and restocking Safeways and Star Markets. Shelving lemon cream, Coconut Dream, and chocolate meringue pies. Dad had a jacket with TEAMSTER embroidered on the back. He liked to brag that he knew the fastest routes in and out of Manhattan, at any point during the day. He knew when best to take the Lincoln Tunnel.

Dad felt that my aristocratic heritage and working-class lineage would make me an ideal political candidate. He cast me as a liberal Democrat and cast himself as my campaign manager. Dad first ran me in third grade for homeroom line leader. I lost to Andorra Rose, whose mother, on election day, made two dozen chocolate cupcakes with pink rosebuds in the center. Dad viewed this loss as a tactical oversight. Our future campaigns always involved The Pie Piper donating dozens of pies and pastries to Holy Angels. In fifth grade, I was class treasurer. In seventh grade, I was student representative to the advisory council on redesigning our school uniforms. Dad imagined I would win the governorship of New Jersey, and from there, if I could find the right Southern running mate, become the first woman president of the United States.

I was twelve the afternoon I caught Dad sprawled out on the Philadelphia Chippendale, one hand holding a silver lighter, the other hand cradling a short ceramic pipe. There'd been a bomb scare at Holy Angels and the nuns had begrudgingly sent us home early. Dad was wearing his boxer shorts and watching a rerun of *The Joker's Wild*. He flung a cashmere blanket over his lap, swung his legs off my mother's two-hundred-year-old sofa, and said, "Honey, come meet James Buchanan." I sat beside my bare-chested father, his blond hair flattened on one side, and watched him twirl his pipe around. "Made this in college. Art class. The clay morphed in the kiln." He showed me the blunt end of the pipe. "Looks just like our bachelor president. His first lady was his niece. Handsome fellow." On the TV, Wink Martindale exclaimed, "Joker! Joker! Joker!" Dad smiled. "Don't worry. Your mom has seen me smoke."

My father confided to me that he'd had panic attacks as a kid. "I'd be paralyzed with fear. Knocked out with it. The only thing that helped was reading almanacs." Dad memorized historical facts, like the years each president served in office, and he'd repeat these dates in an effort to calm himself down. "Zachary Taylor 1849–50, Rutherford Birchard Hayes 1877–81, Franklin Pierce 1853–57." At fifteen, Dad discovered pot.

I loved sitting in the living room while Dad toked up. Marijuana haze drifted around me, settling on the folds of my wool pleated skirt. I'd lean my neck down against my Peter Pan collar and catch the wonderful stink of weed lingering against my blouse. I was a nervous kid. I often threw up before big tests. No one at Holy Angels invited me to their sleepovers anymore, on account of my loud, thrashing night terrors. Even my closest friend, Alana Clinton, often insisted I take a chill pill. I'd attempted hypnosis therapy to treat the warts on my hands, the muscle spasm in my left eye, the mysterious rashes that appeared across my stomach, my inner-ear imbalance, and my tooth-grinding problem. Only breathing in my father's pot smoke truly relaxed me. He never let me inhale directly from Buchanan, but he'd grant me a contact high. Afterward, the two of us would split one of my father's ancestral peach pies. This happened once or twice a week. Mom didn't know.

Mom and I pulled off the Devil's Backbone and stopped for soft-serve at a place called The Frozen Armadillo. She got a chocolate and vanilla twist with a cherry-flavored dip, and I ordered a vanilla cone covered in something advertised as Twinkle-Kote. Outside in the August heat, the ice cream dripped down our arms. We decided to eat the cones in the air-conditioned rental car. I told Mom my theory about LBJ and the Kennedy assassination. I was convinced that Lyndon was the real culprit. Nothing that big could happen in Texas without Lyndon's approval.

"Motive is obvious," I said. "Who gains the most from Kennedy dying? LBJ gets to be president. Who's responsible for the investigation and subsequent cover-up? LBJ gets to appoint the Warren Commission. There's proof that LBJ actually knew Jack Ruby. All

LBJ ever wanted was to be president. Not vice president. He was an old man. Time was running out." I told my mother that there had been talk of Kennedy dropping LBJ from the ticket in '64.

"How do you know so much?" she asked.

"It's Dad's fault," I said.

"You know, your father always wanted to be a high school history teacher."

"What stopped him?" I asked.

"Well, sweetie," Mom said, wiping ice cream off my nose, "convicted felons aren't allowed to teach children."

Mom balanced her own ice cream cone against the steering wheel and turned on the ignition. She headed out toward Johnson City. We drove past brown, sandy hills crowned by patches of cacti with round, thorned leaves.

"Take it back," I told her. "What you said. Take it back."

"You shouldn't idealize your father. You didn't know him as well as you'd like to think."

"From the looks of it," I pointed to Mom's belly, "Dad didn't know you at all." I was deciding between calling my mother a "bitch" and calling her a "fucking bitch" when she chucked the rest of her ice cream cone at the side of my face. The ice cream splattered against my hair and cheek. The wafer cone landed on the side of my leg. I picked it up and threw it back at her. I pulled the top of my own ice cream off of its cone and aimed for Mom's chest. She shrieked, swerving the car and throwing back at me whatever clumps of ice cream she could pull from her cleavage. We each lost sense of our target, hurling any ice cream slop we could get hold of. The rental car's green cloth upholstery and side windows clouded over in a sticky, cherry-flavored film. Chocolate ice cream melted in streams down Mom's chest. The black velvet letters on my Victim T-shirt soaked up my dessert. Mom drove and swore. She called me ungrateful and threatened to leave me right there on the spine of the Devil's Backbone. Mom didn't notice the bend in the road. She screamed in confusion as our rental car lurched through a very real white picket fence, careening down a hill and into an orchard. She pumped and locked the brakes just in time for us to hit a patch of peach trees.

The air bags did not work. No explosion of white pillow. In that brief instant, as I watched the seat belt jerk Mom back and hold her safely in place, I thought of how the pressure and force of the air bag would have crushed Mom's belly, crippling Lyndon, killing the start of him. Mom saved me from the windshield by holding her right arm out straight against my chest. "Holy fuck," she said.

Mom surveyed me. "Are you all right?" she asked. We got out of the car together, the two of us still dripping with ice cream. We marveled at the damage. A peach tree appeared to be growing out of the hood of our rental car. Mom picked up a pink and yellow fruit, brushing the fuzz against her lips before taking a bite. "You and your presidents," she said. "That's it. I'm through. And you can be damned sure I'm not taking you to Yorba Linda. There's no fucking way I'm visiting Nixon."

I insisted on hiking the remaining mile and a half to the LBJ Ranch. The car was not my problem. I was a kid and this was my summer vacation. I stayed a hundred yards in front of my mother. She played with her cell phone the entire time, dialing and redialing numbers. From her loud cursing, I could tell that there was no service, no way to call a tow truck or taxi. No way to complain to her mystery lover about me. I imagined my mother had many young lovers. For all I knew, she didn't know who Lyndon's father was. I didn't want to think about The Lion having sex. I wanted to remember the Saturday mornings when I'd wake up early, sneak into my parents' room, and burrow a narrow tunnel between their sleeping bodies. I'd trace the beauty marks on Mom's back, naming the largest ones. With the tips of my fingers, I'd smooth out the worry lines on my father's forehead. Their bed was an enormous life raft. I would imagine that the three of us were the last family left in the world. I loved my parents best when they were asleep and I was standing guard.

On the LBJ tour bus, the man sitting closest to the door stood up to give my mother his seat. She smiled and said, "Not necessary." We'd taken turns washing up by ourselves in the ladies' room of the park's Visitor Center. While Mom pulled knots of peanut Twinkle-Kote from her hair, I watched a short film about the ranch, the birthplace, and the family cemetery. The birthplace wasn't really the birthplace. The original birthplace had been torn down. LBJ actually had a facsimile of the house rebuilt during his presidency. He decorated the house in period pieces, but none of the furnishings were original except for a rawhide cushioned chair. The film showed Lyndon in a cowboy hat and sports coat posing on the front porch of his make-believe home. Dad would have loved the film. He would have leaned over and repeated the story about LBJ and the goat fucker.

"Do you know about LBJ and the goat fucker?" I said to Mom. "When Johnson first ran for office, he told his campaign manager to spread a rumor that his opponent had sex with farm animals. When the manager pointed out that this wasn't true, Johnson said, 'So what. Force the bastard to admit, "I never fucked a goat." He'll be ruined.'"

"You curse like your father." Mom sighed.

The Reconstructed Birthplace was the first stop on the tour. The park ranger/bus driver was a chatty older woman named Cynthia. She bounced around the bus taking our tickets, sporty and spry in her light green ranger's uniform. A row of bench seats ran along each side of the bus facing a wide center aisle. Another row of seats ran along the back. There were nine other people on the bus: the polite man closest to the door, a pair of elderly, identical twin sisters who wore matching red windbreakers, a middle-aged German couple toting two large canvas backpacks, and a family of four. The mother and father of the family laughed as their young daughter hugged her baby brother and scooped him up onto her lap. The little blond boy had a crazy cowlick I wanted to flatten and fix. Mom and I sat in the very back row, several seats apart from each other.

As we drove past the banks of the Pedernales River, Cynthia described the lawn chair staff meetings Lyndon held at his ranch during Vietnam. She told us that Lady Bird had kindly donated all of the land and the ranch to the National Park Service, but chose to live part-time in the main ranch house. I could feel my shingles sore rubbing against my T-shirt, the pain ratcheting up inside of me. I was still angry at Mom. I held my breath to calm myself and ran through dates: "Andrew Johnson 1865–69, Benjamin Harrison 1889–93, Warren Gamaliel Harding 1921–23." Mom leaned over and said, "Lady Bird is shrewd. Putting the ranch into a trust is an excellent way of avoiding taxes."

We drove past lazy orange and white Hereford cattle grazing by the river. An ibex shot out from behind a sycamore tree, and then another ibex followed, and another. The cows ignored the elegant brown and white horned antelopes. Cynthia said, "Lady Bird also runs an exotic animal safari on the ranch. As exotic animals are legal in Texas, hunters can pay the Johnson family to come and stalk rare creatures from the Dark Continent." My mother whispered, "Lady Bird's a genius."

I'd always thought that Dad liked Mom because her mother's maiden name was Van Buren. One afternoon, my father told me how he and Mom began dating. "You have to be careful with this information," he said. "Your mother doesn't know the whole story." My parents met their freshman year in college. The same day Dad met Mom, he also met another woman, a sculpture major named Lisel. She had wavy black hair, a German accent, and an apartment off-campus. Dad liked both women and was stuck deciding whether to pursue Mom or Lisel. He decided to go after Lisel. He was dressed up and on his way to meet the German sculptress for their first serious date when he bumped into Mom. "She'd been playing rugby and she was totally covered in mud and sweat. She asked me if I wanted to take a shower with her. I went back to her dorm." Dad smiled. "And that's the moment when my life began." He said something else about Mom being a sexy lady, but I clutched my hands to my ears and blocked him out.

The Reconstructed Birthplace was white with green shutters. It was small. Just two bedrooms, a kitchen, and a breezeway. Cynthia showed us the bedroom where Johnson was birthed. A queen-size bed dominated the room. I noticed long, shiny black beetles crawling over the chenille bedspread. One of the beetles flew up and cir-

cled past me. Cynthia said, "His mother claimed that he had it
wrong. She kept insisting that Lyndon was actually born in the
smaller bedroom, but LBJ was adamant."

In the kitchen I saw the rawhide chair, the one authentic piece.
I wanted to run my hand over the cow fur. Right by the kitchen
table stood a baby's wooden highchair with LADY BIRD etched
across the backrest. Cynthia said that the First Lady had been kind
enough to donate her own Roycrafter highchair for the replica.
Mom mouthed "Lady Bird" to herself and rested her hands on her
belly. I pictured a plump, kicking baby fidgeting in the chair.
"Mom, if you want," I said, "I could steal the highchair for you."

"What's a lady bird?" Mom asked Cynthia.

"A lady bird is what we in the South call ladybugs."

Mom looked at me. She shook her head. "Those little killers."

Sometimes when I hung out with my dad while he smoked Buchanan, I'd get paranoid. Even though I understood how girls got
pregnant, I'd imagine one of my father's sperm magically escap-
ing from his boxer shorts, swimming through his pants, landing
on my leg, and inching up my Holy Angels uniform. I imagined
being pregnant with Dad's baby, but I couldn't imagine anything
after that. In her grief Mom had fucked someone. Maybe The Lion
had some Meat after all. She probably couldn't explain her own
pain over losing Dad. At least not to me. I knew harboring a baby
while I looked on could only make her feel alone. While he was
alive, Mom was certain I loved Dad more than her. "The two of you
have your own secret society," she'd say. Now that he was dead,
Mom was convinced I'd love the memory of him more than I'd
ever love her. I wanted to tell her she was dead wrong, but I wasn't
sure that she was.

The Johnson family graveyard, nothing more than a small plot of
land squared off by a stone wall, stood straight across from the
birthplace. Mom and I walked hand in hand in the August heat to
the cemetery. Cynthia and our bus mates were still loitering beside
the house. Mom told me that Dad had been arrested before I was

born. He'd been pulled over for speeding in his pie truck. The cop noticed a baggie of pot in the ashtray. A very big baggie of pot. Dad was arrested, tried, and found guilty of possession with intent to distribute. "Your grandfather could have made the whole thing go away, but instead, he let your father do six months in prison. Minimum security, a life lesson. I was pregnant with you the whole time he was locked up."

Mom tucked a wisp of loose hair behind my left ear. "I figured you should know about your father's past, you know, for your political career."

I wanted to tell her that I was sorry. As much as I loved my father, I was mystified as to why Mom, who worked ninety hours a week, would stay married to a man who was happiest when lying down on a couch, a man who couldn't keep his balance on the roof of his own house. A man who could never find his wallet or remember to tie his shoes. A man who panicked every time the phone rang. I would never understand how she had come to love him.

"I'm sorry about the rental car," I said.

"Insurance will cover it."

Mom and I looked out at the family gravestones. The tallest one was Lyndon's.

"Honey, your dad was a wonderful, frustrating, lovely, ridiculous man."

When we reboarded the bus, our tour guide, Cynthia, smiled and informed us, "You're all very lucky. Lady Bird is in Bermuda this week. The Secret Service has OK'ed us for a drive-by of the ranch house."

Mom shouted down the length of the bus to Cynthia, "Can't we leave the bus and visit the inside of the house?"

"I'm afraid not, ma'am."

"But that's why we came here," the elderly twins said in unison.

"Sorry, ladies. Those are the rules." Cynthia turned the bus onto a red dirt road.

Without even the slightest look in my direction, Mom shouted,

"My daughter has visited every other presidential home in the country. We came all the way from New Jersey."

"Security risk," Cynthia said. "Plus, the ranch house is Lady Bird's primary residence. None of us would want a bunch of strangers trudging through our homes while we were out of town."

"It's fine, Mom," I said.

"Besides, you've seen the birthplace," Cynthia said.

"The reconstructed birthplace," Mom retorted. "Elise, you came here to see the house, and I'm going to make sure you see it." My pregnant mother pushed herself up from her seat on the moving bus, clutched her leather purse, and waddled to the front. Cynthia continued to drive. Mom held on to a railing and leaned into the back of Cynthia's chair. Cynthia shook her head. And then she shook her head so violently that her mirrored sunglasses flung off her face and skittered to the floor of the bus. Mom kept right on talking. She reached into her purse and pulled out her wallet. Everyone on the bus heard Cynthia say, "Ma'am, I am a ranger for the National Park Service. I cannot be intimidated."

While my mother continued to buzz in her ear, Cynthia picked up the microphone on her CB and radioed headquarters. She spoke in a quick, clipped lingo that I did not understand. Then Mom swiped at the CB, grabbing at the spiral speaker cord. The entire bus and I witnessed their slap fight for control over the CB. Neither Mom nor Cynthia could hold on to the gadget, and the black cord snapped and struck against the dashboard console. Mom leaned in and appeared to snare Cynthia in a headlock. None of my fellow passengers moved. The polite man who had offered Mom his seat looked at me and said, "Can't you calm her down?" Then Mom let go of Cynthia and said in a hoarse voice, "You win." Cynthia announced that the bus would return to the Visitor Center, immediately. We would not be driving by the Johnson ranch house today. The German couple spoke German, in quick, violent snatches. The little boy with the cowlick put his hands over his ears and screamed in three sharp blasts before his sister covered his mouth with the back of her hand. I felt my shingles pain run down my neck and arms, felt the ladybug shell on my back harden.

Mom strode down the length of the bus, past identical fierce glares from the twin sisters. She sat beside me. I shook my head and said, "This is not Manhattan. We're in the Republic of Texas. Pushy doesn't work here."

Mom said, "Don't worry, kid. I got it covered."

Cynthia sped back to the Visitor Center. She tried to calm the agitated passengers by turning on the bus's stereo system and blasting Lyndon Johnson's favorite song, "Raindrops Keep Fallin' on My Head." I stared out the window at the terraced farmland and tried to remember why I ever cared about the presidents. I loved them because my father loved them. Since he'd died, I'd been trying every day to reclaim his sense of history. All I'd managed to do was recreate his level of stress and discomfort. The red sore on my back proved to me that I was nothing more than the nervous daughter of a panicked man. That was my place in the passage of time, my inheritance. I could never be president. I was the would-be pothead child of a convicted felon and a whore. I tried to picture my father relaxed, stoned, resigned to his shortcomings. His eyes bloodshot, his smile goofy, a halo of ladybugs flying over his blond head: that was the father I loved.

When Cynthia parked the bus, she pointed to Mom and me and said, "You two stay seated. For the rest of you, I'm sorry but this is the last stop." Mom clutched my arm. As Cynthia ushered our fellow travelers off the bus, I imagined the Secret Service descending upon us. We were a family of felons. I figured the penalty for assaulting a park ranger included a prison sentence. Maybe now, with the threat of incarceration pending, Mom would admit her pregnancy. I was furious with her. She'd ruined our vacation, stained my Victim T-shirt, tarnished my father's reputation.

Through the bus window, Mom watched Cynthia confer with a fellow ranger in the Visitor Center. Mom said, "I told Ranger Cindy to wait ten minutes in case those Germans got curious."

The Johnson ranch house was smaller than I had imagined. The white paint on the outside of the house needed a touch-up. The large bow windows sagged in their rotting casings. Before Cynthia dropped us off she pointed out the security cameras and told us which ones were working. "I'll give you twenty minutes like we agreed. The house is locked, but you can view the grounds and Lyndon Baines Johnson's antique car collection."

A massive live oak stood on the front lawn. Lyndon, or some other hunter, had attached two plaques with enormous stuffed deer's heads directly to the tree's trunk. Mom petted a buck's antlers. I'm not sure what Mom promised or paid Cynthia for our private tour of the Johnson Ranch. Mom believed in cash, and always had at least a thousand dollars stashed on or near her person. She also believed in threats and bribes. With a phone call, Mom could place a lien on your ancestral home or buy you the ostrich farm you'd always dreamed of owning. Mom knew how to bargain. How to make a deal. She was fearless. She knew that she couldn't appreciate the presidents the way Dad and I had, but she could give me something Dad never could. Mom could provide access. She could make things happen. She had what it took to be president.

We walked into the open-air front of the airplane hangar that held Lyndon's cars: a red Ford Phaeton, a Fiat 500 Jolly Ghia, a vintage fire truck, and a little green wagon. The sun had tanned Mom's face. She looked beautiful, victorious. I put my arms around her, rubbed her tummy. "What is it?" I asked. She looked down at me and placed my hand flat on the crown of her belly. "It's a boy."

Inside the hangar, I recognized one of the automobiles, a small blue and white convertible. "This is one of those land-and-sea cars. An amphibious car. Johnson used to drive his friends around the ranch, take them down to the river, and scare everyone by plunging them into the water. The car turns into a boat."

Mom opened the driver's-side door, "Get in," she said.

We sat in the white leather seats, proud of our hard-earned view of the Texas hills. Mom took out a linen handkerchief from her purse and handed it to me. "Your father told me this thing helped you guys relax."

I knew by the weight and size of the gift that it was Buchanan. I unwrapped the pipe. The bowl was still packed with a small amount of pot. I'd never smoked Buchanan before.

"Your father died too young to have a will," Mom said. "Just think of this as your inheritance."

"I don't suppose you have a lighter." Mom handed me a silver Zippo with Dad's initials. She watched me light the pipe. I coughed. The smoke burned my throat. I offered Mom Buchanan, but she shook her head no and pointed to her belly.

"When the baby's older," she said, "I want you to tell him about his dad. I want him to know where he came from."

His dad.

We sat together in this magic convertible, me smoking, Mom breathing in the air at my side. We needed a new getaway car. One that could take us back home and beyond. Up the Hudson and along the Garden State Parkway. I gazed down the hill to the Pedernales. Mom pointed out a zebra. I laughed. It was just a gray spotted pony. Everything was clear. I would skip Nixon. Dad would understand. Instead, I'd take my little brother to Omaha, Nebraska, then to Michigan. Gerald Ford, 1974–77, born Leslie Lynch King. He was renamed after his adopted father. Ford didn't know who his real father was until he was practically an adult. I'd tell my brother about Ford and all the men fate brought to power, the chief executives, all the fearless men in charge. He'd know that Andrew Jackson was thirteen when he fought the British in the Battle of Hanging Rock. I'd explain the difference between John Adams and John Quincy Adams. I'd give him reasons to like Ike, to be grateful for the Monroe Doctrine, to appreciate the irony of William Henry Harrison dying of pneumonia one month into his term, after staying out in the cold to deliver his endless inauguration address.

Mom said, "Now smoke in moderation. Don't get caught. Don't let your grades slip. Promise me."

I could hear the walkie-talkie static and chatter coming from the Secret Service agents. We'd been caught. Mom would certainly be arrested. Cynthia would lose her job. I'd be left to raise Lyndon alone. Dad's pot was strong, but mellow. For the first time in our relationship Mom and I had a deal, an understanding. I began to hum "Hail to the Chief." As the agents approached in their dark, shiny suits, I promised Mom I would tell Lyndon, my running mate and my half brother, all the things I knew about my father, his father.

STEPHANIE DICKINSON

■

A Lynching in Stereoscope

FROM *African-American Review*

Jelly

I TURN UP ELIZABETH STREET. On the sidewalk there's a penny. Lincoln, great emancipator. I decide to kick him rather than pick him up. There's enough Honest Abes in my pocket. I drain my Pepsi, letting the caffeine hit, while the sugar seeps into my teeth and zigzags up my nose. I shiver. Someone's tossed a soda can into the lilac bushes where the scentless buds are hard as BBs. It must be 90 degrees today, but I'm in an ice pocket. The air's getting colder, and I can feel the chill of these rich houses. I'm on my way to a new job as a live-in housekeeper. What could be easier than helping some senior citizens swallow pills? I can make people like me. Any flavor. Old folks. Tough kids. Everyone in Harris County Jail was always saying, "Jelly, your eyes remind us of a Thai girl's, your skin's a hot gingerbread, you're the kind of girl the basketball players like to date. Jelly, what do *you* play? Your arms and thighs are tight." I kept to myself, lifting barbells. "Jelly, why are you trying to be so big?" I have to laugh when I think of the question the quivery male voice kept asking me, on the phone when I called about the job: "Are you strong?"

That's it. A Spanish-style house with low-pitched clay tile roof and white stucco walls. I breathe in the salt cedars, the bushes pearled with skin petals that seem to sweat. I knock at the back door like the man told me to. "Come in, come in. It's not locked." A young guy in jeans and T-shirt opens the door and waves me into the kitchen. He's blond and well-built.

Ciz

I soap myself with the last of the yellow bar. Today is soap-making day, and I'm known in a few shacktowns for my recipes. Honeysuckle and cinnamon, dogwood and toffee. Humming, I run the cloth over my underarms. Sometimes I wish I could adorn myself in leaves, the dirt and stains of wood, not reach for my mended calico. I don't bother with drawers or stockings. The 90 degrees are crowding me as I push my head through the dress neck, and pull the comb through my wild hair that needs three hands to tie it back. I press the tin mirror close to my face, and hunt for the light in my eyes, like once I searched for my son's father. I was thirteen then. Now I'm twenty-five. Brightness is what the mirror gives back, gold flecks in each brown iris, and a nose that fits nice between eyes and cheeks. My lips are full but not to bursting. "Sweet Ciz," my grandpa used to say, "you weren't there when they passed out the feet. Only the inches." But he was wrong. I stand four feet eight inches tall.

"Alp, rise and shine, my sweet potato pie." I sing to my son still asleep behind the curtain that divides the room. "Fried cornmeal mush."

Beautiful heat, already a green steam in the leaves when I cross under the chestnut. Not a whiff of breeze in my bottle tree. Alp and I hung the branches with root beer jugs and bud vases — each filled with colored water to protect us. It's July, so the cook stove is out in the summer kitchen. The embers glow when I stir them. Suddenly the hairs stiffen on my upper lip. The eyes in the back of my head see the dog on the stoop. A white bloodhound. His tongue hangs sideways from his muzzle, and he's panting. A scream knots my throat. I need a griot woman to tell me what this means. Maybe old Sally Joy. The good medicine would keep an evil-spirited dog away. This one must be a benefactor, come to bless my soap making.

Jelly

It's heat I've never walked into before. I almost swoon. Copper pots hang above the stove where a kettle of applesauce simmers. The sink and counters glow avocado green. Sun slants in from a dormer, hitting my silver platform shoes. The blond squints like they hurt his eyes.

"I'm the new live-in," I say, wishing I had sneakers on. To run if anything goes wrong.

He gives me a long look that takes in the leather fringes that lace up the sides of my jean bell-bottoms, my midriff purple top, my dreads tied back in a rubber band.

I don't tell him I picked the clothes out of a pile because they fit; I don't tell him about my arrest, sitting in the Texas Street Greyhound bus depot next to this Mexican woman who had three kids — two boys and a baby girl. She asked if I'd hold the baby while she took her boys to the bathroom. The next thing I knew the cops were arresting me for kidnapping. I did two months in County, before a judge threw the charges out. Two days ago I said goodbye to Houston. I told my mom and baby brother I'd phone from Arkansas. My lucky number is two.

Look what the dog dragged in, he's thinking. *I can't believe the old ashes plan on hiring this one. A black Elvis backup singer in her karate jumpsuit.* He grins to mask himself.

"Who are the old ashes?" Sometimes I can hear inner speech; that's my gift, my one specialness, to pick up sentences now and then, and the voices people talk to themselves in.

His chin jerks. "Natalie and Nathan, the twins." He picks up the spatula from a spoon tray and stirs the applesauce. "I'm Roland. I come Sundays *only.*"

He's friendlier now that he wonders if I can see inside his mind, and shows me the bland diet menus taped to the cupboards, the sea salts and sugar substitutes, the lower cabinet with a Lazy Susan filled with vitamins and medications.

"Why Sundays only?" I edge my shoulder against the sub-zero refrigerator, feel it hum. I'm high on having gotten a job with no questions asked, no lies having to be told.

"I'm not a slave." He daubs his pinkie into the applesauce, and then licks. "Definitely more cinnamon sugar. That's how the old ashes like it. I'm surprised diabetes isn't one of their many afflictions."

"Bring him in, Roland," a man shouts in a papery voice. I hear slippers making a sandpaper scuff over tile, and then a thumping sound.

"Her, Nathan, it's a her." Roland rolls his eyes. He holds open the salon-style door.

Ciz

"Shoo," I say to the bloodhound. "Shoo." I've never seen such whiteness as this hound with his droopy ears and blue eyes like pieces of the sky were cut out and forced into his head. "What do you want with me?" The grease in the skillet is sputtering, crackling, and popping like it's angry. I run to stir it. When I turn back to the screen the dog is gone, and Alp is rubbing his sleepy face about to set himself down on the step. His irises have tiny flecks of yellow in them. Like caught bits of sun. He's a big boy, almost six feet tall and just going on twelve.

"Boy, bring me some creek water, and then you'll eat." Before I send him off, I ask him about the bloodhound.

He shakes his head, brushes off a fly that mistakes his reddish purple lips for plums. "If the dog comes back, can we keep him?"

I tell him no. "Now go on. Get the bucket." He goes. Sweet natured with dimples, give him a white peach and he's happy for a week. Alp likes to carve soldiers out of soap ends. He gathers blackberries and blueberries and mashed cypress bark to dye uniforms with. Then he scratches battlefields in the dirt with a stick, and puts his Battle of the Somme between the sweet gum trees. I don't dare interfere with Alp when he's making a battle. I watch him disappear into the boxwoods and acacia.

Old Sally Joy comes by to borrow some lard. From her dogtrot cabin someone is playing a banjo and singing. Her daughter has a new fine brown man. Bluejays try to stick in their own verses. I get an old newspaper and wrap her up a cone of lard. It's high noon before I get time to fry up some kale and bacon. Alp smells food and comes running to me.

"*The soap needs rainwater. Tend to it,*" *I say straight into his face. He takes after me. The main reason my soap's so fine is that I boil my lye in rainwater, and then add it to the creek water along with sassafras oil, and leftover bones.*

"*Ma, it's too hot to carry water.*"

"*And stir the water in slow, Alp.*"

"*Ma, if lightning struck a tree I was under, would it electrocute me?*"

"*Not if you weren't standing up.*"

"*Ma, if I was swimming and a water moccasin bit me, would I get sick?*"

"*Alp, you're going to wish I was a snake if you don't get that water.*"

It usually takes three times of telling Alp to do something before he does it. But for some reason it tires me today more than usual. The heat is flat-out, and the handle of the fry pan seems heavy in my hand. That feathery shade near the creek starts to call Ciz Ciz and almost puts me to sleep.

Jelly

The old man thumps his cane. His hair is messed like he slept in it. He's tall with a handsome gray face, and dressed in a beige terrycloth robe with brown slippers. He ushers me down a hall. Rounded doors, and grillwork windows. Burgundy throw rugs.

We stop next to earth-colored pottery jugs set in a cluster "You'll be preparing our meals, bathrooming us, doing laundry, lifting if needed. And I am Nathan. You're answerable to mainly me." The old man's eyes squint like he is trying to squeeze a tear from them. "You'll get room and board, and four hundred dollars a week. You look muscular enough to lift us. We weigh hardly anything at all. We're old housecats and our bones stick out like grasshoppers."

I listen to the oars of the ceiling fan stirring the air. He motions me deeper in past the end tables that burgundy pillows sit on. The living room is almost bare except for a wide-screen TV, two hospital beds, and an oxygen tank. A woman lies propped on pillows, absorbed in a talk show.

"We'll have a few words with Natalie. It's just the two of us. We've tried the home health aides sent by the state. Abominations!" His slipper hooks the edge of the burgundy rug, and he catches his balance by grabbing my arm. "You're a sturdy well-built girl, exceptionally strapping." He trips again. "Hell cat, I'll cane you flat," he says, striking the rug with his cane. "Natalie, this is . . ." he falters.

"Cozetta Clark. But I go by Jelly," I tell him, thinking of my mother throwing up her hands when she found me yet again hiding in the curtain with a jar of Welch's grape jelly, almost empty.

He bows. "Cozetta, how lovely. Yet Jelly has its beauty too. Unlike my twin."

Ciz

Midafternoon. The banjo goes quiet, making more room for the heat. The lye-hot sun smolders above the white dogwoods, the blooms curl and suck in their scent. It's that trembling dwarf nectarine time when the heat ripens inside you. I can hardly see for the sweat in my eyes. I force the ladle through the bubbling soap. It feels like a journey. The summer kitchen screen snaps, meaning Alp's going for more cornbread. And then I hear a choking sound — an animal trying to draw breath, like gasping through soggy cheesecloth. I raise the ladle. It's that bloodhound again. The albino. He's barely crawling, dragging himself by his front paws. Did you get into my caustic soda? If you did, you're a goner. He's whining, his mouth foams red-flecked spittle. If he ate caustic, his throat will swell, and his esophagus will burn inside him. I run to the rainwater barrel and fill the dipper. Here, hound, let me clean your mouth. He scratches his nose in the dirt like he is tracking a squirrel; his neck arches in a fantastic snap. I freeze. Suddenly I am more frightened of the dog's death than he, worried over the heart beating so fast I can watch it through the pale belly and rib cage, the heart beating like a drum. The in and out frantic panting stops. Head now clumsy crashes to the ground.

"Alp!" He's sure to have his finger in the molasses can. "Alp, come here."

Jelly

Nathan laughs, "My dear twin."

Two plastic tubes curl into her nose, and a hose connects her to the oxygen. Natalie's eyes are more violet than blue, and she must have been blond in her day, but now the only light hairs left are the ones that grow in the wrinkles around her mouth. I think of desilking sweet corn. She scowls at the huge TV at the foot of her bed where a car growls, turns into a jaguar.

"My sister has emphysema. Sixty cigarettes a day, a waterway of smoke, for forty years creates what you see." He sits on his bed, sliding off his bedroom slippers. "Could you pick my legs up and swing them in?" I think of coffee stirrers when I lift his legs. "Ah, such nice hands." He lies back with a groan. "We'll enjoy the use of them. I'm quite satisfied. Roland will acquaint you with the house. Choose either of the master bedrooms to sleep in."

"I can't take the light," Natalie complains. "Would you close the drapes?"

Arabesques of grillwork. I pity the burglar who chooses this window.

"Oh, Jelly," Nathan calls. "After you settle in, would you look for something for us? It will be in my old closet. At the back I have a bookcase, and on the middle shelf, a box with a tiger on its lid. Since you're such a muscular girl, I have no hesitation in asking you to carry it down."

Ciz

Where is a dog in his mind when he dies? With his prey, digging their bones up from shallow graves, the mice and coon whispering his name. Should I bury him in the garden where the dirt is musky and soft, cover him with the curling squash vines? He'll bring bad luck to my sweet corn. I go for a gunnysack. "Alp," I keep calling. I'm panting by the time I get the dog in the burlap. And just then to see fifty townspeople walking in the sun through the black walnuts and buckthorn and crab apples, makes your heart stop, and then pick up again hard. What do they want? They must be going after someone. Maybe Sally Joy, maybe the banjo player, maybe one of the croppers stole something. "What can I do for you?" *I call out, thinking,* Don't you come out, boy. I've been calling you and you didn't listen, so now you stay where you are, make yourself small.

I recognize Sheriff Garner. His deputies have regular redbone hounds tugging at leashes. The redbones sniff their way to the gunny-sack. "We've found the dog," *the square-headed deputy shouts. He nudges the dead hound; its muzzle expels a clot of blood like a well-fleshed blackish strawberry. Things go on in a dog's hell. The deputy is shaking his head.* "Know who this here dog belongs to? R. E. Lee Wilson."

My blood ices. Mr. R. E. owns the air I'm breathing.

Sheriff Garner walks toward me, rocking the upper part of his body. He's known to visit shack women. Has a girl by one of them in Judsonia. "This dog was trailing the boy who molested his mistress. A nine-year-old girl. Happened this morning!"

"My boy's been with me all day. The folks around here can tell you."

Alp steps out of the summer kitchen, and three or four town men in suspenders and straw hats hustle him over to where I am. The coals under the soap kettle glow sweet-potato orange. "Listen. Whatever he done, whatever you say he done, I did it. He didn't do anything."

"We're going to make us a trial. This animal took down his pants in front of a nine-year-old girl."

They dunk Alp's hand into the scalding soap. His scream rises to the treetops. First time he ever pees himself since he was a baby.

Names fly. Killers, castrated pigs, dirt, shack dung, coons.

Jelly

I choose Nathan's old room for my own. I plop down in the oak chair, put up my feet, and look around. There's too much of something, but I can't figure what it is until I spot the decorative wooden boxes on the dresser top. A box takes every flat-surfaced space: bee boxes, dragon boxes, a lady box, the hair for ring storage and compartments behind her breasts.

"Jelly," Nathan's watery voice rises up the stairs. "Remember the box I asked for."

It's a struggle to climb to my feet. The closet runs almost the length of the room. I switch on the light. Hanging in a row are three-piece suits in blues and grays, tuxedos with long coattails, and shoes in racks, so many men's shoes, brick-brown Oxfords, and black wingtips with such lustrous shine they seem on fire. It doesn't look like Nathan walked far in any of them, let alone danced. Smell of cherry tobacco clings to the dry cleaning bags like the inside of a cold pipe stem.

I find the bookcase in the far back, and on top is a flat ebony box with a tiger panel. Next to it is another of those decorative boxes, this one in the shape of a screaming man. His head is hinged and I open it with my fingernail. What do I expect, a diamond stickpin? Figures I would find a piece of dirt. It feels greasy, tarry, not like dirt at all. Could it be opium? Maybe that's the secret of all these boxes. My baby brother's mother-in-law sews Percodan in the hem of her housecoats. Each of the compartments has a different piece of dirt in it.

I carry the tiger box carefully down the curved staircase and set it on the tray table next to Nathan's bed. The TV is slowly nursing them to sleep.

Ciz

Onlookers shout. Their yells move the road closer, twist and push it around my plot. The steel-spectacled deputy hits my boy in the mouth. Alp shudders like a dog shaking off ditch water. "That's it." A baby shrieks. Here with its mama. Mewling so loud I can't hear what the faces are saying, just see mouths moving up and down.

Men push through the deputies, a bunch of cotton shirts, old-fashioned neckpieces. "Make the bastard talk about what he did to R. E. Lee's girl!"

I jump between them and Alp, cover him with as much of me as I can muster. A boot picks itself up, heel banging my hip. The flat of another lands solid in the small of my back. I think of my mother's hair, her eyebrows that we combed for fun with a toothbrush.

"Leave the woman be," Sheriff Garner bellows.

A kick to the ribs knocks me to the ground. Mother had an amber ring.

"Who's he calling a woman?" A boy's shrill voice. A yellow fog of words. Color of my soap. If I blink and wish hard enough, he'll disappear. Soap's almost ready to pour into tins. "I wouldn't take that not even in pitch dark. How 'bout you, Oscar?" Laughter. "Not with a barge paddle."

A female cries, "Cleanse the sin from R. E. Lee's child."

Not even a regular child, but that man's prize. I crawl to Sheriff Garner's pant leg. "Let my son be. I swear he's good." My heart's rasping. "My boy's been with me all day. He can't fly."

The spectacled deputy takes off his belt. "Let's tend to the boy." One after another the men come, taking turns whipping. None hide their faces. My son's eyes swell shut. At least he's saved from seeing. The deputy dunks my son's other hand in the soap. This time Alp's scream digs a hole in the ground.

Agwe, Aizan. I mouth the names of ancient givers. The dirt road has filled with cars. Like corpses. A covered hack stops at a distance; inside are two women wearing feather and veil hats.

"Let's take them to the river."

They push me after my son. Red water's leaking from Alp's forearms where the skin is ripped. I scream. They ball a handkerchief and stick it in my mouth.

It's not to the river they take Alp, but into the trees. They shove him toward the sweet gums where his soap soldiers wrestle with twigs. I jerk, almost break from their grip. Let me go with him. He's afraid of when the weather changes too many times in one day, he's afraid of ladders and birds. They hold me back.

The mushrooms grow big as fists where they tie him up and pile on the kindling. Fifty, now there's a hundred streaming past me. Laughers, jerkers, spitters. They crash into the woods. A newspaperman takes out his tablet. "We're just swatting a few mosquitoes. That's not news."

Jelly

Nathan gives off mustiness, like those mansions of oil tycoons filled with rosewood music boxes that once played ragtime, old from not being touched except by cyclones of dust. "We were brought up rich, Jelly, but Daddy didn't spoil us."

"Shut up, Nathan," Natalie hisses. She takes love from the TV, laps up her stewed tomatoes when the actors eat their phantom meals.

"She talked like that to Daddy. Can you imagine?" Nathan's eyes brighten. "As a child her skin was smoother than petals. Her face, a breathing flower. Daddy sometimes just stared at her."

"That's it!" Natalie throws her Centrum Silver vitamins at him. The bottle strikes his chest. "Take a walk in the hall or I'll break your head and shit on your neck."

Nathan dutifully sits up, grips his cane, and struggles to stand.

"Now cut it off, cut it off," Natalie orders.

I turn off the oxygen, and take the tubes from her nose. The Pall Malls are next to her nasal spray. This is the holy moment when I light her cigarette, and her mouth sucks in smoke as if it were silk. Afterward I sponge her underarms where the hairs are frail as cobwebs. "Never had a baby, did you, Natalie?"

Her belly is smooth as a girl's, no stretch marks. Just a scar on her buttocks like the glistening ripple a trout makes running under a full moon. I powder her, and she rolls onto her back. Her violet eyes go to the ceiling like she's in a staring contest with it. The sheen of her on my fingers is like dust from a moth's wings.

Ciz

I'm not afraid anymore. Hickory is king of the woods. They're burning my son. I hear his screams. They must pull him from the fire to savor him. For thirty minutes my baby howls. Alp, it's your mama, honey love. You're named Alp after those cold tall mountains far away. Go there in your mind.

They burn him slow. The fine thigh pieces.

I say goodbye to my arms, feel a yank as they cord my wrists behind my back. Someone rips my apron. "Let's go swimming, sweetheart." They walk me to the bridge. Last sun ripples in the sluggish current. This is the river Alp was baptized in. Burning water. Three times the

Methodist preacher took him under. Sweetish smoke. I wanted Alp to have as many safeguards as he could get.

The sun is a honed blade that gouges my heart out. It isn't thumping, and I don't feel it hit the side of my ribs. My heart is gone when they push a charred thing past me in a wheelbarrow. The thing has no legs. It raises up on its haunches, reaching out, no hands on the ends of its blackened wrists. Give me my smoke baby back. I'll plant him in the garden. I'll lie down beside him in the squash blossoms.

A man with a whiskey nose croaks, "I'm going to write the boys down there in Delight. Tell them about the barbeque we had this afternoon."

Townspeople crowd both sides of the river. There's a bunch behind me. Someone is playing an accordion. Someone is selling rock candy. Voices of rumbling earth and burrowed cicadas. Soon I won't know what a cicada is. My own mother will die again. Along with water, corn mush, son.

"Make way, make way, R. E. Wilson's on his way." And then I see the man who owns the dirt where they make me set my feet.

"This is the boy who done it, R. E." They push the blackened thing in the wheelbarrow at him. A burnt offering. He has a golden boy and girl with him, a twin set. Made out of cornsilk, sunlight, heavy cream, and wedding rings. When the great giver is angry it is hard to calm her. But her price is only that of a chicken.

Jelly

Natalie's room. They've sent me to look for their stereoscope.

On the dressing table there's a chrome-plated cigarette case too perfect to have been used much. Not like things in my family that have been touched and touched. You can feel back taxes and second mortgages on the hairbrushes.

The card box sits on the messed bedspread where Roland must have been kicking back, and the stereoscope stares up from the nightstand. I used to fight with my baby brother over who got great-Gran's stereoscope first. You could disappear behind the eye squares for a few minutes, and when you looked up Sunday would be gone, along with the pork chops. My favorite card was of a Forbidden City girl's bound feet, her toes curling under to meet the heel. Lily feet.

What kind of pictures do the twins have? I lift the stereoscope to my face. True old-timer amusement. I feel that drop in temperature again, like when you're swimming and you hit a pocket of deep chill that takes you all the way back to the Ice Age.

The card photograph is of a barefoot corpse. Hanging from a bridge, a pretty woman in a calico dress. I can see the ripples in the brown river, and almost hear the sluggish gurgling. A postcard. Etched into the corner "copyright 1934 — Arkansas — unmailable."

The calico skirt seems to take the wind and still it. Hanging with her head to the side, the woman is graceful like a ballet dancer at rest. Her toes point downward, tiny feet, like lilies below her hem. The trees crowd together. At the edge of the photograph is another hanging body, smaller than the woman's. Badly burned, too burned to tell what sex it is. Like the greasy dirt in the boxes.

Faces on the bridge. A handsome man stands out; his starched trousers set to shine for all time. His children are too pretty to be alive. The girl in a dress of magnolia petals, and the boy her impish double. They are staring, not quite solemn.

I breathe deeply. Take the card out of the stereoscope? Who is she? Why did they hang her on this afternoon? No, she wasn't a stunt actress of the day. I shrug, and slide the card into my pocket. Who can care about a still photograph after all the moving blood and dismemberment on TV? Maybe it's the silence that makes it so haunted, the subdued brown color like everything is drying leaves — the faces, the bridge, the water, the rope — ready to crumble but when you try to blow the leaves away they end up back in your face.

I'm about to cut the light off when I see the studio portrait on top of the dresser. A heavy brass frame encloses the twins holding hands in a mock apple orchard. It's supposed to be summer, the long hot American summer. They must be eight or nine. Too blond-skinned. Like things from comets or the Milky Way. Nathan, in a miniature three-piece suit, a handkerchief in the breast pocket, smiles at Natalie, whose hair hangs in sausage curls to her waist. Her dress is chiffon. The dog would catch anyone's attention. A white bloodhound. Its leash — a charm bracelet around Natalie's wrist. They are the same children as those inside the stereoscope card.

"I saw the dog you had when you were kids," I say, setting up a TV-tray table beside Natalie's bed to hold the stereoscope and card box.

"That's Blue," Natalie says in an irritated voice. "Where's dinner?"

Five minutes is all their strained asparagus and turkey meatloaf take in the microwave. I smell cinnamon, as if the ghosts of apples are boiling on the stove.

Nathan holds forth while Natalie gobbles meatloaf as if it were rare filet. "I can still see that noon when Daddy told us, 'Hurry, dress, wear your old shoes. Blue has been found!' We expected a picnic on the river. Tongue sandwiches, a feast of wild strawberries and grape peaches."

The twins stay up poring over their stereoscope. When they are asleep, I walk far enough from the house so that it is not their ground, and then I get to my knees and bury the card.

Ciz

Devil is the name the old griot women give the evil hounds. Devil is the name I give the one who puts a rope around my neck. A man ties my torn apron. For an instant I think kindness. Then his hands fill my pockets with pebbles. I want to think about the rock doves singing when Alp and I played with our chessmen all through the slow part of the day. Alp, they're going to hang you too, even if you're already dead. A stone hits me in the stomach, then a stick. Wrens winding down, day almost done. Luscious dusk. I raise my face, even as a peach pit hits my forehead. Alp, there's still so much cornmeal mush left, I should have let you eat every whisper of it.

"Let the woman go," someone shouts, but is drowned out.

Where could I possibly go now that I've been here? The cypress roots

*are whispering my name; be strong, the river bottom calls. Ciz, Ciz,
your boy is safe.*

It's Mr. R. E. who decides what to do with me, who nods his head.

Sheriff says, "OK, Ciz, let's get it over with." He pulls his pants up,
takes a hop as he adjusts the belt. A habit. He'll get to do that ten thousand more times before he dies. A rope has been tied to a joint, the noose
end coils in the dust.

*My ashy son hangs over the water; my son who has no hands is bur-
ied in the air on the summer vines. A breeze twitches through the silver
maples, their naked undersides shine. The photographer is moving
closer, his camera like a box lunch at an ice cream social.* "Let's see you
do a jig, Ciz." *Is it true when they take a photograph at the moment of
death, that's where your soul stays?*

Jelly

I'm late with their breakfast, but when I serve them their toast
burnt black, neither complains. They smack and ask for more. In
the kitchen I find the bread that has green in the middle, toast it,
and cover the mold with grape jelly. I can hear them fighting.

"I'll throw this plate at you, Nathan. I'll really bean you. I don't
know where your stinking card went. What do I care? You have a
box full of them."

"But that one. Natalie, that was our history."

When I bring them their toast, which both find delicious, I hear
myself asking about the dog.

Nathan looks at me thoughtfully as he sips his decaf coffee
through a crazy straw. "Blue was from the medieval white Talbot
Hound, who died out as a breed around 600 A.D. My father was
amazed when he came upon a Talbot birthed in an Arkansas
sharecropper's lean-to. An immaculate conception. Poor Blue."
He pulls his terrycloth robe around him. "We saved the bastard's
ashes to mix with our own."

"So that's what all that dirt upstairs in those boxes is?" I ask.

"I'm not sure I know what you're talking about." Nathan's
waterless blue eyes follow me as I carry the tops of the TV trays

into the kitchen. Does he know that I know? What is it I know? That he witnessed something? That he keeps it with him, worships it, relic of a lost place and time? That he's enchanted by a calico dress? A sluggish river? I don't worry about that old filthy rag of a world that he comes from. Whatever he and his kind thought was the cat's meow has been chewed under. There's worse things to be afraid of these days.

Ciz

I drop. Ripples of heat rise from the trees. I'm listening to the leaves turn over, tinkling, showing off their silver undersides.

"Does it hurt, Mama?" Alp asks. I spit the handkerchief from my mouth, a honeydew voice flows through my tongue — we're the angels, not the murdered ones.

The blond children play on the riverbank while the limbs of the black walnuts drift in the current. The girl looks out from behind her brother, half-smiles, and ducks. Peek-a-boo, I see you. Wind caresses. A sickle moon waits in the sky. Barn swallows offer up pitifully glad songs.

I blink and walk out into air. Giver, let me live.

■

Heavy Metal Mercenary

FROM *Rolling Stone*

WOLF WEISS IS BEHIND THE WHEEL of the black GMC Yukon, speed-weaving through rush-hour traffic in Baghdad. He's headed for the border with Kuwait, 340 miles to the south, and he intends to keep "hard" — that is, make instantly and absolutely clear to anyone who is thinking about wasting us that they will be wasted first. The vehicle is an arsenal on wheels. It's loaded with shoulder-launched antitank rockets, fragmentation grenades that have a "kill radius" of five meters, and a box bolted to the hump between the seats that contains 2,000 rounds of ammunition. Weiss, a thirty-six-year-old American, has an AKS-47 slung over his shoulder with parachute cord, which he uses to leverage the weapon when he needs to shoot and steer at the same time. Next to him is a British-trained Nepalese Gurkha named Kedar, who has his own AK pointed out the passenger-side window. His job is to guard our right flank, from two o'clock to five o'clock. Next to me in the back is an Iraqi in tan combat gear who goes by "D" — as in, "Don't be alarmed if D here starts to fire over your head" — and behind us is our follow-on vehicle, a gray Yukon driven by an American named Scott, which has a belt-fed, fully automatic machine gun capable of firing 700 rounds a minute pointed out the back window.

"Locked, cocked, and ready to rock!" Scott shouts to Weiss over the radio. As he guns the Yukon through the crowded streets, Weiss views the drivers all around us not as fellow motorists but as potential terrorists — and we are their target. The director of a private security company that escorts supply convoys between cities and ferries clients to work, Weiss is a private gun for hire, part of the vast and growing army of for-profit contractors who are providing much of the firepower in Iraq. There are now an estimated 20,000 "operators" or "shooters," as they're known on the ground, making corporate soldiers the second-largest contingent in Iraq after the American military. For better or worse, these private military contractors have become an integral part of the occupation, the only force available to protect workers and officials as they attempt to rebuild schools and restore power. By government estimates, the for-profit militias could wind up costing American taxpayers more than $4 billion — a quarter of the cost budgeted for reconstruction. "A lot of people are calling us private armies — and that's basically what we are," says Weiss. "This is not a security company. This is a paramilitary force."

Some of the private warriors sport such neat haircuts and tidy polo shirts that they look, at first, more like golf pros than gunslingers. Wolf Weiss, as his name suggests, is not the polo-shirt sort. He wears his body armor, and his bravado, at all times. He is not tall — only five feet eight — but his barrel chest is bursting out of his black bulletproof vest. His dark, crinkly hair, which hangs halfway down his back, is pulled back in a braid. His left biceps features a long, curling tattoo of a panther; the right displays a smaller one of the Grim Reaper playing the guitar. Beneath his vest, covering every inch of his back, is a tattoo that Weiss considers "a good representation of myself and my ideals in a nutshell" — a full-color, full-face rendering of a wolf about to pounce. "If you look into the eyeball," he tells me later, "you'll see a hunter with his hands up." Sure enough, in one of the gleaming oracular pools, there is a tiny reflection of a predator, helpless in the knowledge that he has become the prey.

"The wolf is obviously me," Weiss says. "The man in the eyeball is Evil." As he drives, Weiss keeps changing lanes abruptly, cutting off other drivers in a high-octane dash for the desert. "Speed is security," he likes to say. If anyone evil manages to get close enough to look in on us, the first thing he sees will not be faces but muzzles poised to fire. So when a car pulls alongside the Yukon, Weiss floors it and swerves away. "Kedar, get him!" he yells. "*Get him!*"

Kedar swings his weapon around and trains it on the car. The driver takes the hint and immediately peels off.

Other contractors, especially the British, view such shows of force as unnecessary and insanely provocative. Treating everyone as hostile, they say, helps make people hostile: The more you point your weapons at innocent civilians, the harder it is to convince them that you're only here to help. Then again, Wolf isn't violating any industry standards, because for all practical purposes there are no industry standards. Anyone willing to carry a gun in Iraq can have a job in Iraq — and those hired as shooters know that no matter how crazy or dangerous they act, they can almost certainly get a job with another company. "They didn't check crap," one operator told me in disgust after a prospective employer didn't even bother to verify his credentials. "They hired me over the phone and had me on a plane the next day." As a Special Forces veteran, Weiss is considered a Tier One operator — someone with extensive experience in combat and overseas deployments. But many private contractors are drawn from what some call the Bubba Tier, guys who have worked as small-town cops or prison guards. The demand for private security in Iraq is so high that the supply simply doesn't matter.

As the offending driver falls back, Weiss tells me he has never actually fired at anyone for menacing him in traffic. But he did shoot out someone's engine once, and though he is somber about it, he has killed Iraqis in the course of four firefights, give or take, during the past year. His own marketing material, a poster-size photo of Wolf and the eight-man team of "wolverines" he commands, spells out his credo: "Protect the weak, defend the innocent, strike down thine enemies and vanquish all evil by the right hand of God. Strength and honor to all who live by the code of the warrior."

In the SUV, a CD is blaring a crazy soundtrack to go with the crazy moving picture outside the windows. "What is that?" I howl above the music. "Judas Priest!" Wolf howls back. *"Screaming for Vengeance!"*

The whole idea of vengeance is very big with Weiss, and it has been for a very long time. "My father was assassinated when I was eleven," he tells me. "He was found with over seventy percent of his bones broken, shot twice at point-blank range in the back of the head, wrapped up in a blanket with a yellow ribbon and a bow tie, and then put in the back of his Rolls-Royce." Weiss says this in an almost neutral tone, as if he's stating where he went to high school.

He springs this on me just as things are starting to feel slightly less weird. We have made it out of Baghdad and traveled a few miles south on the MSR (Main Supply Route) Tampa, which runs the length of Iraq, from Kuwait to Turkey. Thanks to the abundance of improvised explosive devices that are planted along it, this particular stretch of the MSR is known as IED Alley. At the moment, though, it feels deceptively serene. There are fewer cars on the road here than in the city, and the setting sun is bathing the Iraqi desert in a gentle glow. Weiss has popped another CD into the dashboard player. Actually, it is *his* CD. When he isn't a hired gun, Weiss is a rock musician, albeit one with the sensibilities of a hired gun: The album is called *Code of the Warrior,* and he wrote almost all of the songs himself. It sounds sort of like Mötley Crüe, if Mötley Crüe were a bunch of gung-ho patriots trained to kill men with their bare hands. As each song comes up, Weiss explains what it is about. "911" is about 9/11. "Rising Son" is about — well, actually, it's for — his son. "The Wheel Goes 'Round," he says, is about confronting the killers of his father.

Vic Weiss, a sports promoter and businessman, was murdered in 1979. He was a charismatic player who liked to flash diamond rings and Rolexes. According to the *Los Angeles Times,* the elder Weiss "privately rubbed shoulders with criminals, ran up huge debts on sports betting, and skimmed off the top of laundered money he delivered to mobsters." His murder, although widely presumed to have been a Mafia execution, has never been solved.

It might seem far too simplistic to say that Wolf's whole life is about confronting his father's killers — but that's pretty much how he puts it himself. "That's what definitely fueled and spawned my hatred for evil," he says. It also fueled and spawned his development as a self-described "no-good two-bit son-of-a-bitch asshole drug addict." When Wolf enlisted in the Marine Corps at eighteen, it was partly because he wanted to clean up his act. It was also because he intended to acquire the strength and the skills necessary to bring his father's killers to justice. In the course of almost fourteen years in the Marines, he served as a hostage rescuer, a combat diver, a free-fall parachutist, and a scout sniper. At one point he even started "actively planning" to hunt down his father's killers, but his mother talked him out of it over dinner at a Chinese restaurant. He eventually let his father's death go, got married, had three kids, and gave the Lord center stage in his life. ("I am not afraid of dying," he tells me. "To be absent from the body is to be present with the Lord.") But that doesn't mean he settled down. In 1999, six years short of qualifying for full retirement, Weiss quit the Marines.

"Why are you doing this?" his commanding officer asked. "Nobody does this."

"Sir," Weiss replied, "I am going to be a rock and roll star."

It didn't work out that way. Weiss supported himself as a tattoo artist while he booked gigs and sold tickets and produced his own album — but he didn't like the pressure to compromise his artistic vision. "Because I was unwilling to change for the corporate machine known as the music industry, the business of arms continues to call me back," he says. So when American forces invaded Iraq last year, Weiss decided to fall back on his old skills. "There's only a few things in this world I can do really, really well," he says. "War is one."

Night has fallen, and we are driving through the desert. Actually, it feels more like we're bouncing through it. We have hit a seventy-kilometer stretch that Wolf calls the I-70, but it's no highway. The route is mostly a car-killing patchwork of ruts and pebbles and dust. Strips of gravel alternate with sand traps. Every now and then, to obscure the Yukon, Weiss drops down onto something that he calls the "low road." No self-respecting city park would label it a path.

"At night, you're not going to see the threat," says Wolf. "A lot of times you won't even hear it. You have to key in on flashes in the desert." Turning some knobs on a box on the dashboard, Weiss shines an eerily roving spotlight on the surrounding dunes. He doesn't expect to see any terrorists — they prefer to make their attacks closer to the cities where they are based — but there are plenty of other wild cards: tire-punching spikes left by insurgents, people driving with no headlights, dust storms, dead camels. Experienced vets such as Weiss can make as much as $20,000 a month as private contractors — fifteen times what they'd get in the military. "Guys like me don't come cheap," Wolf says. The pay is so lucrative, U.S. troops are eagerly defecting to the for-profit ranks; a manager at one company told me he never goes through a military checkpoint without soldiers asking him for his business card. But Weiss is quick to insist that he and other hired guns aren't mercenaries in the traditional sense. In fact, he confides, he sometimes performs "sensitive" government missions for free, out of loyalty to the United States, handling jobs the military would rather distance itself from. "I trust my country and I trust my flag," he says. "I trust that they're making the right decision, even if I don't understand it."

The high pay can come at a high price. For-profit militias are often rushed into hostile territory without adequate training and with no reliable means to identify, let alone communicate with, the various militaries on the ground here — the Iraqi police, the civil-defense corps, other security companies. "There's been twice when we almost got lit right up by a .50-caliber machine gun from our own countrymen," Weiss says. "Our own people don't always know who we are." So far, at least eighty contractors have been killed in action — suffering more casualties than any U.S. ally. The most notorious deaths occurred in March, when four contractors with Blackwater Security were killed and mutilated in Fallujah, prompting an American siege of the city.

"Iraq is the biggest marketplace in the short history of the privatized military industry," says P. W. Singer, the national security fellow at the Brookings Institution and the author of *Corporate Warriors.* "Private militaries are playing a pivotal role in warfare to an extent not seen since the advent of the mass nation-state armies in the Napoleonic age."

The boom has happened so quickly — and with so little oversight — that the Pentagon can't reliably count the private troops in Iraq, let alone monitor their conduct. For-profit contractors are pretty much making up the rules of engagement as they go along — and breaking them, too. Weiss recalls one rainy winter night right after he arrived in Iraq. The company team, which was then led by another director, had headed north with a large convoy of trucks. Along the way, Weiss says, the boss kept lighting into the truck drivers for no good reason. When they finally reached their destination, Weiss got a frantic call from his superior, who needed a first-aid kit. Weiss rushed over with it, only to find that the director had stabbed one of the drivers in the heart. "I did keep the guy from bleeding out," he says. The director was arrested, Weiss adds, but never wound up serving time for the assault.

When we reach Talil Air Base, near Nasiriyah, Weiss stops to fuel up. Because he never knows when he will have to "e and e" — escape and evade attack — he never passes up a chance to fill the tank. In the early days of the invasion, before reliable fuel drops were set up, there were times when Weiss simply commandeered gas stations at gunpoint and took what he needed, terrifying the Iraqi civilians who had been waiting in line all night. "It makes you feel bad when you basically assault a gas station, secure the perimeter, and just barge your way right in front of the line," he says. "But you need the fuel, you got to fill it up, you know?" To make amends, Weiss would throw money out the window before speeding off.

Weiss takes me around to the second Yukon to have a look at the "rear security." Under coalition regulations, the belt-fed machine gun perched in the back is supposed to be off-limits to private security companies. So are many of the other weapons in the SUV, including the shoulder-launched rockets and the fragmentation grenades. "I need to match the firepower that is out there," Weiss says with a shrug. He declines to tell me exactly where he gets his weapons, but it is not hard to guess. Many, if not most, security companies buy their weapons on the black market, providing cash to the same arms dealers who supply the Iraqi insurgents who are killing American soldiers, to say nothing of the mafias that are killing average Iraqis and the religious militias that are getting ready to kill one another. Operators know that a Kurdish arms trader with an SUV full of high-quality, value-for-money armaments is just a phone call away. An American contractor named Ken Walker bought some AKs in a hotel parking lot in Kurdistan but allows that obtaining rocket-propelled grenades would have been no problem. "It's easier to get an RPG than a receipt," he told me with a laugh.

It's as if coalition authorities had banned all recreational drug use in Iraq — and then paid enormous sums to private contractors to identify and enrich all the drug suppliers they could find. I once spent an afternoon in one of the wealthiest parts of Baghdad, visiting a prosperous arms dealer who basically was running an all-day, all-night implements-of-destruction sale out of his house. Outside, there was a line of cars waiting for deliveries, which the man's preadolescent son was carrying out to the customers like groceries. The phone was ringing so incessantly with fresh orders that the arms dealer finally took it off the hook.

Once Weiss and his team are fueled up, they head for the city of Basra, 115 miles away. When we reach the outskirts of the city, flares are rising and falling here and there, white and red in the night sky. Over their radio, Wolf and Scott begin to speculate about the fireworks. Have the British got some operation going on? Are the bad guys signaling one another? We head for the port, which is shut tight as a screw and quiet as death. Stopping the Yukon, Weiss contemplates the silence. "In all my time here, this is the first time I've seen this," he says, a slight edge of surprise in his voice. He honks the horn, honks it again. For several minutes, we sit, waiting. Then Weiss turns to the Iraqi gunman who has been riding beside me in the back seat — carefully pulling a mask over his face whenever we ride through cities. "D," he orders, "do your switch. Make it quick."

This is a central moment in the operation. To avoid exposing himself as a collaborator, D needs to switch from his combat gear and put on a white *dishdasha*, transforming himself from a soldier of fortune into an ordinary Iraqi so he can sneak into the company's safe house in Basra undetected. But as D hops out of the car, a white BMW suddenly appears out of nowhere, a ghostly image in the pitch-black port.

"Go! Go!" Wolf and company bark at the car, weapons pointed.

The car does not budge. The men inside stare at us.

"*Rooh!*" I hear D cry out the Arabic translation, urgently and gutturally. "*Rooh!*"

Oh my God, I think, *we are going to waste these guys.* Then I wonder what these men are doing, driving around the port at midnight. *No,* I think. *These guys are going to waste us.*

Mercifully, the white BMW peels off prior to the wasting of anyone. When D climbs back into the seat beside me, his head is wrapped in a tribal-looking scarf, no weapon to be seen. A few minutes later, we drop him off at the safe house and he slips into the street, just another ordinary Iraqi going about his business.

A little later, at the border, Weiss is obliged to unload all the weapons, legal and otherwise, from the SUV. Private contractors are forbidden to carry their weapons into Kuwait, and Wolf's men are met by a team of Iraqis, who collect the rockets and machine guns and grenades and run them back up to the safe house in Basra. We cross the border into Kuwait City. The team breaks up, and Weiss takes me home to his apartment to meet the wife and kids.

They're not exactly what I expected from a guy with a tattoo of a wolf on his back and an illegal arsenal in his SUV. While his wife, Kitt, makes French toast, his six-year-old daughter, Teresa, invites me to look at her turtles. "This is Mary," she says, pointing to the big one. There are five extremely little ones. Naming them is the responsibility of her younger brother, Michael, who can't be bothered. He's busy eating cereal and watching *Shrek*.

"I try not to let the kids really know," says Kitt, an attractive, startlingly normal woman who pronounces herself "not worried" about her husband's job. "They know Dad goes to work, but they don't know the extent of what could happen." The phone rings, and Weiss answers it. He listens for a moment, then asks, "How many trucks did they hit?"

It's his boss. Three supply trucks coming down from Nasiriyah tonight were attacked right at the Kuwaiti border, in the town of Safwan, even though they were under the protection of soldiers from an American-allied military. One of the company's drivers was killed, two seriously wounded.

"Oh, no . . . you mean . . . with the glasses?" Weiss says. "They stabbed him in the head?"

Wolf's boss owns the company that was sending the supplies, and this is the third time in six weeks that one of his convoys has been hit. Like other suppliers, he has a clause in his contract: If his convoys keep getting ambushed while under military protection, he retains the right to send in his own security guys to help guard future transports. "The companies that own the cargo do not trust the military to run the convoys by themselves," says Weiss. To me, the idea that a military — any military — might need protection is mind-blowing. To Wolf, it's par for the course.

"The coalition forces rotate every three to six months," he says. "That's just enough to get your feet wet, and you're gone. Some of these new guys have never been to Iraq, never pushed a convoy or anything else. In the last part of last year, who did they have running the show? National Guardsmen, Reserve units, a lot of weekend warriors — they were losing convoys left and right."

The next morning, Weiss reassembles his team and starts back to Baghdad. Just over the border, where the spaces are wide open, he has his men test their weapons by firing them out the windows of the SUVs. "Watch out for the desert people," he cautions. The sound of gunshots echoes in the air. Weiss had a convoy scheduled to run north this morning, but it has been canceled; there is unrest in Basra, and the client has decided that the road is just too dangerous. Since this leaves Weiss with nothing to transport but me, I offer to fly out of Kuwait City. He won't hear of it. He's making this run up to Baghdad for fun. He knows nothing is likely to happen — but he also knows that anything could. "When you're getting shot at and returning fire, it's the same, regardless of who you're working for — the adrenaline, the chaos, the sheer horror at times," he says. "There's always a void to fill with me. I'm an adrenaline junkie of some kind."

STEPHEN ELLIOTT

■

My Little Brother Ruined My Life

FROM *Maisonneuve*

"ARE YOU A MASOCHIST?" It's the first thing Bosco asks me. He's fourteen years old now, almost my height, five foot eight, creamy white skin, and a small German nose from my stepmother's side of the family. He's wearing pajama bottoms and my father's green bomber jacket. We're in a cab returning from the airport. He's here to stay with me for ten days. And I'm realizing I've made a terrible mistake.

"Why would you think that?" I ask. I'm tired myself. I just flew into San Francisco two hours earlier. I haven't been home in weeks.

"Dad says you're a masochist. He read it."

"I'm a fiction writer," I say. "It's fiction."

"Sure it is," he says.

We go to a party for people from the university. Bosco grabs two beers from the fridge and hands me one. "He's a little young to be drinking, isn't he?" Claire asks. Claire's a poet from Georgia. The house is filled with poets and short story writers. Jackets are piled on the bed in the bedroom and people are lying on them or on the floor telling stories about losing their virginity. Everybody has an MFA so every story has a small inappropriate observation. "He put his hand between my legs at the movie theater. I was wearing my mother's skirt." "I was fifteen, she was nineteen. It was the day after my best friend committed suicide." My brother hangs on the front steps with Kaui's boyfriend, Andy, and Andy tells him not to do heroin. "Everything else is OK," Andy says.

"That guy was cool," Bosco says.

I don't know my little brother as well as I should. I left home before I was his age. I ran away just after my mother died and slept on rooftops and hallways for all of eighth grade. I ate from the garbage behind Dominick's, food thrown away just past the due date. The state took custody of me and charged my father with abuse and neglect.

My father and I never really mended our relationship. He remarried, made money, moved to the suburbs, had children. I wrote a book about growing up in group homes and the violence there. My father thinks I have exaggerated my victimhood at his expense. We get along for months at a time and then I'll get some note explaining how he wasn't that bad of a father, how he didn't shave my head, he gave me haircuts, and I'll remember waking up to my father's fists and being dragged along the floor into the kitchen. My father likes to joke that he only handcuffed me to a pipe that one time and look how many stories I've written about it. He says he should have been a worse father because it would have helped my writing. Sometimes I tell my father it's best we don't talk for a while. So I was surprised when he suggested Bosco come out and stay with me. I was more surprised when, after saying yes, I found out the ticket was for ten days.

What I have to keep telling myself is that Bosco is a kid and being a kid is hard. I'm not jealous that he's growing up with two parents in a big house in the suburbs. I just want to be a good brother, but the truth is that I don't have the skills. I've borrowed a sleeping bag for him. My studio is so small; he sleeps on the wooden floor, his feet inches from my head. His feet smell and I'm going to have to tell him about that.

"Stop walking into me," I say. We're on Sixteenth Street and Bosco keeps brushing against me and I keep moving farther away until I am against the buildings.

"I'm not. You're walking into me."

"From now on I'm going to call you Underfoot," I say. "You see these lines on the sidewalk? Stay on your side of the line."

"You stay on your side of the line." The streets are crowded and the fruit vendors are out, so it's hard for either of us to stick to our grids. We pass the Victoria Theater where *Hedwig and the Angry Inch* is in its final week.

"It's like my feet are magnets and you have a metal head."

We try, we try. We watch a basketball game at my friend's house and I lose fifty dollars. "What were you thinking?" Bosco asks. "Syracuse is sooo much better."

"You're fourteen years old. You don't know anything about college basketball."

"Neither do you, apparently."

We head to the Orbit Room, where my ex-girlfriend is getting drunk with her friends. I worry that my brother will think I drink too much. Then I worry that maybe I do drink too much.

Theresa is wearing blue jeans and a torn black shirt. It's always tough to see an ex-girlfriend and realize she's getting better-looking. Theresa has been at the protests all day in Oakland. "They fired rubber bullets at us," she says proudly. "It was amazing."

The Orbit Room has round cement tables that are four feet high and people sit around them on tall stools. Bosco is off talking to someone. I say to Theresa, "This is awful. It's like coming face to face with a part of yourself you had no interest in knowing."

"You'll do fine," she says.

"No," I tell her. "I don't like children. Also, my apartment is too small. And I've been sick recently, I have this ringing in my ears."

"Don't think about yourself," Theresa says. "Think about your brother."

"Why do I have to think about him?" I ask. "He has everything. Can we stay with you?"

"No. I'm getting on with my life."

It's almost one in the morning and we're walking home. "Why'd you break up with her?" Bosco asks. "She's the whole package."

He sounds like my father. My father always spoke of women as if they were frozen meat.

"Yeah, she's great," I say, and I think of how if I hadn't broken up with her we would be at her place now. Bosco would be in her extra bedroom and I would be on the inside of the spoon.

"You'll never get a girlfriend like that again."

A child sleeps on my floor. The morning is full of rain. I watch my hands as I type. I have scars up and down my wrist from all of my suicide attempts.

My father writes to say that my fourteen-year-old cousin went to a concert once and became a doper and now my uncle is going to throw him out. I hate e-mail for this reason. I tell my father that I was doing dope long before my first concert and that maybe my uncle should be a little more thoughtful in assigning blame. My father tells me my uncle has a family to think about. It's my father's favorite notion. The situation where the family must abandon one of its own for the good of the whole. That's why he moved while I was living on the streets at fourteen, he says. Because I was a drug addict and he had to think of the family. Which is why, when the police found me, after a year on the streets, lying in a hallway, shivering and bleeding, and asked where my parents were, I answered, "I don't know." Honestly, I didn't. But my family was just two people then, my father and my sister. So I've always been skeptical of that argument. I've always been skeptical of parents who abandon children for the good of the family.

I introduce Bosco to Amber, a sixteen-year-old girl from the writing program where I volunteer as a tutor. We go to a movie that isn't very good and then eat dessert at an overpriced coffee shop. "So how long are you here for?" Amber asks Bosco.

"Until next Sunday."

"Wow. A whole week more." Amber is young and pretty. She's an *A* student, the editor of her school newspaper. She can make Bosco into a better person. Young boys are so easy to manipulate. They only think of one thing. Someday, when he's older, Bosco will also think of his place in the world and how people don't appreciate him enough. He'll worry about how hard it is to make a living. He'll feel jealousy and anger when he is passed over for a promotion and then self-loathing for his own small-mindedness.

Amber takes Bosco back to her home in the Haight District. I take the opportunity to get some work done, do the dishes, and push his things into the back of the studio. When he comes home, we both have one of those Smirnoff Ice drinks that I have in my fridge.

"What did you guys talk about?" I ask.

"Drugs mostly."

"Yeah?"

"Yeah. She likes to do mushrooms."

"Oh. Yeah, mushrooms are good. When I was your age, I loved acid."

"My friend does acid," he says.

"Acid is bad for you," I tell him, though I know I'm too late. I can tell he's going to become a horrible drug addict and the next time he visits he'll steal my laptop and sell it for crack.

"She said I was weird." He's leaning against the wall, below the lip of the window. I live on a busy street. Dirt from exhaust pipes builds up along the sill. My little brother has something more to say. He has that kid smile. He thinks he's so cool. I raise my eyebrow.

"I shook her hand, but she wanted a hug," he says. "I might have been able to score, but I didn't try."

My brother and I have a card-playing ancestry. Our grandfather played cards every day of his adult life. He was an absentee father. He worked during the day and played cards at night. My uncle said he nearly gambled away their house. Because I'm the best euchre player at Stanford, people are always trying to take me down a peg. I get paired up with my brother.

"That's a spade," I say, pointing to the jack of clubs.

"No, it isn't." He's on his third beer. He's sucking them down like water. He'll be an alcoholic before he turns eighteen. Everybody's half-drunk and they holler at Bosco to bring them drinks. He's become the beer boy.

"It is a fucking spade."

"Why are you swearing at your brother?"

"When spades are trump, the jack of the same color becomes the second-highest trump."

"You should have told me," he says. He turns everything back that way.

"I did tell you."

"No, you didn't."

"Why don't you just admit you're wrong?" I say. "Why don't you take responsibility for your actions?"

"Why don't you admit you're wrong?"

"Your grandfather would turn over in his grave if he saw you playing cards that way."

After one more beer apiece, Bosco and I stumble home arm in arm. The restaurants are closed; the world is asleep. "That's nothing," Bosco says, peeing on the wall of a live-work loft building. "Me and my friend Jimmy drank a whole bottle of whiskey. I don't get hung over."

"That's one more thing you can look forward to."

He'll be leaving in a few days and we haven't done anything. We haven't seen either bridge, Golden Gate Park, the ocean, or the bay. We haven't been to any museums. We haven't hiked the Lands End or gone rock climbing. When people ask him what he did in San Francisco, Bosco will say he got drunk. But the thing is, I don't have television. I don't have Playstation. I don't have Internet. There is absolutely nothing to do in my apartment except read, write, and get drunk. There's a message on the machine from my father. "I just wanted to check in on my boys, make sure you're having a good time." Anyway, there's only a few days left and I'm counting them off. Walking near Polk Street, I offer to pay for Bosco to go to bed with a transvestite prostitute.

"Shut up," he says.

"You won't notice the difference," I tell him.

"You're sick."

"I'm going to tell everybody you did it anyway, and they'll believe me because I'm older than you."

It's late on Thursday night and there's been a party at the tutoring center with raffles and piñatas. Friends of mine are drinking at the bar, but they won't let Bosco in. Bosco says I should go without him; he'll wander the Mission District. I tell him I don't think that's a good idea. We stop to see Theresa at a reading in a used bookstore.

"I'm leaving him with you. I'm going out."

"Like hell you are." She's wearing a charcoal gray skirt. Her legs are tight and tanned, swimmer's legs. I slip my foot under her foot, which dangles off the armrest of a comfy chair. She moves it away. There's a blond boy with her, smiling awkwardly.

"Let's all go back to your place," I say. "I'll buy."

"You'll buy what?"

"Anything. I don't care."

"No. I'm doing things."

"What kind of things?"

"This is Sherman."

"Hello, Sherman."

Later, at the Pakistani restaurant near Guerrero, we split rice, naan, and an order of chicken tikka masala. "I take back what I said about her," Bosco says. "She's not that nice." He's on my side.

Bosco wants to go to a concert with Amber and her friends, but I say no, not unless I chaperone. Bosco says please, so I tell him we'll have to ask his parents. We call and they say no. He calls my stepmother back and begs her. "Why?" he says. "That's stupid. But Mom. But Mom." He hangs up the phone.

"Did you just hang up on your mother?"

"Yes."

We meet the girls at the station and I find myself wanting to impress them, but I can't. Young girls talk a lot, act dramatic, dance around, and sing inside trains. I feel so old.

The club is near the warehouses and the waterfront. Teenagers are sprawled across the sidewalk. I go inside, sway to the punk music. I want to dance, but I don't want to be the old dancing guy.

The first band poured motor oil on the floor so people can slide while they listen to music. I help the cleanup crew mop up the mess and Bosco disappears with some of the girls. When he comes back, he's smiling, and I think he's stoned.

"Don't worry," Amber says. "We'll take care of him. You can leave him with us."

I say no, I'll stick around. I go to the bar across the street for a drink.

On the way to the train Bosco walks with his new friend Mickey. It makes me happy to see him bonding. These are good kids, except that they are stoners and two years older than him. They are very kind children, environmentalists. They don't think guns are cool. And that's what I want for Bosco, to introduce him to kids who don't think violence is a good thing. Because his uncle has swastika tattoos and closets full of guns and his cousin was given a shotgun for his fourteenth birthday. It's after midnight now, and parents are calling these children, who are out so late, on their cell phones. The children say they are doing fine.

I think of my own mother, who died painfully for five years on the living room couch. She used to pee in a bucket and I would have to walk her pee to the bathroom and flush it down the toilet. "Give me money," I would tell her. And she would refuse, so I would yell and scream. And then she would give in, because she was too ill and weak to fight. Then my father stopped giving her money. Sometimes I would yell at her and other times I would curl up with her, laying my head on the quilted blanket covering her legs. I remember loving her and hating her. I remember how often she cried. Despite what people might say, I don't think she liked me very much in the end. Children are horrible. Children are monsters.

And yet most people my age have them. I do too, in a way. I was a sperm donor for about a year when I was living in my car. I checked the box that said they could look me up when they turn eighteen. Fifteen years from now I expect to meet the genetic experiment I made at $45 a toss.

Bosco says he wants to stay out and I say OK. It's an impulse decision. I give him forty bucks and tell him to take a cab home. It's one in the morning. He asked and I said yes. The second he gets off the train, I wonder if I would say yes if asked again. The city is a dangerous place.

Back in the apartment I watch the dangerous city from my window. I can see a chocolate factory and the Twin Peaks and the lights of the cars driving up the hills. Bosco calls. He's having a good time. His friends are having dinner in a twenty-four-hour diner. I used to wait tables in a place like that. I know the kind of kids that come in at two in the morning. They have too much freedom. "We're going to Liz's place in the West Portal," Bosco tells me.

"No," I tell him.

"C'mon."

"Use the money I gave you to get in a cab. It's time to come home." And he does.

On Bosco's last night we go to Andrew's to play cards. First we watch *Orgazmo* at Ben's house. Then we walk along Valencia to Dolores Park and I point across my adopted city to the Oakland Bay Bridge. "You see," I say. "It's so much more colorful here than in Chicago."

"And that's a good thing?"

"There are more parks. Did you know there's more park per square foot than in any other major city?"

"I'm hungry. When are we going to eat?"

"Did you have fun while you were here?"

"It beats being in school."

At Andrew's, there are so many people that we have to split into two games of cards. I tell Bosco I'm going to set a good example for him by not drinking tonight, but I have a few beers anyway. Bosco wants to know if he can drink too and I tell him he can have a beer if more than half the people in attendance say it's OK. "This is democracy," I say. He's too shy to ask.

Bosco partners with Adam and I partner with Geoff. He wins every game and I win every game and in the end it's Geoff and me against my brother, Adam, and Tom. The score's nine to six. Geoff and I are in the barn. "Should I call it?" Bosco asks Adam, and Adam spreads his large hands and says, "Last time you called that, you got euchred."

"I think we should," Bosco says. He's got that look in his eye, the look of a gambler. We're not playing for money, but somewhere inside his head the little synapses are firing. He has a keen understanding of the game for his age, a rational mind, an ability to learn from his mistakes, but he doesn't have the ability to read other people and he doesn't take instruction well. I slowplay a king of trump and when Geoff takes it with the left bower I lay down the rest of my cards. Game over.

"That's a great game," Bosco says on the way home. "I only lost to you tonight."

"You'll never beat me in cards," I tell him. "It's your burden to bear."

I wanted to steer my brother in the right direction. Instead we drank and played cards. Sunday morning and the streets are still wet.

"Is there anything I can do to convince you to stay?" I ask.

"You'd have to give me more money."

"You've already spent all my money."

"Oh," he says. "Thanks."

When the big red van pulls up, we put his bag in the back. I go to hug and he goes to slap hands and we end up in this awkward embrace with our biceps against each other's necks. "You choked me," he says, climbing into his seat. I point my index finger at him with my thumb up, as if that was some kind of cool sign. The driver gives me a small nod and closes the door. My little brother looks into his lap, fiddling with his CD Walkman. I step back toward the metal grating of my building's entryway. The driver smiles at me like everything is going to be OK. Like he knows this is my little brother and he understands my concern and will take good care of him and get him to the airport safely and once at the airport the boy will board a plane that will not crash and he will get home fine. And then Bosco will tell the whole world how cool his big brother is, and his father will leave me messages saying how much better I am at this child-raising thing than he was. And I won't return his messages because my father and I still have so many unresolved issues, but I'll know and he'll know I'm right and I've been right all along. I see all of this in the driver's calming placid eyes. But he doesn't know anything, he's just a van driver.

■

Tearaway Burkas
and Tinplate Menorahs

FROM *Mother Jones*

I NEVER SERVED in our nation's armed forces. I was of draft age during the Vietnam War, in college from 1969 to 1973, and the Selective Service people felt, in their wisdom, that it was more important for me to complete my undergraduate education so I could prepare for my chosen profession — comedian.

Three decades later, I was asked to give back — by going on a USO Tour in 1999 to, among other places, Bosnia and Kosovo. It changed my view of the military. I returned home with nothing but admiration for our troops and their leaders. That's what happens when you go on a USO Tour. There's no way around it.

So, this article — about my recent tour to Iraq and Afghanistan — is not going to be what you might expect from me or from this magazine. As you probably know, I've been very critical of our current president, whom I consider arrogant, dishonest, petulant, and not a teeny bit stupid. And I've been critical of the hubris that led us into the war in Iraq, particularly the way it misled the American people, isolated us from most of the rest of the world, and seemed to plan for nothing other than a best-case scenario once we arrived.

Nevertheless, this is a story of a traveling troupe of "show folk" humbly doing our best to bring a little joy, laughter, music, and

Christmas cheer to the men and women who bear the burden of this administration's policies. As I said to every soldier who thanked me for coming, "It's my honor."

And a talented group of show folk we were. The Army band — every one a brilliant musician. Top country artists — Mark Wills, who had the number-one country hit "Nineteen Something" (OK, I've never heard it either — but he's huge), and Darryl Worley, who wrote his number-one single "Have You Forgotten?" after visiting our troops in Afghanistan in 2002. If you listen to the lyrics (which evidently a lot of idiots do not), "Have You Forgotten?" is an emotional and somewhat jingoistic call of support for Operation Enduring Freedom in Afghanistan and not an explicit call for the war in Iraq.

Nevertheless, Darryl does support Operation Iraqi Freedom wholeheartedly, and he told me on the last day of our trip that he'd become incensed when he first heard I was on the tour because he'd been looking forward to eight days when he didn't have to defend his position. He sees these USO Tours as a kind of vacation from controversy, and now he thought he was going to have to debate me the whole eight days.

When Darryl told me this, I asked if he'd been worried I'd start the show in Baghdad like this: "Your president lied to you, and you are dying for no reason!!! Ladies and gentlemen, Darryl Worley!"

Darryl howled. He is a hilarious guy, and I have to say, we laughed our way through Southwest Asia. I love the guy.

There were other self-proclaimed "rednecks." Darryl and Mark brought their guitarists, their mutual road manager, and personal manager. There was also Bradshaw, the World Wrestling Entertainment star from Texas, who is nowhere near as stupid as he likes to make out.

So, we had a Rednecks vs. the New York Jews dynamic set up. Which meant constant good-natured shit flying back and forth. With me, there was my brother, Owen, who was the trip's photographer; former *Saturday Night Live* writer Andy Breckman, who was writing the comedy portions of the show with me; and Steve Kurtz, manager of No Illusion, a three-gal "urban" singing group who are beautiful and sing like angels. They're young — 19, 20, and 22 — and given my rule that I don't allow myself to be sexually attracted to women younger than my daughter, I behaved paternalistically toward No Illusion. That was not entirely true with the two Washington Redskins cheerleaders. No USO Tour is complete without NFL cheerleaders, and the Redskins sent two, Kelley and Katie Cornwell, whom the troops seemed happier to see than me. As I told the soldiers, "I don't know how you guys do it for nine months. I've been over here a week, and the first thing I'm going to do when I get home is have sex with my wife — while thinking about the cheerleaders. Not so different from you guys, except I won't be alone."

I acted as co-emcee with Karri Turner, the attractive blond star of the popular CBS show *JAG*, which I'd never seen, but which is carried by the armed forces network and is very popular with the soldiers. So, our traveling troupe of show folk included musicians, composers, an actor, a writer, a comedian, singers, and dancers. My wife said to me before I left, "You don't see Bill O'Reilly doing a USO Tour."

"That's not fair, honey. O'Reilly has no talent."

Rounding out the show was singer Bonnie Tilley, a talented LA pop singer who sang in a Disney movie and happens to be the niece of the sergeant major of the Army, Jack Tilley, the leader of our tour. The sergeant major of the Army is the Army's highest-ranking enlisted soldier and as such is loved and revered by the troops. Tilley had accompanied me on one of our tours to the Balkans and was happy to have me along; nevertheless, he got peeved at me once in Baghdad and used the occasion to inform me that he is "a killer." Later in the tour, with just a hint of mist in his eyes, Tilley told me that prior to this trip, he had never met his niece. A life in the Army carries with it more than a few sacrifices.

We took off from Andrews Air Force Base on a cramped KC-10 (a converted DC-10 that doubles as a cargo and refueling plane) for the fourteen-hour flight to Kuwait, our first stop. Breckman and I wrote most of the way. The idea was to make this a variety show, a throwback to Bob Hope. After the Army band played a few songs, Karri would take the stage and say a few sincere words of her choosing, then introduce me.

Andy wrote my opening line: "Anybody here from out of town?" Then a couple more quick jokes: "Say, that Army chow isn't sitting well with me. So far I've had five MREs [meals ready-to-eat] and none of them seem to have an exit strategy."

Then into a bit with Karri, designed to get a soldier onstage.

AL: Karri, congratulations on the success of *JAG*.

KARRI: Thank you, Al. We're on our ninth season.

AL: Wow. Nine seasons! You must have had thousands of guest stars appear on your show.

KARRI: Not thousands. But we've had a lot of great people. We've been very lucky.

AL: Well, I've never been on the show.

KARRI: As I say, we've been very lucky.

AL: I was thinking that maybe before the ninth season is over, I could do a guest shot.

KARRI: Well, y'know, *JAG* is really a drama show, and you're such a terrific comedian. Maybe it's not a fit.

AL: So, anyway, I've taken the liberty of writing a little audition piece to show my range. [*Handing Karri the script.*] I play a prosecutor sent in by the Pentagon to shake things up around the JAG office.

KARRI: You wrote this?

AL: Yeah. I'm a writer, comedian, dramatic actor. [*Beat.*] It's your line.

KARRI: Oh. [*Reading from script.*] Lieutenant Hardgrove, what are you doing here in JAG OPS?

AL: I told you, Harriet. Call me Lance.

KARRI: Lieutenant Hardgrove, this is JAG OPS. It's all business here.

AL: Is it? Then why are you wearing that negligee?

KARRI: [*Off-script.*] Al, my character would never wear a negligee to the office!

AL: You would if you were madly in love with Lieutenant Lance Hardgrove.

KARRI: Al, I'm married in the show! I have two kids —

AL: Yeah, yeah, yeah. Keep reading.

KARRI: [*Reading script.*] Lance, I'm wearing this negligee because I want tonight to be very special. I want to give myself to you completely. Now kiss me! [*Al grabs Karri and kisses her. Karri fights him off.*]

KARRI: Now, wait a minute! You just wrote this so you could kiss me! If I was gonna kiss anybody, it'd be a real soldier. Like one of these brave men . . . or women. Who wants to help me out? You, soldier. [*Karri points to soldier in front.*]

AL: OK. I guess we *are* here to entertain the troops.

[*The soldier comes up. Al hands him script. Improvise name, rank, where you from, etc. Karri and the soldier do the script. . . .*]

KARRI: Lieutenant Hardgrove, this is JAG OPS. It's all business here.

SOLDIER: Is it? Then why are you wearing that negligee?

KARRI: Lance, I'm wearing this negligee because I want tonight to be very special. I want to give myself to you completely. Now kiss me! [*They kiss a long, deep kiss. Cheers, etc. After kiss . . .*]

AL: Wait! It's not over. There's another line.

KARRI: There is?

[*Al points out line to soldier.*]

AL: Go ahead. Read it.

SOLDIER: [*Reading.*] You know, Harriet, a woman your age should have a thorough breast examination every year. Lucky for you, Dr. Al Franken is here.

[*Al approaches Karri.*]

KARRI: Al!!! At ease!

AL: [*Looking down at his crotch.*] Too late for that now.

KARRI: Oh! Ewww. Let's just bring out our first guest.

This Hope-style bit never failed to get huge laughs and giant cheers. Each time the soldier kissed Karri, it was as if every soldier had kissed her. Sex, in general, seemed a safe bet as a subject for sure laughs. By and large, these are men and women in their early twenties, a time of life when I recall thinking about sex almost constantly.

There are at least five men for every woman serving in the Persian Gulf (observation, not raw data), and one soldier told me at a base in Afghanistan that they had just sent five women back pregnant. "After you've been in the desert a while, a 2 begins to look like a 10," he said. Actually, I saw a lot of attractive women in uniform. I particularly liked an MP in Kuwait named Davis who was just a little mean. And who knows, maybe it was the uniform. Mark Wills's guitarist said he was picking up some desert fatigues for his wife.

My brother, Owen, is an expatriate who lives in Paris. You probably couldn't find someone more against the war in Iraq than Owen. But during the trip, he was moved to tears on a number of occasions, and when we dropped him in Germany on the way home, he asked the whole group to sing "God Bless America" one last time. (We ended each show with it.)

It was a doubly emotional trip for both of us. Our mom had died about ten days before the tour, and it was good that we got to spend this time together. (After it was announced in the press that my mom had died, some guy wrote this review of my latest book on Amazon: "See, if you write mean things about people, your mom might die." Six of 37 people found the review "helpful.")

We arrived in Kuwait tired. We were given some quarters, men separated from women, about three or four to a room. After a brief rest, I met with the cheerleaders and one of the girls from No Illusion to run through and choreograph the Taliban Cheerleader number.

I had borrowed some burkas from *Saturday Night Live,* and the idea was to introduce them saying, "All the way from Kabul, please welcome the Taliban Cheerleaders!" The girls enter in burkas, and

I ask them to do a number. Through her burka, the lead Taliban Cheerleader whispers in my ear. I act puzzled. "You're not allowed to dance?" I ask. "Or even listen to music?" She shakes her head, no. "But," I point out, "we liberated Afghanistan from the Taliban. Certainly you can do one number? Whatta ya say, guys?" The troops cheer. The cheerleaders consult, and the leader nods — OK, one. "All right!" I say. "Hit it!" and we blast "Gonna Make You Sweat!" by C+C Music Factory. The girls do a bump-and-grind dance in their tearaway burkas, then peel them off and continue in their Redskins cheerleader outfits as the guys go nuts.

Worked like a charm every time.

The second day we take off in a Chinook to do meet-and-greets at various camps. Except for Kuwait City — which we were not allowed to visit (some Americans had been attacked there just before we arrived) — Kuwait is a fucking wasteland.

The troops in these outposts are incredibly appreciative. "Where you from?" I ask. "How long you been here?" "Reservist? National Guard?" They're from all over. A lot from small towns, some from the Bronx or Brooklyn. Some from Puerto Rico. A lot from the South, from Montana, Minnesota, upstate New York. I ask reservists if they plan to reenlist. "Hell no!" more than a few say. But their reenlistment rate is 70 percent, I'm later told. Most of all, they're grateful we came all this way.

The second night in Kuwait is our first show. At Camp Arifjan. The place isn't too bad. There's a Burger King, an equivalent of a Pizza Hut, and an Internet café where soldiers can instant-message with loved ones at home. The show lasts two and a half hours, and the troops love everything. Darryl's up last and ends his set with "Have You Forgotten?" They all know the lyrics:

> Have you forgotten how it felt that day
> To see your homeland under fire
> And her people blown away? . . .
> Some say this country's just out looking for a fight.
> After 9/11, man, I'd have to say that's right.

The song climaxes on an emotional high and a standing ovation. The next day Andy Breckman deadpans to Darryl: "You know what you should sing in the next show? That 9/11 song." Andy repeats that every day until our last show, when he slips a note into Darryl's guitar case: "Don't forget the 9/11 song."

That first night I got all teary-eyed when we ended with "God Bless America." In the front row I saw a black male soldier linking arms with a white male soldier and a woman soldier, swaying back and forth and really meaning it. I thought how the military could teach our colleges and universities a thing or two about affirmative action. Then I noticed that the woman soldier was holding the hand of a gay soldier, who was holding the hand of a transgender soldier. . . . OK, that's not true.

Early the next morning we were off to Baghdad. The plan had been to do a show that night and the next at Baghdad International Airport, but there was a change in plan. World Wrestling Entertainment was doing a show there, and there was nowhere to put us. We would split up the group and do smaller shows at different bases around Iraq, specifically in Saddam's hometown of Tikrit, in Mosul, and at a base called Camp Junction City.

It was decided that Tikrit was the most dangerous of the three. Steve Kurtz, the manager of No Illusion, had promised the girls' parents he'd do everything possible to keep them safe. So he chose Mosul. I agreed to go to Tikrit if we could visit the hole. The hole where they had found Saddam. My goal was to get a picture of myself in the hole with the Redskins cheerleaders. Sergeant Major of the Army Tilley said he'd try to make it happen but couldn't guarantee anything.

Karri, the cheerleaders, the Army band, Andy, my brother, and I flew to Tikrit in two Black Hawks. My understanding was that the most dangerous part of the trip was landing and taking off from the Baghdad airport, flying across Iraq in a helicopter, then landing in Tikrit, the Baathist stronghold. Wearing flak jackets and helmets, we headed out, flying incredibly fast and incredibly low with two gunners looking for insurgents with shoulder-launched rockets designed to kill us. The point of flying low is that it makes it harder to get a bead on the chopper from the ground; in addition, we were constantly taking evasive action, swerving and making sudden changes in altitude, usually to jump power wires. A singer in the Army band threw up.

Flying over Baghdad, I had a flash of the movie *Black Hawk Down*. But in a good way — at least I got a glimpse of what life looked like in an impoverished Third World Arab city.

As we headed north, the country got greener. I saw shepherds grazing sheep. Two and a half days of Army food and I was already hoping for a lamb chop. An hour later, flying over Tikrit, you could see that Saddam had spread some cash around his hometown. Nice little city.

Once we landed inside the Army compound in Tikrit, we felt safe. It was an amazing complex, a couple of square miles comprising a ridiculously huge and ornate Saddam palace and smaller guest palaces for members of the Baath Party and Uday's friends. It was easy to envision the place as a Ritz-Carlton in about fifteen years, perfect for corporate conferences.

We arrived early in the afternoon and settled into Uday's guesthouse. We had some time before our show, so I started working on getting to the hole. The military brass was not encouraging, but I ran into a high-ranking member of the Coalition Provisional Authority, the civilian group that "runs" Iraq under Paul Bremer. This guy was in his forties, also Jewish, and a fan of my work. He'd meet us at 3:30 to take us to the hole. But just me, Andy, and Owen. No picture of me in the hole with the cheerleaders. At 3:30, he tells us that Colonel Hickey is in a meeting, and we need his permission to go to the hole. We'll have to go in the morning. Later that night, we get the word. No hole. Fuck.

But the show that night goes great. We're doing it for the unit that actually caught Hussein, so they especially like the Saddam bit. I had borrowed a Saddam uniform, beret, and a mustache from *Saturday Night Live,* and Andy and I wrote a piece in the style of the old *Tonight Show* Mighty Carson Art Players. (As Saddam, with my faux Arabic accent, I didn't sound so different from Triumph the Insult Comic Dog.)

KARRI: For reasons you'll understand, we didn't want to announce our next guest ahead of time. He's a very special, very secret surprise. Former Iraqi president Saddam Hussein!!! [*Two MPs lead Al up in handcuffs.*]

AL: Thank you! Thank you! If they allowed me to carry an AK-47, I'd be firing it into the air. Hi, Karri. It's great to be back in Baghdad. Listen, before you say anything — I've been thinking, and I've decided to let the inspectors back in.

KARRI: Well, it's kind of late for that.

AL: Oohh! I was afraid you'd say that.

KARRI: We've been looking for you, Saddam. Where have you been the last eight months?

AL: Well, you know, basically in the Tikrit area, visiting family, friends, socializing.

KARRI: Saddam, we captured you in a tiny hole.

AL: Yes, that's true. I've been spending a lot of time in holes. I have many holes around the country. Actually the hole you found me in — that was one of my favorite holes. It's my winter hole.

KARRI: Your winter hole?

AL: Oh, Karri, you should see it. It had everything. It had the air duct. I could roll over. The dirt was very nicely packed. As you know, Karri, I used to have twenty, thirty palaces. But the kids had grown. You want to downsize. So . . . the hole.

KARRI: I see. Anyway, I have to say, you're looking a lot better than when we first found you.

AL: Yes, you know, any mass murderer on the run sooner or later ends up looking like Ted Kaczynski. . . . But I've had a shave, a haircut, I've been deloused. I'm feeling great.

KARRI: You're looking great.

AL: Thank you. I've been working out in the hole. Rolling over. First this way, then that way. It's a good regimen.

KARRI: Saddam, I guess the thing that's on everyone's mind is the weapons of mass destruction.

AL: You'd like to know, wouldn't you? The WMD. Where are they? Are they in Samarra? Maybe. Are they in Kirkuk? Could be. Maybe yes, maybe no. How 'bout Tikrit? Maybe they're in my hole. Maybe while you were sleeping I put them in your hole. Who knows?

KARRI: Now, Saddam!

AL: I'm sorry. I kid. I kid because I love. I tell you what, Karri. I like you so much, I'm going to make you a deal. One time only. I give you the weapons — you leave Iraq. Let me return to power and resume killing and torturing anyone I want. Take it or leave it.

KARRI: I don't know. Whatta ya say, guys? [*Nos, boos, etc.*]

AL: Well, OK, forget it. The important thing is, I'm back in Baghdad.

KARRI: Yes, and now that the hiding is over, what are you looking forward to?

AL: Two things, really. One — being deloused some more. They missed some. In the pubes mainly. I don't have to tell you, Karri, what that's like. Hey, I kid. Out of love. But, seriously, most of all, I am looking forward to being reunited with my beloved sons, Uday and Qusay.

KARRI: Oh.

AL: I didn't like the sound of that "oh."

KARRI: I guess you haven't heard the news. . . .

AL: They're in trouble again? Don't tell me. It was Uday. Ooooh, that Uday!

KARRI: Well . . . let's just say that everybody here is hoping you and your sons can be reunited very, very soon. [*Applause, cheers.*]

By the second day of the trip, "Ooooh, that Uday!" had become the catchphrase for the tour. It was as if Uday were just an irrepressible kid who'd broken curfew a few times.

It turned out that while we were in Tikrit, the three young ladies from No Illusion, who supposedly had been given the safer assignment, were in almost constant danger. That day they visited four different bases, traveling between them in convoys. In the city of Mosul, their convoy took a wrong turn, à la Jessica Lynch, and ended up at a dead end in a crowded market area, necessitating what's known in the military as a "backing out" maneuver. They were sitting ducks, and the terrified young women and Steve, their manager, were ordered to lie down on the floor of their Humvees. This is how you get killed in Iraq. But by the time they settled in for the night at a base outside Mosul, a soldier offered Steve some reassurance: "Don't worry. The two Iraqis who jumped the fence with the AK-47s have been apprehended."

We flew back to Baghdad with $1.4 million of Saddam's cash, which was stashed in tin containers. We landed midway at an outpost to drop off a chaplain because a soldier had been killed there the day before. When we landed at the Baghdad airport, the pilots seemed more interested in getting the $1.4 million to the right place than in us, and for the first time on the trip we were dropped off nowhere in particular.

We wandered into a bombed-out terminal where a unit of infantry had set up some makeshift bunks. These weren't the guys from the public-affairs office who usually greet us, and their hollow eyes suggested they'd seen some shit — including, according to a private from Long Island, a recent suicide by a member of their unit. This was our little *Apocalypse Now* part of the tour, and we did a small show right there for about a dozen guys.

Reunited with our group, we did our regular show that afternoon in the same hangar where Bush had served Thanksgiving dinner. Afterward, a soldier went up to Steve and said, "It's an honor to meet you."

"No, no," Steve replied. "I'm just the manager of the three girl singers."

"You don't understand," the soldier said. "I'm a soldier. I have to be here. I met Bush, but he's the president, so he really had to come. I'd rather meet you, because you don't have to be here. You came because you care."

There was a lot of that. Our just being there meant so much to these guys. Doing the show was gravy.

That night we stayed in another of Saddam's palaces. Again, obscenely ornate, tons and tons of marble, his initials etched into every pillar and inlaid with gold. An Army chaplain had given me a Hanukkah kit comprising a flimsy menorah and some candles.

Andy said that the kit was to Hanukkah as the MREs were to food. But that night in the main room of Saddam's palace — in our little "fuck you" to Saddam — we celebrated the second night of Hanukkah under the biggest cut-glass chandelier I've ever seen.

The next day, on our way to the plane, our driver pointed to his right. "Saddam's being held in there." I wanted to ask if I could meet him. I thought I could do the Saddam bit for him and see what he thought. But since they didn't even let me go to the hole, I let it go.

The following morning, off to Afghanistan. During the show in Kandahar, Andy called his fiancée in New York and found out that *Time* had just named the American Soldier as Person of the Year. Word spread fast. What a rush! To be performing to about a thousand Persons of the Year.

As we drove through Kandahar the next day, our driver, a private, saw a colonel walking up ahead of us. "That's Colonel Garrett. He runs Afghanistan."

"Let's say hi," I said from the backseat. We pulled beside him and I said, "Hi, colonel."

"Hi, Al! Great show last night! I'm headed up to the airstrip to see you guys off."

"We'll give you a lift," I said.

"No, thanks, my vehicle's up ahead about 150 yards."

"We'll give you a lift to your vehicle. We've heard how lazy you are." Our driver was suddenly freaked out.

"Yeah," added Andy. "All we've been hearing is how lazy you are."

"I'm not that lazy." The colonel got it, but acted slightly insulted. "I can make it to my vehicle."

The poor private weakly told the colonel, "I didn't say you were lazy." Colonel Garrett nodded, as if he didn't believe him, and walked ahead. As we passed him, the private told us, "Actually, he's one of the finest officers I've ever known."

"Then why," I asked, "did you keep calling him lazy?"

"I didn't!"

On the tarmac at Kandahar, Sergeant Major Grippe, one of many gruff Sergeant Rock knockoffs we met along the way, gave us a send-off that included references to our troops being in Tehran and Damascus same time next year. It gave the New York Jews on the trip a bit of a chill.

We had been told during a safety briefing in Afghanistan not to step off the pavement. Soviet mines. I told the briefer I was an avid bird watcher and asked if I could find anything in the field beyond the airstrip. "Yeah," he said, "just walk till the first *boom*."

It was cold in Afghanistan, and one night about ten of us guys stayed in a tent heated by pumped-in hot air. When the air was on, the tent was about 100 degrees. Twenty minutes after we turned it off, the temperature dropped to about 40. After a lot of arguing, I arrived at a solution. We'd turn it off before we went to sleep. The first guy to wake up to piss would turn it back on, the next guy would turn it off, etc. As it turned out, I was the first guy up, and it was fucking freezing.

Next stop was Uzbekistan — the K-2 air base across the Afghan border. As in Iraq and Afghanistan, every soldier carries a gun. But there's really no danger inside the base itself. The biggest enemy is monotony, and the soldiers call the camp "Groundhog Day" because every day is the same.

It was our last show, and during "God Bless America," there were a lot of tears onstage. Sergeant Major of the Army Tilley was retiring, and this was his last hurrah. Eight days and I found myself irrationally attached to these people, including the "killer," who's lived a life totally at odds from my own. (I'm a lover.)

We didn't spend the night at K-2, flying instead to Germany, where awards were given out. I won a Distinguished Civilian Service medal from the secretary of the Army, which I plan to wear whenever I debate a conservative on TV.

We flew home and arrived at Andrews on Christmas Eve. I said goodbye to my fellow show folk and took the shuttle home to New York for Christmas with my family. But I couldn't relate to them. They hadn't been through what I had the last eight days, and they'd never know the hardships I had experienced and the horrors I had witnessed.

Actually, we had a nice dinner.

JEFF GORDINIER

■

The Lost Boys

FROM *Details*

Excommunication for Beginners

THE VOICE OF THE PROPHET wasn't what you'd expect. It was soft. The prophet didn't raise his voice, not even when he was doling out the worst of punishments, not even when he was talking about the wickedness of the Negro or the Jew or the homosexual. There was a daintiness to the way he spoke, a lilt, and a kind of hypnotic, grinding slowness. Warren Jeffs spoke very, very slowly. Tom Steed liked to joke to himself that the prophet must be stoned out of his mind.

A lot of the Cricker families had cassette tapes of the prophet's sermons. They'd sit around and listen to them. You'd pay a visit to one of the big polygamist houses and hear that slow, soft voice — the omnipotent voice of Warren Jeffs, prophet and president of the Fundamentalist Church of Jesus Christ of Latter-day Saints — droning away like an old lady. You got to know that voice real well.

Between the sermons and the constant physical labor, there wasn't much to do out there on the border between Utah and Arizona, in the towns of Hildale and Colorado City. An outsider, hearing the words *polygamist compound*, would probably think right away of something kinky, a free-love carnival, but the truth is the prophet had so many rules that the place was beginning to feel like a gulag. More than a mere cleric, the prophet was almost a feudal lord — a civic and corporate godfather who controlled every acre of land, oversaw every bank account, and made every major decision regarding jobs, schools, law enforcement, and marriage. Things were already getting strict when Warren Jeffs's father, Rulon T. Jeffs, was the prophet of FLDS, but after Rulon died in 2002 and Warren took control, the roughly 10,000 believers found it hard to keep up with the expanding list of potential transgressions: no movies, no TV other than the occasional nature program, no video games, no Internet, no smokes, no cussing, no showing attitude, no talking to girls outside of the family, no short-sleeve shirts, no facial hair, no hair down past your ears. "Perfect obedience produces perfect faith," President Jeffs would say. He would also say that those who failed to achieve perfect obedience would be cast into eternal damnation.

You found stuff to do, though, in spite of the rules, and that's what got you into trouble. In fact, it wasn't long after Warren Jeffs moved down from Salt Lake City and formally rose to the seat of sacred power that something strange began to happen to hundreds of teenage boys in Hildale and Colorado City. Now, for even the most minuscule of infractions, they were being cast out. They were being excommunicated. Pretty soon the pruning of young males would kick into overdrive, and eventually the number of the banished would reach the neighborhood of four hundred. The boys developed a theory — that these "infractions" were a smokescreen, and that the prophet's real goal was to weed out the younger men so that there were plenty of wives left for the older generation. Families would scatter and disintegrate, lawsuits would gather like massive storm clouds over Canaan Mountain, and TV reporters would descend with their microphones and their empathetic eyes. It was around then, naturally, that someone started calling the kids the Lost Boys.

In the beginning, though, Tom Sam Steed considered himself a true believer. Yes, he'd gotten in trouble for seeing movies. He'd watched *Charlie's Angels* at a theater in Salt Lake City, and for this, the impure and diabolical influence of Cameron Diaz, Tom had been put on probation. He was floating in limbo on the margins of the church, but he badly wanted back in. To this end, Tom had been lobbying for a face-to-face meeting with Warren Jeffs, and finally, around his seventeenth birthday, Tom received word that the hour of reckoning was upon him.

It was a warm day, not yet winter. Without changing out of his work shirt, Tom walked to a printing shop across the street from Warren Jeffs's house — a gigantic walled and gated community of its own, really, since Jeffs was said to have anywhere from forty to seventy wives. Jeffs, a reed of a man in his forties, sat behind a desk, while an uncle of Tom's grabbed a free chair. Tom shook the prophet's hand and learned that it, too, was soft: a smooth sac of filigreed bones. Tom sat down.

With their white-blond hair and ice-blue eyes, most of the kids in the Crick looked like little Vikings, but Tom stood out, not only because his skin and hair were darker, vaguely Navajo or Latino, but also because his brown eyes flashed with a quality that just about anyone would recognize as independence. The prophet's questions, though . . . they tripped him up. At first, Tom shot right back with a response to each one, but as Warren Jeffs persisted with his line of inquiry, kept knitting away in that soft and slow voice, Tom found himself turning mute.

Are you a homosexual?

Who is your father?

Something was happening. Tom could answer only with movements of his head. As everyone in the room knew, there were complicated reasons why Tom could not give a simple response to questions about his father. This did not feel like a welcome back into the bosom of the church he loved so much, and months later a handful of closing words would still fester in his memory: *You won't have a chance for salvation in this lifetime. You're welcome to the scriptures, but that is all.* Tom was told he could no longer associate with his family. He could no longer set foot on church property — i.e., the entire town. Almost as an afterthought, Jeffs pointed out that Tom would be wiped off the face of the earth when the destructions came.

Not much time passed, maybe twenty minutes, before Tom was sitting in the driver's seat of his silver Nissan pickup, flooring the accelerator as he rode through the peach-colored buttes of the desert, heading for the town of Hurricane, having decided to kill himself. He planned to drive the truck off a cliff. The church had told him he was worthless, dogshit, and at that point you might as well get it over with, right? He had the windows rolled down, and the only sound he would later remember hearing was a sound that was in fact inaudible — a voice, slow and soft, tape-looping in his head.

Tom changed his mind only at the last moment. He was coming down the hill into Hurricane when he halfheartedly banged his front tire on a guard rail, thought twice, turned the steering wheel fast, hit the brakes, and felt the back part of the truck skidding toward the right and thudding into the rail.

A Brief Layman's Guide to the Crick

Polygamy is against the law, but there are thousands of polygamists in the American Southwest.

Even though the mainstream Mormon church banned the practice of "plural marriage" in 1890, pockets of fundamentalists have continued to cling to it for over a century, believing that Joseph Smith, the prophet who founded the Latter-day Saints religion, always meant for polygamy to be a core principle of the faith. Seeking extreme isolation, many of these polygamist families live on a baking patch of land on the border between Utah and Arizona, a short ways up from the Grand Canyon. In the strip-mall parking lots of nearby towns like Hurricane and St. George, you'll see groups of polygamist women done up like they're off to a casting call for *Little House on the Prairie,* in blue and lavender nineteenth-century dresses, with their hair pulled back in matching double braids. You find the most fervent and insular of all the polygamist clusters in a place that goes by many names. The government people see it as two towns: Hildale, Utah, and Colorado City, Arizona. The prophet and other leaders of the FLDS polygamist sect consider the land communally owned by the church, and therefore refer to it as the United Effort Plan, or UEP. Old-timers tend to think of the area as Short Creek, but the boys who are born into these families call it the Crick and call themselves Crickers. "Lost Boys" — that's something the reporters came up with later.

Very few Americans are aware of the existence of this micro-theocracy within our own borders — a state of affairs that writer Jon Krakauer, whose *Under the Banner of Heaven* introduced Colorado City to middle America, likens to having the Taliban right up the street from Caesar's Palace. (Published in 2003 and instantly locust-swarmed by controversy, Krakauer's book deals with the dangerous undercurrents of fundamentalist Mormonism but stops short of delving into the Lost Boys phenomenon, news of which only seeped up from the underground months later.) Here are some of the things the FLDS sect is said to believe: Global apocalypse is right around the corner. Government is the enemy. The moon landings never happened. The purity of the white race must be preserved. The submissiveness of women must be maintained. Whatever the prophet says is the direct word of God. Men and women must marry whomever the prophet tells them to. If the prophet delivers a verdict — such as the excommunication of a boy — the family must abide by that ruling. Should the family refuse, the prophet can force the father into a predicament called "repenting from afar" — exile, more or less — while the father's wives and children will be reassigned to other men.

Those who leave the church are apostates and are to be shunned; outsiders are to be ignored if not chased off UEP land. Even high-ranking state officials have encountered the collective allergy to the presence of outsiders. "Oh, we've had our investigators down there, and as soon as you hit the town limits, somebody is literally following you around, trying to figure out why you're there," says Kirk Torgensen, Utah's chief deputy attorney general. "And oftentimes they'll come up and just flat-out confront you. 'What are you doing here? Who are you? What are you looking for? This is private property.'"

That insularity might be fine, merely a splash of local color for the tourists passing through the Vermillion Cliffs, were polygamy the only offense associated with the Crick. After all, adultery and fornication are also on the books as crimes in Utah, but nobody really considers it worth the time, money, and effort to prosecute the sexual behavior of consenting adults. Still, there are disturbing customs associated with polygamy that the attorneys general in both Arizona and Utah find it perilous to ignore. "We know it for a fact that young people are taught to accept a lifestyle which in the past has absolutely been the marrying of young girls — not upon their choosing — to whomever the prophet decides is worthy," Torgensen says. "Now, what I've told the polygamists is, this has nothing to do with your religion. I'm treating you exactly the same way I treat everybody else. You go out and have sex with a thirteen-year-old or a fourteen-year-old or a fifteen-year-old, I'm comin' after you." Lately, officials across the Southwest have figured out that young girls aren't the only ones who get a raw deal from the practice of plural marriage. It's simple math. If you've got a closed community with equal numbers of boys and girls, and you've got older men who want to marry twenty of the girls, you're going to have a population imbalance. Warren Jeffs apparently found a solution: shear off some of the boys.

Crickers Take Refuge in the Butt Hut

Tom Steed did not drive his truck over the cliff, so before long he wound up in Hurricane, a town where the air has the unmistakable aroma of global-conglomerate cheeseburgers. Here he started seeing kid after kid cast out of the Crick, and each had a different story to tell. Some, like Tom, felt the cold, severing blade of instant expulsion. Among the banished were a couple of boys, friends of Tom's, who had sidestepped the prophet's rules against consorting with girls by hitting on a creative solution: They experimented with each other. The prophet found out — one of the boys, overcome with guilt, could not resist the urge to confess — and he excommunicated them on the spot. For other kids, the process was more amorphous. Maybe you stuck around Colorado City for a while, but people stopped talking to you and opportunities vanished, and finally, tired of being treated like a ghost, you ran away. Maybe the church kept you around as a hired hand — you'd live in your car or in a tool shed, you'd work in an envelope factory or in a quarry — until the humiliation became too much to stomach. Maybe, like one thirteen-year-old, you got sick of living in such a dumb and boring place, so one night you trucked it over to Hurricane for a little . . . *vacation* . . . and when your family tracked you down, they said the prophet had caught wind of your hegira and you might as well not bother coming back.

Some went to St. George, some to Salt Lake City, some to Las Vegas. A lot of the boys passed through Hurricane. That's where the Butt Hut was.

To understand the nature of the ex-Crickers' collision with the modern world, you need to see it from their vantage point. Several of them had been lucky enough to travel with their families to Idaho or California, yes, but others had been born within the perimeter of the compound and had rarely, if ever, ventured more than a few miles away. They couldn't name the president of the United States, didn't know how to spend or save money, had rarely watched television, knew zip about drugs or sex or American pop culture, and were equipped with an education that had been largely fenced in by *The Book of Mormon* — no science, no world history. Were they to enter a room and meet a black person, they might reflexively address him as "nigger," unaware that such a word was unacceptable. A lot of them, Tom noticed, didn't know a thing about how the world worked.

So things got pretty crazy at the Butt Hut. It was half a duplex, two bedrooms and a garage, yet at one point there might have been seventeen ex-Crickers crashing there, only three or four of whom had jobs and paid rent. They subsisted on mac and cheese, bitched about who got to use the shower, partied until four in the morning, slept on the floor. Richard Gilbert couldn't walk from his bed to the front door without stepping on eight kids.

Richard was in his late teens, and he had the straight-necked carriage and searchlight eyes of a budding tribal chieftain. Back in the Crick, Richard had been considered one of the good boys — someone who knew how to please the prophet — and he'd fallen into the slough of disfavor only after a decree went out that FLDS boys and girls were no longer permitted to attend public school. Richard thought: *Your knowledge is what gives you your power.* He decided to go to the school anyway, and as a result he got kicked out of the church. Frankly, he'd say, it was a relief. Kids he'd known since kindergarten now averted their eyes when the good boy said hello. His parents had been kicked out, too. Richard lived with them in Snowflake, Arizona, until their own residue of fundamentalist dogma got to be too much for him — or, hell, maybe he was just getting kind of old to live with his parents — and one day he just walked to the side of the road. It took about sixteen hours to hitchhike to Hurricane; he scored rides with Navajos from the nearby rez.

Now Richard was here in the Butt Hut, with the future looking about as shiny as a sewage pipe, with the quest for knowledge periodically reduced to ex-Crickers glutting themselves in front of the idiot box for twelve hours at a stretch. Each kid tasted freedom differently. For Raymond Hardy, a computer geek who had found a way to watch the *Lord of the Rings* movies in the FLDS compound, breaking away meant an all-access pass to the Elysian Fields of technology. He spent days playing computer games. He went to the city, bought a pair of bondage pants and a Metallica T-shirt tongued with green flames, and walked up and down the streets of the Crick just to see what weird looks he got.

For other kids, it was beer and drugs. Pot, coke, crystal meth, X, 'shrooms. Finding a party was just a matter of making a phone call or two. Richard saw boys experimenting and going off the deep end; they had no common sense when it came to sex and drugs, didn't know how to stop, weren't aware that stopping was even a necessity. (Besides, they were already going to hell.) Every now and then a cop would come by the Butt Hut and ask about a particular kid; if the kid was underage, maybe the parents had filed a runaway report. Richard would tell the cop: *What am I supposed to do? Let 'em sleep on the side of the road?* Alone, over time, ex-Crickers felt a throb of desolation and futility. "I talked personally with quite a few of them," Richard would later say. "And in most cases all they needed was somebody to sit there and say 'It's OK, I'm listening to you.' Because for a lot of those boys, being from a large family, getting listening time with parents is kind of hard when you've got, you know, fifty brothers and sisters."

All things considered, maybe the Butt Hut qualified as a kind of grotty salvation. The ex-Crickers stayed close with a network of cell phones, but now and then they'd hear stories about other Lost Boys who'd gone off to Las Vegas and wound up working as hustlers. By keeping in touch, maybe they could prevent that from happening, and prevent other things too. Another story went around about a party in the Arizona Strip, the stretch of nothing-ness north of the Grand Canyon; *Mad Max*–style revels took place there with great frequency, half-crazed with bonfires and beer kegs and desert shadows. One time, according to the story, a kid had a six-cylinder pistol. He was drinking a lot, telling people good-bye, saying weird shit. Finally he put the pistol to his head and snapped the trigger. *Click, click, click, click, click, click.* When the kid wasn't looking, a friend of his had removed all six of the bullets from the gun.

After a few months Tom Steed moved out of the Butt Hut. By then he'd witnessed a level of debauchery that he would come to prefer not to discuss. As he'd say, "I still had a few morals and standards."

Pursuit of the Fugitive

Sam Brower, private detective, sees a car. "OK now, this is odd," he says. It might be anyone's car, but it is parked outside the walls of the biggest home in Hildale, a tentacled pod of buildings belong-ing to Prophet Warren Jeffs, and for this reason the car is the bar-est signal that the prophet, or someone close to the prophet, might be in the vicinity. Warren Jeffs: *Here? Now?* "Stand by, man," Sam says. Orange dust spins in the hot air as Sam, dressed precisely the way you'd imagine a private dick and licensed bounty hunter would dress for desert operations (cowboy boots, shades, Hawaiian shirt, Utah Jazz cap), pulls his Saturn VUE to the side of the road, jumps out, and starts fishing through the debris in the back seat to find the legal papers.

Just days ago, Warren Jeffs was named as a defendant in a couple of lawsuits. In one, a civil case that's based on the RICO Act and the same brand of racketeering charges you might throw at the Mafia, six of the Lost Boys are claiming that the prophet and his inner circle systematically conspired to lock them out of jobs, school, and family relationships — pretty much everything a free society would allow. In the complaint filed in the other lawsuit, a twenty-one-year-old man named Brent Jeffs, one of the prophet's nephews, accuses Warren Jeffs and two of the prophet's brothers of repeatedly sodomizing him when he was a child; the prophet's legal representatives deny the charges from Brent Jeffs and call them "total fabrications."

In both cases, the attorney dropping the legal bomb is Joanne Suder, a Baltimore trial lawyer who has handled cases involving sexual-abuse accusations against the Catholic Church; Suder has hired Sam Brower as a legman. He's collecting information about Warren Jeffs and the FLDS compound, and for several days he's been trying to serve the prophet his legal papers — a complicated task, since just about nobody here will speak to him, and it seems as though Jeffs has vanished.

The town is flanked by beautiful red rock formations, which look, to anyone who was a child in the seventies, like sets from the TV show *Land of the Lost*. As you drive around it feels like a normal rural village, then incongruous images appear. Small boys in long-sleeve flannel shirts riding bulldozers and ponies down the street. Mothers covered from collar to wrist to ankle in dresses whose style you might find in a pioneer museum. Little girls playing in their yards but racing to get back inside their houses at the first glimpse of an interloper's vehicle. You pass a dingy roadside motel that looks like an artifact from a Hitchcock movie. "This is the infamous Mark Twain Inn, where marriages are consummated,"

Sam says. You pass an empty field marked here and there by mounds of soil. "This is one of the most bizarre things," Sam says. "This is the baby cemetery. I guess they have a lot of dead babies. This is my theory — it's because of all the inbreeding. Everybody here is related." You wouldn't feel a pressing sense of danger had Sam not conceded that, yes, he's gotten threats. Someone recently called and said, "You need to back off. I'm just tellin' you if you don't back off, you're gonna get burned."

Isolation, blind trust in the authority of a lone commander, a collective yearning for Armageddon, a siege mentality — all of these factors have led a few people to hypothesize that any major intervention into Hildale and Colorado City could bring about a disaster comparable to what went down in Waco or Ruby Ridge. ("With all due respect," says Kirk Torgensen back in the Utah attorney general's office, "that's one question I'm not going to get into. I'm just not going to go there.") Yet the stories that continue to radiate from Hildale and Colorado City — stories of incest, pedophilia, and families wedged apart — suggest that some kind of intrusion might be inevitable.

One of the youngest Lost Boys — we'll call him Walker — remembers the day he heard the news that Warren Jeffs had married off Walker's seventeen-year-old sister to a church leader who was roughly double her age. He says the bride's mother had been left in the dark. "I'd been going through hell, and when I heard about that I wanted to kill him," Walker says. "If I would've had a gun, I would've. That's exactly how I felt." Another ex-Cricker, a twenty-two-year-old truck driver named Richard Ream, paints a picture of an entire society being ripped up by its tangled roots. "It tears my heart out to see it," Ream says. "Men can get their families taken away from 'em for infractions as simple as having a television in their home, or letting their children read novels. That's why I'm involved with the lawsuit against Warren Jeffs. Not because I want financial recovery — I don't need their damn money — but because I want to see families be forever."

Warren Jeffs has never done an interview, but his legal mouthpiece of many years, Salt Lake City lawyer Rodney Parker, forty-five, denies and dismisses several elements of the Lost Boys saga. "I don't think that the story that these individuals are telling is the truth," Parker says. "The church doesn't throw people out because they watched television or they used a computer or they looked at a girl. I mean, that just isn't the way they work. They're serious down there. It's a serious church and they're serious about their religion. And they don't do things like that." Parker makes the case that the boys were cast out for a more debased brand of mischief — "some of these people have been involved in alcohol and drugs, which is inconsistent with the church" — and that, regardless, every religious group in America has a right to select or reject whomever it chooses. "Legally, you can't sue a church for excommunicating a member," the lawyer says. "That just seems so fundamental: If a church can't do that, how do they define themselves?" Parker doesn't dispute the reports that FLDS families have been split up, but he suggests that wives who have been reassigned go willingly and happily, and that "there's a spin being put on it by people that are trying to destroy the church." As for the notion that boys are being plucked out in order to give the older men a more plentiful supply of ripe young females, well, "there's no truth at all to that," Parker says. "They're just makin' it up."

In a minute or two Sam Brower gathers the legal papers and steers the Saturn back to the prophet's headquarters, but the car he spotted is no longer here. "They bolted already," Sam says, impressed. "They're gone." He tools around the block again, but the car has evaporated. "Shit, man. Just thirty seconds earlier we might've had 'em."

Lost Boys Storm the Capitol

Word spread among the ex-Crickers: There was this rich guy in SLC, a former polyg who was willing and able to help them. His name was Dan Fischer. Fischer ran a charity called Smiles for Diversity, and he wanted to use it to help get the boys back in school and find them places to live. He even had a toll-free number: 1-877-GET-A-DAD.

White-haired, virile, and fond of the grand oratorical flourish, Fischer was the kind of fiftysomething businessman of the American West whose dynamism and entrepreneurial zest were automatically expressed in his handshake: not only was it very firm, but it would actually lift your arm into the air. Trained as a dentist, he'd become a millionaire as the force behind Ultradent, a company that supplied equipment to dentists around the world.

Fischer grew up during one of the most tumultuous periods in the history of American polygamy. He was raised by three mothers, and his family lived down a dirt lane in an area of Salt Lake City that was smirkingly known as Polygville. Fischer's father, in fact, suffered a familiar fate. He was excommunicated, his wives and children scattered. "It's one thing when your parents separate. It's another thing when the whole family is virtually annihilated," Fischer said. "You come to realize there are some things that are simply evil."

As a young man, Dan Fischer himself had three wives, none of whom he really liked or even knew before getting married, and all of whom were assigned to him by LeRoy S. Johnson, a fundamentalist prophet who preceded Rulon Jeffs. The first two wives were sisters; he later divorced the first and dissolved the "spiritual marriage" to the third, which was never technically legal. He has sixteen children. "I'm so thankful I'm not a polygamist today," he said. "I know many wonderful people that are. But tragically I know more of the fallout victims of it."

The Crickers didn't trust the government — after all, they'd been trained to despise it — but they were prone to trust a man like Fischer, whose background was the same as theirs. In August, Fischer invited about one hundred of the Lost Boys to Salt Lake City — offered to pay their way — and put together a press event in which they sat on the steps of the Utah State Capitol building. Fischer wore a bulletproof vest. It was up there, alongside Fischer and Utah Attorney General Mark Shurtleff and Jon Krakauer, that two boys volunteered to step up to the microphone. They were Tom Steed and Richard Gilbert.

Tom had met Krakauer a few days earlier. He had no idea who

Krakauer was — couldn't have imagined that a best-selling author would dress like some seven-grain hacky-sacker from Boulder — but there was something about the guy that coaxed Tom to open up. He told Krakauer about being excommunicated, about the house in Hurricane, about how he'd moved up to Idaho and tried to expand his carpet-cleaning business and got buried in $10,000 of debt. A few days later, Tom got a call from the Diversity people: Jon Krakauer had signed on to be Tom's mentor, and he was going to get the relationship rolling by paying off that debt.

Fischer gathered the boys in a ballroom at the Grand America Hotel and gave them a speech. He said he wanted to send them to Washington, where they could see the monuments and museums and learn what freedom was all about. He wanted them to know, among other things, that astronauts had landed on the moon. Some of the Crickers had been taught that if a man ever set foot on the moon, the moon would turn blood red.

You Can't Pray a Lie

The smell hits you right away: dishes piled in the sink, half-eaten chicken fingers left on the counter, sweaty clothes dropped on the floor. It's a smell, with a fermented sweetness verging on rot, that is unique to the natural habitat of young men living in close quarters, and which seems to be a source of pleasure only to the flies darting from one end of the room to the other.

The Butt Hut was abandoned long ago, its denizens dispersed, but these days the Lost Boys come together here, in an apartment on Dan Fischer's property near the Wasatch Mountains. The place serves as a way station for ex-Crickers; a few sleep here, while most hang out between classes at local high schools and colleges. The conversation, like the scent, tells you as much as anything about how three nineteen-year-olds in the den are adjusting to twenty-first-century America.

Raymond Hardy wears a black T-shirt that says ANIME FREAK and talks about how the *Matrix* franchise degenerated after the first installment. Edward Timpson says he dreams of traveling to Berlin to join the Love Parade, "the biggest rave in the world." Richard Gilbert has a newly shaved head; he wanted to see what that was like. For many of the ex-Crickers, there are moments when they cannot help but hear a voice that eggs them on toward guilt, weakness, and doom. "I mean, you'll get that panic attack for a couple of seconds — *I am going to hell I am going to hell* — and then you're just like, no, I'm not, no, I'm not, OK. That's how it is for me sometimes," Richard says. "I'll get a panic attack just from what I've been taught my whole life, all of a sudden jumping on me out of nowhere." As for their current spiritual affiliation, they don't hesitate for a second.

"We are no religion," says Edward.

"Yeah," says Raymond. "Pretty much every one of us is no religion."

Edward mulls it over for a moment, then says, "We're . . . *humanitarians.*"

"Let me put it this way," says Richard. "If a baseball player hits you in the back of the head with a baseball bat, are you ever going to want to turn your back on another baseball player again? That's the kind of the situation we're in. It feels like church just reamed us good."

Tom Steed is sitting in a parking lot in St. George, Utah, with the car door hanging open and the summer sky darkening over the freeway that leads to Las Vegas. When it gets dark out here, it gets *dark;* it's like a giant wing has blotted out the sky. Tom's talking about going to college, maybe moving to Colorado, inching forward in life. Across the parking lot, a man is piling groceries into a minivan; the man wears a familiar long-sleeve work shirt. "Oh, there's a polygie right there," Tom says quietly. "He used to work with me."

This happens now and then. A flashback, a split second of cross-culture friction. "I wave at 'em, or put my hand out to shake their hand, and I just get glares," Tom says. "Which is fine." Although he doesn't direct his anger toward those people, it would be a mistake to presume, because of his smile, or because of the forgiving stillness in his voice, that Tom Steed has somehow moved beyond anger itself. "My intentions aren't to harm the people there," he says. "But I want the monster stopped. I want him behind bars for this shit he's done."

■

Roadkill

FROM *Creative Nonfiction*

THE TEETH WON'T COME OUT, even when I pull hard. It's because the carcass isn't old enough. The skull wants to keep the teeth, refuses to be broken apart. Sometimes the teeth shatter in the jaws of the Leatherman tool I keep, along with a pair of work gloves and a Ziploc bag, under the front seat of my car. Long incisors are choice for my art; deer, elk, antelope, porcupines, and coyotes all have excellent teeth. I harvest them, bleach them, and eventually implant them into giant papier-mâché fish that I sculpt when I am frustrated with writing.

The last months of my pregnancy correspond to high roadkill season. In northern Colorado, late summer and autumn are punctuated by dead animals on the highway. I count — often there are several casualties per mile of pavement. Skunks are the most common victims, but porcupines and deer and foxes also bloom on the highways, dead, sometimes fixed in horrible contorted poses, sometimes looking bloated and uncomfortable, other times squished into the pavement such that a few tufts of fur grow out of the blacktop, as if there had never been an animal, never been pain, never been a life at all.

Where animals are dead on the road, others are likely to have died before them. I realized this on lonely Highway 13 near the Colorado/Wyoming border, where I once stopped to take pictures. A fence along the road boasted Burma-Shave signs, each only a foot across and half as high, stuck on fence posts about twenty yards apart. The first sign said TAKE STEAK, the next IN AMERICA, then BEEF UP YOUR LIFE, and finally just EAT BEEF. A long-time vegetarian, I decided to set the self-timer on my camera and pose, affecting an exaggerated bodybuilder posture, under each of the signs.

I parked near a newly dead deer. Between the road and the fence, I walked over three skeletons; along the fence, within a hundred yards of one another, were eight or ten more. I puzzled a few moments over the wreckage of life, wondering how an animal could deserve death by automobile. On the windburned Wyoming plain, over the corpse of a spike buck, I yelled out a few lines from E. E. Cummings: "I who have died am alive again today, and this the sun's birthday . . ." Two semis roared by on the highway behind me, invading the prayer. I judged them to be moving at about eighty miles per hour. One driver pulled his horn, and before the sound was finished, the trucks had disappeared over a rise in the road. Gone like phantoms.

Fancying myself some sort of Georgia O'Keeffe renegade in a Subaru, I picked up three deer skulls and tossed them under the hatchback door.

I don't exactly enjoy pulling teeth. It's a stinky business; often there are maggots to contend with, sometimes blood, fur, dried entrails. Usually the eye sockets are empty, and I wonder when the animal last had vision. I know pain is gone, but pulling, I utter the Buddhist prayer for a favorable rebirth, "*Om mani padme hum.*" Or I say to the animal, "Hope you're in heaven." I yank the teeth with a disquieting notion of having taken reincarnation upon myself.

In pregnancy, the process of scouting out dead animals and extracting their teeth is fundamentally altered by my shape. I'm not so agile; I must squat instead of bending. I have to get closer to the bodies. I have to get closer to death.

For the first time in my life, I start feeling like an animal. I can't move very quickly, and I am vulnerable. The child inside me squirms and rolls. My breasts are swollen to twice their normal size, demanding that my attention constantly turn to nurturing and sustenance. The explosion of my olfactory capability makes me believe I could, if need be, sniff out food, or danger. I feel strong but also desperate and tender. The weight of technology seems heightened. I feel complicit in death every time I drive. When I see carcasses by the side of the road, I whisper to my baby, "I love you." I tell her I'll take care of her. I tell him I'll protect him with my life.

Near home, I find a small, long-dead deer by the side of the highway. After soaking the skull in bleach for a day, I rinse it with the garden hose, at first superficially, but then with unabashed interest. I put my fingers in the eyeholes and survey the bone. It's easy enough to tell where the spinal cord went into the skull at the base of the brain. Aiming the hose here, I watch the water flow in. A few dry maggot casings get pushed out of the sinuses, as little rivers spurt from two openings that led to the deer's nostrils when there was still skin and cartilage to connect everything.

I put my finger to the tip of my own nose and roll the flesh while I sit on the lawn, speculating. It won't hurt, I reason, to decompose. By the time the maggots are at me, I'll be good and dead, already unfeeling, like this deer, whose head I have in my hand. Straight overhead, the sun seethes casually on.

I dig my toes into the grass. I think about birth and rebirth and God. It's late August. A few leaves have already turned on the cottonwoods in our yard, and the changing season seems to recognize me. Even now, pregnant and unusual to myself, autumn does not just come: it bears me — baby and all — along in its golden stream. I lift the deer skull to eye level and scrutinize again. The child inside me kicks to tell me that birthing in fall is perhaps the ultimate paradox.

My intrigue with fish began when I was an undergraduate and flew to Alaska for a summer to gut salmon for money. We worked eight-hour shifts, with only three or four hours between, for weeks at a time. In a constant state of half-wakefulness, I performed the various jobs in the plant — heading, gulleting, washing, sorting the fish, which came in a steady barrage. The actions were repetitive, at first monotonous, but as the hours and the summer wore on, everything fell into a rhythmic lull. Although I knew nothing about Zen at the time, the actions associated with killing and cleaning fish became, ironically, meditative. Standing at the wash table at 3 A.M., cutting the blood line at the backbone — scooping the clots that resembled thick strawberry jam away from the spines, then placing the fish back on the conveyor belt to be sorted, frozen, and eventually sent to Japan — began to be nearly pleasant.

The packing process was cold and clean; the fish were firm and silver. I expected to be horrified at the sheer volume of life being raked from the ocean. In one small packing plant with a crew of thirty people, we processed 20,000 pounds of salmon every hour. But instinct betrayed me. A false, quiet sense of abundance prevailed. The constant pouring forth of fish gave me the feeling the ocean was fecund and inexhaustible.

In school the following semester, I was required to write a paper on a modern novel of my choice. Near the end of Virginia Woolf's *Between the Acts,* a giant carp surfaces in a garden pond. The dreamlike image of the carp resonated with my memories of salmon, and after hours in the basement of the university library thumbing through dusty books of symbols, I found out that fish represent fertility.

Having a baby has never been a life objective for me. I didn't presume that I would not be a mother, but while friends waited and yearned for children, maternal longing only skirted my consciousness. When I began sculpting fish, it was with the concept of fertility in mind, not of reproduction, necessarily. I thought of fertility of imagination and spirit, proliferation of thought and creativity as jostling shoulder to shoulder in one category. The fish were a way I could be creative, could be fertile when I was not writing.

Fish I have made range in length from about eight inches to over six feet. Beginning with cardboard, I cut two identical fish shapes and tape them together, stuffing the form with paper to give it dimension. I crumple up drafts of particularly bad stories and seal them inside. I add fins, also cut from cardboard. When the shape is finished, the papier-mâché process begins; two or three layers are required for structural integrity. A mosaic of colored fabric pieces goes on in decoupage fashion over the paper. This is the most time-consuming part of the process, but also the part by which each fish takes on its distinctive look. Several layers of sealers are applied over the fabric to give a shiny, finished effect. Eyes are difficult to decide on — sometimes I use colored clay, sometimes painted sand dollars, sometimes various hardware-store items, such as faucet handles or dish-drain covers painted with bright nail polish. The finishing touch is adding the teeth.

Teeth are chosen according to the size of the fish, the size of the mouth, and the "personality" the fish has acquired over the course of its creation. Using a power drill, I make holes in the papier-mâché, then glue in the teeth. The dental work transforms the art. The teeth make the fish look fiendish and determined. I use this idea to remind myself to be relentless about thought, to be committed to ideas, to be terrible and foreboding in pursuit of mind-fulness, gentleness, and fertility.

When I decided I wanted to get pregnant, I hung the fish all around the bedroom and conceived on the first go-round.

In a conference room in the hospital basement, we sit around an oak table strewn with handouts on how to time contractions and our options of cloth or disposable diapers. We have already discussed colostrum and preterm labor, prolapsed umbilical cords and jaundice. Everyone is starting to yawn, the prospective mothers rubbing their bellies, the fathers-to-be tipping their baseball caps back to scratch at their hairlines.

The instructor says, "An episiotomy is when the doctor snips the skin of the perineum to let the baby come out more easily." Everyone nods, and then there is silence.

The term is not new to me; still, it takes some effort to remain calm. "But it's not skin, exactly, right?" Several eyes shift my way but dart just as quickly back to the tabletop or the clock on the wall. The instructor looks as if she hasn't understood my question.

There's silence until I go on. "I mean, the perineum is a muscle; when the doctor cuts it, he or she is cutting a muscular wall, right?"

"Well, yes," she says. She runs her fingers quickly through her bangs. She has a tiny waist. If I hadn't seen her around town with her two children, I wouldn't believe anything she said about birthing. "But when the doctor cuts it, it is stretched paper thin by the baby's head."

I have to think about this for a minute. I fold my hands and rest them on top of my belly, even with my chest. "OK, but when the baby is out, the perineum will no longer be stretched paper thin, so when the doctor is sewing, we're talking about muscle, right?"

My husband, John, squeezes my knee under the table. People are staring at me now.

"That's right, but it doesn't hurt as much as you think." I must still be wearing a question mark on my face, because she adds quickly, "The sewing, I mean." Then she smiles right at me and says, "I promise."

The first week in childbirth class we get to know one another by introducing ourselves and our partners and then saying what we associate with the word *labor*. Of thirteen women in the class, eleven say *pain*. I say that I hope labor will be a time when I am able to concentrate and focus in order to bring my baby into the world. I start wondering if pain is a bad thing. I start paying attention to what *pain* means.

I notice that ads for cell phones, mortgage companies, and oil changes all use the word *painless* to mean fast or handy. Looking around the faces in my class, I try to translate what that means to childbirth. *Pain* has lapsed in the vernacular to the same status as annoying and inconvenient. To feel is presented not only as upsetting to fast-paced living, but also as a competitive disadvantage.

When I am not paying attention in childbirth class, I think about dead animals and their pain and their teeth. I remember a time two years ago when I killed a cat on a state highway. Heading home at ten or eleven at night during the first real snowstorm of the year, large flakes rushed my headlights. Yellow lane lines and silver reflectors marked the dimensions of the road, everything else lost in white. I saw the animal maybe a second before hearing the thick sound of its head connecting with my axle. Immediately I thought *skunk,* but after driving on, agitated, for half a mile or more, I thought, *no, maybe it was a cat.* Finding a place to turn around, I measured the relative values of cats and skunks: It didn't matter to me. I might actually prefer skunks, with their shuffling little steps, heads to the ground, sniffing things out. But I had hit the animal close to a ranch house, and it was my moral obligation to tell the owners if I had smashed their kitty.

Letting the car creep onto the scene, I saw the animal in the road, a black blotch on the highway between the stripes left by my tires in the snow. No other vehicles had passed. It was a cat. I gagged, half out of sympathy for the unfortunate cat, half in dread that I would have to go knock on the ranch-house door.

The porch light was on, and an upstairs light. I resolved to be swift and honest, ringing the bell and clearing my throat. I waited. There was the sound of people mumbling inside. There was clumping down the stairs. Finally the door opened a crack. I tried to appear meek and harmless, standing there in the snow. A man, maybe thirty, maybe less, wearing only boxer shorts stood shivering.

"I'm sorry to disturb you," I mustered. "I know it's late, but I think . . ." I stopped and looked at my feet, pushed some snow against my boot with the other foot, then looked at the man again. "I'm so sorry. I think I killed your cat."

"Oh," he said. He said it thoughtfully, raised his eyebrows while he surveyed me. He stood there, saying nothing, for ten or fifteen seconds. He rattled the doorknob in his hand. He closed his eyes slowly, as if he would fall asleep standing right there. Then he opened them again, leaned toward me, and said, "Actually, we don't have a cat."

On the way back out of the driveway, my headlights fell exactly on the cat. I looked hard; there was no blood. The thought that it might not be dead burst first into the pit of my stomach, then worked its way into my head. I set the brake and left the lights shining on the animal. I went to it and leaned over, terrified, snowflakes stinging my skin. It was breathing. It could not move; its spine was probably broken. Maybe it was in terrible pain. Maybe it couldn't feel anything. The cat looked up at me with unadulterated terror.

I reached out to pet it. To comfort it. To try to pick it up and take it to a vet, even though it was the middle of the night and there wasn't a vet for twenty miles in either direction. I didn't know how to help, and it hardly mattered. When my hand came near, the cat lifted its head, hissed, and tried to bite, even though it was unable to use its legs to scratch or run away.

Tears were freezing on my face. I kept telling the cat I was sorry — sorry that it had to die so that I could drive on the highway after dark, sorry it had to die at all. I said the Lord's Prayer, then thought the best, most merciful thing to do would be to get in the car, take aim with the tires, and run it over again, eliminate its current suffering, kill it absolutely.

I told the cat again that I was sorry, then got into the car. I held the wheel in rigid hands, alternately watching the cat and the clock buried in my dashboard. Two minutes passed, then three, then five. I sat until a snowplow advanced over the horizon. Surely the plow would finish the cat, send it tumbling into the ditch, with all its metal, diesel force. The flashing blue light was a harbinger of mercy, and I pulled away and drove home.

I think about it now, in the late months of pregnancy. If the cat had belonged to the man in the boxer shorts, of course it would have been worse. His pet would have been violently and tragically killed. There would have been tears and loss. As it was, I felt bad for a few days, but eventually, in my mind, the cat became roadkill. So it seemed it was not I, or even the car I was driving, that was responsible for the death. The cat became *roadkill,* as if the highway itself rose up from its embankments and strangled the animal where it walked, as if neither the cat nor I had ever been possessed of feeling.

Clearly, people have intense feelings about birthing and raising children. An unborn baby evokes unsolicited and inexplicable love. A friend from far away has me hold the phone to my belly so she can whisper to the child. Neighbors arrive at the door with casseroles and flowers. Everyone wants to touch my stomach. I get the feeling that, through pregnancy, I have assumed responsibility for a child's pain, forever. Of course, the child's joy will come running with it, hand in hand, and the mystery of it all is too great to brush against intellectually. No one tells me this, but everyone knows it. They let this vast, shapeless secret shimmer just behind their eyes when they meet me on the street and just smile and nod in recognition of my burgeoning figure.

At the final childbirth class, graduates from the previous class come with their newborns. They use words like *amazing, miraculous,* and *magical.* They hold their children and whisper, "Just new to us, from God."

But I get confused when the fathers talk to us about labor. Referring to his wife, one says, "After she got the epidural, she was like herself again, happy and laughing."

Another says, "I loved the monitor! I could watch the screen and tell her when to push."

A new mother confirms, "It was great. I really couldn't feel anything." My heart rate goes up, and I feel it like the pulse of a pink neon sign. The mother is glowing; she's radiant; her baby is perfect. Everyone in the room is happy for the woman; I am happy for her, and for the tiny girl she cradles. Then she says, "Really, it was almost painless," and I start to feel as if we are all on television. I keep thinking, *I hope childbirth isn't like a commercial.* I keep thinking, *I want to feel the pain.*

I call the nurses' station at the hospital. Home alone, I take the phone into the bedroom so I can stretch and do pelvic tilts on the bed while I make the call. I tell the nurse that I have been researching the use of the fetal monitor and anesthesia, and I have some questions.

"Of course, anesthesia makes things easier for everyone," she says, "but it is optional." So I tell her what I've read about fetal monitoring — that the monitor has no benefit for low-risk mothers and that the chances of having a cesarean go up with the use of the technology.

It feels like she is using her knowledge against me when she says, "Yes, unfortunately, there is a lot of negative lay literature out there." She goes on to explain why the medical staff needs the monitors, for the health and safety of my baby and me.

The monitor wraps around the mother's middle and has two devices, one that measures the intensity of contractions, one that monitors the baby's heart rate. Each of these is a disc about three or four inches in diameter. There is a sensor on the back of each disc that goes on the mother's stomach; it is not invasive. Thick straps hold the discs against the mother's belly.

The nurse throws in some medical jargon as she tells me what I already know. Her voice remains even and pleasant. She explains the theory of the monitor, which is the same, basically, as what I've read in the books, but she has nothing negative to say. She finishes her speech with a sweetly phrased question. "You do want to have a healthy baby, don't you?"

I'm helpless and vulnerable. I consider shouting, "No, I hope it pops out with four heads and a mustache!" But I also want to cry. I don't know what to believe. The nurse implies that wearing the monitor during labor will somehow make my baby healthy, that the well-being of my child depends not on what I eat, how I take care of myself, or even how I prepare for labor. She must be right. She's an informed professional, and she's articulate. But in the eighth month of keeping someone I've never met alive with my own body, science doesn't make a lot sense to me.

I take a deep breath, consider, and try again. "I am concerned that the monitor will interfere with my ability to relax and concentrate and birth my child." I explain that I'm sensitive. I think having a monitor will not only distract me, it will inhibit me from concentrating on the work at hand.

The nurse doesn't hear me. She ignores my words and says, "Are you afraid the sound waves from the monitor will hurt your baby?" She launches into another speech, but I cut her off. I decide to quit being rational and instead to be honest.

I'm not afraid the sound waves will hurt the baby. I tell her I'm going to tell her the truth; does she really want to know why I don't want the monitor?

"Yes, all right," she says, and I can practically hear her rolling her eyes on the other end of the line.

I tell the nurse that my problem is one of imagery. I know, in theory, what the monitor does and what it is for, but I can't seem to move beyond the visual impact the machine has on me.

"What do you mean?" the nurse asks. "I'm not sure I understand what you are saying."

I give up being delicate. I've already exposed myself as an irrational being, unable to grasp simple concepts and reason, so I tell her. "Well, in the diagrams and photos I've seen, the woman is lying on her back against the white sheets of a hospital bed. She's got an IV in her arm and two wide straps around her stomach, and it looks to me like she is being executed."

I debate about going on about death and roadkill and how now, in pregnancy, I understand that we are bound to our parents and children in a huge circle of pain and love and birth and feeling that has nothing at all to do with fetal monitoring or epidural anesthesia. But I don't say anything.

After a pause, she says, "Wearing the monitor is just the first of many sacrifices you will make as a mother. Surely you realize that we are not going to electrocute you."

"Yes," I say. "Surely. Thank you." I hang up the phone and cry for some time, patting my stomach and telling my baby, "Don't worry. I'll take care of you." I tell him that any way he comes into the world, I will love him. I tell her not to be afraid, because I am not afraid. I cry wholeheartedly and enjoy it — the hot tears that hit the pillow, the air entering my throat. I watch my belly heave with every sob. I tell the baby, "Your mama is sad; can you feel it? It's not a bad thing." I lie on the bed, looking out the window. "I am so happy that you are coming," I say. A few golden leaves flutter to the ground, and the toothy fish swim through the air over my head.

∎

Hell-Heaven

FROM *The New Yorker*

PRANAB CHAKRABORTY wasn't technically my father's younger brother. He was a fellow Bengali from Calcutta who had washed up on the barren shores of my parents' social life in the early seventies, when they lived in a rented apartment in Central Square and could number their acquaintances on one hand. But I had no real uncles in America, and so I was taught to call him Pranab Kaku. Accordingly, he called my father Shyamal Da, always addressing him in the polite form, and he called my mother Boudi, which is how Bengalis are supposed to address an older brother's wife, instead of using her first name, Aparna. After Pranab Kaku was befriended by my parents, he confessed that on the day we first met him he had followed my mother and me for the better part of an afternoon around the streets of Cambridge, where she and I tended to roam after I got out of school. He had trailed behind us along Massachusetts Avenue, and in and out of the Harvard Coop, where my mother liked to look at discounted housewares. He wandered with us into Harvard Yard, where my mother often sat on the grass on pleasant days and watched the stream of students and professors filing busily along the paths, until, finally, as we were climbing the steps to Widener Library so that I could use the bathroom, he tapped my mother on the shoulder and inquired, in English, if she might be a Bengali. The answer to his question was clear, given that my mother was wearing the red and white bangles unique to Bengali married women, and a common Tangail sari, and had a thick stem of vermillion powder in the center parting of her hair, and the full round face and large dark eyes that are so typical of Bengali women. He noticed the two or three safety pins she wore fastened to the thin gold bangles that were behind the red and white ones, which she would use to replace a missing hook on a blouse or to draw a string through a petticoat at a moment's notice, a practice he associated strictly with his mother and sisters and aunts in Calcutta. Moreover, Pranab Kaku had overheard my mother speaking to me in Bengali, telling me that I couldn't buy an issue of *Archie* at the Coop. But back then, he also confessed, he was so new to America that he took nothing for granted, and doubted even the obvious.

My parents and I had lived in Central Square for three years prior to that day; before that, we had lived in Berlin, where I was born and where my father had finished his training in microbiology before accepting a position as a researcher at Mass General, and before Berlin my mother and father had lived in India, where they had been strangers to each other, and where their marriage had been arranged. Central Square is the first place I can recall living, and in my memories of our apartment, in a dark-brown shingled house on Ashburton Place, Pranab Kaku is always there. According to the story he liked to recall often, my mother invited him to accompany us back to our apartment that very afternoon, and prepared tea for the two of them; then, after learning that he had not had a proper Bengali meal in more than three months, she served him the leftover curried mackerel and rice that we had eaten for dinner the night before. He remained into the evening, for a second dinner, after my father got home, and after that he showed up for dinner almost every night, occupying the fourth chair at our square Formica kitchen table, and becoming a part of our family in practice as well as in name.

He was from a wealthy family in Calcutta and had never had to do so much as pour himself a glass of water before moving to America, to study engineering at MIT. Life as a graduate student in Boston was a cruel shock, and in his first month he lost nearly twenty pounds. He had arrived in January, in the middle of a snowstorm, and at the end of a week he had packed his bags and gone to Logan, prepared to abandon the opportunity he'd worked toward all his life, only to change his mind at the last minute. He was living on Trowbridge Street in the home of a divorced woman with two young children who were always screaming and crying. He rented a room in the attic and was permitted to use the kitchen only at specified times of the day, and instructed always to wipe down the stove with Windex and a sponge. My parents agreed that it was a terrible situation, and if they'd had a bedroom to spare they would have offered it to him. Instead, they welcomed him to our meals, and opened up our apartment to him at any time, and soon it was there he went between classes and on his days off, always leaving behind some vestige of himself: a nearly finished pack of cigarettes, a newspaper, a piece of mail he had not bothered to open, a sweater he had taken off and forgotten in the course of his stay.

I remember vividly the sound of his exuberant laughter and the sight of his lanky body slouched or sprawled on the dull, mismatched furniture that had come with our apartment. He had a striking face, with a high forehead and a thick mustache, and overgrown, untamed hair that my mother said made him look like the American hippies who were everywhere in those days. His long legs jiggled rapidly up and down wherever he sat, and his elegant hands trembled when he held a cigarette between his fingers, tapping the ashes into a teacup that my mother began to set aside for this exclusive purpose. Though he was a scientist by training, there was nothing rigid or predictable or orderly about him. He always seemed to be starving, walking through the door and announcing that he hadn't had lunch, and then he would eat ravenously, reaching behind my mother to steal cutlets as she was frying them, before she had a chance to set them properly on a plate with red-onion salad. In private, my parents remarked that he was a brilliant student, a star at Jadavpur who had come to MIT with an impressive assistantship, but Pranab Kaku was cavalier about his classes, skipping them with frequency. "These Americans are learning equations I knew at Usha's age," he would complain. He was stunned that my second-grade teacher didn't assign any homework, and that at the age of seven I hadn't yet been taught square roots or the concept of pi.

He appeared without warning, never phoning beforehand but simply knocking on the door the way people did in Calcutta and calling out "Boudi!" as he waited for my mother to let him in. Before we met him, I would return from school and find my mother with her purse in her lap and her trench coat on, desperate to escape the apartment where she had spent the day alone. But now I would find her in the kitchen, rolling out dough for *luchis,* which she normally made only on Sundays for my father and me, or putting up new curtains she'd bought at Woolworth's. I did not know, back then, that Pranab Kaku's visits were what my mother looked forward to all day, that she changed into a new sari and combed her hair in anticipation of his arrival, and that she planned, days in advance, the snacks she would serve him with such nonchalance. That she lived for the moment she heard him call out "Boudi!" from the porch, and that she was in a foul humor on the days he didn't materialize.

It must have pleased her that I looked forward to his visits as well. He showed me card tricks and an optical illusion in which he appeared to be severing his own thumb with enormous struggle and strength, and taught me to memorize multiplication tables well before I had to learn them in school. His hobby was photography. He owned an expensive camera that required thought before you pressed the shutter, and I quickly became his favorite subject, round-faced, missing teeth, my thick bangs in need of a trim. They are still the pictures of myself I like best, for they convey that confidence of youth I no longer possess, especially in front of a camera. I remember having to run back and forth in Harvard Yard as he stood with the camera, trying to capture me in motion, or posing on the steps of university buildings and on the street and against the trunks of trees. There is only one photograph in which my mother appears; she is holding me as I sit straddling her lap, her head tilted toward me, her hands pressed to my ears as if to prevent me from hearing something. In that picture, Pranab Kaku's shadow, his two arms raised at angles to hold the camera to his face, hovers in the corner of the frame, his darkened, featureless shape superimposed on one side of my mother's body. It was always the three of us. I was always there when he visited. It would have been inappropriate for my mother to receive him in the apartment alone; this was something that went without saying.

They had in common all the things she and my father did not: a love of music, film, leftist politics, poetry. They were from the same neighborhood in North Calcutta, their family homes within walking distance, the façades familiar to them once the exact locations were described. They knew the same shops, the same bus and tram routes, the same holes-in-the-wall for the best *jelabis* and *moghlai parathas*. My father, on the other hand, came from a suburb twenty miles outside Calcutta, an area that my mother considered the wilderness, and even in her bleakest hours of homesickness she was grateful that my father had at least spared her a life in the stern house of her in-laws, where she would have had to keep her head covered with the end of her sari at all times and use an outhouse that was nothing but a raised platform with a hole, and where, in the rooms, there was not a single painting hanging on the walls. Within a few weeks, Pranab Kaku had brought his reel-to-reel over to our apartment, and he played for my mother medley after medley of songs from the Hindi films of their youth. They were cheerful songs of courtship, which transformed the quiet life in our apartment and transported my mother back to the world she'd left behind in order to marry my father. She and Pranab Kaku would try to recall which scene in which movie the songs were from, who the actors were and what they were wearing. My mother would describe Raj Kapoor and Nargis singing under umbrellas in the rain, or Dev Anand strumming a guitar on the beach in Goa. She and Pranab Kaku would argue passionately about these matters, raising their voices in playful combat, confronting each other in a way she and my father never did.

Because he played the part of a younger brother, she felt free to call him Pranab, whereas she never called my father by his first name. My father was thirty-seven then, nine years older than my mother. Pranab Kaku was twenty-five. My father was monkish by nature, a lover of silence and solitude. He had married my mother to placate his parents; they were willing to accept his desertion as long as he had a wife. He was wedded to his work, his research, and he existed in a shell that neither my mother nor I could penetrate. Conversation was a chore for him; it required an effort he preferred to expend at the lab. He disliked excess in anything, voiced no cravings or needs apart from the frugal elements of his daily routine: cereal and tea in the mornings, a cup of tea after he got home, and two different vegetable dishes every night with dinner. He did not eat with the reckless appetite of Pranab Kaku. My father had a survivor's mentality. From time to time, he liked to remark, in mixed company and often with no relevant provocation, that starving Russians under Stalin had resorted to eating the glue off the back of their wallpaper. One might think that he would have felt slightly jealous, or at the very least suspicious, about the regularity of Pranab Kaku's visits and the effect they had on my mother's behavior and mood. But my guess is that my father was grateful to Pranab Kaku for the companionship he provided, freed from the sense of responsibility he must have felt for forcing her to leave India, and relieved, perhaps, to see her happy for a change.

In the summer, Pranab Kaku bought a navy-blue Volkswagen Beetle, and began to take my mother and me for drives through Boston and Cambridge, and soon outside the city, flying down the highway. He would take us to India Tea and Spices in Watertown, and one time he drove us all the way to New Hampshire to look at the mountains. As the weather grew hotter, we started going, once or twice a week, to Walden Pond. My mother always prepared a picnic of hard-boiled eggs and cucumber sandwiches, and talked fondly about the winter picnics of her youth, grand expeditions with fifty of her relatives, all taking the train into the West Bengal countryside. Pranab Kaku listened to these stories with interest, absorbing the vanishing details of her past. He did not turn a deaf ear to her nostalgia, like my father, or listen uncomprehending, like me. At Walden Pond, Pranab Kaku would coax my mother through the woods, and lead her down the steep slope to the water's edge. She would unpack the picnic things and sit and watch us as we swam. His chest was matted with thick dark hair, all the way to his waist. He was an odd sight, with his pole-thin legs and a small, flaccid belly, like an otherwise svelte woman who has had a baby and not bothered to tone her abdomen. "You're making me fat, Boudi," he would complain after gorging himself on my mother's cooking. He swam noisily, clumsily, his head always above the water; he didn't know how to blow bubbles or hold his breath, as I had learned in swimming class. Wherever we went, any stranger would have naturally assumed that Pranab Kaku was my father, that my mother was his wife.

It is clear to me now that my mother was in love with him. He wooed her as no other man had, with the innocent affection of a brother-in-law. In my mind, he was just a family member, a cross between an uncle and a much older brother, for in certain respects my parents sheltered and cared for him in much the same way they cared for me. He was respectful of my father, always seeking his advice about making a life in the West, about setting up a bank account and getting a job, and deferring to his opinions about Kissinger and Watergate. Occasionally, my mother would tease him about women, asking about female Indian students at MIT, or showing him pictures of her younger cousins in India. "What do you think of her?" she would ask. "Isn't she pretty?" She knew that she could never have Pranab Kaku for herself, and I suppose it was her attempt to keep him in the family. But, most important, in the beginning he was totally dependent on her, needing her for those months in a way my father never did in the whole history of their marriage. He brought to my mother the first and, I suspect, the only pure happiness she ever felt. I don't think even my birth made her as happy. I was evidence of her marriage to my father, an assumed consequence of the life she had been raised to lead. But Pranab Kaku was different. He was the one totally unanticipated pleasure in her life.

*

In the fall of 1974, Pranab Kaku met a student at Radcliffe named Deborah, an American, and she began to accompany him to our house. I called Deborah by her first name, as my parents did, but Pranab Kaku taught her to call my father Shyamal Da and my mother Boudi, something with which Deborah gladly complied. Before they came to dinner for the first time, I asked my mother, as she was straightening up the living room, if I ought to address her as Deborah Kakima, turning her into an aunt as I had turned Pranab into an uncle. "What's the point?" my mother said, looking back at me sharply. "In a few weeks, the fun will be over and she'll leave him." And yet Deborah remained by his side, attending the weekend parties that Pranab Kaku and my parents were becoming more involved with, gatherings that were exclusively Bengali with the exception of her. Deborah was very tall, taller than both my parents and nearly as tall as Pranab Kaku. She wore her long brass-colored hair center-parted, as my mother did, but it was gathered into a low ponytail instead of a braid, or it spilled messily over her shoulders and down her back in a way that my mother considered indecent. She wore small silver spectacles and not a trace of makeup, and she studied philosophy. I found her utterly beautiful, but according to my mother she had spots on her face, and her hips were too small.

For a while, Pranab Kaku still showed up once a week for dinner on his own, mostly asking my mother what she thought of Deborah. He sought her approval, telling her that Deborah was the daughter of professors at Boston College, that her father published poetry, and that both her parents had Ph.D.s. When he wasn't around, my mother complained about Deborah's visits, about having to make the food less spicy even though Deborah said she liked spicy food, and feeling embarrassed to put a fried fish head in the dal. Pranab Kaku taught Deborah to say *khub bhalo* and *aacha* and to pick up certain foods with her fingers instead of with a fork. Sometimes they ended up feeding each other, allowing their fingers to linger in each other's mouth, causing my parents to look down at their plates and wait for the moment to pass. At larger gatherings, they kissed and held hands in front of everyone, and when they were out of earshot my mother would talk to the other Bengali women. "He used to be so different. I don't understand how a person can change so suddenly. It's just hell-heaven, the difference," she would say, always using the English words for her self-concocted, backward metaphor.

The more my mother began to resent Deborah's visits, the more I began to anticipate them. I fell in love with Deborah, the way young girls often fall in love with women who are not their mothers. I loved her serene gray eyes, the ponchos and denim wrap skirts and sandals she wore, her straight hair that she let me manipulate into all sorts of silly styles. I longed for her casual appearance; my mother insisted whenever there was a gathering that I wear one of my ankle-length, faintly Victorian dresses, which she referred to as maxis, and have party hair, which meant taking a strand from either side of my head and joining them with a barrette at the back. At parties, Deborah would, eventually, politely slip away, much to the relief of the Bengali women with whom she was expected to carry on a conversation, and she would play with me. I was older than all my parents' friends' children, but with Deborah I had a companion. She knew all about the books I read, about Pippi Longstocking and Anne of Green Gables. She gave me the sorts of gifts my parents had neither the money nor the inspiration to buy: a large book of Grimms' fairy tales with watercolor illustrations on thick, silken pages, wooden puppets with hair fashioned from yarn. She told me about her family, three older sisters and two brothers, the youngest of whom was closer to my age than to hers. Once, after visiting her parents, she brought back three Nancy Drews, her name written in a girlish hand at the top of the first page, and an old toy she'd had, a small paper theater set with interchangeable backdrops, the exterior of a castle and a ballroom and an open field. Deborah and I spoke freely in English, a language in which, by that age, I expressed myself more easily than Bengali, which I was required to speak at home. Sometimes she asked me how to say this or that in Bengali; once, she asked me what *asobbho* meant. I hesitated, then told her it was what my mother called me if I had done something extremely naughty, and

Deborah's face clouded. I felt protective of her, aware that she was unwanted, that she was resented, aware of the nasty things people said.

Outings in the Volkswagen now involved the four of us, Deborah in the front, her hand over Pranab Kaku's while it rested on the gearshift, my mother and I in the back. Soon, my mother began coming up with reasons to excuse herself, headaches and incipient colds, and so I became part of a new triangle. To my surprise, my mother allowed me to go with them, to the Museum of Fine Arts and the Public Garden and the aquarium. She was waiting for the affair to end, for Deborah to break Pranab Kaku's heart and for him to return to us, scarred and penitent. I saw no sign of their relationship foundering. Their open affection for each other, their easily expressed happiness, was a new and romantic thing to me. Having me in the back seat allowed Pranab Kaku and Deborah to practice for the future, to try on the idea of a family of their own. Countless photographs were taken of me and Deborah, of me sitting on Deborah's lap, holding her hand, kissing her on the cheek. We exchanged what I believed were secret smiles, and in those moments I felt that she understood me better than anyone else in the world. Anyone would have said that Deborah would make an excellent mother one day. But my mother refused to acknowledge such a thing. I did not know at the time that my mother allowed me to go off with Pranab Kaku and Deborah because she was pregnant for the fifth time since my birth, and was so sick and exhausted and fearful of losing another baby that she slept most of the day. After ten weeks, she miscarried once again and was advised by her doctor to stop trying.

By summer, there was a diamond on Deborah's left hand, something my mother had never been given. Because his own family lived so far away, Pranab Kaku came to the house alone one day, to ask for my parents' blessing before giving her the ring. He showed us the box, opening it and taking out the diamond nestled inside. "I want to see how it looks on someone," he said, urging my mother to try it on, but she refused. I was the one who stuck out my hand, feeling the weight of the ring suspended at the base of my finger. Then he asked for a second thing: He wanted my parents to write to his parents, saying that they had met Deborah and that they thought highly of her. He was nervous, naturally, about telling his family that he intended to marry an American girl. He had told his parents all about us, and at one point my parents had received a letter from them, expressing appreciation for taking such good care of their son and for giving him a proper home in America. "It needn't be long," Pranab Kaku said. "Just a few lines. They'll accept it more easily if it comes from you." My father thought neither ill nor well of Deborah, never commenting or criticizing as my mother did, but he assured Pranab Kaku that a letter of endorsement would be on its way to Calcutta by the end of the week. My mother nodded her assent, but the following day I saw the teacup Pranab Kaku had used all this time as an ashtray in the kitchen garbage can, in pieces, and three Band-Aids taped to my mother's hand.

Pranab Kaku's parents were horrified by the thought of their only son marrying an American woman, and a few weeks later our telephone rang in the middle of the night: It was Mr. Chakraborty telling my father that they could not possibly bless such a marriage, that it was out of the question, that if Pranab Kaku dared to marry Deborah he would no longer acknowledge him as a son. Then his wife got on the phone, asking to speak to my mother, and attacked her as if they were intimate, blaming my mother for allowing the affair to develop. She said that they had already chosen a wife for him in Calcutta, that he'd left for America with the understanding that he'd go back after he had finished his studies, and marry this girl. They had bought the neighboring flat in their building for Pranab and his betrothed, and it was sitting empty, waiting for his return. "We thought we could trust you, and yet you have betrayed us so deeply," his mother said, taking out her anger on a stranger in a way she could not with her son. "Is this what happens to people in America?" For Pranab Kaku's sake, my mother defended the engagement, telling his mother that Deborah was a polite girl from a decent family. Pranab Kaku's parents pleaded with mine to talk him out of the engagement, but my father refused, deciding that it was not their place to get embroiled in a situation that had nothing to do with them. "We are not his parents," he told my mother. "We can tell him they don't approve but nothing more." And so my parents told Pranab Kaku nothing about how his parents had berated them, and blamed them, and threatened to disown Pranab Kaku, only that they had refused to give him their blessing. In the face of this refusal, Pranab Kaku shrugged. "I don't care. Not everyone can be as open-minded as you," he told my parents. "Your blessing is blessing enough."

After the engagement, Pranab Kaku and Deborah began drifting out of our lives. They moved in together, to an apartment in Boston, in the South End, a part of the city my parents considered unsafe. We moved as well, to a house in Natick. Though my parents had bought the house, they occupied it as if they were still tenants, touching up scuff marks with leftover paint and reluctant to put holes in the walls, and every afternoon when the sun shone through the living-room window my mother closed the blinds so that our new furniture would not fade. A few weeks before the wedding, my parents invited Pranab Kaku to the house alone, and my mother prepared a special meal to mark the end of his bachelorhood. It would be the only Bengali aspect of the wedding; the rest of it would be strictly American, with a cake and a minister and Deborah in a long white dress and veil. There is a photograph of the dinner, taken by my father, the only picture, to my knowledge, in which my mother and Pranab Kaku appear together. The picture is slightly blurry; I remember Pranab Kaku explaining to my father how to work the camera, and so he is captured looking up from the kitchen table and the elaborate array of food my mother had prepared in his honor, his mouth open, his long arm outstretched and his finger pointing, instructing my father how to read the light meter or some such thing. My mother stands beside him, one hand placed on top of his head in a gesture of blessing, the first and last time she was to touch him in her life. "She will leave him," my mother told her friends afterward. "He is throwing his life away."

The wedding was at a church in Ipswich, with a reception at a country club. It was going to be a small ceremony, which my parents took to mean one or two hundred people as opposed to three or four hundred. My mother was shocked that fewer than thirty people had been invited, and she was more perplexed than honored that, of all the Bengalis Pranab Kaku knew by then, we were the only ones on the list. At the wedding, we sat, like the other guests, first on the hard wooden pews of the church and then at a long table that had been set up for lunch.

Though we were the closest thing Pranab Kaku had to a family that day, we were not included in the group photographs that were taken on the grounds of the country club, with Deborah's parents and grandparents and her many siblings, and neither my mother nor my father got up to make a toast. My mother did not appreciate the fact that Deborah had made sure that my parents, who did not eat beef, were given fish instead of filet mignon like everyone else. She kept speaking in Bengali, complaining about the formality of the proceedings, and the fact that Pranab Kaku, wearing a tuxedo, barely said a word to us because he was too busy leaning over the shoulders of his new American in-laws as he circled the table. As usual, my father said nothing in response to my mother's commentary, quietly and methodically working through his meal, his fork and knife occasionally squeaking against the surface of the china, because he was accustomed to eating with his hands. He cleared his plate and then my mother's, for she had pronounced the food inedible, and then he announced that he had overeaten and had a stomachache. The only time my mother forced a smile was when Deborah appeared behind her chair, kissing her on the cheek and asking if we were enjoying ourselves. When the dancing started, my parents remained at the table, drinking tea, and after two or three songs they decided that it was time for us to go home, my mother shooting me looks to that effect across the room, where I was dancing in a circle with Pranab Kaku and Deborah and the other children at the wedding. I wanted to stay, and when, reluctantly, I walked over to where my parents sat Deborah followed me. "Boudi, let Usha stay. She's having such a good time," she said to my mother. "Lots of people will be heading back your way, someone can drop her off in a little while." But my mother said no, I had had plenty of fun already, and forced me to put on my coat over my long puff-sleeved dress. As we drove home from the wedding I told my mother, for the first but not the last time in my life, that I hated her.

The following year, we received a birth announcement from the Chakrabortys, a picture of twin girls, which my mother did not paste into an album or display on the refrigerator door. The girls were named Srabani and Sabitri, but were called Bonny and Sara. Apart from a thank-you card for our wedding gift, it was their only communication; we were not invited to the new house in Marblehead, bought after Pranab Kaku got a high-paying job at Stone & Webster. For a while, my parents and their friends continued to invite the Chakrabortys to gatherings, but because they never came, or left after staying only an hour, the invitations stopped. Their absences were attributed, by my parents and their circle, to Deborah, and it was universally agreed that she had stripped Pranab Kaku not only of his origins but of his independence. She was the enemy, he was her prey, and their example was invoked as a warning, and as vindication, that mixed marriages were a doomed enterprise. Occasionally, they surprised everyone, appearing at a *pujo* for a few hours with their two identical little girls who barely looked Bengali and spoke only English and were being raised so differently from me and most of the other children. They were not taken to Calcutta every summer, they did not have parents who were clinging to another way of life and exhorting their children to do the same. Because of Deborah, they were exempt from all that, and for this reason I envied them. "Usha, look at you, all grown up and so pretty," Deborah would say whenever she saw me, rekindling, if only for a minute, our bond of years before. She had cut off her beautiful long hair by then, and had a bob. "I bet you'll be old enough to baby-sit soon," she would say. "I'll call you — the girls would love that." But she never did.

I began to grow out of my girlhood, entering middle school and developing crushes on the American boys in my class. The crushes amounted to nothing; in spite of Deborah's compliments,

I was always overlooked at that age. But my mother must have picked up on something, for she forbade me to attend the dances that were held the last Friday of every month in the school cafeteria, and it was an unspoken law that I was not allowed to date. "Don't think you'll get away with marrying an American, the way Pranab Kaku did," she would say from time to time. I was thirteen, the thought of marriage irrelevant to my life. Still, her words upset me, and I felt her grip on me tighten. She would fly into a rage when I told her I wanted to start wearing a bra, or if I wanted to go to Harvard Square with a friend. In the middle of our arguments, she often conjured Deborah as her antithesis, the sort of woman she refused to be. "If *she* were your mother, she would let you do whatever you wanted, because she wouldn't care. Is that what you want, Usha, a mother who doesn't care?" When I began menstruating, the summer before I started ninth grade, my mother gave me a speech, telling me that I was to let no boy touch me, and then she asked if I knew how a woman became pregnant. I told her what I had been taught in science, about the sperm fertilizing the egg, and then she asked if I knew how, exactly, that happened. I saw the terror in her eyes and so, though I knew that aspect of procreation as well, I lied, and told her it hadn't been explained to us.

I began keeping other secrets from her, evading her with the aid of my friends. I told her I was sleeping over at a friend's when really I went to parties, drinking beer and allowing boys to kiss me and fondle my breasts and press their erections against my hip as we lay groping on a sofa or the back seat of a car. I began to pity my mother; the older I got, the more I saw what a desolate life she led. She had never worked, and during the day she watched soap operas to pass the time. Her only job, every day, was to clean and cook for my father and me. We rarely went to restaurants, my father always pointing out, even in cheap ones, how expensive they were compared with eating at home. When my mother complained to him about how much she hated life in the suburbs and how lonely she felt, he said nothing to placate her. "If you are so unhappy, go back to Calcutta," he would offer, making it clear that their separation would not affect him one way or the other. I began to take my cues from my father in dealing with her, isolating her doubly. When she screamed at me for talking too long on the telephone, or for staying too long in my room, I learned to scream back, telling her that she was pathetic, that she knew nothing about me, and it was clear to us both that I had stopped needing her, definitively and abruptly, just as Pranab Kaku had.

Then, the year before I went off to college, my parents and I were invited to the Chakrabortys' home for Thanksgiving. We were not the only guests from my parents' old Cambridge crowd; it turned out that Pranab Kaku and Deborah wanted to have a sort of reunion of all the people they had been friendly with back then. Normally, my parents did not celebrate Thanksgiving; the ritual of a large sit-down dinner and the foods that one was supposed to eat was lost on them. They treated it as if it were Memorial Day or Veterans Day — just another holiday in the American year. But we drove out to Marblehead, to an impressive stone-faced house with a semicircular gravel driveway clogged with cars. The house was a short walk from the ocean; on our way, we had driven by the harbor overlooking the cold, glittering Atlantic, and when we stepped out of the car we were greeted by the sound of gulls and waves. Most of the living-room furniture had been moved to the basement, and extra tables joined to the main one to form a giant U. They were covered with tablecloths, set with white plates and silverware, and had centerpieces of gourds. I was struck by the toys and dolls that were everywhere, dogs that shed long yellow hairs on everything, all the photographs of Bonny and Sara and Deborah decorating the walls, still more plastering the refrigerator door. Food was being prepared when we arrived, something my mother always frowned upon, the kitchen a chaos of people and smells and enormous dirtied bowls.

Deborah's family, whom we remembered dimly from the wedding, was there, her parents and her brothers and sisters and their husbands and wives and boyfriends and babies. Her sisters were in their thirties, but, like Deborah, they could have been mistaken for college students, wearing jeans and clogs and fisherman

sweaters, and her brother Matty, with whom I had danced in a circle at the wedding, was now a freshman at Amherst, with wide-set
green eyes and wispy brown hair and a complexion that reddened
easily. As soon as I saw Deborah's siblings, joking with one another as they chopped and stirred things in the kitchen, I was furious with my mother for making a scene before we left the house
and forcing me to wear a shalwar kameez. I knew they assumed,
from my clothing, that I had more in common with the other Bengalis than with them. But Deborah insisted on including me, setting me to work peeling apples with Matty, and out of my parents'
sight I was given beer to drink. When the meal was ready, we were
told where to sit, in an alternating boy-girl formation that made
the Bengalis uncomfortable. Bottles of wine were lined up on the
table. Two turkeys were brought out, one stuffed with sausage and
one without. My mouth watered at the food, but I knew that afterward, on our way home, my mother would complain that it was all
tasteless and bland. "Impossible," my mother said, shaking her
hand over the top of her glass when someone tried to pour her a
little wine.

Deborah's father, Gene, got up to say grace, and asked everyone
at the table to join hands. He bowed his head and closed his eyes.
"Dear Lord, we thank you today for the food we are about to receive," he began. My parents were seated next to each other, and I
was stunned to see that they complied, that my father's brown
fingers lightly clasped my mother's pale ones. I noticed Matty
seated on the other side of the room, and saw him glancing at me
as his father spoke. After the chorus of amens, Gene raised his
glass and said, "Forgive me, but I never thought I'd have the opportunity to say this: Here's to Thanksgiving with the Indians."
Only a few people laughed at the joke.

Then Pranab Kaku stood up and thanked everyone for coming.
He was relaxed from alcohol, his once wiry body beginning to
thicken. He started to talk sentimentally about his early days in
Cambridge, and then suddenly he recounted the story of meeting
me and my mother for the first time, telling the guests about how
he had followed us that afternoon. The people who did not know

us laughed, amused by the description of the encounter, and by Pranab Kaku's desperation. He walked around the room to where my mother was sitting and draped a lanky arm around her shoulder, forcing her, for a brief moment, to stand up. "This woman," he declared, pulling her close to his side, "this woman hosted my first real Thanksgiving in America. It might have been an afternoon in May, but that first meal at Boudi's table was Thanksgiving to me. If it weren't for that meal, I would have gone back to Calcutta." My mother looked away, embarrassed. She was thirty-eight, already going gray, and she looked closer to my father's age than to Pranab Kaku's; regardless of his waistline, he retained his handsome, carefree looks. Pranab Kaku went back to his place at the head of the table, next to Deborah, and concluded, "And if that had been the case I'd have never met you, my darling," and he kissed her on the mouth in front of everyone, to much applause, as if it were their wedding day all over again.

After the turkey, smaller forks were distributed and orders were taken for three different kinds of pie, written on small pads by Deborah's sisters, as if they were waitresses. After dessert, the dogs needed to go out, and Pranab Kaku volunteered to take them. "How about a walk on the beach?" he suggested, and Deborah's side of the family agreed that that was an excellent idea. None of the Bengalis wanted to go, preferring to sit with their tea and cluster together, at last, at one end of the room, speaking freely after the forced chitchat with the Americans during the meal. Matty came over and sat in the chair beside me that was now empty, encouraging me to join the walk. When I hesitated, pointing to my inappropriate clothes and shoes but also aware of my mother's silent fury at the sight of us together, he said, "I'm sure Deb can lend you something." So I went upstairs, where Deborah gave me a pair of her jeans and a thick sweater and some sneakers, so that I looked like her and her sisters.

She sat on the edge of her bed, watching me change, as if we were girlfriends, and she asked if I had a boyfriend. When I told her no, she said, "Matty thinks you're cute."

"He told you?"

"No, but I can tell."

As I walked back downstairs, emboldened by this information, in the jeans I'd had to roll up and in which I felt finally like myself, I noticed my mother lift her eyes from her teacup and stare at me, but she said nothing, and off I went, with Pranab Kaku and his dogs and his in-laws, along a road and then down some steep wooden steps to the water. Deborah and one of her sisters stayed behind, to begin the cleanup and see to the needs of those who remained. Initially, we all walked together, in a single row across the sand, but then I noticed Matty hanging back, and so the two of us trailed behind, the distance between us and the others increasing. We began flirting, talking of things I no longer remember, and eventually we wandered into a rocky inlet and Matty fished a joint out of his pocket. We turned our backs to the wind and smoked it, our cold fingers touching in the process, our lips pressed to the same damp section of the rolling paper. At first I didn't feel any effect, but then, listening to him talk about the band he was in, I was aware that his voice sounded miles away, and that I had the urge to laugh, even though what he was saying was not terribly funny. It felt as if we were apart from the group for hours, but when we wandered back to the sand we could still see them, walking out onto a rocky promontory to watch the sun set. It was dark by the time we all headed back to the house, and I dreaded seeing my parents while I was still high. But when we got there Deborah told me that my parents, feeling tired, had left, agreeing to let someone drive me home later. A fire had been lit and I was told to relax and have more pie as the leftovers were put away and the living room slowly put back in order. Of course, it was Matty who drove me home, and sitting in my parents' driveway I kissed him, at once thrilled and terrified that my mother might walk onto the lawn in her nightgown and discover us. I gave Matty my phone number, and for a few weeks I thought of him constantly, and hoped foolishly that he would call.

In the end, my mother was right, and fourteen years after that Thanksgiving, after twenty-three years of marriage, Pranab Kaku and Deborah got divorced. It was he who had strayed, falling in love with a married Bengali woman, destroying two families in the process. The other woman was someone my parents knew, though not very well. Deborah was in her forties by then, Bonny and Sara away at college. In her shock and grief, it was my mother whom Deborah turned to, calling and weeping into the phone. Somehow, through all the years, she had continued to regard us as quasi in-laws, sending flowers when my grandparents died, and giving me a compact edition of the OED as a college-graduation present. "You knew him so well. How could he do something like this?" Deborah asked my mother. And then, "Did you know anything about it?" My mother answered truthfully that she did not. Their hearts had been broken by the same man, only my mother's had long ago mended, and in an odd way, as my parents approached their old age, she and my father had grown fond of each other, out of habit if nothing else. I believe my absence from the house, once I left for college, had something to do with this, because over the years, when I visited, I noticed a warmth between my parents that had not been there before, a quiet teasing, a solidarity, a concern when one of them fell ill. My mother and I had also made peace; she had accepted the fact that I was not only her daughter but a child of America as well. Slowly, she accepted that I dated one American man, and then another, and then yet another, that I slept with them, and even that I lived with one though we were not married. She welcomed my boyfriends into our home and when things didn't work out she told me I would find someone better. After years of being idle, she decided, when she turned fifty, to get a degree in library science at a nearby university.

On the phone, Deborah admitted something that surprised my mother: that all these years she had felt hopelessly shut out of a part of Pranab Kaku's life. "I was so horribly jealous of you back then, for knowing him, understanding him in a way I never could. He turned his back on his family, on all of you, really, but I still felt threatened. I could never get over that." She told my mother that she had tried, for years, to get Pranab Kaku to reconcile with his parents, and that she had also encouraged him to maintain ties with other Bengalis, but he had resisted. It had been Deborah's idea to invite us to their Thanksgiving; ironically, the other woman had been there, too. "I hope you don't blame me for taking him away from your lives, Boudi. I always worried that you did."

My mother assured Deborah that she blamed her for nothing. She confessed nothing to Deborah about her own jealousy of decades before, only that she was sorry for what had happened, that it was a sad and terrible thing for their family. She did not tell Deborah that a few weeks after Pranab Kaku's wedding, while I was at a Girl Scout meeting and my father was at work, she had gone through the house, gathering up all the safety pins that lurked in drawers and tins, and adding them to the few fastened to her bracelets. When she'd found enough, she pinned them to her sari one by one, attaching the front piece to the layer of material underneath, so that no one would be able to pull the garment off her body. Then she took a can of lighter fluid and a box of kitchen matches and stepped outside, into our chilly backyard, which was full of leaves needing to be raked. Over her sari she was wearing a knee-length lilac trench coat, and to any neighbor she must have looked as though she'd simply stepped out for some fresh air. She opened up the coat and removed the tip from the can of lighter fluid and doused herself, then buttoned and belted the coat. She walked over to the garbage barrel behind our house and disposed of the fluid, then returned to the middle of the yard with the box of matches in her coat pocket. For nearly an hour she stood there, looking at our house, trying to work up the courage to strike a match. It was not I who saved her, or my father, but our next-door neighbor, Mrs. Holcomb, with whom my mother had never been particularly friendly. She came out to rake the leaves in her yard, calling out to my mother and remarking how beautiful the sunset was. "I see you've been admiring it for a while now," she said. My mother agreed, and then she went back into the house. By the time my father and I came home in the early evening, she was in the kitchen boiling rice for our dinner, as if it were any other day.

My mother told Deborah none of this. It was to me that she confessed, after my own heart was broken by a man I'd hoped to marry.

■

At the Café Lovely

FROM *Zoetrope*

EVERY SO OFTEN I dream of my brother's face on fire, his brown eyes — eyes very much like my own — staring at me through a terrible mask of flames. I wake to the scent of burning flesh, his fiery face looming before me as an afterimage, and in that darkness I am eleven again. I have not yet learned to trespass. I have not yet learned to grieve. Nor have I learned to pity us — my brother, my mother, and me — and Anek and I are in Bangkok sitting on the roof of our mother's house smoking cigarettes, watching people drift by on their bicycles while the neighbors release their mangy dogs for the night to roam the city's streets.

It was a Saturday. Saturdays meant the city didn't burn the dump behind our house. We could breathe freely again. We wouldn't have to shut all the windows to keep out the stench, sleep in suffocating heat. Downstairs, we could hear Ma cooking in the outdoor kitchen, the clang of pots and pans, the warm smell of rice curling up toward us.

"Hey, kid," Anek said, stubbing his cigarette on the corrugated tin roof. "What's for dinner?" I sniffed the air. I had a keen sense of smell in those days. *Like a dog,* Anek told his friends once. *My little brother can smell your ma taking a crap on the other side of town.*

"Rice."

"Sure."

"Green beans. Fried egg."

"No meat?"

"No. I don't smell any meat."

"Oi." Anek threw a leaf over the edge of the roof. It hovered for a second before dropping swiftly to the street. "I'm tired of this. I'm tired of green beans."

Our father had been dead for four months. The insurance money from the factory was running out. There had been a malfunctioning crane and a crate the size of our house full of little wooden toys waiting to be sent to the children of America. Not a very large crate when I think about the size of the house, but big enough to kill a man when the crate fell on him from a height of ten meters. At the funeral, I was surprised by how little sadness I felt, as if it wasn't our father laid out before the mourners at all — wasn't him lying there in that rubberwood box, wasn't his body popping and crackling in the temple furnace like kindling — but a striking replica of our father in a state of rest. Pa had taken us to the wax museum once, and I remember thinking that he had somehow commissioned the museum to make a beautiful replica of himself and would be appearing any minute now at his own funeral.

After the cremation, we went with Ma to scatter the ashes at Pak Nam. We rode a small six-seater boat out to where the brown river emptied into the green sea. We leaned over the side — all three of us tipping the tiny tin urn together — while Ma tried to mutter a prayer through her tears.

Anek lit another cigarette.

"Are you going out tonight?" I asked.

"Yeah."

"Can I come with?"

"I don't think so."

"But you said last time —"

"Stop whining. I know what I said last time. I said I might. I said maybe. I made no promises, kid. I told you no lies. Last I checked, 'maybe' didn't mean 'yes.'"

A month before, for my birthday, Anek had taken me to the new American fast-food place at Sogo Mall. I was happy that day. I had dreamed all week of hamburgers and French fries and a nice cold soda and the air-conditioning of the place. During the ride to the mall, my arms wrapped around my brother's waist, the motorcycle sputtering under us, I imagined sitting at one of those shiny plastic tables across from my brother. We would look like those university students I had seen through the floor-to-ceiling windows, the ones who laughed and sipped at their sodas. Afterward, we would walk into the summer sun with soft-serve sundaes, my brother's arm around my shoulder.

The place was packed, full of students and families clamoring for a taste of American fast food. All around us, people hungrily devoured their meals. I could smell beef cooking on the grill, hear peanut oil bubbling in the deep fryers. I stared at the illuminated menu above the counter.

"What should I get, Anek?"

"Don't worry, kid. I know just what you'd like."

We waited in line, ordered at the counter, took our tray to an empty booth. Anek said he wasn't hungry, but I knew he had only enough money to order for me: a small burger and some fries. I decided not to ask him about it. I wasn't going to piss him off, what with it being my birthday and what with people being so touchy about money ever since Pa died. As we walked to the booth, I told Anek we could share the meal, I probably wouldn't be able to finish it all myself anyway.

Even though he had been telling me all month about how delicious and great the place was, my brother looked a little uncomfortable. He kept glancing around nervously. It occurred to me then that it was probably his first time there as well. We had on our best clothes that day — Anek in his blue jeans and white polo shirt, me in my khakis and red button-down — but even then I knew our clothes couldn't compare to the other kids' clothes. Their clothes had been bought in the mall; ours had been bought at the weekend bazaar and were cheap imitations of what they wore.

Anek stared across the table at me. He smiled. He tousled my hair. "Happy birthday, kid. Eat up."

"Thanks, Anek."

I unwrapped the burger. I peeked under the bun at the gray meat, the limp green pickles, the swirl of yellow mustard and red ketchup. Anek stared out the window at the road in front of the

mall. For some reason, I suddenly felt like I should eat as quickly
as possible so we could get the hell out of there. I didn't feel so excited anymore. And I noticed that the place smelled strange — a
scent I'd never encountered before — a bit rancid, like palaa fish
left too long in the sun. Later, I would find out it was cheese.

I took a few apprehensive bites at the bun. I bit into the brittle
meat. I chewed and I chewed and I chewed and finally swallowed,
the thick mass inching slowly down my throat. I took another bite.
Then I felt my stomach shoot up to my throat like one of those bottle rockets Anek and I used to set off in front of Apae's convenience store just to piss him off. I remember thinking, *Oh fuck, oh
fuck, please no,* but before I could take a deep breath to settle
things, it all came rushing out of me. I threw up all over that shiny
American linoleum floor.

A hush fell over the place, followed by a smattering of giggles.

"Oh, you fucking pussy," Anek hissed.

"I'm sorry, Anek."

"You goddamn, motherfucking, monkey-cock-sucking piece of
low-class *pussy.*"

I wiped my lips with my forearm. Anek pulled me to my feet,
led me out through the glass double doors, his hand on my collar.
I tried to say sorry again, but before I could mouth the words my
heart felt like it might explode and — just as we cleared the doors
— I sent a stream of gray-green vomit splashing against the hot
concrete.

"Oh. My. Fucking. Lord. Why?" Anek moaned, lifting his face to
the sky. "Oh why, Lord? Why hast thou forsaken me?" Anek and I
had been watching a lot of Christian movies on TV lately.

When we came to a traffic stop an hour later, I was leaning
against my brother's back, still feeling ill, thick traffic smoke whipping around us. Anek turned to me and said: "That's the first and
last time, kid. I can't believe you. All that money for a bunch of
puke. No more fucking hamburgers for you."

We finished watching the sun set over the neighborhood, a pano-
ply of red and orange and purple and blue. Anek told me that
Bangkok sunsets were the most beautiful sunsets in the world.

"It's the pollution," he said. "Brings out the colors in the sky." Then after Anek and I smoked the last of the cigarettes, we climbed down from the roof.

At dinner, as usual, we barely said a word to each other. Ma had been saying less and less ever since that crate of toys killed our father. She was all headshakes and nods, headshakes and nods. We picked at our green beans, slathered fish sauce on our rice.

"Thanks for the meal, Ma."

Ma nodded.

"Yeah, Ma, this is delicious."

She nodded again.

Besides the silence, Ma's cooking was also getting worse, but we couldn't bring ourselves to say anything about it. What's more, she had perfected the art of moving silently through the house. She seemed an apparition in those days. She'd retreated into herself. She no longer watched over us. She simply watched. I'd be doodling in my book at the kitchen table and all of a sudden Ma would just be sitting there, watching me with her chin in one hand. Or Anek and I would be horsing around in the outdoor kitchen after dinner, throwing buckets of dirty dishwater on each other, and we'd look over our shoulders to find Ma standing against the crumbling concrete siding of the house. Anek told me she caught him masturbating in the bathroom once. He didn't even realize she had opened the door until he heard it shut, a loud slam so he could know that she'd seen him. Anek didn't masturbate for weeks after that and neither did I.

One night I caught Ma staring at her own image in the bedroom mirror with an astonished look on her face, as if she no longer recognized her own sallow reflection. It seemed Pa's death had made our mother a curious spectator of her own life, though when I think of her now I wonder if she was simply waiting for us to notice her grief. But we were just children, Anek and I, and when children learn to acknowledge the gravity of their loved ones' sorrows they're no longer children.

"That woman needs help," Anek said, after we washed the dishes that evening.

"She's just sad, Anek."

"Listen, kid, I'm sad too, OK? Do you see me walking around like a mute though? Do you see me sneaking around the house like I'm some fucking ninja?"

I dropped it. I didn't feel like talking about the state of things that night, not with Anek. I knew he would get angry if we talked about Pa, if we talked about his death, if we talked about what it was doing to Ma. I never knew what to do with my brother's anger in those days. I simply and desperately needed his love.

I think Anek felt bad about the hamburger incident because he started giving me lessons on the motorcycle, an old 350cc Honda our father had ridden to the factory every morning. After Pa died, Ma wanted to sell the bike, but Anek convinced her not to. He told her the bike wasn't worth much. He claimed it needed too many repairs. But I knew that aside from some superficial damage — chipped paint, an ugly crack in the rear mudguard, rusted-through places in the exhaust pipe — the bike was in fine working condition. Anek wanted the bike for himself. He'd been complaining all year about being the only one among his friends without a bike. We'd spent countless hours at the mall showroom, my brother wandering among the gleaming new bikes while I trailed behind him absentmindedly. And though I thought then that my brother had lied to my mother about the bike out of selfishness, I know now that Pa did not leave us much. That Honda was Anek's inheritance.

He'd kick-start it for me — I didn't have the strength to do it myself — and I'd hop on in front and ride slowly through the neighborhood with Anek behind me.

"I'll kill you, you little shit. I'll kill you if you break my bike," he'd yell when I approached a turn too fast or when I had trouble steadying the handlebars after coming out of one. "I'm gonna nail you to a fucking cross like Jesus-fucking-Christ himself."

My feet barely reached the gear pedal, but I'd learned, within a week, to shift into second by sliding off the seat. I'd accelerate out of first, snap the clutch, slide off the seat just so, then pop the gear into place. We'd putter by the city dump at twenty, twenty-five kilos an hour, and some of the *dek khaya*, the garbage children whose families lived in shanties on the dump, would race alongside us, urging me to go faster, asking Anek if they could ride too.

I began to understand the way Anek had eyed those showroom bikes. I began to get a taste for speed.

"That's as fast as I'm letting you go," Anek once said when we got home. "Second gear's good enough for now."

"But I can do it, Anek. I can do it."

"Get taller, kid. Get stronger."

"C'mon, Anek. Please. Second is so slow. It's stupid."

"I'll tell you what's stupid, little brother. What's stupid is you're eleven years old. What's stupid is you go into turns like a drunkard. What's stupid is you can't even reach the gear pedal. Grow, kid. Give me twenty more centimeters. Then maybe we'll talk about letting you do third. Maybe."

"Why can't I come?"

"Because you can't, that's why."

"But you said last week —"

"I already told you, vomit-boy. I know what I said last week. I said maybe. Which part of that didn't you understand? I didn't say, 'Oh yes! Of course, buddy! I love you so much! You're my super pal! I'd love to take you out next Saturday!' now did I?"

"Just this once, Anek. I promise I won't bother you."

"I don't think so."

"Please?"

"Please nothing, little brother. Sit at home and watch a soap with Ma or something."

"But why, Anek? Why can't I go with you?"

"Because I'm going where grown men go, that's why. Because last I checked, last time I saw you naked, you were far from being grown."

"I promise I won't bother you, Anek. I'll just sit in a corner or something. Really. I promise. I'll stay out of your way. Just don't leave me here with Ma tonight."

When we were young, our mother would put on her perfume every evening before Pa came home. She would smell like jasmine, fresh picked off a tree. Pa, he would smell of the cologne he dabbed on after he got out of the shower. Although I would never smell the ocean until we went out to Pak Nam to scatter his ashes, I knew that my father smelled like the sea. I just knew it. Anek and I would sit between them, watching some soap opera on TV, and I would inhale their scents, the scents of my parents, and imagine millions of tiny white flowers floating on the surface of a wide and green and bottomless ocean.

But those scents are lost to me now, and I've often wondered if, in my belated sorrow, with all my tardy regrets, I've imagined them all these years.

Anek finally gave in and took me. We rode out to Minburi District along the new speedway, the engine squealing beneath us. We were going so fast that my face felt stretched impossibly tight. I wanted to tell Anek to slow down but I remembered that I had promised to stay out of his way.

We were wearing our best clothes again that night, the same old outfits: Anek in his blue jeans and white polo shirt, me in my khakis and red button-down. When we walked out of the house Ma glanced up from the TV with a look that said, *What are you all dressed up for?*, and Anek told her he was taking me out to the new ice-skating rink, he heard it was all the rage. I even said, "Imagine that, Ma. Ice-skating in Bangkok," but she just nodded, her lips a straight thin line, and went back to watching television.

"*Imagine that, Ma . . .*" Anek teased when we walked out.

"Eat shit, Anek."

"Whoa there. Be careful, little one. Don't make me change my mind."

When we arrived at the place, it was not what I had imagined at all. I expected mirror balls and multicolored lights and loud American music and hundreds of people dancing inside — like places I'd seen in the district west of our neighborhood, places all the *farangs* frequented at night. It didn't look like that. It was only a shophouse, like the thousands of tiny two-story shophouses all over the city — short and common, square and concrete, in need of a new paint job. A pink neon sign blinked in the tinted window.

CAFÉ LOVELY, it said in English. I could hear the soft, muffled sounds of upcountry music reaching across the street.

"This is it?"

"I can take you home," Anek said. "That's not a problem."

The place smelled of mothballs. There was an old jukebox in the corner. A couple of girls in miniskirts and tanktops and heavy makeup danced and swayed with two balding, middle-aged local men. The men looked awkward with those girls in their arms, feet moving out of time, their large hands gripping slender waists. In a dark corner, more girls were seated at a table, laughing. They sounded like a flock of excited birds. I'd never seen so many girls in my life.

Three of Anek's friends were already at a table.

"What's with the babysitting?" one of them asked, grinning.

"Sorry," Anek said sheepishly as we sat down. "Couldn't bear to leave him home with my crazy ma."

"You hungry, kid?" said another. "Want a hamburger?"

"No, thanks."

"Hey," Anek said. "Leave him alone. Let's just pretend he's not here."

The song ended. I saw one of the girls go up a set of stairs at the back, leading one of the men by the hand. I didn't even have to ask. I wondered if Anek, too, would be going up those stairs at the end of the night. And although I had been disappointed at first by the café's shoddy façade, I found myself excited now by its possibilities.

Anek must've seen me staring because he slapped me hard across the back of the head. "Ow," I cried, rubbing my head with a palm. "That fucking hurt."

"Keep your eyes to yourself, little man."

"That's right," one of his friends intoned, the one who'd asked me if I wanted a hamburger. "Be careful what you wish for, boy. The AIDS might eat your dick."

"Not before it eats your mom's, though," I replied, and they all laughed, even my brother, Anek, who said, "Awesome," and smiled at me for the first time all evening.

*

Anek had come home one night when I was nine and told me that Pa had taken him out for his fifteenth birthday. The city dump was burning; there was a light red glow in the sky from the pyre. Even though our windows were shut, I could still smell the putrid scent of tires and plastic and garbage burning, the sour odor seeping through our windows. I was sleeping in my underwear, two fans turned on high, both fixed in my direction. Anek walked into the room, stripped down to his underwear, and thrust out his hand.

"Bet you can't tell me what this smell is."

I sniffed his fingers. It smelled like *awsuan:* oysters simmered in egg yolk. But somehow I knew it wasn't food.

"What is it?"

Anek chuckled.

"What is it, Anek?"

"That, my dear brother, is the smell of" — he put his hand up to his face, sniffed it hungrily — "heaven."

I blinked at him.

"A woman, kid. You know what that is? Pa took me to a *sophaeni* tonight. And let me tell you, little one, when he takes you for *your* fifteenth birthday, you'll never be the same again. This scent" — he raised his hand to his face again — "it'll change your fucking life."

Anek and his friends had already poured themselves a few drinks while I sat there sipping my cola — half listening to their banter, half watching the girls across the room — when one of Anek's friends stood up and said: "It's getting to that time of night, guys."

I didn't know what the hell was going on, I just thought he was a funny drunk, but then Anek got up and told the bartender we were going outside for a breath of fresh air. One of the girls came up to us, put a hand on Anek's shoulder, and said, "Leaving so soon?" but Anek told her not to worry, to be patient, he'd be back to give her what she wanted. The girl winked at me and said, "Who's the handsome little boy?" and I smiled back, but Anek had to be an asshole, so he said, "Oh, that's my virgin brother," which annoyed me because no girl had ever winked at me before and I thought she was beautiful.

I followed Anek and his friends out of the Café Lovely and into a small alley off the shophouse row. Anek didn't want to leave me by myself. He said it didn't look good — leaving a little boy alone in a place like that — but I could tell that he didn't want me to come either. As we cut into the dark alley, I had a feeling that a breath of fresh air was the last thing we were going to get.

When we stopped, one of Anek's friends pulled out a small container of paint thinner from a plastic bag. "All right," he said, prying at the lid with a small pocketknife. The lid flew open with a loud pop and rolled down the dark alley, swirling to a stop by a dumpster. I saw the quick shadows of roaches scattering in its wake. That's what the alley smelled like — roaches: dank and humid like the back room where Ma put away our father's belongings. Anek's friend poured half the can into the plastic bag, the liquid thick and translucent, the bag sagging from the weight, while the others flicked their cigarettes into the sewer ditch along the side of the alley. The thinner gave off a sharp, strong odor, punched little pinpricks in my nostrils, and reminded me of days when Pa and Anek used to fumigate the house. Anek's friend pulled out another plastic bag from his back pocket and put the first bag with the thinner inside it.

"OK." He held out the double bag with one hand, offering it to his friends, the way I'd seen butchers at the market holding dead chickens by the necks. I could hear the jukebox starting up again in the café, another old upcountry tune echoing softly down the alley. "Who's first?"

For a second, they all stood with their hands in their pockets. Then Anek reached out and took the bag with a quick, impatient gesture.

"Let's just get this over with," he said. "I tell you guys, though, one hit and I'm done. I don't like having my little brother around this shit."

I realized then what they were doing. I knew what huffers were, but I'd always imagined little kids and strung-out homeless guys in the Klong Toey slum with their heads buried in pots of rubber cement. I suddenly became very afraid — I wanted to grab the bag out of my brother's hands — even as I longed to watch Anek do it, wanted, in fact, to do it myself, to show Anek and his friends my indifference.

Anek brought the mouth of the bag to his chin. He took a big, deep breath, pulled his entire body back like it was a slingshot, then blew into the bag, inflating it like a balloon, the loose ends covering half his face, and it made a sound like a quick wind blowing through a sail. The bag grew larger and larger and I was afraid that it might burst, that the thinner would go flying everywhere. Anek looked at me the whole time he blew, his eyes growing wider and wider. He kept blowing and blowing and blowing, and I knew that my brother was blowing for a long time because one of the guys said, "Fucking inhale already, Anek," but he kept on blowing and blowing and all that time he kept looking at me with those eyes about to pop out of his head. I don't know what he was trying to tell me then, looking at me like that, but I remember noticing for the first time that he had our mother's eyes. He finally inhaled, sucked his breath back into his chest, the plastic balloon collapsing in on itself, and then my brother was blinking hard, teetering, like a boxer stunned by a swift and surprising blow, and I knew that whatever it was he had smelled, whatever scent he had just inhaled, it was knocking him off his feet. He handed the bag to one of the other guys and said, "C'mon, kid, let's get out of here," and I followed my brother out of the dark alley, back into the dimly lit street.

Years later, I'd be in a different alley with friends of my own, and one of the guys, high off a can of spray paint, would absentmindedly light a cigarette after taking a hit and his face would burst into a sheet of blue flames. He ran around the alley wild with panic, running into the sides of the buildings, stumbling and falling and getting back to his feet again, hands flying violently around his burning face as if trying to beat back a swarm of attacking insects. He never made a sound, just ran around that alley with his face on fire, the flames catching in his hair and his clothes, looking like some giant ignited match in the shape of a man. For a second, we couldn't quite comprehend what was happening — some of us laughed, most of us were just stunned — before I managed to chase the boy down, tackle him to the ground, and beat out the flames from his face with my T-shirt. His eyes were wild with terror and we just stared at each other for a moment before he started to weep hysterically, his body shaking under mine, the terrible scent of burnt flesh and singed hair filling the alley. His lashes and eyebrows had been burned cleanly off his face. His eyelids were raw, pink. His face began to swell immediately, large white welts blooming here and there. And he just kept on crying beneath me, calling for his mother and father, blubbering incoherently in the high, desperate voice of a child.

Back at the café, I could tell that the thinner was setting in. Anek kept tilting back in his seat, dilating his eyes. He took a long swig of his rye, poured himself another. I knew we wouldn't be going home for a while. The same girl who had winked at me earlier walked across the room and sat down at our table. She put her arm around my shoulder. I felt my body tense. She smelled like menthol, like the prickly-heat powder Anek and I sprinkled on ourselves to keep cool at night.

"Hi, handsome."

"Hi."

I sipped at the last of my cola. Across the room, I noticed the girls looking our way, giggling.

"That's my brother," Anek drawled.

"I know, Anek."

"He's a little high," I laughed.

"Looks like it."

"Yeah." Anek smiled, slow and lazy. "Just a little."

"Where are the rest?" she asked me.

"Outside."

"What about you, handsome? Are you high?"

"No."

"Ever been?"

"Yeah. Of course. Plenty of times."

She laughed, threw her head far back. Menthol. I felt my heart pounding in my chest. I wanted to smear her carmine lips with my hands. I reached across the table for Anek's Krong Thips and lit one.

"You're adorable," she said, pinching one of my cheeks. I felt myself blush. "But you shouldn't be smoking those things at your age."

"I know," I said, smiling at her, taking a drag. "Cigarettes are bad."

"C'mon," Anek said, getting up abruptly, swaying a little bit. He reached out and grabbed her hand from my shoulder. "C'mon." He nodded toward the staircase. "Let's go."

She stood up, her hand dangling in my brother's, while I sat between them.

"What about the kid?" she asked, looking down at me.

"Oh, he'll be fine."

"Maybe not tonight, Anek. We shouldn't leave the kid by himself."

"Hey, barfboy," Anek said. "You gonna be OK?"

I looked up at my brother. He still had the girl's hand in his own. I took a long drag of my cigarette.

"Yeah. I'll be fine, Anek. I'm not a kid anymore."

Anek smiled as if he found me amusing. I wanted to wipe the smile off his face. I felt angry. I didn't want to be abandoned. Anek must've sensed this because there suddenly seemed something sad about my brother's smile. He dropped the girl's hand. He reached out and tapped me lightly on the head.

"OK, kid. You don't have to be so tough all the time," he said finally. He took a deep breath, his voice a little steadier, his eyes a little wider. "Tell you what. I'm just gonna go put some music in the jukebox. Then Nong and I are gonna dance. Then we're gonna go upstairs for a while. Just a short while. We won't be long. I promise. Then, if you want, we'll go home, OK?" But I just took another drag of my cigarette, watched the girls in the corner, tried not to meet my brother's eyes.

She led him out to the dance floor. They stood by the jukebox and he slipped a few coins into the machine, steadying himself with one hand. A record came on, the sound of high Isan flutes and xylophones and a hand drum striking up the first few bars. Anek clumsily took one of the girl's hands, hooked an arm around her waist, and they started moving to the music. They stood close, their chins on each other's shoulders, though perhaps a little too close for the girl, because she leaned away from my brother a few times. But then again, maybe it was because my brother was high, drunk, and they kept losing their balance. They didn't look like dancers at all after a while; they looked like they were just holding each other up, falling into and out of each other's body.

I hadn't recognized the tune at first — I thought it was just another generic upcountry ballad — but then a woman's falsetto came soaring over the instruments and I remembered that it was an old record of Ma's, something she and Pa used to listen to in the early afternoon hours before the endlessly growing mass of garbage burned behind our house. Those days curry and fish in tamarind sauce would be cooking on the stove, the aroma wafting into the house, and I swear that right then, listening to that music, I could smell it on the tip of my nose.

Oh beloved, so sad was my departure . . .

I looked at Anek and the girl. She couldn't have been more than sixteen years old — younger than my brother — but it seemed clear to me now that she was the one holding him up, directing his course, leading him. I wondered how many men she had already held up tonight, how many more she would hold in the thousands of nights before her. I wondered whether she was already finding the force of their weight unbearable. I wondered whether I would be adding my weight to that mass one day. She held him close now and he pulled away, fell out of sync, though they continued to move across the floor as slowly and languorously as the music in the café.

. . . I am tired, I am broken, I am lost . . .

When the song ended, they pulled away from each other, and Anek took the girl by the hand and led her toward the staircase. As they began to mount the stairs, the girl said something to my brother and they both stopped to look back at me. My brother smiled weakly then, raised a hand in my direction. I looked away, pretended not to see the gesture, stirring the ash in the tray with my cigarette. When I looked back they were gone.

The place fell silent. A balding, middle-aged man walked down the stairs. He made for the door, his steps quick and certain, as if he couldn't wait to leave. When he passed by my table, I caught a whiff of him, and his scent lingered on my nostrils for a while. He smelled like okra.

I stood up. I don't know why I walked toward that staircase. Perhaps it was childish curiosity. Or perhaps I wanted to see, once and for all, what secrets, what sins, what comforts those stairs led one to. Or perhaps I wanted to retrieve Anek before he did whatever it was I thought he might do.

I had imagined darkness and was surprised, when I arrived at the top of the stairs, to find a brightly lit hallway flanked on both sides by closed doors. The corridor smelled sweet, sickly, as if it had been perfumed to cover up some stench. The bare walls gleamed under the buzzing fluorescent fixtures. I heard another song start up downstairs, laughter again from the table of girls. I walked slowly down the hallway, the noises downstairs faded to a murmur. I felt like I had surfaced into another world and left those distant, muffled sounds beneath me, underwater. As I crept along, careful to be silent, I began to hear a chorus of ghostly, guttural groans coming from behind the doors. I heard a man whimper; I heard another cry out incoherently. After a while, those rooms seemed — with their grunting and moaning — like torture chambers in which faceless men suffered untold cruelties. I wondered if my brother was making any of these noises. I thought of the video Anek had borrowed from one of his friends, the women in them cooing and squealing perversely, and how strange it was now that none of the women could be heard. Instead, I could hear only the men growling away as if in some terrible, solitary animal pain. I imagined the men writhing against the women, and I wondered how these women — those girls sitting downstairs — could possibly endure in such silence.

Just as I turned the corner, a hand grabbed me by the collar, choking me. I was certain, for a moment, that I would now be dragged into one of the rooms and made to join that chorus of howling men.

"Little boy," a voice hissed in my ear. "Where do you think you're going?"

It was the bartender from downstairs. He looked down at me, brow furrowed, beads of spittle glistening at the corners of his lips. I smelled whiskey on his breath, felt his large, chapped hands on my neck as he pulled me toward him and lifted me off the concrete floor.

"You're in the wrong place," he whispered into my ear, while I struggled against his grip. "I should kill you for being up here. I should snap your head right off your fucking neck."

I screamed for Anek then. I sent my brother's name echoing down that empty hallway. I screamed his name over and over again as the bartender lifted me up into his thick, ropey arms. The more I struggled against the bartender, the more dire my predicament seemed, and I cried out for my brother as I had never cried out before. The men seemed to stop their moaning then and, for a moment, I felt as if my cries were the only sound in the world. I saw a few doors open, a couple of women sticking out their heads to look at the commotion. The bartender walked backward with me, toward the staircase, as I kicked and struggled against his suffocating embrace.

Then, I saw my brother hobbling in his underwear, his blue jeans shackling his feet.

"Hey!" Anek yelled, staggering, bending down to gather up his jeans. "Hey!" The man stopped, loosened his grip on my body. "Hey!" Anek yelled again, getting closer now. "That's my little brother, you cocksucker. Put him down."

The bartender still had me, his breath hot on my neck. As Anek struggled to pull up his jeans I glimpsed the purple, bulbous head of his penis peeking over the waistband of his underwear. The bartender must've seen this too; he began to chuckle obscenely.

"Get him out of here, Anek," he said. Anek nodded grimly. The bartender put me down, shoved me lightly toward my brother. "You know I can't have him up here," he said.

"You OK, kid?" Anek asked, breathless, ignoring the bartender, bending down to look me in the eyes. I saw the girl standing in the hallway behind Anek, a towel wrapped loosely around her small body. She waved at me, smiling, and then walked back into the room. The other women disappeared as well. I heard the bartender going downstairs, the steps creaking under his weight. Soon, Anek and I were the only people left in that hallway, and for some reason — despite my attempts to steel myself — I began to cry. I tried to apologize to my brother through the tears.

"Oh shit," my brother muttered, pulling me to his chest. "C'mon, kid," he said. "Let's just go home."

We went to the bathroom. I stood sniveling by a urinal while Anek leaned over a sink and dashed water on his face. When we came back out, his steps were no longer unsteady, though his voice still quavered slightly. Beads of water glistened on his face. He lit a cigarette at the door and waved to the bartender and the girls in the corner. I couldn't look at them now.

We stepped into the street. His friends were still in the alley, laughing and stumbling, flinging pieces of garbage from the dumpster at each other. We stood at the mouth of the alley and Anek said, "See you later, boys," and one of them yelled back saying, "Wait, Anek! Wait! I have an idea! Let's put your kid brother in the dump!" But Anek just put an arm around my shoulder and said, "Maybe next time."

We crossed the street. Anek kick-started the motorcycle. It sputtered and wheezed and coughed before settling into a soft, persistent purr. I started to climb onto the back, but Anek said, "What the hell are you doing? Can't you see I'm in no shape to take us home?"

"You can't be serious, Anek."

"Serious as our pa is dead, kid."

I stood there for a moment, dumbfounded. I climbed onto the front seat.

"I swear to God, though, you make so much as a dent on my bike and I'll —"

But I had already cocked the accelerator and we were on our

way. Slowly, of course. I slipped off the seat a little so I could reach the pedal, snapped the clutch with my left hand, and popped the bike into second gear. We sputtered for a while like that along the streets of Minburi, crawling at fifteen kilos, and I made a sharp right onto the bridge that would take us out to the new speedway.

Years later, I would ask Anek if he remembered this night. He would say that I made it up. He never would've taken me to the Café Lovely at such a young age, he'd say, never would've let me drive that bike home. He denies it now because he doesn't want to feel responsible for the way things turned out, for the way we abandoned our mother to that hot and empty house, for the thoughtless, desperate things I would learn to do. Later that same year, my mother would wake me up in the middle of the night. She would be crying. She would ask me to sleep again in her bed. And, for the first time, I would refuse her. I would deny Ma the comfort of my body.

After Anek moved to an apartment across the river in Thonburi, I gathered my father's belongings from the back room and pawned them while Ma was at work. I used the money to buy myself a motorcycle. When I got home, my mother was waiting for me. She came at me with a thousand impotent fists, and when she was finished, spent and exhausted, her small body quivering in my arms, she asked me to leave her house. I did. And I did not return to that house again until it was too late, until Anek called to say our mother was ill, that she wanted us by her side to accompany her through her final hours.

That night, as we rode back from the Café Lovely, I felt my brother's arms around my waist, his head slumped on my shoulder. I remember thinking then about how I'd never felt the weight of my brother's head before. His hot, measured breaths warmed my neck. I could still smell the thinner's faint, sour scent wafting from his face. I suddenly became afraid that Anek had fallen asleep and would tumble off the bike at any moment.

"Are you awake, Anek?"

"Yeah, I'm awake."

"Good."

"Do me a favor. Eyes on the road."

"I'm glad you're awake, Anek."

"Third."

"What's that?"

"I said third."

"You sure?"

"It's a one-time offer, little man."

I slipped off the seat, accelerated a little, squeezed the clutch, and tapped the gear pedal just as we hit the speedway. I was so excited we might as well have broken the sound barrier, but the engine jolted us forward just enough that my grip weakened and we went swerving along the empty speedway, weaving wildly back and forth at thirty kilometers an hour.

"Easy now. Easy. There, there, you have it. Just take a deep breath now. Holy shit, I almost had to break your ass back there. You almost had us kissing the pavement."

I could feel the palms of my hands slick against the handle grips. Even at thirty kilos, the wind blew hot against our faces.

"Accelerate," Anek said.

"No fucking way."

"I said accelerate. This is a speedway, you know. Not a slow-way. I'd like to get home before dawn."

"You're out of your mind, Anek. That's the thinner talking."

"Listen, if you won't do it, I'll do it myself," he said, reaching over me for the throttle.

"Fine," I said, brushing his hand away. "I'll do it. Just give me a second."

We slowly gathered speed along the empty highway — thirty-five, forty, forty-five — and after a while, the concrete moving swiftly and steadily below our feet, I was beginning to feel a little more comfortable. Anek put his arms around my waist again, his chin still on my shoulder.

"Good," he whispered into my ear. "Good, good. You've got it. You're fucking doing it. You're really coasting now, boy. Welcome to the third gear, my little man.

"Now," he said. "Try fourth."

I didn't argue this time. I just twisted the accelerator some more, popped the bike into fourth, sliding smoothly off the seat then quickly back on. This time, to my surprise, our course didn't even waver. It was an easy transition. We were cruising comfortably now at sixty, sixty-five, seventy, seventy-five, faster and faster and faster still, the engine singing a high note beneath us as we flew along that straight and empty speedway. We didn't say a word to each other the rest of the way. And nothing seemed lovelier to me than that hot wind howling in my ears, the night blurring around us, the smell of the engine furiously burning gasoline.

MOLLY MCNETT

■

Catalogue Sales

FROM *New England Review*

OUR PARENTS DIVORCED when I was nine and my sister Amy was eleven. That was the year that Amy and I moved to town with my mom, and spent weekends with my dad in our old house in the country. While we were there, he would sometimes go out to do chores or errands or something, and I used that time to snoop around. At first, I found only a few things that I'd never noticed when we lived there full-time. There was an enema two-pack in the bathroom, with only one of the two left. And the bedroom closet that used to be my mom's was entirely full of Angel Soft toilet tissue, all the way up to the bar you were supposed to hang clothes on. That was funny to look at, but, since my dad was a notorious cheapskate, not mysterious or anything.

Then one day I looked through his roll-top desk and found a U.S. passport. This was strange for a couple of reasons. First, it was hard to imagine my dad going to another country. His brother Ron had been a foreign exchange student back when they were in high school, and my dad always said, "Ron means well, but he don't have a brain in his skull." Uncle Ron had wanted to go to Europe, but he got sent to Africa instead and came back weighing a hundred-thirty, which is actually not very much for a tall person. My dad would bring that up at Thanksgiving, and Uncle Ron would say, "Well, it was something different, anyway," and Dad would repeat, "Something different," and roll his eyes at us.

Also, there was the money. According to Amy, it was why our parents divorced. Before the divorce, my dad used to own a farm. Now someone else owned it, and he cash-rented from that person. My mom used to own the Little Dancers' Studio in town, and now she just taught there, so it was kind of the same thing, except that my mom liked to spend money. My dad didn't. You wouldn't think of my dad going on vacation, unless it was a place you could camp and maybe catch your own fish.

I had the feeling if I kept snooping I'd find something else, and pretty soon I did: a phone bill, stuffed between some papers on his roll-top desk.

"Two hundred sixty-two dollars. That's a lot for long distance, right?" Amy was in the kitchen making frosting, which was always the first thing she did when she was unsupervised. She liked to eat it straight from the bowl.

Underneath the phone bill was a Farm and Fleet sale flyer. "Huffy bikes for sixty-five dollars," I yelled to Amy. "Roller-blades, forty-eight."

"That's too expensive," she said. "You can get them for forty some places."

"Which can you get for forty? The bikes?"

Under the sale flyer was a softcover catalogue with a row of black-and-white pictures on it. It looked like a junior high yearbook. It was folded back to one page, and a few pictures were circled in red pen.

"#45902 Cherry," it said under one picture. "Age: 19. I am pleasant friendly I enjoy cooking dancing and singing in a band. Seeking marriage with family values man and loving with responsibility."

I looked at the phone bill again. Two calls on the bill to Manila, the Philippines.

"Dad's going to the Philippines," I yelled.

Amy ran into the room and we started flipping through the catalogue. There was more than one woman circled. Some had their hair pinned up with flowers on one side.

Amy grabbed the magazine.

"I had it first."

"Stop, Vicki, it'll rip." I let go and read over her shoulder. Some of the descriptions said the girls liked to cook or clean house. The word *pleasant* was in two of the ads my dad had circled. I thought about that. My mom was many things but she wasn't really pleasant. On some days it seemed to me that she argued with almost everything anyone said. The girls my dad had circled were nineteen, eighteen, and twenty-three.

"How old's Dad?" I asked.

"Forty-six." Amy was turning the pages fast so that I could read only part of the entries. I saw a girl who looked about my age, wearing a plaid skirt with some kind of sweatpants under it instead of tights and a striped top that looked like a tennis uniform. Her hair was long and tangled. She was missing a tooth in front, but her smile was wide and proud, as if she considered this a good feature. "Looking for some companion to write letters," it said.

"Wait," I said. "That one wants a pen pal." I liked the idea of a foreign pen pal. If I wrote to this one, I would ask why she wore sweatpants under her skirt and why she didn't match a solid color with the plaid, instead of stripes. Was it the fashion there?

"You think you can get a pen pal from the same place Dad is getting a girlfriend?"

"No," I said, though I wasn't sure why I couldn't.

We replaced the roll-top desk the way we found it, with the phone bill and catalogue between the junk mail. Then we went outside to feed the horses. My mom and dad used to ride together but not anymore, so the horses just grazed all summer and got very fat. Lately their manes always had burrs in them. We tried to throw at the same time so they wouldn't fight but it never worked. The brown horse would follow the black from one pile to the other, pushing him away. The black horse hardly got to eat, but neither did the brown one, he was so busy defending both the piles. Amy and I stood there watching them, thinking about our dad and the catalogue and wondering exactly what to make of it.

"Maybe he wants to do something different," said Amy.

The family Uncle Ron had stayed with in Africa ate only balls of raw dough and they all washed with just one sponge. One of these reasons was why he got worms. After Uncle Ron got home the father of the family kept writing letters, asking Ron to send him a car. Every Christmas my dad would read Uncle Ron's Christmas cards out loud until he got to the one that said "Joyous Noel! I am still awaiting my car!" Everybody would laugh and laugh. When I first heard this I was pretty little, and I pictured Uncle Ron putting stamps over the windshield of his car and parking it on a street corner next to the out-of-town mailbox. I thought you would have to cover the whole windshield, maybe the entire car with stamps. But he actually never sent it.

We went inside and finished the frosting and then drank some water, because eating straight frosting makes you very thirsty, and all that time we tried to think about how we could get more information about the catalogue and the pictures and whether we should say anything, and Amy decided that we should just ask my dad when he got back.

So that is what she did, just like that, and he told us: He had already gone to the Philippines. If we had done a better job of snooping we would have seen the stamp on his passport. Then he cleared his throat and said that actually, see, the fact was that we would see her in person because she was coming here in a week. Her tourist visa would expire in three months. Sometime before that, they would get married.

"Next week?" Amy asked. "She's coming next week?"

"Don't tell your mother about the marriage part right away," he said. "You know how she gets about things."

So when our mother picked us up that Sunday, Amy told her about Dad and the woman and the visit, but she didn't say anything about the marriage, just like our dad had asked. It was raining and the defrost was broken on our van, and our mom kept wiping a little spot with her hand and leaning forward to see out of it, muttering "Unbelievable," as the wipers clicked back and forth.

Then she said: "How old is she?"

"Twenty-three," I said. At the same time Amy said, "We don't know." Then she shot me a look.

"She dresses cheap," said Amy.

"I bet," my mom snapped.

"So do we," I whispered to Amy. Amy just clucked her tongue, but she knew it was true. Ever since the divorce there was a lot of economizing on everything. We didn't get an allowance anymore, and my mom drove an old car that needed a new muffler and sometimes broke down so that we had to get rides from our aunt Becky, and the piping on our couch ripped out and we just cut it off with scissors instead of buying a new couch or even a slipcover, which my dad told my mom was too expensive.

That was how their fights used to start before the divorce. She got piles of catalogues in the mail. She would show him something she wanted and he would say it was too expensive and she'd say, but look, it's the most beautiful thing. Have you ever seen a blue so bright and cheery like that, or it's lined, it's loden, it's so well-made, but he would just repeat: It's too expensive. A lot of times she bought it anyway, and he'd say she had a problem with money. Sometimes back then I would think he was just being mean to her, but lately I thought it might be true. She didn't have a Visa card since the divorce, but the UPS truck came at least once a week to our house in town. A lot of times she'd blow through her checking and have to return what she bought. Then my dad started bringing cash instead of his usual child support checks. They would sit together at the table, and he would divide the cash into envelopes for each category of spending — food, clothing, propane — and my dad would go through it with her — "You see? You see?" — and she would nod, although usually her eyes would be glazed over or she'd be chewing on a nail or shaking a foot or something.

Once after they had been doing this a few months my mom took the cash from two envelopes at once and we went shopping for school clothes, but then she saw a purse she wanted to buy — she kind of collected purses — and we only had enough money left for Cokes and a Cinnabon, split between the three of us.

The next month we got lucky and she bought us Abercrombie shirts in melon and blueberry, with bell sleeves. Then she had to go to my dad for more money before the month was over. After that, my dad took over buying clothes for Amy and me.

What this meant was Goodwill Boxes, the kind you get when they are trying to clear their stock and you get all you can cram into a box for two dollars. Let's just say that they weren't the kind of things my mom used to get us. The actual boxes you filled up at the Box Sales were the ones that people had donated stuff in, and they usually said things like GARAGE SALE or JUNK on the side.

Some of the clothes *were* junk — they smelled like mothballs and were worn-looking or out of style, but to tell you the truth I didn't mind it. I had a best friend, Jen, and two other friends, Madeline and another Jen, and when they came over we'd try on the worst-looking things, like pink Lycra tights that were pilled from the dryer, and striped knit caps, the kind with the tassel down to your knees. Then we'd top it off with some protective goggles or cheater reading glasses I'd tucked in the box when my dad wasn't looking. When we looked truly obnoxious we'd put whole packs of gum in our mouths at one time and walk to the Dollar Store and ask the clerk the price of one thing after another:

"How much is this?"

"A dollar."

"What about this one?"

"I'm sorry, I can't hardly understand you —"

"What's it cost?"

"Well, everything's a dollar . . ."

"So how much is this, then?"

That was how we were, doing stupid things like that. We didn't care about what we looked like. Although one time when my best friend, Jen, and I were standing at our bathroom mirror, trying on some herbicide caps, she said, "We're not raving beauties, you know." That surprised me. Not where Jen was concerned, because her teeth stuck out in every direction, like someone had squeezed her head really hard, and she had huge octagon glasses like her mother's — only her mother's were on a chain. But when I looked at myself, my teeth and face looked normal, and nice enough.

All of this was different for Amy. Her year was seventh grade, and that was when people divided up in a much more permanent way. Amy and her friends — Terri, Jill, Lisa — were the most popular group. They dressed in a very specific way — nothing like what we got from the Goodwill Boxes. But since my dad had taken over, that was almost all we'd been getting. Amy's wide-leg jeans from last year were a size too small, and when wide-legs get short you can't pretend they're capri pants or anything. When you sit down your socks show, and sometimes part of your bare leg if you don't wear knee socks. My dad even noticed this was happening and bought a pair of new jeans on clearance at Farm and Fleet. Amy said she wouldn't wear those because they smelled like tires. The waist was high, too, like old women's jeans, which was the real reason she wouldn't wear them.

He got us tennis shoes at the same Farm and Fleet sale, but Amy's said "Ladies' Walkers" on the tongue, which she said was mortifying. Whenever we left the house, she wore her stacked platforms, which were half a size too small. At the end of the day her pinkie toes would be very red and squished-looking.

When you wear jeans or shoes that are too small you can get a pinched feeling about everything, and that's how she was to be around. She was acting different with everybody, even her own friends. She never invited them over or went bike riding or downtown with them like she used to. Still, when she was in a mood to talk, that was who she talked about. I knew Cheryl had a new dog and that Jill was using pepper polish to stop biting her nails and that Terri wanted to switch to the flute and the band director said Terri had more of a clarinet personality, and Terri's mother had read him the riot act and now Terri had a new flute, the most expensive kind. Amy and I were not in band.

So I was surprised when Amy said that she was not going to tell any of her friends about my dad and his new girlfriend from the Philippines. We started talking about this that same Sunday night, when we were cleaning up from dinner. I was drying and Amy was squirting dishwashing soap right on the brush and scrubbing the plates with it, which would get you in trouble at my dad's place.

"Why would I want to? It makes him look like a pervert," Amy said.

"Exactly," my mother agreed. She was sitting at the table with her feet up, ashing her cigarettes on a dinner plate.

I thought about the word "pervert" and how what my dad was doing was strange but not the same as being a peeping Tom or anything, and without thinking I said, "But he is going to marry her." Amy cupped her forehead with her palm. "Jesus," she said.

"He's going to marry her?" My mom's voice got very high when she said "marry." Then she started to cry. We quit the dishes and sat on either side of her. Amy lifted one of her curls out of the cigarette plate and rubbed it off with a napkin.

I didn't really think about my mom loving my dad too often. Just the weekend before, when she was dropping us off, he'd come down the sidewalk in a tight flannel shirt and black buckle boots and she'd said, "Good Lord, will you look at that?" He had gained weight since the divorce, but the truth is, he had always been kind of fat.

That didn't seem to matter to my mom anymore. It surprised me, but I understood it, too. When I pictured them sitting there at our table together while they did the envelopes, or the way he would come into town to replace the dryer vent or caulk the tub, it seemed like we all had a life together even though we didn't stay overnight in the same place.

She took a Kleenex and emptied one nostril very loudly, then switched to the other. When she was done she said, "Promise not to tell anyone at school about this, like Amy was saying."

"Of course not," said Amy.

I was not good at keeping secrets. Even secrets I didn't want to tell I usually ended up telling without thinking about it. Especially things that I was supposed to keep to myself but wasn't exactly sure why I had to.

"Vicki," said Amy.

"Vicki!" said my mom.

Of course, as soon as I promised, my mom proceeded to get on the phone and tell everyone who would listen while Amy and I went back to the dishes. My mom hadn't washed anything all weekend, and she used about ten glasses and coffee mugs per day because she was always pouring coffee and forgetting where she'd put it. Amy and I kept washing, going and going, and my mom kept on talking. When all of the people she called got busy and had to go she called a catalogue company to try to return some boots she'd bought a long time ago.

"You never explicitly stated I couldn't wear them outside," she kept saying, tracing the words *explicitly stated* on a piece of scratch paper.

"When are you going to tell people?" I asked Amy.

"Never, OK? It's embarrassing."

"You'll have to say something sometime," I said.

Amy dropped the skillet she was washing into the sink. "Look, Vicki," she said, "maybe you don't care what people think, but I do."

"I care what people think."

"No you don't. You and your friends don't take anything seriously."

Was that true? Just Friday while we were playing Bombardment in gym we decided to fall down when we got hit with the ball, like we were at a Civil War reenactment, and that was exactly what the gym teacher had told us, that we would have to sit out until we could take things more seriously. Still, it made me mad when Amy said it, as if we didn't matter just because we were funny.

"At least I can tell my friends things," I said. "At least we have fun."

Amy peeled off her dishwashing gloves and whipped them into the sink, then raised the Dawn in one hand like she wanted to throw it at me, with her mouth all bunched up. Instead she turned and slammed the bottle into the sink, and then ran out of the room. The plastic bottle cracked on the edge of the skillet and the soap oozed out of the crack, down over the skillet and into the drain.

My mom raised her eyebrows at me and I shrugged. That was how Amy got sometimes. For no reason she'd start yelling at you or crying, and it could happen really fast. The next time you saw her, it would be like none of it ever happened.

Which was how it was that night. After the dishes and the phone calls were finished, we got ready for bed. My mom followed us to the bathroom like she always did, to check our dental hygiene. She usually did barre work at the same time, using the bathroom counter, but not tonight. She just looked in the mirror the whole time with her eyes wide and sad, sighing and drumming her fingernails on the counter. She was a nail-biter — we all were — but lately she had been growing them out and you could see quite a bit of white on the ends. They made a strong click when she drummed them. Suddenly I felt irritated with her. "Your hands are too dry, Mom," I said. "You should use more lotion."

She sighed. "I suppose," she said, and she drew me in on one side, and Amy on the other, and smooched us on the heads. "What a day, women," she said. "What a day."

That Monday they rotated our lunch hour so that mine overlapped with Amy's by fifteen minutes. Jen and Jen had different homerooms than me and Madeline, so lunch was the first time I could tell everyone about my dad and the girl. While we waited for hot lunch I was watching the clock, thinking about how I could give some hints and have them guess and promise not to tell by the time Amy and her friends came down the stairs. I had to be quick. If Amy saw my face while I was talking about it, she'd know right away. And I knew she'd tell my mom.

But Jen, the other Jen and not my best friend, was telling a long story about her mother and how they'd gotten rear-ended that weekend. Jen's mother got rear-ended about once a month and it was always the other driver's fault. It was like she was just this unlucky person that these bad drivers followed around on purpose, like friends who try to slam you on the bumper cars or something. Anyway, Jen said her mom wanted to exchange insurance information with the pickup who rear-ended them even though there was no damage to either vehicle, and I was thinking that I'd say, when she finished, "I can't tell you what happened, but it's about my dad," when all of a sudden Madeline said, "Isn't that Amy over there?"

There she was, about four tables over, sitting on the end of the bench with a space between her and Cheryl the size of three or four people. Amy was facing Cheryl and Jill and Terri, but Cheryl and Jill and Terri were not facing Amy. They were turned in the opposite direction, toward a girl I didn't recognize. The girl had a long brown coat on and the others were listening to her talk and nodding and laughing. I wondered if this girl was new in school. She was the kind of person you would notice and know, even if she just went to your school at all. Maybe it had something to do with the coat. It was tan suede with this trim around the cuffs and collar that was off-white and soft like a collie's fur. The girl's hair was long and blond, and she kept throwing her head back and laughing with her knees pulled up to her chest so her hair blended with the fur trim.

Amy was listening to this new girl, too, leaning in toward all of them with her chin stuck way up, and laughing when the others did. It was not her real laugh. It was too loud, and it kept going after the others stopped for a second or two. When that happened, it made it really obvious how far she was sitting from them. It was like they never made room for her in the first place.

And that wasn't the only thing that made her stick out. She was wearing the melon bell-sleeve shirt that my mom had bought her at Abercrombie, but the sleeves were about two inches short of her wrist, instead of down to her knuckles like they're supposed to be. Finally she'd given in and worn her new Farm and Fleet jeans, but because the Abercrombie shirt was too small it didn't quite come to her waist when she sat down, so you could see the label of the jeans entirely. She'd taken a black marker and crossed out the brand on the leather patch at the waist. And on her feet were those white Ladies' Walkers. Even though my dad had measured her, the Farm and Fleet jeans were short enough that you could see the gray reinforced heel of her gym sock, just above her shoe.

"I didn't know Amy was still friends with Terri and them," said Madeline.

"She isn't," said Jen.

I felt sick to my stomach. We got to the front of the line and I was supposed to decide on Taco Salad or Health Plate and they both looked vomitous to me, and I stood there, thinking of a comeback, like where does a person get off making comments if that person's teeth are sticking out all directions and their glasses are butt-ugly, but instead I set my tray next to Madeline's, facing Amy and her table. Jen and Jen sat across from us.

I waited for somebody to tell me about what happened, or when. Or who the other girl was. But nobody said anything. Jen kept talking even though her story was finished, about her mother and the policeman and bad drivers in general, people on cell phones or eating or just sleep-deprived, which was as dangerous as driving drunk. . . .

By the time I saw Amy again, there were other things to think about. It was the night my dad was picking up the bride at the airport. When my mom got us from school she was wearing a new dress: red and backless. She went out to a bar with my aunt Becky and left Amy and me to baby-sit ourselves.

We watched TV and ate caramel corn and went to bed without brushing our teeth. Then we lay there in bed, not sleeping. Not even feeling tired. It was white in the room, the white moon on our white bedspread and everything so light it felt like morning. By now my dad's bride was sitting in his car, or looking around our house, maybe putting her things in the drawers of the medicine cabinet. But what had happened in the cafeteria that day was even harder for me to believe. I wanted it to be a mistake.

"I saw you at lunch," I said.

Her head turned toward me, just a little.

"Did you tell anyone?" It was not what I wanted to ask, but it came out like that anyway.

"No," she said. "Did you?"

"No."

"Good."

She put her hands on her stomach and lay still. *Say something,* I thought. *Say it.* I looked at her, the small gleam from her eyes and the white of the sheet, and her body so still I couldn't feel her breathe, and I felt a fear in my chest, as if there was someone in her place: a stranger or a ghost.

When we were smaller sometimes I'd get scared in the dark. Are you Amy? I'd ask her. Or are you a woof? I'm Amy, she'd say. Now go to sleep.

*

On Saturdays, our mom drove us to our dad's for the weekend. Usually she went inside to talk for a minute, or at least helped us with our suitcase. This week it was different. She dropped us all the way at the end of the driveway, then drove away, spinning out on the gravel without even waiting to see if anyone was there to get us.

The door of the house opened and there was a little girl, waving and smiling at us. For a minute I was confused. It seemed like the girl must be the daughter of the bride I was expecting, and that this daughter had been sent before the mother. Then my dad came out and took our suitcase and we followed him back inside. There was no other person there, so it was not a daughter that I had seen, it was her.

Nineteen and eighteen and twenty-three were the ages circled in Dad's catalogue, and all of those ages were very old compared to me and Amy, while this girl didn't seem all that much older at all.

I raised my eyebrows at Amy and she raised hers back at me. "Amy and Vicki," Dad said, touching the girl's arm, "this is Daisy."

Sometimes when you first look at someone they seem like they might be pretty and then it is a relief to find that they bite their nails, for example. You can think, *Well, it's all fine, but it doesn't really count.* Daisy was not like that. Everything about her was pretty. Her smile was pretty and her face was pretty and her hair was very long and very pretty.

And her clothes were pretty. I mean they really were. Not like teachers, who sometimes have a pair of wide-leg jeans or something that's stylish, but then they button their blouse up all the way to the neck or they wear a pair of Birkenstocks with the wide-legs or they have their hair cut in a bob, so everything gets ruined. She was wearing a button-down white blouse and a lettuce-edge skirt that came just above the knee and a pair of tight brown boots with heels, a kind I had seen on a TV show once, but not yet on anybody at school. And her hair was so long and black and shiny, the kind that you wanted to ask permission to touch. The whole picture she made was perfect, like girls in magazines. In that same way, it was almost too much.

You had to wonder what my dad thought about that. I could remember lots of shows I watched on TV where the man was very old or ugly and he had a wife who looked young and beautiful. It always seemed ridiculous to me, like a musical where kids are singing the adult parts and you have to just imagine what the real characters might look like. But my dad didn't seem bothered. It was like he thought he deserved it, or something.

And Daisy was even prettier than my mom — my mom's body was very beautiful in a bony way, but her skin was so white that you could see veins and freckles all over it, and there were lines be-tween her eyes when she got mad or when she concentrated on something. Daisy's skin was smooth and tan and her breasts were full but very high, too, the way boys like them. Wouldn't all kinds of them be trying to ask her on a date?

Then my dad announced that Daisy was making a big dinner for us, with all Filipino food, and wouldn't it be interesting? He put his hand behind Daisy's back, down toward her bottom, and she smiled up at him.

Suddenly Amy took off and ran up the stairs, and the three of us were left standing there. Daisy looked at my dad with a worried ex-pression and he just shook his head, like this kind of thing hap-pened all the time. Of course it did, but this time was different. It wasn't exactly fun for me, either. On the other hand, when some-one is so pretty you can't help it: You want them to like you.

"Do you need help?" I asked Daisy. "With the cooking?"

She patted my head, and because she wasn't taller than me she had to reach up to do it. It gave me a warm shiver.

"Nice," she said to my dad.

"She's a good girl," he nodded. "A good help."

Daisy smiled at me. "It's finished," she said. "Just wait for cook-ing." I realized that my hair was pulled straight back and probably looked greasy. "My mom's doing laundry," I said. "That's why I have sweats on." Smiling back at her made me feel even uglier, like the smile was the only thing I had going for me.

"Ahh," she said, nodding in the way you do when little kids tell you something and you don't understand them.

My dad pulled Daisy in to him and brushed his lips against the top of her head, and she giggled a little, and then I really wanted to run up the stairs, too. I was not an idiot and I knew what married and engaged people did, but it just seemed crazy to me that someone like her would let an old, ugly guy touch her on the bottom or take her clothes off. My eyes started to mist up a little. I felt uncomfortable there, in the same house that used to be my house, and I wanted to go back to my mom's or get away from there.

"Do we have chores?" I asked my dad. He handed me a bag with some old bones in it, and I went out to the barn and dumped them in the old pie tin for the barn cats. It felt better to be outside, and even though it was very cold I stood there, wasting time. The only cat that came was an old gray tom with one eye matted shut. He started in on a bone, looking up to cough and hiss at me.

"Dummy," I told him, "I'm the one who gave you that."

I got more hay for the horses and when I was done I brought some to the cows, too, just for an excuse to be outside longer. A couple of them walked over and started eating, but most of them just stared at me, too dumb to push their way in or even smell where the hay was. Cows are like that. Every time they see you they'll stand and stare like it's the very first time they've encountered such a specimen.

By that time my hands and nose were freezing off and I knew I'd better go inside to see if Amy was OK. I found her upstairs, standing in my mom and dad's room. Only it didn't look like that room anymore. It was like a dressing room, or something. There were clothes everywhere. New clothes. Girls' clothes, it looked like. In our size. Good clothes with their tags still on. They were on the bed, on the dresser, hanging in the closet where the toilet paper used to be. There were sweaters and twin sets and tanks and belts, black slide shoes and black boots and button-down shirts in all colors: bright orange, blue, pink, lemon yellow. Three pairs of hip-slung jeans, and one was even dirty wash. And right in the middle of the closet, hanging by itself, was a suede coat, with fur on the hem and the cuffs, just like the new girl had at school.

"Who is it for?" I asked. I suppose for a second I thought it might be for us. I had a recurring dream like that when I was little, only it was about dolls.

"Her," said Amy. "Who do you think?" She stood in the middle of the braided rug in her training bra, zipping up a pair of the jeans. The hem spilled onto the floor a little, like it was supposed to, and the waist was so low that her butt crack almost showed in the back. They were perfect.

"Did she say you could?" I asked.

"Dad paid for them." She pulled a cowl-neck sweater over her head and examined herself in the mirror. Amy's hair was long and naturally curly like my mom's but it was blond, which looked glamorous with the light blue of the sweater.

"Maybe she bought it herself," I said. "Just because she's from a poor country doesn't mean that she's poor. That's a generalization."

She snorted. "That explains why she married an old fat guy."

I couldn't think of a comeback. I knew what she said was true, and it made me feel stupid. I had stood downstairs looking at Daisy and my dad together, wondering why they were together, when the answer was obvious. He had more money than she did. He was fat; she was beautiful and wanted nice things. That was probably what all those girls in the catalogue wanted. But how would Daisy even know what was in style anyway if she was from a poor country like that? Was it from TV? Did they have TV there?

One thing I knew for sure was that I didn't like it. I felt like one of the cows who didn't even notice that there was food around and other cows were eating first, and I got that feeling like I wanted to pick up something and smash it.

"Crap," I said.

"What's the matter with you, Vicki? Try something on." Amy took the coat off its hanger and tossed it on my lap. I lifted the tag out of the sleeve: $249.95.

"I can't put this on," I said. "There's hay in my hair."

"Suit yourself."

I put the suede against my face. It was softer than anything, softer than skin. It wasn't fake, for sure. There was a deep smell to it, like rich food. And the trim was so light next to it, as light and fluffy-looking as that girl and her little laugh and her blond hair.

Amy took an eye pencil and a lipstick from Daisy's kit and sat next to me on the bed.

"Close your eyes." She took the pencil and drew around my lids. Then she colored in my lips in dark red and blotted it with a Kleenex. Her face had that mentholated smell from the Noxzema base, and up close you could see the tiny white hairs on her face coated over in orangey-brown.

"You're all set," she said. "Now try something on."

"There's tags on these," I said. "We should at least wait until the tags are off."

Amy rummaged under some of the pants and held up a camisole set.

"No tags," she said, waving it. "Maybe she used them already. Hubba hubba."

"You're weird," I said, but when I took them from her they felt very soft and silky, and the fabric was my favorite color — teal.

I stood up and pulled off my sweats and my underwear and my T-shirt and pulled the camisole over my head. It was only a little too big, and the panties fit. I went to stand at the full-length mirror, next to Amy.

It's not like I never had makeup on before, but this time my eyes seemed like eyes from magazines, and when I half shut them, looking sideways, letting my mouth open a little, I felt something, a hope and a strangeness, maybe it started because there was something sexy in the outfit, it even made it look like I had breasts, though that was more the design of the fabric, because there were little starbursts where the nipples were, but I was running my hands over it, moving and looking in the mirror and the fabric was so smooth and shiny I kept going, running my hands over it.

"What's the matter, are you in love with yourself, or what?" Amy said.

My face felt hot. "Shut up," I said. "Are you in love with yourself? That's what I want to know."

"Good comeback."

"Amy, Vicki!" Dad yelled. "Dinner!"

I stepped out of the panties, pulled off the camisole top, and put them both in the top drawer of the dresser, and when I was done putting my sweats on I started hanging up all the other clothes. The colored blouses. All the jeans. The sweaters. The stuff that was not on hangers I piled on top of the dresser in the closet. Then I picked up the suede coat and took one of my mom's padded pink silk hangers and buttoned the top button. I hung it all the way in the back of the closet, so you couldn't even see it there, the way you do in a store with a shirt you don't have money for and don't want anyone else to get.

Amy had put her hair up and was pulling little curls out along the nape of her neck.

I shoved the slides and shoes and boots into the bottom of the closet and shut the door. Then I ran to the bathroom and scrubbed my face with Dial soap, very fast. There was a brown smudge under one eye that didn't come off all the way but you couldn't tell unless you were very close. When I came back through the bedroom, Amy was still standing there in the clothes, looking in the mirror.

"Hurry," I said. "What if they come up?"

"Go ahead."

I ran down by myself and there were Dad and Daisy, sitting at the table.

"Where's your sister?" asked Dad.

"Bathroom."

Daisy served me and Dad. "This is called *pants-it*," said Dad, beaming.

"*Pahn-seet*," she corrected him. I felt embarrassed, even though I didn't know how to pronounce it either. It was clear noodles with pieces of meat and vegetables. There was also a dish of pork with pineapple rings on top of it, and a sweet-smelling soup.

Then we could hear Amy, clicking down the stairs in Daisy's new Italian slides. Click, clickety, click. She came in wearing Daisy's jeans and Daisy's blue sweater with the tags tucked inside the neck.

"Nice war paint, Kemosabe," Dad said.

Amy sat down in the empty chair.

"Soup, Vicki," said Daisy.

"Thank you," I said. I had not rinsed the soap well enough and my face felt tight.

"And soup for Amy," she said. Daisy didn't look at Amy when

she served her. But she had noticed the outfit. She was sitting stiffly on the edge of her chair and after she gave Amy the soup she started blinking fast, blinking and looking away into the corner like there was dust blowing in her face.

We ate. My dad took seconds and Daisy brought him another beer.

Amy went to the fridge, added more ice to her lemonade, and sat down again. Dad looked right at her and kept eating. He wasn't going to notice the outfit. He ate, and he looked up with his jaw hanging open a little. His tongue was kind of big, and when he got tired or relaxed, sometimes it hung over his bottom lip and made him look slow. You could just picture him as a fat teacher that Daisy might make fun of with her popular friends at school, the same way my mom made fun of him coming down the lane.

It made you wonder if he bought my mom new things too, when he first met her. And if you thought about it, he was the one with the money problem. He had the most expensive taste of all: people who liked beautiful things.

Amy lifted the soup to her mouth and drank it, the way we'd seen Daisy do. She had a tiny smile on her lips, and I could guess what she was thinking. There were three or four pairs of jeans to spare and even more sweaters and shoes. She could slip some things into her suitcase. Maybe there would even be enough to last the week.

The thing was, it was only partly about the clothes, and Amy didn't get that, and that made her seem pitiful or something. It made me want to say something to hurt her.

"It won't make a difference," I said.

She stopped smiling. "What do you mean?"

I put some pineapple in my mouth. A whole ring at one time. "They won't notice," I said.

"What do you mean, Vicki?" she said. "Who are you talking about?"

I felt bad then. I wanted her to yell at me, or have one of her fits where she ran out of the room, but she didn't. She wasn't even looking at me, but I knew how she felt. Terrible. Like dirt. I knew because when you have a sister, it's like what happens to them happens to you.

But it was not too late for me. I would be the right size next year, and maybe I would be friends with Daisy by then. Maybe she would let me borrow whatever I wanted. So far, though, she didn't seem very happy about the idea. I didn't blame her. If they were my clothes, I wouldn't want to lend them to anyone. Even now, when I thought about that coat hanging on our new hall tree at my mom's, or on the hook at my locker at school, I did not like the thought of returning it.

A ladybug landed on the lampshade, fanned its tail, and drew it in again.

"How do we get those damn things?" my dad said. "It's the middle of winter."

"I want more pineapple," I said. I had taken three slices of the pineapple already, and I knew I had finished it. My right eyelid was getting some sort of tic. It fluttered, I pressed my palm over it, and it fluttered again.

"There is no pineapple, more," Daisy said. Her voice was tired-sounding, like this was an old routine, for me to ask for what I wanted, and it was up to her to get it for me.

■

Bohemians

FROM *The New Yorker*

IN A LOVELY URBAN COINCIDENCE, the last two houses on our block were both occupied by widows who had lost their husbands in Eastern European pogroms. Dad called them the Bohemians. He called anyone white with an accent a Bohemian. Whenever he saw one of the Bohemians, he greeted her by mispronouncing the Czech word for "door." Neither Bohemian was Czech, but both were polite, so when Dad said "door" to them they answered cordially, as if he weren't perennially schlockered.

Mrs. Poltoi, the stouter Bohemian, had spent the war in a crawl-space, splitting a daily potato with five cousins. Consequently she was bitter and claustrophobic and loved food. If you ate something while standing near her, she stared at it going into your mouth. She wore only black. She said the Catholic Church was a jeweled harlot drinking the blood of the poor. She said America was a spoiled child ignorant of grief. When our ball rolled onto her property, she seized it and waddled into her backyard and pitched it into the quarry.

Mrs. Hopanlitski, on the other hand, was thin, and joyfully made pipe-cleaner animals. When I brought home one of her crude dogs in top hats, Mom said, "Take over your Mold-A-Hero. To her, it will seem like the toy of a king." To Mom, the camps, massacres, and railroad sidings of twenty years before were as unreal as covered wagons. When Mrs. H. claimed her family had once owned serfs, Mom's attention wandered. She had a tract house in mind. No way was she getting one. We were renting a remodeled garage behind the Giancarlos, and Dad was basically drinking up the sporting-goods store. His NFL helmets were years out of date. I'd stop by after school and find the store closed and Dad getting sloshed among the fake legs with Bennie Delmonico at Prosthetics World.

Using the Mold-A-Hero, I cast Mrs. H. a plastic Lafayette, and she said she'd keep it forever on her sill. Within a week, she'd given it to Elizabeth the Raccoon. I didn't mind. Raccoon, an only child like me, had nothing. The Kletz brothers called her Raccoon for the bags she had under her eyes from never sleeping. Her parents fought nonstop. They fought over breakfast. They fought in the yard in their underwear. At dusk they stood on their porch whacking each other with lengths of weather stripping. Raccoon practically had spinal curvature from spending so much time slumped over with misery. When the Kletz brothers called her Raccoon, she indulged them by rubbing her hands together ferally. The nickname was the most attention she'd ever had. Sometimes she'd wish to be hit by a car so she could come back as a true raccoon and track down the Kletzes and give them rabies.

"Never wish harm on yourself or others," Mrs. H. said. "You are a lovely child." Her English was flat and clear, almost like ours.

"Raccoon, you mean," Raccoon said. "A lovely raccoon."

"A lovely child of God," Mrs. H. said.

"Yeah, right," Raccoon said. "Tell again about the prince."

So Mrs. H. told again how she'd stood rapt in her yard watching an actual prince powder his birthmark to invisibility. She remembered the smell of burning compost from the fields, and men in colorful leggings dragging a gutted boar across a wooden bridge. This was before she was forced to become a human pack animal in the Carpathians, carrying the personal belongings of cruel officers. At night, they chained her to a tree. Sometimes they burned her calves with a machine-gun barrel for fun. Which was why she always wore kneesocks. After three years, she'd come home to find her babies in tiny graves. They were, she would say, short-lived but wonderful gifts. She did not now begrudge God for taking them. A falling star is brief, but isn't one nonetheless glad to have seen it? Her grace made us hate Mrs. Poltoi all the more. What was eating a sixth of a potato every day compared to being chained to a tree? What was being crammed in with a bunch of your cousins compared to having your kids killed?

The summer I was ten, Raccoon and I, already borderline rejects due to our mutually unraveling households, were joined by Art Siminiak, who had recently made the mistake of inviting the Kletzes in for lemonade. There was no lemonade. Instead, there was Art's mom and a sailor from Great Lakes passed out naked across the paper-drive stacks on the Siminiaks' sun porch.

This new, three-way friendship consisted of slumping in gangways, playing gloveless catch with a Wiffle, trailing hopefully behind kids whose homes could be entered without fear of fiasco.

Over on Mozart lived Eddie the Vacant. Eddie was seventeen, huge and simple. He could crush a walnut in his bare hand, but first you had to put it there and tell him to do it. Once he'd pinned a VACANT sign to his shirt and walked around the neighborhood that way, and the name had stuck. Eddie claimed to see birds. Different birds appeared on different days of the week. Also, there was a Halloween bird and a Christmas bird.

One day, as Eddie hobbled by, we asked what kind of birds he was seeing.

"Party birds," he said. "They got big streamers coming out they butts."

"You having a party?" said Art. "You having a homo party?"

"I gone have a birthday party," said Eddie, blinking shyly.

"Your dad know?" Raccoon said.

"No, he don't yet," said Eddie.

His plans for the party were private and illogical. We peppered him with questions, hoping to get him to further embarrass himself. The party would be held in his garage. As far as the junk car in there, he would push it out by hand. As far as the oil on the floor, he would soak it up using Handi Wipes. As far as music, he would play a trumpet.

"What are you going to play the trumpet with?" said Art. "Your asshole?"

"No, I not gone play it with that," Eddie said. "I just gone use my lips, OK?"

As far as girls, there would be girls; he knew many girls, from his job managing the Drake Hotel, he said. As far as food, there would be food, including pudding dumplings.

"You're the manager of the Drake Hotel," Raccoon said.

"Hey, I know how to get the money for pudding dumplings!" Eddie said.

Then he rang Poltoi's bell and asked for a contribution. She said for what. He said for him. She said to what end. He looked at her blankly and asked for a contribution. She asked him to leave the porch. He asked for a contribution. Somewhere, he'd got the idea that, when asking for a contribution, one angled to sit on the couch. He started in, and she pushed him back with a thick forearm. Down the front steps he went, ringing the iron banister with his massive head.

He got up and staggered away, a little blood on his scalp.

"Learn to leave people be!" Poltoi shouted after him.

Ten minutes later, Eddie Sr. stood on Poltoi's porch, a hulking effeminate tailor too cowed to use his bulk for anything but butting open the jamming door at his shop.

"Since when has it become the sport to knock unfortunates down stairs?" he asked.

"He was not listen," she said. "I tell him no. He try to come inside."

"With all respect," he said, "it is in my son's nature to perhaps be not so responsive."

"Someone so unresponse, keep him indoors," she said. "He is big as a man. And I am old lady."

"Never has Eddie presented a danger to anyone," Eddie Sr. said.

"I know my rights," she said. "Next time, I call police."

But, having been pushed down the stairs, Eddie the Vacant couldn't seem to stay away.

"Off this porch," Poltoi said through the screen when he

showed up the next day, offering her an empty cold-cream jar for three dollars.

"We gone have so many snacks," he said. "And if I drink a alcohol drink, then watch out. Because I ain't allowed. I dance too fast."

He was trying the doorknob now, showing how fast he would dance if alcohol was served.

"Please, off this porch!" she shouted.

"Please, off this porch!" he shouted back, doubling at the waist in wacky laughter.

Poltoi called the cops. Normally, Lieutenant Brusci would have asked Eddie what bird was in effect that day and given him a ride home in his squad. But this was during the OneCity fiasco. To cut graft, cops were being yanked off their regular beats and replaced by cops from other parts of town. A couple of Armenians from South Shore showed up and dragged Eddie off the porch in a club lock so tight he claimed the birds he was seeing were beakless.

"I'll give you a beak, Frankenstein," said one of the Armenians, tightening the chokehold.

Eddie entered the squad with all the fluidity of a hat rack. Art and Raccoon and I ran over to Eddie Sr.'s tailor shop, above the Marquee, which had sunk to porn. When Eddie Sr. saw us, he stopped his Singer by kicking out the plug. From downstairs came a series of erotic moans.

Eddie Sr. rushed to the hospital with his Purple Heart and some photos of Eddie as a grinning, wet-chinned kid on a pony. He found Eddie handcuffed to a bed, with an IV drip and a smashed face. Apparently, he'd bitten one of the Armenians. Bail was set at three hundred. The tailor shop made zilch. Eddie Sr.'s fabrics were a lexicon of yesteryear. Dust coated a bright-yellow sign that read ZIPPERS REPAIRED IN JIFFY.

"Jail for that kid, I admit, don't make total sense," the judge said. "Three months in the Anston. Best I can do."

The Anston Center for Youth was a red-brick former forge now yarded in barbed wire. After their shifts, the guards held loud, hooting orgies kitty-corner at Zem's Lamplighter. Skinny immi-

grant women arrived at Zem's in station wagons and emerged
hours later adjusting their stockings. From all over Chicago kids
were sent to the Anston, kids who'd only ever been praised for the
level of beatings they gave and received and their willingness to
carve themselves up. One Anston kid had famously hired another
kid to run over his foot. Another had killed his mother's lover with
a can opener. A third had sliced open his own eyelid with a pop-top
on a dare.

Eddie the Vacant disappeared into the Anston in January and
came out in March.

To welcome him home, Eddie Sr. had the neighborhood kids
over. Eddie the Vacant looked so bad even the Kletzes didn't joke
about how bad he looked. His nose was off center and a scald
mark ran from ear to chin. When you got too close, his hands shot
up. When the cake was served, he dropped his plate, shouting,
"Leave a guy alone!"

Our natural meanness now found a purpose. Led by the
Kletzes, we cut through Poltoi's hose, bashed out her basement
windows with ball-peens, pushed her little shopping cart over the
edge of the quarry, and watched it end-over-end into the former
Slag Ravine.

Then it was spring and the quarry got busy. When the noon
blast went off, our windows rattled. The three-o'clock blast was
even bigger. Raccoon and Art and I made a fort from the cardboard shipping containers the Cline frames came in. One day,
while pretending the three-o'clock blast was atomic, we saw Eddie
the Vacant bounding toward our fort through the weeds, like some
lover in a commercial, only fatter and falling occasionally.

His trauma had made us kinder toward him.

"Eddie," Art said. "You tell your dad where you're at?"

"It no big problem," Eddie said. "I was gone leave my dad a
note."

"But did you?" said Art.

"I'll leave him a note when I get back," said Eddie. "I gone come
in with you now."

"No room," said Raccoon. "You're too huge."

"That a good one!" said Eddie, crowding in.

Down in the quarry were the sad cats, the slumping watchman's shack, the piles of reddish, discarded dynamite wrappings that occasionally rose erratically up the hillside like startled birds.

Along the quarryside trail came Mrs. Poltoi, dragging a new shopping cart.

"Look at that pig," said Raccoon. "Eddie, that's the pig that put you away."

"What did they do to you in there, Ed?" said Art. "Did they mess with you?"

"No, they didn't," said Eddie. "I just a say to them, 'Leave a guy alone!' I mean, sometime they did, OK? Sometime that one guy say, 'Hey, Eddie, pull your thing! We gone watch you.'"

"OK, OK," said Art.

At dusk, the three of us would go to Mrs. H.'s porch. She'd bring out cookies and urge forgiveness. It wasn't Poltoi's fault her heart was small, she told us. She, Mrs. H., had seen a great number of things, and seeing so many things had enlarged her heart. Once, she had seen Göring. Once, she had seen Einstein. Once, during the war, she had seen a whole city block, formerly thick with furriers, bombed black overnight. In the morning, charred bodies had crawled along the street, begging for mercy. One such body had grabbed her by the ankle, and she recognized it as Bergen, a friend of her father's.

"What did you do?" said Raccoon.

"Not important now," said Mrs. H., gulping back tears, looking off into the quarry.

Then disaster. Dad got a check for shoulder pads for all six district football teams and, trying to work things out with Mom, decided to take her on a cruise to Jamaica. Nobody in our neighborhood had ever been on a cruise. Nobody had even been to Wisconsin. The disaster was, I was staying with Poltoi. Ours was a liquor household, where you could ask a question over and over in utter sincerity and never get a straight answer. I asked and asked, "Why her?" And was told and told, "It will be an adventure."

I asked, "Why not Grammy?"

I was told, "Grammy don't feel well."

I asked, "Why not Hopanlitski?"

Dad did this like snort.

"Like that's gonna happen," said Mom.

"Why not, why not?" I kept asking.

"Because shut up," they kept answering.

Just after Easter, over I went, with my little green suitcase.

I was a night panicker and occasional bed wetter. I'd wake drenched and panting. Had they told her? I doubted it. Then I knew they hadn't, from the look on her face the first night, when I peed myself and woke up screaming.

"What's this?" she said.

"Pee," I said, humiliated beyond any ability to lie.

"Ach, well," she said. "Who don't? This also used to be me. Pee pee pee. I used to dream of a fish who cursed me."

She changed the sheets gently, with no petulance — a new one on me. Often Ma, still half asleep, popped me with the wet sheet, saying when at last I had a wife, she herself could finally get some freaking sleep.

Then the bed was ready, and Poltoi made a sweeping gesture, like, Please.

I got in.

She stayed standing there.

"You know," she said. "I know they say things. About me, what I done to that boy. But I had a bad time in the past with a big stupid boy. You don't gotta know. But I did like I did that day for good reason. I was scared at him, due to something what happened for real to me."

She stood in the half-light, looking down at her feet.

"Do you get?" she said. "Do you? Can you get it, what I am saying?"

"I think so," I said.

"Tell to him," she said. "Tell to him sorry, explain about it, tell your friends also. If you please. You have a good brain. That is why I am saying to you."

Something in me rose to this. I'd never heard it before but I believed it: I had a good brain. I could be trusted to effect a change.

Next day was Saturday. She made soup. We played a game using three slivers of soap. We made placemats out of colored strips of paper, and she let me teach her my spelling words.

Around noon, the doorbell rang. At the door stood Mrs. H.

"Everything OK?" she said, poking her head in.

"Yes, fine," said Poltoi. "I did not eat him yet."

"Is everything really fine?" Mrs. H. said to me. "You can say."

"It's fine," I said.

"You can say," she said fiercely.

Then she gave Poltoi a look that seemed to say, Hurt him and you will deal with me.

"You silly woman," said Poltoi. "You are going now."

Mrs. H. went.

We resumed our spelling. It was tense in a quiet-house way. Things ticked. When Poltoi missed a word, she pinched her own hand, but not hard. It was like symbolic pinching. Once when she pinched, she looked at me looking at her, and we laughed.

Then we were quiet again.

"That lady?" she finally said. "She like to lie. Maybe you don't know. She say she is come from where I come from?"

"Yes," I said.

"She is lie," she said. "She act so sweet and everything but she lie. She been born in Skokie. Live here all her life, in America. Why you think she talk so good?"

All week, Poltoi made sausage, noodles, potato pancakes; we ate like pigs. She had tea and cakes ready when I came home from school. At night, if necessary, she dried me off, moved me to her bed, changed the sheets, put me back, with never an unkind word.

"Will pass, will pass," she'd hum.

Mom and Dad came home tanned, with a sailor cap for me, and, in a burst of post-vacation honesty, confirmed it: Mrs. H. was a liar. A liar and a kook. Nothing she said was true. She'd been a cashier at Goldblatt's but had been caught stealing. When caught stealing, she'd claimed to be with the Main Office. When a guy from the Main Office came down, she'd claimed to be with the FBI. Then she'd produced a letter from Lady Bird Johnson, but in her own handwriting, with "Johnson" spelled "Jonsen."

I told the other kids what I knew, and in time they came to believe it, even the Kletzes.

And, once we believed it, we couldn't imagine we hadn't seen it all along.

Another spring came, once again birds nested in bushes on the sides of the quarry. A thrown rock excited a thrilling upward explosion. Thin rivers originated in our swampy backyards, and we sailed boats made of flattened shoeboxes, Twinkie wrappers, crimped tinfoil. Raccoon glued together three balsa-wood planes and placed on this boat a turd from her dog, Svengooli, and, as Svengooli's turd went over a little waterfall and disappeared into the quarry, we cheered.

GEORGE SAUNDERS

■

Manifesto

A Press Release from PRKA

FROM *Slate*

LAST THURSDAY, my organization, People Reluctant to Kill for an
Abstraction, orchestrated an overwhelming show of force around
the globe.

At precisely nine in the morning, working with focus and stealth,
our entire membership succeeded in simultaneously beheading
no one. At ten, Phase II began, during which our entire membership did not force a single man to suck another man's penis. Also,
none of us blew himself/herself up in a crowded public place. No
civilians were literally turned inside out via our powerful explo-
sives. In addition, at eleven, in Phase III, zero (0) planes were
flown into buildings.

During Phase IV, just after lunch, we were able to avoid bull-
dozing a single home. Furthermore, we set, on roads in every city,
in every nation in the world, a total of zero (0) roadside bombs,
which, not being there, did not subsequently explode, killing/
maiming a total of nobody. No bombs were dropped, during the
lazy afternoon hours, on crowded civilian neighborhoods, from
which, it was observed, no postbomb momentary silences were
then heard. These silences were, in all cases, followed by no uni-
maginable, grief-stricken bellows of rage, and/or frantic impreca-
tions to a deity. No sleeping baby was awakened from an afternoon

nap by the sudden collapse and/or bursting into flame of his/her domicile during Phase IV.

In the late afternoon (Phase V), our membership focused on using zero (o) trained dogs to bite/terrorize naked prisoners. In addition, no stun guns, rubber batons, rubber bullets, tear gas, or bullets were used by our membership on any individual, anywhere in the world. No one was forced to don a hood. No teeth were pulled in darkened rooms. No drills were used on human flesh, nor were whips or flames. No one was reduced to hysterical tears via a series of blows to the head or body by us. Our membership, while casting no racial or ethnic aspersions, skillfully continued not to rape, gang rape, or sexually assault a single person. On the contrary, during this late-afternoon phase, many of our membership flirted happily and even consoled, in a nonsexual way, individuals to whom they were attracted, putting aside their sexual feelings out of a sudden welling of empathy.

As night fell, our membership harbored no secret feelings of rage or, if they did, meditated, or discussed these feelings with a friend until such time as the feelings abated, or were understood to be symptomatic of some deeper sadness.

It should be noted that, in addition to the above-listed and planned activities completed by our members, a number of unplanned activities were completed by part-time members, or even nonmembers.

In London, a bitter homophobic grandfather whose grocery bag broke open gave a loaf of very nice bread to a balding gay man who stopped to help him. A stooped toothless woman in Tokyo pounded her head with her hands, tired beyond belief of her lifelong feelings of anger and negativity, and silently prayed that her heart would somehow be opened before it was too late. In Syracuse, New York, holding the broken body of his kitten, a man felt a sudden kinship for all small things.

Even declared nonmembers, it would appear, responded to our efforts. In Chitral, Pakistan, for example, a recent al-Qaeda recruit remembered the way an elderly American tourist once made an encouraging remark about his English, and how, as she made the remark, she touched his arm, like a mother. In Gaza, an Israeli soldier and a young Palestinian, just before averting their eyes and muttering insults in their respective languages, exchanged a brief look of mutual shame.

Who are we? A word about our membership.

Since the world began, we have gone about our work quietly, resisting the urge to generalize, valuing the individual over the group, the actual over the conceptual, the inherent sweetness of the present moment over the theoretically peaceful future to be obtained via murder. Many of us have trouble sleeping and lie awake at night, worrying about something catastrophic befalling someone we love. We rise in the morning with no plans to convert anyone via beating, humiliation, or invasion. To tell the truth, we are tired. We work. We would just like some peace and quiet. When wrong, we think about it a while, then apologize. We stand under awnings during urban thunderstorms, moved to thoughtfulness by the troubled, umbrella-tinged faces rushing by. In moments of crisis, we pat one another awkwardly on the back, mumbling shy truisms. Rushing to an appointment, remembering a friend who has passed away, our eyes well with tears and we think: *Well, my God, he could be a pain, but still I'm lucky to have known him.*

This is PRKA. To those who would oppose us, I would simply say: We are many. We are worldwide. We, in fact, outnumber you. Though you are louder, though you create a momentary ripple on the water of life, we will endure, and prevail.

Join us.

Resistance is futile.

J. DAVID STEVENS

■

The Joke

FROM *Mid-American Review*

A PRIEST, a housewife, a chicken, and a bag of chocolate bars are on the bank of a river. They are not sure how they got there but know, collectively, that they are there for the purpose of the joke yet to be told. Uncomfortable as a unit, they take up different positions on the riverbank, waiting for the joke to commence. The sun shines brightly, but a breeze off the river cools the skin. There is a boat nearby: a rowboat, red with white and yellow splashes of paint. The trees on the river's far side bear fruit, though from a distance no one can tell what kind of fruit it is.

Meanwhile the joker is not telling his joke. He sees the characters in his head: an oversexed priest, a voluptuous housewife, a chicken with a Napoleon complex, some chocolate. But he cannot figure out where to go with them. He's had a rough day at work. He's knocked back a few gin-and-tonics already — less tonic, more gin. He promises himself to try again tomorrow.

Things grow restless on the riverbank. The priest has missed afternoon confession, and the housewife — whose name is Lila — worries that she forgot to turn off the oven. The chicken, who has been watching the Asian markets and contemplating a major purchase in Chinese poultry feed, curses the malevolent spirit that caused him to leave the coop without his cell phone. Only the bag of candy seems calm. A few feet from the rest of the group, it discovers its own sentience and repeatedly counts the number of chocolate bars it contains. It wonders if the others recognize its new level of consciousness. It resolves to learn how to speak.

Days pass. The chicken would give his tail feathers for a single glimpse at the S&P Index. Lila has unbuttoned much of her shirt and tied the bottom in a knot. She describes the riverbank as an adventure that she often longs for but never undertakes. Her husband is a corporate lawyer with a Jaguar and a seven handicap who gets free T-shirts and gym bags from the tobacco companies he defends. Lila worries about her two sons — fears they will smoke, then hang out with leather-clad women, get tattooed, drop out of school, buy an RV. Her breasts heave slightly. The priest, whose name is Father Ron, watches the heaving breasts. The bag of candy composes, in a difficult Italian meter, an ode in which the river serves as a metaphor for their situation: both movement and stasis. It longs to recite its ode to the others. It pities Lila, and it pities Father Ron, who is now thinking about leather-clad women and an RV known to its neighbors as *Lovin' On Wheels*.

The joker cannot get the characters out of his head. At work, he sits in front of a computer screen all day, entering tiny numbers into tiny charts that he has been told are instrumental to corporate success. Sometimes he receives messages from friends, usually of the hey-how-you-doing-isn't-life-boring-as-hell ilk, but sometimes jokes. Funny jokes. Complex jokes. Joke lists. Listservs. He is on many lists. He cannot laugh out loud because his boss's secretary might hear him. She knows numbers are not funny. She does not like him because he is somewhat fat, and deep down they both know that fat men are supposed to be funny. In a man, fat without funny is just . . . well, fat. Or Winston Churchill. Or Alfred Hitchcock. He thinks that maybe there is humor in such a realization. His boss's secretary looks up from her *Southern Living*, testing the air. He reverts to numbers. Thinks chicken, candy, housewife, priest.

The chicken decides that the joke is a hell of his own making. Hubris compels him to believe that, if he can resolve the joke from the inside, he might break out of it. He tries the conventional approach. Why did the chicken cross the road? But here there are no roads, only a river. Somewhere from his youth he remembers a riddle about a farmer with a fox, a goose, and a bag of grain that must all ford a stream in a particular order to prevent any from eating the other. His mind works out variations. In the rowboat he paddles priest, housewife, and candy across in different permutations — making sure never to leave priest alone with housewife, housewife alone with chocolate. The task is daunting. The oars are insecure. The chicken's muscles ache, and his red comb becomes redder beneath the midsummer sun. The fruit trees on the opposite shore turn out to be lemon trees, ripe with yellow fire. The silence of the lemons makes the chicken uneasy. He thinks of recipes in which he might use their gutted pulp. Lemonade. Lemon Chess Pie. Lemon drops. Lemon . . . *chicken*. When nothing has changed by dusk, the chicken piles everyone back into the rowboat and returns them to the original shore. He learns to sleep with one eye open, trained on the lemon branches whose shadows reach like dark arms across the water's surface.

The mind is stuck on itself, he decides. It thinks that the world cannot function without it. If a housewife falls in a river but there is no one to hear her scream, no priest to pull her out . . . well, the mind sees the world merely as an extension of such musing. It says, hypothetically, that a chicken walks into a bar. But if a chicken *actually* walked into a bar and made a ranting beeline for the back table where the mind was talking up a couple of Rutgers coeds, it's unlikely that the mind could continue to see the universe as a place of its own invention. In fact, it's likely that the mind would do a screaming tarantella atop the back table until the bartender shooed the chicken out with a broom. This assumes, of course, that the chicken is not a bar regular, and that one of the coeds is not his steady girl, Henrietta, and that most of the bar's patrons do not want to buy him a Sam Adams because he is a well-known power broker around town. The mind would have trouble wrapping around such a chicken, but it would be one hell of a joke.

Meanwhile, Father Ron observes the supple curves of Lila's body. They have now been stranded together for weeks, but she has shown no interest in him. Or, more precisely, she has shown interest in him only as a spiritual confidant — someone with whom she can share all of the problems of her marriage, including her unrequited sexual needs. Father Ron thinks of Job. He wonders if the joke is a test of his spiritual resolve. Thinking along these lines, he notices the chicken, the supple curves of the chicken's body. He tells himself that he is not thinking in a serious way, but in a trapped-on-a-riverbank-with-only-these-questions-to-keep-me-sane way. This is philosophy. He begins to understand why women are called "chicks" — breasts, thighs, white meat, dark. He starts to dream about chicken. He wonders how egregious some sins might seem before God. The chicken, sensing something amiss, gives up on sleep altogether.

There is only frustration. Frustration and desire, the joker tells himself, which are really the same thing in the end. He watches the popular men at the bar whose jokes rise above the smoke and waft into the corner where he sits alone with his domestic beer. How do they begin? Two sisters in Montana must buy a bull for their ranch. An old Jew and a Chinese man are sitting on a park bench. Three hobos eat corn on a train. A doctor's office. A farmer's daughter. A moose. These are items ripe with humor, but when he envisions his joke, he can manage only slight changes: a duck, a rabbi, a librarian, a cherry pie. In the end the joke is futilely the same. Returning from the restroom, he steals a dart from the dart board and scratches his name into the oak table — then adds some eyes, a nose, and a mouth that resemble a once-famous cartoon cat. His mother always liked his drawings. She hung a few around the house and called him her *artiste*. She said that they would take a trip to France one day, though the closest they ever got was flipping through some travel brochures on Quebec at a rest stop near his cousin's place in Syracuse. At home, after last call at the bar, he will leave two Hungry Man dinners to thaw on the counter of his un-air-conditioned kitchen, then eat them both for breakfast the following morning without cooking them. Later he'll have a bagel at the office, extra cream cheese.

Egocentrism gets them only so far. At last they decide that the joke is not designed to punish any of them individually. It is merely a random confluence of cosmic forces, the teapot tempest in which they are tossed. They assume that they will be freed eventually, but, in the name of order and civilization, agree to establish rules by which their small society might run. After several halting drafts, they create a constitutional theocracy with the chicken as president, Father Ron as chancellor, and Lila as minister of culture and good taste. The bag of chocolate bars, because someone must, becomes the democratic masses. It redoubles its efforts at speech and thinks of the best way for a bag of candy to communicate with the outer world. It could pop its cellophane on a rock and attract throngs of approbative ants. It could melt into symbols on the sand. The First National Assembly is scheduled for a year hence: Father Ron will lead the country in prayer, followed by the chicken's address on the health-care system, then Lila's unveiling of the new army uniforms made of couch grass and lemon rind. The candy plans a Homeric hymn to commemorate the founding of the state. If it has time, it will fashion some scenery for its performance — perhaps a frieze of the chicken and Father Ron commuting their household gods across the river and onto the riverbank promised in the mystical covenants of their forebears.

Of course, a joke should be easier to tell. He finally decides that the problem is his mother. When he was a child, she trained him to laugh at misfortune — every accident met with a smile. In this way he learned that pain was comedy. Pratfalls. Pies to the face. A well-placed boot in the groin. He imagines the chicken writhing on the sand, wings to his crotch, moaning, "Oh, my nuggets," and he cannot help smiling. His apartment is dark except for the late-night TV. His undershirt rides up his belly where he sticks his hand beneath the elastic of his shorts and cradles his testicles, an unconscious gesture. He sucks an ice cube from his whiskey glass and spits it out the open window, wondering if it might kill a man twelve stories down. Gravity is hilarious, he decides, hefting his paunch with a forearm. The TV audience roars at the host's one-liners. He resolves to get a bigger chin.

But nothing can help at this point. Long before the National Assembly, friction arises when Father Ron abolishes the institution of marriage and criticizes the chicken's population control plan. They both fear Lila, who has taken to wearing the new army uniform, stockpiling stones, and telling stories of how the Amazons each burned off one breast so as not to impede their bowstrings. An uneasy truce is called. They doff their official vestments, sacrifice the candy bars to a recipe that Lila dubs Couch Grass S'mores, then part ways. As the chicken slips downriver in the rowboat, he dreams of the new society that he will form out of the misfits he finds along his way — characters from bad jokes or other jokes never to be told: one-legged midgets, gay hairdressers, most of Poland. From here on in, until his death, he will strive to view himself as a fowl in charge of his own destiny. But even years later, in his tent beneath the mountains — the sultana's warm body reposed beside him, the drifting incense, and the sound of their many camels spitting in the distance — he will wake with the irrational fear that he is still part of the joke, that he is still working toward some inevitable punch line. There is a spirit at the door of the tent, waiting to sweep in. The chicken stares through the darkness. He sees only the image of his youngest daughter — a redhaired, smoke-eyed beauty who maligns him when she is angry. *Silly bird,* she chastises. *Silly, silly bird.*

Fat man in a little car. Fat man bowling. Fat man in bikini briefs. Fat man doing the cha-cha. Cellulite, he concludes, is the sole of wit. In all honesty, he can do no more with these characters. He detests the chicken and Father Ron. He desires the chocolate bars and Lila. He has grown too close to his material. He's trying too hard. Humor, he knows from somewhere, cannot be forced but must spring from the mind like snakebite. *It will come,* he assures himself. He just has to wait for it. And when his mind does manage to coil like a rattler, the world will finally see him for the hero that he is. The men will buy him drinks; the women will come home with him, and they will titter in the lavishness of their unair-conditioned sweat. There will be no calories that laughter cannot melt away. They will love him high and low, the Bobos in their Versace drinking Sea Breezes by the Sound, the Guidos in their leather pants drinking forties down the shore. The elevator door opens onto his boss's secretary who greets him with a sneer. But he exalts in the stale office air, anticipating the day when he is boss and can send her back out because she has not brought a pickle with his egg salad. She, above all, will be forced to acknowledge her treachery, the wanton ignorance of her kind. When the new *him* arrives at the office one day — the joke, the wit, the mind itself — then she will know how wrong she has been. She will see him in the glory of a new light and swear that everywhere she goes they want to be like him: the Bobos, the Guidos, the bosses, the masses. He is his own religion and not the antimiracle she sees now. Fat man in a cubicle. Fat man at a desk. Fat man who sweats too much. Fat man in off-the-rack pants.

JONATHAN TEL

■

The Myth of the Frequent Flier

FROM *Open City*

I THINK YOU COULD fairly trace my obsession to a conversation that took place some years ago on Aerolineas Argentinas flight AR185 from Buenos Aires to Auckland, the redeye that departed at 22:30, if my memory serves me right; reasonably commodious; I had been upgraded to first class; I accepted the champagne but waved away the food — and after I had put in an hour or two at my laptop, and listened to a snatch of Mozart through the headphones, it occurred to me it might be for the best if I napped, however (my internal clock was not corresponding to that of the longitude), I felt not in the least tired, and so, contrary to what had been my self-imposed rule, listened gravely while a stewardess (in her early forties, I should judge; some wrinkles around the eyes [the flying does that to them: they try to counteract it with moisturizer, but even so] and a pleasant smile, I thought, and a poppy in her lapel [though possibly it was a pin in the shape of a heart this particular stewardess was wearing {the flower having pertained to a stewardess six months or so earlier on Alitalia 406 from Naples to Capri (among the most scenic flights I have ever had the pleasure of)}]) told me a story.

She did not vouch for it personally. She said she had been told it by another stewardess, an employee of Cathay Pacific, in an airport washroom in Vientiane; the Cathay Pacific person herself had learned it from a Swissair purser. All the same, the Argentinean said, it could very well be true.

In brief, the story was about a man (she was fairly certain the person was male; the name she had forgotten, if she had ever been told it) who travels on scheduled airlines. As do we all: but the point is he never does anything but. (Not literally "never" — he has to transfer from flight to flight, of course, involving walking from gate to gate, and waiting patiently to board the next flight; and should the flight be international he would be required to go through Customs and Immigration — but as much as anyone ever could, he flies nonstop.) He sits in an airline seat; he eats airline food; he listens to airline music through airline headphones and watches airline films; he reads airline magazines; he makes the kind of conversation with the person or persons next to him that one does make on airlines; airline socks go on his airline feet, airline earplugs in his airline ears, an airline mask over his airline eyes, and he dreams airline dreams.

He has adopted this lifestyle by choice. He is presumed to be not unhappy.

As to how this had come about . . . She had been told he had won a competition of the I LOVE BRITISH AIRWAYS BE-CAUSE _____ (complete in not more than ten words) sort, for which the prize had been a pass entitling the bearer to travel as much as desired, for life. Naturally the airline had supposed the winner would use the pass a few times a year; little had they suspected he would choose to stay aloft whenever possible. They had offered him a lump sum in lieu; he had refused to accept it.

And was the airline he flew on in fact British Airways? I sought to make the story more specific, and so more verifiable.

She wasn't certain, but she thought that was what the woman in the Vientiane washroom had told her she'd been told. But possibly she (the woman from Aerolineas Argentinas, that is) was misremembering the detail, she conceded; or then again, Cathay Pacific might not have got it quite right; or the fault might lie in Swissair, or somewhere further back.

I did not think much of the story; I filed it to the back of my mind. And then, about two and a half months later, in a seafood bar in the new Denver airport (notorious for its automated baggage transfer system that kept breaking down) from the man serving the lobster salad, I heard another version. In this retelling, the traveler was from North America, and his name (the lobster salad thought) began with a *J*, or at least had a *J* in it — John, Jack, Jean-Jacques, Roger — something like that . . . I had a 727 to catch to Mexico City, and heard no further details.

But by then I was alerted and listened out for further installments. Over the years since, whenever I have had need to travel, I have made a point of chatting with the aircrew and the ground crew, and airport employees, and I'm no longer surprised by how often variations on this story come up. An urban myth, you could call it; but not exactly urban, since it is told (to the best of my knowledge) only in the air world. Call it an airborne myth, then. An updated version of an ancient legend.

Who is he? Where is he from? What impels him to keep doing it? Will he ever stop?

In all the variora I have come across, the frequent flier is described as male (though it is conceivable a female avatar may exist somewhere). He is middle-aged to elderly, never young. His country of citizenship, though, is open to question. The one constant is that he is always a foreigner, never the same nationality as the informant. In the curious airport in Jakarta, modeled on a traditional Javanese longhouse yet constructed in concrete and glass, a security guard told me the eternal traveler is Malay. In the Albuquerque airport, a vendor of Native American turquoise trinkets assured me he is Salvadorian. The fellow employed to chivvy goats off the Axum airstrip swore he is Somali. During the short hop from Sikkim to Katmandu, he is Chinese. In Heathrow he is Irish. In O'Hare he is Canadian. On the polar route from Osaka to Copenhagen, he is Australian.

I was not too surprised to come across (indeed, with the wisdom of hindsight one might characterize it as inevitable) a version of the tale in which he finds a mate. It was a Filipina, employed as a toilet cleaner in the Dubai airport, who first revealed this aspect of his character. The cleaner herself had a Harlequin romance in Tagalog translation stuffed in the pocket of her apron, yet the story she told me was not one of love.

You see, she explained, there was a clause in his prize to the effect that he could take a spouse with him on his travels. And somewhere on his journeys, at some random terminal, he had found a woman who had agreed to marry him — a woman much like herself, in fact, in her mid-thirties, originally from Zamboanga, who might well have dreamed of an aristocrat with flashing green eyes but who had known that a hunched, rumpled middle-aged frequent flier was the best she could hope for. The nuptials had been celebrated in an airport chapel. Thereafter the two of them were flying the world together.

Mrs. Frequent Flier never complains. She sits beside her husband, whether in economy, business, or first class. She massages his swollen feet. She serves him his dinner, selecting choice morsels from the reheated airline tray. She talks when he wants to hear her voice, and listens when he wants to speak, and when he needs silence, she sits beside him, awake, gazing beyond him at the ailerons shifting on the wing.

One cannot help wondering what else the two of them get up to. It is late at night, on a redeye, and I am unable to sleep. Are they, at that very moment, side by side on some other jet, slumped and snoring in economy? Or are they crammed conjointly in the washroom? Or — give them the benefit of the doubt — they are in first, a blanket is draped over them, sweet romantic music is wafting from the headsets . . . their coupling might be lovelier than we'll ever know. Or, of course, in their time zone it might be midday. Wide-awake, he pages through the *Financial Times*. Her knitting needles click.

And it should be stressed that the wife is evanescent. In the majority of versions she does not exist, or is unmentioned at least. She is as noncanonical as Mrs. Noah. And when she does manifest herself, her ethnicity and appearance vary as much as his. In Abu Dhabi she is from Ghana. During the Kunming-Chiang Mai shuttle, she is Hmong. In Stockholm he has a gay partner (though given the appearance and mannerisms of the flight attendant who told me, I wouldn't put too much credence in that).

Just a few months ago, on Ryanair from Liverpool to Dublin (in retrospect, amazing this version had not turned up sooner), a sauntering copilot advised me that the frequent flier, a French-man, is a proud father. His German wife gave birth in the first-class washroom during the Rome-Tripoli run. The child, a healthy three-kilogram boy, was named Alitalia by the proud parents.

A legend is not a fixed thing. It evolves; it grows. Since then, I have heard several times that he and his wife have twins, a boy and a girl. (Always the child or children are described as babies, mind you. Impossible to imagine their adolescence; the myth would shatter.) Personally, I can swallow the wife but not the children; let's face it, a jetliner is no place to bring up a family; and if one uses proper precautions, it need never happen. And even the wife, she too may yet prove to be apocryphal, and fade out of the tale.

But here we come to the crux. Is this legend based on a true story? Several times I have questioned British Airways flight atten-dants during Heathrow-JFK — they declared no such traveler ex-isted on their airline, indeed the prize of a lifetime pass had never been offered. Of course this does not preclude the possibility they were mistaken, or lying, or that the frequent flier was in fact on a different airline. And the whole prize shenanigans might be a red herring anyway. There are versions with much circumstantial de-tail asserting the frequent flier is a millionaire eccentric, a retiree with an American Express platinum card and time on his hands. There are related versions in which he is doing it for a bet, or he has a moneyed backer, or he is obsessive-compulsively research-ing an article for a travel magazine, or he is an independently wealthy performance artist or freak or monk. Indeed, he would not need to be particularly well-funded. I performed a rough calcu-lation on the back of my Emirates Airlines in-flight magazine. Assume he restricts himself to the cheapest long-distance runs (London–New York, Hong Kong–Kuwait, and so forth). Assume he travels by night, and spends daytimes in transit lounges. Assume he buys his tickets through consolidators and "bucket shops" and quasilegal resellers of bump-tickets and unneeded mileage, via the Internet or in those markets where the vagaries of currency and airline pricing policies result in the cheapest possible rates (I could recommend Penang). If so, I guesstimate he could travel for as little as $170 per day, 365 days per year (366 in a leap year): call it $60,000 per annum. Granted, he would need to cover out-of-pocket expenses, and of course the total would be greater if he chose to fly by way of more exotic airports, say Ouagadougou or Aspen . . . but still, his outgoings would be no greater than those of a settled man with a house and a mortgage in any city in the developed world.

And what is his motive? Is he running away from something, or is he in search of it? Is he cursed or is he blessed? Will he ever find peace? There are those who say they have met him personally, though none has absolute proof. Once or a few times I think I might have glimpsed him myself — being turned away from the Royal Orchid lounge at Bangkok airport; asking the way to the Kansas City Terminal 2 Burger King in impeccable Spanish; running to make the connection at Keflavik . . . but I could tell you nothing that would convince a skeptic.

Yet I am sure he exists. I keep traveling from airplane to airplane, from airport to airport, from departures to arrivals to departures again . . . One day I shall find him.

■

Girls I Know

FROM *Epoch*

GINGER AND I CAREENED along Storrow Drive in her black Lexus, on our way to the Brighton Cryobank for Oncologic and Reproductive Donors. Ginger was a shitty driver in ways that I assume most spoiled rich girls are — blithe disregard for others' rights-of-way, refusal to slow down for pedestrians, etc. — but I can't be sure since Ginger is the only spoiled rich girl I've ever known. As she cut off a ComElectric truck I thought of Robert Lowell, the subject of my dissertation, and the time he had Jean Stafford in his father's car and ran into a wall, smashing her nose to bits. "There was about a 25 percent reduction in the aesthetic value of her face," Lowell's friend, Blair Clark, said. A short time later, Lowell asked Stafford to marry him. It was the honorable thing to do, marry the woman whose face he had ruined, and Lowell was nearing the height of his honorable phase, although I don't think he became a worse person necessarily as he grew older. The idea of virtue was always mesmerizing to him, only he could never live up to his ideals for very long. His life was filled with these bold gestures of magnanimity that were always, in the end, withdrawn — not out of insincerity as much as an insufficient attention span. The mania and mad delusions were symptoms, not causes, of his alternating embrace of piety and savageness, at least that's how I understood him back then. I don't think of Lowell that much now, at least not Lowell the person, although I still read his poems fairly regularly.

Shifting gears with her bare feet, her mouth filled with bubble gum, Ginger gave me a sidelong glance. "What you thinking over there, retard?" She dropped the second *r* out of the last word to imitate a Southie accent, which she did pretty well.

I told her about Lowell's car accident, how he lived — in part — off the royalties of Stafford's first book, *A Boston Adventure,* for several years before openly cheating on her with a visitor to their Maine home, prompting separation and then divorce. "If we got in a car wreck today and I fractured all my vertebrae," I cut to the point, "would you marry me?"

We had been hanging out a lot over the past month or so, ever since she had moved into my building at the end of May and mentioned casually — in response to the bewildering description I offered of my intellectual interests — that her grandfather had known Lowell at Harvard. They had played tennis together a few times, hung out some socially in the Yard, before Lowell decided to transfer to study with John Crowe Ransom and Allen Tate, first at Vanderbilt and then at Kenyon. That made Ginger, so knobby-kneed and awkward, suddenly shimmer in my eyes; she was two degrees separated from a major American poet, even if he had died right before she had been born. Growing up in Burlington, Vermont, the only people my childhood friends were two degrees separated from were French-Canadian prostitutes. So my motives for getting to know her were compromised from the beginning, but I don't fault myself for that. I came to Boston to enter Lowell's world as best I could and now — years after basically giving up on that enterprise — Ginger had fallen into my lap.

"I don't think I'd marry you," she said slowly as we rounded a corner, "but my family would help you out financially — you know, redo your kitchen so you could reach all the cabinets from your wheelchair."

"Well, that's definitely something."

She adjusted the volume of one of her Radiohead bootlegs via an inconspicuous button on her steering wheel. "You should be writing on Elizabeth Bishop anyway," she said. "She's the one who grew up with her grandparents, not Lowell."

Early on I had let slip that I had never known my father and that my mother had died of ovarian cancer when I was eleven. Ginger never let go of the information and tried to read it into everything I did, so if I nursed a cup of coffee, or that hideous green tea she was continually brewing, and claimed it was because the beverage was too hot to drink, she'd shake her head knowingly, tap me on the arm, and whisper, "Detachment anxiety." I had wanted her to see me as transcending my background, even if I didn't believe such a thing was possible. That was the problem with Bishop: Writing about someone who came from nowhere, or someplace even farther away than nowhere, Nova Scotia, would have just taken me back again and again to the clapboard house of my grandparents: the three of us playing Parcheesi while a PBS show on the National Park Service droned on in the background and Easter bread baked in the kitchen. So I tried to ignore her poems altogether, even though they spoke to me keenly.

"But I like the Brahmins," I replied that day, using the same hollow justification I always did. "I like their self-indulgence. Bishop, Stevens, Williams, they're all too sincere."

"You're a retard, Walt. Wallace Stevens kicks Lowell's ass, and he was an insurance lawyer. An insurance lawyer! No, Lowell knew he sucked; that's why, when he rewrote his poems, he tried to ruin them."

She baited me like this all the time, which I secretly loved. My retorts were invariably pathetic, though. "His genius was self-consuming . . ." I mumbled.

Every other Wednesday was my drop day at the sperm bank. If I could persuade her, Ginger would give me a ride, and sometimes after I was done we'd spend the day together, either driving around Boston or trading Lowell lines back and forth over gin gimlets at her place. If she weren't around, I'd take the T out to Brighton by myself, do my drop, then come home and try to work on the dissertation. The premise of "Robert Lowell and the Poetics of Yankee Peerage" was, I had realized with some shame two years before, pathetically simple: Lowell's poetry was shaped by where he chose to live and who his parents were. Although I had been in graduate school in the English Department at BU for seven years, I had yet to complete a draft of my introduction, not to mention any of the other chapters. The project had long since lost the interest of my advisor, and the poetry world as well seemed to have lost interest in Lowell, although every thin volume of autobiographical lyrics published still owed its shape — I was convinced — to *Life Studies*, published in 1959. Outside of Boston, I learned second-hand from the few graduates of our program who had managed to secure assistant professorships, Lowell was thought to be unteachable. No one cared about the old South Boston Aquarium anymore, and Lowell's pedigree made him deeply suspect in curricula shaped by identity politics — even if he had stood as a conscientious objector to World War II, was in and out of mental wards his entire adult life, and traveled with Eugene McCarthy in his hopeless bid for the Democratic Party's presidential nomination. He had also broken Stafford's nose not just once, in their car accident, but also another time with his bare hand, versified excerpts from the letters of his second wife without her permission, even drowned three kittens given to him by a friend, although this last damning bit of information was never fully substantiated. Ginger was right; Bishop had become the preeminent poet of her generation, if posthumously, which meant that even while I had picked the right city in which to study poetry, I had also managed to pick the wrong poet.

There were faster ways to Brighton than Storrow Drive but that was the route we'd always take. It gave Ginger the opportunity to identify her Harvard classmates to me as they jogged along the Charles, the ones who had opted to spend the summer in Boston, taking over spacious apartments like the one she had sublet on the top floor of the building where I was the super. I'd ask endless questions about her acquaintances and she'd answer as many as she could, knowing how much I hungered for telling details: "Her dad invented antidepressants," she'd say, or "He's in line for the Dutch throne." Half the time she was probably lying but I gobbled up the morsels she threw my way regardless. It was harder to get Ginger to talk about her own life, but the pace she kept revealed a

lot. She was always having to rush to New York for a family obligation, or drive to Mattapoisett for some aunt's anniversary. When
she wasn't on the move she'd complain to me about what a boring
and dreary summer she was having and how much nicer it would
be to have no such encumbrances. "To have nothing to do but
masturbate for money and read poetry," she'd say. "That sounds
awesome." She never figured out, or at least never acknowledged,
how absolutely broke I was, but that was probably just her trying
to go easy on me. I so wanted her to see me as viable in some way,
even though I was eleven years her senior and half her intelligence.

We turned onto Commonwealth Avenue, drove past those beautiful homes that poke out behind arbors, brick walls, and elm
trees, then merged onto North Beacon. I can't remember when
I've been happier than right then: in that beautiful car, angst rock
blaring on the speakers. Since taking a year off from school to
write *Girls I Know*, the book for which she would receive a six-fig-
ure advance at the end of that summer, Ginger hasn't phoned me
once. That's my fault, though, not hers, which is the odd thing: My
self-pity crested that summer but I was the one, at the end of the
day, who was bent on hurting others. It serves me right that now I
orbit around those images I have of Ginger's self-conscious, en-
dearing beauty, or recall the clever phrases she'd coin without any
effort, all while I labored to be witty and edgy in her presence.
How odd to think that it was me standing on the precipice that
summer even as I did nothing. How odd that the inaugural moment for *Girls I Know* would mark my own entry into that unap-
preciated demographic of single men who — rather than be invited to the Cape with the young families squirting up like daisies
all around — are instead pent in glass and sent floating through
Boston to gaze all too surreptitiously on the unknowable gaggles
of the city's borrowed beauties.

"What's it like, collecting jiz all day?" Ginger had produced a
small, leather-bound notebook I had never seen before from her
oversized straw bag while I signed in at the cryobank. The heavy-

set black nurse shot Ginger a cold stare before affixing labels to a couple of sample jars and walking around the counter. They had started two-cupping me a few months before, when my sperm count began to drop. Now I had to separate the first shot, in which my sperm concentration was the greatest, from the second. It was not an easy maneuver, not that anyone ever asked.

The nurse led me down the hallway toward one of the small private rooms. "Think of me, darling," Ginger shouted as she began to thumb through a *McCall's* in the waiting room. The donor rooms were filled with porn, but the waiting room didn't push the envelope at all — just your typical pile of outdated magazines, a few condensed books, and some pamphlets on STDs and bulimia.

I never used any of the donor aids; the magazines smelled of unwashed men's hands, the videos were too long and involved, and the VCRs were typically broken anyway. I would think of the girl who worked at the convenience store across the street from our building, her pierced eyebrow, the apron she wore smeared with nacho cheese drippings, or that Israeli student I taught at BU a few years before with jet black hair and leather everything. I never thought of Ginger.

Just a few months ago, Irena, a woman I know who works at the Victor Hugo Bookshop on Newbury Street, asked about my sperm. I don't know how she had learned about me whoring my DNA, but I had seen her more than once in the back row at the Grolier poetry readings with a woman I assumed was her girlfriend and I figured my part-time job was gossip that had bubbled up at one point. I told her that I was flattered by her interest and she quickly corrected me. "I don't want your seed," she replied. "I just want to know your lot number." It turned out, she explained, that some of the banks had a reputation for lying about the characteristics and backgrounds of their donors. I was intrigued and gave her my information. A week later I saw her in the bookstore, perched back behind that enclosed counter they have, chopsticks sticking out of her hair. "They say you're a six-one Ivy Leaguer with blue eyes," she said. *Was there,* I thought, *nothing of me worth ad-*

vertising? "You should be thrilled," she went on, knowing — I inferred later — enough of my intellectual interests to see the irony of it all. "In twenty years, every adopted WASP in Boston will look like you."

After I finished my drop that day we got on the Turnpike and raced back into town. No more meandering along the Charles — Ginger was either in a hurry to catch the shuttle back to New York or just feeling antsy, I wasn't sure which.

"What's with the notebook?" Its corner had poked out of her straw purse, reminding me of its earlier appearance at the sperm bank.

"Idea I have," she shrugged, "for a book."

My eyebrows arched.

"It'll be called *Girls I Know* and will be comprised of interviews I'll do with women from all walks of life: secretaries, custodians, lawyers, strippers, women who collect ejaculates at sperm banks —"

"Is that a word, 'ejaculates'?"

"I think so."

I shifted in the leather seat. "Did she talk to you, that woman, after your line about jiz?"

"She warmed up to me when I told her about the book project. Women like it when other women write down what they say."

"Is that right." I was feeling crabby suddenly, I wasn't sure why.

"She says it's a good job. They have really great benefits. She said lots of times the men can't produce their first time in. Did you have any problems?"

"No." We drove by a group of daycare kids walking in twos, holding on to a rope. "When did we start treating our young like cattle?" I wondered aloud.

"We love our children too much," she said. "We gag them with the idea of childhood as idyllic. 'Hold on to this rope and you'll be just fine.' It's ridiculous."

I loved it when she generalized facilely from her Upper East Side upbringing. She pulled behind the building, into her reserved parking place, and we got out.

It was Ginger's book concept that had changed my mood; *Girls I Know* had begun to work on me, at first I wasn't sure why.

"How'd you come up with the idea for your book?" I asked.

"I want to write something without my own voice," she said. "I want to get out of myself."

"Don't we all," I replied, but I was kidding myself, I realize now. At the time I assumed that I was just as self-loathing as the next guy, or girl, but what I took to be self-evisceration back then was really just an artistic form of narcissism that characterized all the poems to which I found myself drawn. I was reading the same thing over and over again, and when I didn't find what I was looking for I projected it. Every poem was about the need to register one's self-disgust. Every poem was written with me in mind.

We walked into the building and she pushed the button for the elevator.

"Do you want to take a nap or something, after expending yourself?"

"No, I'm not tired."

We waited for the doors to open, then stepped inside the car. In her own at once vulnerable and sassy way, Ginger had been trying to seduce me for weeks, but I had resisted, mainly because I couldn't understand her attraction to me and thought — admittedly in a paranoid way — that if our bodies ever coupled she would never have anything to do with me again and I would lose my glimpse into American aristocracy once and for all. After rejecting her for the third time the week before, she had refrained from asking me up since, but that day I didn't really ask for an invitation; I just tagged along.

Although the apartment she was subletting from a family friend was a fully furnished two-bedroom, Ginger had pitched her camp in the living room. Her white futon was on the floor, her trunk open next to it, with expensive clothes piled around it, partially covering an enormous boom box and a bunch of worn paperbacks — books by Hans Küng, Sylvia Plath, and Cormac McCarthy. There were also snake droppings on the floor, left by her pet python, Sid, and the lingering odor of green curry, which she put in everything she cooked.

. We sat on the edge of the futon, our feet touching, and began to kiss. I placed my hand on her nub of a breast and she leaned back but I didn't follow her lead. She stared up at the ceiling for a moment, then asked if I wanted some warm tap water and walked into the kitchen. "'When you left,'" I called to her as she walked out, "'I thought of you each hour of the day.'" "'Each minute of the hour, each second of the minute,'" she hollered back. It was remarkable; after a single measly poetry survey course, Ginger had somehow managed to commit a whole pile of Lowell lines to memory. She came back in with Sid wrapped around her neck, having forgotten about the water. I was actually relieved to see the snake, hoping he'd give us something to talk about so that we wouldn't have to address why I was leading Ginger on and then pulling back.

"Look," she whispered to her pet, her fingers tickling his skin a few inches below his mouth, "it's the superintendent of the building, here to enforce the 'No Pets' rule and take you away." She held him out toward me.

"I, uh . . . that's OK." I didn't like to touch Sid; he scared the hell out of me. What's more, I knew — at the end of the summer — that I'd be the one scraping python shit off the floor. Ginger sat down a good three feet away from me, depositing her pet between us. He curled around her and slithered back into the kitchen.

I looked over at her, at her torn and patched denim cutoffs, the Green Day T-shirt off of which she had ripped the neckband. In a moment I was lost in one of those reveries that constantly sucked me in that summer: the two of us living in one of her family's seven vacation homes, dividend checks piled on Louis XIV dressers, my dog-eared copies of Lowell replaced with first editions. Through a staggering manipulation of connections, a professorship at Brown University had been secured for me. On the weekends we boated off Martha's Vineyard.

"I want a Twinkie," she said. I nodded my head eagerly. She grabbed her purse, and we left.

*

The first day of her residency in my building, just a few scant hours after she had revealed her connection to Lowell while supervising the professional movers she had hired to drive a barely filled van one-and-a-half miles from Harvard Square to the corner of Beacon and Mass Ave., I visited Ginger in her sublet. It had been my intention to leave her alone for a full day but I couldn't stop myself. In addition to her trunk, she had two enormous duffel bags, neither of which she would ever fully unpack, their unzipped tops disgorging clothes as if alive. In one of the bags, under a pair of silk pajamas, I thought I made out the hull of a vibrator. In another were piles of letters, bound with string, written — I would discover much later — by her grandmother, who, before dying of liver cancer, suffered from insomnia and wrote Ginger every night for three-and-a-half years, mostly to complain of the infidelities of her long-dead husband and rail against the inadequate disposal of our nation's spent nuclear reactor rods, apparently her one current-events obsession.

Ginger watched me look over her belongings without making small talk. I asked her about the classes she had taken the previous year. "I don't remember the course titles," she said, "just the stuff we read."

"Well," I tried again, "what did you read?"

"In one class we read Aquinas. I remember his ontological proof for the existence of God: 'But as soon as the signification of the name *God* is understood, it is at once seen that God exists. For by this name is signified that thing than which nothing greater can be conceived. But that which exists actually and mentally is greater than that which exists only mentally. Therefore, since as soon as the name *God* is understood it exists mentally, it also follows that it exists actually. Therefore the proposition *God exists* is self-evident.'"

"Do all of your friends have photographic memories?"

She wrinkled her mouth. "I don't know. I don't have friends. I have acquaintances, classmates, cousins." She sat down on the floor, having yet to unfurl her futon. "In another class we read Faulkner. All I remember is Cash's line about Darl at the very end of *As I Lay Dying*: 'This world is not his world; this life his life.'"

I just smiled. I had never read a word of Faulkner — still haven't.

"I read Roethke in the same class that had some Lowell in it. Do you know 'I Knew a Woman'? 'These old bones live to learn her wanton ways.'"

"'I measure time by how a body sways.'"

"I like his poems more than Lowell's."

"Roethke!"

She smiled with her head bent down so that her eyes had to roll up in their sockets to look at me.

"Did your grandfather," I figured it was fair game now, since she had mentioned him before, "did he by chance remain friends with Lowell after he left Harvard?" I was on the hunt for an unknown correspondence, perhaps a letter or two that hadn't been picked over by other scholars.

"Nope. Sorry." She noticed me looking down at her own collection of yellowing envelopes and added, "No one in my family ever wrote, or received a letter from, Lowell. I don't think Grandfather liked him very much — something about his temper."

"He didn't have his first manic attack," here I had the opportunity to defend the patrician poet against his patrician detractor and I took it up eagerly, "until he was about thirty-two. But he was violent, even as a child. He beat up kids all the time at St. Mark's, punched his father out. That's why everyone called him Cal, for Caliban, or Caligula."

She didn't try to reclaim the conversation; she just let me go on for a while. I peppered her with a sampling of my Lowell anecdotes: him climbing up on a statue naked while in Argentina during a breakdown, getting lost in Caroline Blackwood's mansion the night before he died, refusing President Lyndon Johnson's invitation to read at the White House. She seemed neither entirely interested in what I had to say nor altogether bored.

"Do you ever feel so cramped in your own skin," she asked when I had exhausted myself, "that you'd do anything to crawl out? Do you ever look in the mirror and just want to erase your face?"

I paused, not sure how to respond.

"I think it's a girl thing," she added, "wanting to make yourself disappear. Boys think of shooting people; girls think of starvation."

After eating Twinkies and drinking Mountain Dew at the convenience store across the street from our building, Ginger decided to begin her research for *Girls I Know* and I tagged along. We went to the Glass Slipper. It's nice, entering a strip club with a young girl. The enormous black bouncer gave me a knowing nod and we were quickly ushered to a choice booth right in front just as the next dancer came down the staircase and onto the stage. The DJ situated in a booth on our left began to spin some techno music, but the speakers were blown and the sound came out muffled. As my eyes adjusted to the half-light I noticed that the place was basically deserted. The stripper had on a business suit that was about two sizes too small and was holding a briefcase that she set down in the middle of the stage while looking menacingly at Ginger, her tongue heavy on her lower lip.

"Her tits are busting out," Ginger said. "I wish my tits busted out." She took out her notebook, looked around the place a little bit, then began to scribble furiously.

"It's the people who don't have any reason to give a shit that do things with their lives," I said, watching her write. "Why is that?"

She held up an index finger, finished her thought, then shut her book. "I don't know," she said in response, waving at one of the waitresses. "Maybe it's just easier than doing nothing."

I had been trying, roughly since Ginger was in middle school, to do something other than nothing, to get my Ph.D., and I wasn't finding it easy at all. A thin waitress in fishnet stockings and a strapless tanktop sauntered over. She had dirty black hair tied off in a ponytail, dark eye shadow, and lipstick.

"What can I get you?" Like everyone else in the place, she looked at Ginger, not me.

"I'm writing a book about women," Ginger said, sliding over toward me and nodding at the space next to her. "Tell me your story."

The woman looked over her shoulder, then over at me. "You want something to drink?"

"Bud."

She nodded and looked at Ginger, who ordered a gin gimlet.

When the waitress walked away I knocked Ginger with my elbow to tease her about being shut down but she ignored me. On stage, the stripper had opened her briefcase and taken out an enormous dildo that she waved at us like a handgun. Ginger pointed up at the ceiling, where there were mirrors I hadn't noticed. The dancer walked up the stairs, then came back down minus the suit and dildo, in a black teddy. She put her arms around the pole in the middle of the stage and began to buck and twist, the lingerie slipping to the ground. Looking at the woman's back as it was reflected off the mirrors behind the stage, I noticed a purple stain on her skin.

"Birthmark?" I asked Ginger.

"I'm thinking more burn than birth." She nodded her head authoritatively. We both looked at it for a few seconds. "It's shaped like Rhode Island," she added.

The waitress came back with our drinks. She asked me for nine dollars. I pointed at Ginger, who gave her twenty.

"So you're writing a book?"

Ginger nodded. "*Girls I Know.*"

"Sheila," the woman nodded at another waitress, "can you get a scotch and soda for the guy at eight?"

I couldn't see Sheila's reaction but I did watch as the waitress set her tray down on our table and squeezed in next to Ginger. After the stripper in front of us had crawled over to pick a twenty out of Ginger's hand with her mouth, she told us about her life.

"I ran away from home at thirteen," she began. "We were living with my mom's boyfriend in Rumford, Maine, a piece of shit town. I don't remember the guy's name. He had two kids. One of them was mental — really big and strong but would spit up his food and crap on himself. The other went to juvenile hall cuz he kept on trying to rape the girls in his homeroom. He was a year older than me.

"Mom was diabetic and didn't work. She got disability money because her left eye was no good. The guy she was with then was real fat. He didn't work neither. The two of them would sit around, drink, and watch TV. Whenever I was alone with him, he would smile at me in a fucked-up way. He never touched me, though. I heard them talking about it one night and my mom was like, 'If you want it so bad go give it a try, just don't hurt her,' so I left.

"It wasn't like I meant to run away for good. I was really just planning on walking around. I went into a grocery store and decided I was going to buy some cigarettes only I didn't have any money, so I swiped a pack and then out in the parking lot this guy came up to me and said he had seen what I had done with the Marlboro Lights and he was going to turn me in. I begged him not to, I actually thought he could get me into trouble, and he said he wouldn't but that I should get home and he'd give me a ride. So I got in his car with him.

"He took me to his house all the way up near Oquossoc, me screaming the whole way, pounding on the window. No one in any of the cars we passed looked over at us. When we got to his place he locked me in his basement. A couple times a day he'd give me food. There was a sink and shower down there. I'd go to the bathroom in the sink. A few days later he came downstairs with a mattress and another man. The man gave him money to rape me. I don't know how much. I found out later that the guy had taken out ads in porn magazines. 'Young Girl Who Likes Pain.' It took me a month of getting the shit raped out of me to figure out a way out of there. I ended up knocking the door down with a section of pipe when he was gone one day.

"I didn't feel like I could go home after that so I moved to Waterville, then Berlin, New Hampshire, then Manchester. I did tricks, worked in a convenience store for a while. I didn't look like I was thirteen no more. I got arrested for stuff, nothing serious, mostly just cuz I had nowhere to go. Then I started doing speed and LSD and other shit guys would give me to fuck them or suck them off. I'm eighteen now. I take Concord Trailways down from Manchester on Monday and waitress and dance here through Wednesday. I can't dance on the weekends because they say my tits aren't big enough and I can't afford no enlargements. So I work and buy my shit down here for the week. One of my girlfriends looks after my boy while I'm gone in exchange for speed. I had him two years ago, Jayce. I work down here so it won't ever get back to him, how I make money."

A guy sitting a few tables away gave her a wave and she stood up, picked up her tray, and went back to work. As she walked off, I couldn't bear to look at Ginger. She had started scribbling notes again and I didn't want her to read my face. I was thinking that she might end up with a pretty good book.

When we got outside, we found broken glass all over the sidewalk on the passenger side of the Lexus. Someone had taken a crowbar to her dashboard in an attempt to swipe her disc player but had only gotten it halfway out. "At least finish the job," she said, surveying the damage.

An older man walked out of an adult bookstore across the street. "Is that your car?" Ginger nodded. "The alarm's been howling for the last twenty minutes. It just stopped."

She looked at him. "That's what alarms do, they howl."

He walked away while I tried to use one of my Birkenstock clogs to brush the broken glass off the front seats. It didn't work too well. We got in and took off.

Ginger drove through the city streets just as she did on Storrow Drive, carelessly aggressive. It wasn't rush hour yet but there were lots of pedestrians walking around and I stared at them, wondering what they were thinking, how it must have felt to have to get dressed up every day for work — exhausting, but then again you've got money in the bank at the end of the month and that doesn't sound all bad. I glanced over and noticed she was smiling. Ginger had three kinds of smiles: There was one that wasn't really a smile but a smirk, which she used when needling me about Lowell, another one that was a smile on the outside only, eyes vacant, kind of a social mask she had probably developed just to simplify her family encounters. The third smile was a girlish grin; it was my favorite one — very rare, but also very sweet. That was the one I glimpsed for a moment right then.

"What?" I asked her.

She shook her head.

"No, what?"

She shrugged. "I can feel shards of glass in my ass."

"Me too." We laughed.

She turned onto Mass Ave. In a few minutes we'd be home. I'd be listening to the phone messages left by tenants who needed their toilets fixed; I'd be wondering how to avoid my dissertation on my own.

"'We're knotted together in innocence and guile,'" she said. She had settled on my favorite of all of Lowell's sonnets.

"'Yet we are not equal,'" I replied. I didn't say the rest of the line, not right then. We sat at a light that didn't want to change. Finally she turned to me.

"You know, Walt, it's not my fault that I have the background I do."

I was barely listening. The ingenuously simple premise of *Girls I Know* had reasserted itself in my mind and, horrifically, I found myself comparing it to my hieroglyphic of a dissertation, with envisioned chapters on Lowell and Boston infrastructure, the discernible metrical cadence of lithium, and an allegorical reading of "Sailing Home from Rapallo" as an anticolonial critique of French Symbolic Poetry. I thought of Ginger on the shuttle to New York, headed back for a weekend filled with parties, or having lunch with one of her professors at the Harvard Faculty Club, or just applying to Harvard in the first place. Had she even bothered to write a personal statement, or did people with last names like hers skip that step? And I thought of my grandfather up in Burlington, probably at that moment attempting once more to make it through some of Lowell's verse so that he could talk to me about my work, ask pertinent questions — try to be my father.

Now, in hindsight, I see it differently; I see, in her clumsy self-defense, one last attempt to reach out across the distance that I insisted existed between us, a distance made up of privilege and want that I felt — like some key to all mythologies — could explain every person or poem I encountered. Now I see her trying to become my friend.

"Yes it is," I said.

After reading poems from *Life Studies* that he sent her as he put the collection together, Elizabeth Bishop wrote Lowell a letter about what it felt like for her to see him write about his illustrious family. "I am green with envy of your kind of assurance," she said. "I feel that I could write in as much detail about my Uncle Artie, say — but what would be the significance? Nothing at all." She had an uncle, like everyone, but Lowell had something different, his genealogy. "All you have to do," she went on, "is put down the names!"

It has to be the most exasperated she ever sounded, at least on paper, but Bishop got over it; she continued to write her own kind of poems, and kept up her friendship with Lowell until the day he died. When he moved to England, Bishop took his place at Harvard, teaching poetry to kids like Ginger. He had so much acclaim in his life, she had some but not as much. When Lowell was playing as a boy on Revere Street in Boston, Bishop was up in Nova Scotia, watching her grandparents grow older still. Where is her bitterness? It must be somewhere in her work and yet I can't seem to find it. For a time she seemed to consider wrecking herself — becoming an alcoholic, writing nothing at all — but she didn't. She went on in her quiet, quizzical way. I don't see how she did it.

"I have lived without sense so long the loss no longer hurts." That's the next line in the sonnet Ginger started to speak in her car that day. Like I said, it's a great poem.

There were other days we spent together after that one but not many. Ginger began to avoid me. I, as a result, started to pine for her — copying poems and leaving them on her door, even assembling a pyramid of Twinkies on her welcome mat late one night. She didn't tell me about her advance until the day she moved out, when her parents sent up their driver to take her stuff not over the Harvard Bridge and back into Cambridge but rather down to New

York. "I'm going to write my book, I thought it might be easier in the city," she said with a shrug. I had to pry the monetary amount out of her by guessing incrementally larger dollar figures. When she pulled away it occurred to me that I had never seen Ginger with anyone other than me since I had met her — that maybe those acquaintances of hers that jogged every afternoon along the Charles were just that, acquaintances, and that her summer had probably been a lonely one, even with all the engagements.

In the past year I haven't gone anywhere; I'm still the super at the same building, although my dissertation has been re-designated in my mind as no longer stalled but abandoned. Generational shifts occur in Boston every four years; you last through one cycle of college students and suddenly you're on the inside of the outside, as close as you'll ever get to being *from* here, even if you grew up in a New England outpost, rooting for the Red Sox like everyone else. It's been almost a decade for me but I finally feel settled into life here, if in a permanently qualified way.

On the T yesterday I thought of those of us who migrated here for ridiculous reasons, because of a few lines of poetry, those of us whom the city has permitted to burrow into its hide even though we have nothing to offer, and I imagined, years down the road, when my artificially inseminated sons have grown into boys, stepping onto the Red Line and suddenly finding myself surrounded by my likenesses. They might be slightly different shades of me, maybe different features here and there, but I will recognize them as my own, all squeezed together for a chance stop or two, reading their library books or just gazing out the window, oblivious to the presence of their father, the man who provided them with their ghostly parentage: with the unknowable lines of a peculiar, faint family.

WILLIAM T. VOLLMANN

■

They Came Out Like Ants!

FROM *Harper's Magazine*

IT WAS ON GOOD FRIDAY NIGHT, at the threshold of that church on Avenida Reforma, in Mexicali, Mexico, with the Virgin of Guadalupe's image invisible overhead and the border wall faintly discernible, like a phosphorescent log in a dark forest, that I first met the sisters Hernández. When the loudspeaker sighed *María, la Madre de Jesús,* I thought they looked sincerely distressed, Susana in particular. The Crucifixion had just occurred again. When they mentioned Jesus, Mary, and Judas, they were speaking of people they knew intimately. Later our talk turned to Mexicali, and they began to tell me about the time of the great fire when all the Chinese who lived secretly and illegally under the ground came out "like ants," to escape the burning, and everybody was shocked at how many of them there were. Susana and Rebeca had not yet been born when that happened, but it remained as real to them as the betrayal of Christ. I couldn't decide whether to believe them. When was this great fire? They weren't sure. But they knew that Chinese — *many, many* Chinese, as they kept saying — used to hide in tunnels in Mexicali.

Chinese tunnels. Well, why shouldn't there be Chinese tunnels in Mexicali? I'd seen the Valley of the Queens in Egypt (dirt and gravel hills, sharp-edged rock shards, then caves); I'd convinced myself of the existence of Pompeii's Anfiteatro, which is mainly a collar of grass now, with a few concentric ribs of stone beneath. Havre, Montana, still maintains its underground quarter as a source of tourist revenue: Here's the bordello; there's the purple-glassed skylight; and don't forget to see the old black leather dentist drill, a foot drill, actually, which was operated by the patient! Why shouldn't there be more than sand beneath Mexicali?

José Lopez, a freelance tour guide with two blackened front teeth, told me that a year or two ago a friend of his had delivered a truckload of fresh fish from San Felipe up to a certain Chinese produce market in Mexicali. What was the address of this market? José couldn't say. It was surely somewhere in the Chinesca, the Chinatown. The merchant opened a door, and José's friend glimpsed a long dark tunnel walled with earth. What's that? he asked. You don't need to know, came the answer. José's understanding was that even now the Chinese didn't trust banks. They kept their money under the ground.

The owner of the Golden China Restaurant believed that there were four or five thousand Chinese in Mexicali. A certain Mr. Auyón, said to be a world-famous painter of horses, informed me that there were currently eight thousand Chinese, thirty-two thousand half-Chinese, and a hundred Chinese restaurants.

Most of the Chinese were legal now, but in the old days they'd come illegally from San Felipe, and then their relatives or Tong associates had concealed them in those tunnels, which, it was widely believed, still extended under "all downtown," and there was even supposed to be a passageway to Calexico, California, though none of the storytellers had seen it, and some allowed that it might have been discovered and sealed off decades ago by the Border Patrol. I've read that during Prohibition *in the Chinese district of Mexicali, tunnels led to opium dens and brothels, and for the convenience of bootleggers, one of them burrowed under the international line to Calexico,* which might have been that tunnel, or a precursor, under the cantina around the corner from the Hotel Malibu. Mexicans bought me drinks there and insisted that the tunnel still existed.

A tunnel under the Hotel Del Norte was discovered and closed in the 1980s; the Chinese didn't have anything to do with that one,

I'm told. In the autumn of 2003, people with guns and uniforms found another tunnel that began in a mechanic's shop east of the Chinesca and came up in Calexico — in a fireplace, I was told — but it wasn't a Chinese tunnel. A whore in the Hotel Altamirano said she knew for a fact that the Chinese had been behind that tunnel, because *they always work in secret.* Frank Waters recalls in his memoir of the days when the Colorado River still flowed to the sea that in 1925 Chinese were smuggled across the border *in crates of melons, disguised as old Mexican señoras, and even carried by plane from Laguna Salada.* Perhaps they traveled by tunnel as well. From the Chinatown in Mexicali to the one in Los Angeles, both of which have since burned. *They came out like ants!*

My own mental image of the tunnels grew strangely similar to those long aboveground arcades on both sides of the border; on certain very hot summer nights when I have been under a fever's sway, with sweat bursting out on the back of my neck and running down my sides, the archways have seemed endless; their sidewalks pulse red like some science fiction nightmare about plunging into the sun, and as I walk home out of Mexico, the drunken woman and the empty throne of the shoeshine man are but artifacts, lonely and sparse, within those immense corridors of night. I wander down below the street and up again for the border formalities, which pass like a dream, and suddenly I find myself in the continuation of those same arcades, which are quieter and cooler than their Mexican equivalents. Bereft of the sulfur-sweet stink of the feculent New River, which loops northwest as soon as it enters the United States, they extend block after block in the same late-night dream.

It seemed that everyone knew about these tunnels — everybody in Mexicali, that is. But when I crossed the border to inquire at the Pioneers Museum, two old white men who'd lived in Imperial County all their lives stared at me, not amused at all, and replied they'd never heard anything about any tunnels. Up in Brawley, Stella Mendoza, wife, mother, ex-director and continuing representative of her Imperial Irrigation District, passionate defender and lifelong resident of Mexican America, who spoke Spanish, traced back her ancestry to Sonora, and went to Mexicali "all the time," said that the tunnels were likewise news to her. But why should we Americans know anything about Chinese tunnels in Mexico?

Vampires and Cigarettes

The clandestine nature of the tunnels lent itself to supernatural evocations. About thirty years ago a rumor had settled on Mexicali that the Chinese were harboring a vampire down there. Later it came out that the creature was human but a "mutant," very hairy, two of whose lower teeth had grown like fangs right through the skin above his upper lip. He "escaped," said the woman who'd seen him, but the Chinese recaptured him, and that was the end of the story. I asked José Lopez whether he believed this tale, and he said, "Look. You have to keep an open mind. In the 1960s the Devil himself came to Mexicali. He actually killed a woman! Everybody knew it was the Devil. If you keep a closed mind, you can't believe it. But why not believe it?"

They live like cigarettes, said a Mexican journalist on a Sunday, cramming all his upright fingers together as if he'd shoved them into a box. He advised me to search for people who looked *like this* (pulling his eye corners upward), because only they could tell me everything. Although he'd never seen one, his sources inclined him to believe that there might be a tunnel under Condominios Montealbán, those ill-famed grimy concrete apartments beside the Río Nuevo, where tired women, some Chinese-looking, some not, complained about the illnesses of their children, and teenagers sat day after day in the shade of an old stone lion. It had been at Condominios Montealbán that a Mexican mother had compared her country and my country thus: "Here we're free. Over there they live like robots." We live like robots; Chinese lived like cigarettes. And they protected a vampire, and they *came out like ants.*

The people I met on the street didn't like the Chinese; nor, it seemed, did many of the intelligentsia, the journalists, or the archivists. A young boy I met, who had worked in a Chinese restaurant for five years, told me: "They come from far away from here, so their character is different from ours, and it's bad. They don't share." I asked him if he'd ever heard anything about tunnels? "Never," he said, "because these kinda people, they don't wanna talk to no one about their life." A white-haired, pleasant, round-faced lady named Lupita, who had once worked in the office of a semi company, had graduated to being a security guard in a prostitute discotheque, and now held afternoon duty as the moneytaker for a parking lot beside a shut-down supermarket, allowed that her favorite aspect of Mexicali was her friends, and her second favorite was the Chinese food. Would she consider marrying a Chinese? I inquired. "No! I'm not a racist, but no Chinese, no nigger!"

"Them Damned Nagurs"

Imperial, by which I mean not only the Imperial Valley but also that valley's continuation south of the border, is a boarded-up billiard arcade, white and tan; Imperial is Calexico's rows of palms, flat tan sand, oleanders, and squarish buildings, namely the Golden China Restaurant, Yum Yum Chinese Food, McDonald's, Mexican insurance; Imperial contains a photograph of a charred building and a heap of dirt: *Planta Despepitadora de Algodón "Chino-Mexicana."* Imperial is a map of the way to wealth, but the map has been sun-bleached back to blankness. Leave an opened newspaper outside for a month and step on it; the way it crumbles, that's Imperial. Imperial is a Mexicali wall at twilight: tan, crudely smoothed, and hot to the touch. Imperial is a siltscape so featureless that every little dip made by last century's flood gets a christening, even if the name is only X Wash. In spite of its wide, flat streets and buildings, Imperial is actually a mountain, Gold Mountain to be precise.

By 1849, word of the California gold rush had reached China. Mr. Chung Ming got rich right away. Hearing the news, his friend Cheong Yum rushed to California and achieved equal success. In 1852, 20,000 Chinese, mostly Cantonese,* made the journey to

---

* According to the owner of the Golden China Restaurant, in 2003 this was still the case, although a number of Mexicali's Chinese also came from Shanghai.

try their luck. A little more than a decade later, there were 12,000 of them digging, blasting, mortaring, and shoveling on the transcontinental railroad. *Wherever we put them we found them good,* reported a white magnate who happily paid them less than he did his Irishmen. The Irishmen noticed. One of them lamented: *Begad if it wasn't for them damned nagurs we would get $50 and not do half the work.*

"Chinamen" and Indians received preference for employment in the vineyards around Los Angeles, and in 1860 a contingent of white laborers gave up and departed for Texas. In 1876 a chronicle of Los Angeles reports this news: *City still rapidly improving. During June anti-Chinese meetings were the order of the day.* Those words were written a mere five years after the infamous Chinese Massacre.* In spite of the anti-Asian movement's best efforts, *An Illustrated History of Los Angeles County,* published in 1889, estimates that between two and three thousand Chinese walked the streets: *The Chinese are a prominent factor in the population of Los Angeles. . . . The Chinaman, as a rule, with occasional exceptions, is not desirable help in the household. On the ranch . . . he can be tolerated, when white men are not obtainable.*

Meanwhile, in 1898, the Britannica Company contracted with Mr. Ma You Yong to bring a thousand Chinese to Mexico for railroad work. A tunnel cave-in killed seventy-seven. And they kept right on, from Oaxaca all the way to Salinas Cruz and Jesús Carranza. Onlookers no doubt remarked that they live together like cigarettes. In the sixth year of their labors, Jack London published a bitterly logical little essay entitled "The Scab." *When a striker kills with a brick the man who has taken his place, he has no sense of wrong-doing . . . Behind every brick thrown by the striker is the*

---

* The way one county history tells it, two rival Chinese mobs fighting over a woman "on either side of Negro alley" began shooting at each other on 23 October 1871. On the following day, a policeman and two citizens who were doing what they could to bring peace got wounded in the crossfire; one citizen died. "The news of his death spread like wild-fire, and brought together a large crowd, composed principally of the lower class of Mexicans and the scum of the foreigners." The predictable result: lynchings, shootings, arson, pillaging. Nineteen Chinese were murdered. (Another source gives the casualty figure of a probably inflated seventy-two.)

selfish will "to live" of himself, and the slightly altruistic will "to live" of his family.

Under capitalism, continues London, we are all scabs, and we all hate scabs. But not everyone takes his reasoning that far. The Chinese coolie, whom London mentions in the same breath as the Caucasian professor who scabs by being meeker than his predecessor, was to haters of *damned nagurs* a dangerously particular case. You see, in California the Chinese do more than we, in exchange for less. In that case, we'd better make it hot for the Chinese. Hence anti-Chinese riots; hence the Chinese Exclusion Act of 1882 and its many descendants.

"The Scab" saw print the same year as Mexicali's founding. The Chinese were already there.

They Came for the Work

A soft-spoken old Chinese shoe-store owner at Altamirano and Juárez (who became less open with me once I started badgering him about tunnels) told me that his grandfather came in 1906 to pick cotton. He worked for an American company, but he couldn't remember the name. I suspect it was the Colorado River Land Company, which had already hired Mariano Ma. In later years he'd be seen at the racetrack with the governor of Baja California, but in 1903 he spent his days with Chang Peio and the other *braceros,* leveling roads, digging canals, all for a wage of fifty centavos (twenty-five additional for food); whether this was paid daily or weekly is not recorded. Señor Ma remarks: *In that place there were a lot of mosquitoes. Many people died on account of the various sicknesses caused by insect bites, rattlesnakes, and the intense heat. Some people were buried underground by quicksand and whirlwinds.*

The old Chinese-Mexican mestiza Carmen Jaham told it this way: *Mexicali began with about a hundred or a hundred and fifty Chinese.* And between 1902 and 1921, 40,000 or 50,000 Chinese came to Mexico. In 1913 there were a thousand in Mexicali alone. And they kept coming.

Steve Leung, the owner of a shop on Calle Altamirano, a middle-aged third-generation Chinese, told me that most of the Chinese workers who came here had been farmers. They saw the desert wasteland standing fallow and they cultivated it. Later, when the Mexicans started moving in, the Chinese ran grocery stores and laundries. They were successful with the groceries, but then the Mexicans started taking over that business, so the Chinese pulled back to restaurants. "Mexican people have not been able to take that over, since Chinese work longer hours," Mr. Leung said. "They don't fight with the local people; they let them come in; they just pull back."

And in my mind's eye, as Mr. Leung said this, I could see them pulling back into the tunnels. Whether or not his version of events correctly explains the facts, it certainly fits in with them, for the photo albums in the Archivo Histórico del Municipio de Mexicali do show an awful lot of Chinese grocery stores.

"A High-Pitched Voice Was Screaming Chinese Orders"

The historian Hubert H. Bancroft, whose many-volumed work on California is a monument nearly as eminent as the border wall, expresses his epoch when he tells us: *These people were truly, in every sense, aliens. The color of their skins, the repulsiveness of their features, their under-size of figure, their incomprehensible language, strange customs, and heathen religion . . . conspired to set them apart.*

In around 1905 we find Mr. Hutchins, the Chinese inspector, carrying out his task at Jacumba, *which is to allow no unentitled Mongolian to cross from Mexico into the United States.* When he catches them, they're jailed and tried.

In one of Zane Grey's novels, published in 1913, a rancher on the Arizona side of Sonora explains to a cowboy that *of course, my job is to keep tab on Chinese and Japs trying to get into the U.S. from Magdalena Bay.* (That same year, the Colorado River Land Company imports another five hundred Chinese into Mexico from Hong Kong.)

In 2003 the man in the *casa de cambio* on First Street assured me in a gleeful murmur that of course there were tunnels *every-where* in Calexico because if they started over *there* in Mexico then it stood to reason that they'd come up over *here*. He was Chinese. His building had three tunnel entrances, he said, but unfortunately he couldn't show them to me because they were closed. But he knew for a fact that the old building that now housed the Sam Ellis store had a tunnel. The kindly old proprietor of the latter establishment showed me photographs of the way the border used to be; he advised me to go to the Chamber of Commerce for an interpreter; as for the tunnels, every time I asked if I could just take a peek in his basement he didn't seem to hear me, but he did say: *You're never gonna find any of those tunnels.*

In 1925, Dashiell Hammett's crime story "Dead Yellow Women" envisions Chinese tunnels in San Francisco, all the while keeping faithful to the expectations of his public: *The passageway was solid and alive with stinking bodies. Hands and teeth began to take my clothes away from me . . . A high-pitched voice was screaming Chinese orders . . .* That was one passageway to alienness. In another, which the protagonist reached through a trap door, *the queen of something stood there! . . . A butterfly-shaped headdress decked with the loot of a dozen jewelry stores exaggerated her height.*

When Fu Manchu movies went out of fashion, new authentications of menacing alienness became available. Zulema Rashid, born in Calexico in 1945, remembers being scared every time she had to buy something in the Chinese store on Imperial Avenue *because the Chinese were Communists who tortured people.*

A fighting-cock breeder, from near San Luis Río de Colorado, told me during a match in Islas Agrarias that *of course the Chinese are all into slavery.* That was why one never saw any Chinese beggars. He got even more animated in the course of telling me that seven years ago the authorities had rounded up many illegal Chinese in Mexicali and sequestered them in a stadium under heavy guard, but some had mysteriously escaped, an occurrence that he considered both uncanny and hateful; he turned bitter when he mentioned it. He supposed that they had disappeared into one of their tunnels.

"A Raw Smell"

They came out of the ground like ants. So why shouldn't there be tunnels? They exist, asserted Beatriz Limón, who was a reporter for *La Crónica*. She, however, had never seen one. One of her colleagues had entered a tunnel with Chinese guides, but the smell had been too terrible for her — a *raw* smell, said Beatriz with distaste, a smell like sewage.

Oscar Sanchez from the Archivo Histórico looked up at me from behind his desk and said: "They are there. But I can tell you nothing concrete. Originally they were there for shelter from the heat, but then they started to install the casinos. Oh, but it is difficult. These people are very closed!"

Men said that there once had been tunnels beneath the dance hall Thirteen Negro, which was whitewashed over its ancientness and cracked through its whitewash, doing business on and on at the center of the brick-fringed archways of arcades, lord of not quite closed sidewalk gratings, with blackness beneath. Why wouldn't there be tunnels under the Thirteen Negro? And if they were there, why wouldn't they still be there? But the waiter denied it. What did his denial mean? I asked him how often he got Chinese customers and he said every night. I asked him if he could introduce me to a Chinese regular; maybe I could buy the man a drink. But the waiter said he didn't want any trouble.

The Tale of the Air Ducts

My next tactic was to bang on Mexicali's nearest prominently ideogrammed metal gate, and that is how, ushered down a tree-shaded walkway and into a courtyard, I had the inestimable pleasure of meeting Professor Eduardo Auyón Gerardo of the Chinese Association Chung Shan.

This *world-renowned painter, known especially for his paintings of horses and nude women,* had a Chinese mother and a Mexican father. In 1960, when he was thirteen years old, his father brought him to Mexicali to join his grandmother.

Mr. Auyón was not especially pleased to see me. He told me that I really should have made an appointment. In fact I'd banged on the gate two days ago and made an appointment through his nephew. This did not mollify the *world-renowned painter,* who sat unsmiling amidst his *sumi* paintings and brass lions. Well, to business: First he tried to sell me a gold-plated commemorative medallion, which he had designed. It was pretty but expensive. Then he offered me a dusty copy of his book, *El Dragón en el Desierto: Los Pioneros Chinos en Mexicali,* for the special price of thirty dollars. Comprehending that if I didn't buy something from him my interview would be terminated, I paid for *El Dragón en el Desierto,* after which he brightened slightly and began to relate snippets of Chinese-Mexican history.

I asked him if I could please meet a Chinese family.

It's very difficult, he explained, because my countrymen are not very communicative. But *El Dragón en el Desierto* does have ten chapters. You can read all about the Chinese in there. That was perfect. My research was now at an end. We agreed that if and only if I read his book thoroughly and maybe memorized it, then came back in a month, it was possible that he might have found a Chinese family to tell me something innocuous.

That point having been settled, I asked him about the Chinese tunnels. They don't exist, the world-renowned painter of horses assured me. The people couldn't survive in them if they did. They could not sleep. It would be too hot down there.

Just in case there were tunnels after all, Mr. Auyón, where do you think they might be?

That heat, the body cannot withstand it, he replied. In the nighttime one has to sleep. One has to live down there — that's why the snakes live underground — but in the summer it's too hot.

So there are no tunnels?

Every locality has tunnels like a house has a cellar. There are businesses that have two or three branches. They have cellars and connections. On Juárez at Reforma, one man has seven businesses. Underneath, it looks like another city.

Could I see one of those cellars? He didn't think that that was possible. Then, looking into my face, and this was the one moment when I felt that he was actually being genuine with me, he said: Do you want to know the history of Mexicali? *Every ten acres, one Chinese died.*

I'm sorry, I said. He looked at his watch. The world-renowned medallionist had an important appointment.

I asked him if he could show me one of the cellars that he'd mentioned. He took me into the Hotel Chinesca next door and past the fancy lobby into the open-air courtyard giving onto tiny double-bedded rooms, and from a chambermaid he got the key to the cellar, which looked and smelled like a cellar. There he pointed to a "communication" passage in the corner of the wall. It was small and square and had a screen over it; it was, he said, an air duct. Inside it I could see light and stoneworked walls. A small child could have hidden there. Triumphantly, Mr. Auyón declared: This is what they call a tunnel.

Under the Volleyball Court

So it went. I could tell you about my interview with the taxi driver who knew for a fact that a tunnel had once led from the Chinesca right across the border, but they closed it; or the tale of Leonardo, the "tour guide" from Tijuana who was down on his luck, so he followed me down the street at around midnight, trying to interest me in young girls. Did I want fifteen-year-olds? I did not. Well, then, he could get me twelve-year-olds. He could deliver them right to me if I went to the Hotel Mexico. He had a hatchet-shaped, smooth little face, and he was little and vicious. Since he could do anything (he'd already told me the story of how he'd obtained excellent false papers for *pollos* in T.J.), I told him to take me into the Chinese tunnels, about which he'd never heard. So he did research. It took him a day. He found me an underground casino that would be possible to visit before opening time, but I had to promise not to talk to anyone, and he couldn't guarantee that I could take photographs. When he saw that I really wanted to take photographs, he said that he could work it out. Leonardo was the man, all right. Why shouldn't it be true? There'd been gaming houses in Mexicali since 1909. He described so well how it would be that I could almost see it. Soon a note was waiting for me at the Hotel Chinesca: The tour would cost me fifty dollars, and I had to pay in advance. Leonardo went first to give the password; he'd be back in two minutes. I waited for him in the pitch-dark alley on the edge of the Río Nuevo; the moon resembled an orange darkly pitted by cyanide fumigation injury, and I waited and waited for admission to that splendid underground world that Leonardo had promised me.

To my rescue came Professor Yolanda Sánchez Ogás, lifelong resident of Mexicali (born in 1940), historian, anthropologist, and author of *Bajo el Sol de Mexicali* and *A La Orilla del Rio Colorado: Los Cucapá,* both of which she sold me out of the closet of her house. The first time I asked her about Chinese tunnels, she said that she didn't know anything about them but would find out. The next time I saw her she calmly said: I went into the tunnels. That entire area under La Chinesca has a subterranean level. As for the casino, I know there *was* one, but right now I don't think so. But under the volleyball court many *Chinos* live.

Have you seen them living there?

No, but I have heard. And I met an old man who lived all his life under Restaurant Ocho.

Rats and Cockroaches

Next morning in Callejón Chinesca the proprietors of the watch stores and clothing stores were already rolling up their gratings. We were looking for the Restaurant Jing Tung. Nobody in the street had ever heard of it. But that didn't mean it wasn't there. Yolanda led us to the Hotel Cecil, which I'm told was the labor of love of a Chinese named Cecil Chin. We went upstairs. Yolanda said that there had once been a tunnel with bars, casinos, and a restaurant.

This is all new, said the manager, gesturing around him. When they constructed this hotel in 1947, the tunnel was already there. There used to be an entrance on the first floor.

Can we go into the tunnel? I asked.

The manager wearily spread his hands. It's closed, he said. He didn't care to nourish any myths.

Across the street from the Cecil, in another roofed passageway called Pasajes Prendes, there was an ancient barbershop whose owner's white hair resembled his ribbed and whitewashed concrete ceiling, and he said: No, you walked in from the street, and the restaurant was on the left by the bar, and it had really big chairs and a piano, and there was a man who played the piano. They took the piano away many years ago. In the tunnel there was a store, and right here in front there was a butcher shop aboveground. The hotel was finished in April of '47, and there was nothing here before, he said, beaming through his round glasses. Oh, he was happy, smiling, talking about the past.

So what's in the tunnels now? I asked.

Pure trash.

His single customer, who was tub-shaped, chimed in: And rats!

Yolanda said nothing. I knew that she hated rats.

I went down there, said the customer, and it's all trash. Rats, cockroaches, because of the humidity . . .

A woman over here had a store, said the barber. There is still an entrance over there, and it's full of water. There was a cantina below. Cecil Chin owned the cantina. The whole building, there's tunnels all over the place. Anyone could go in. It was public property.

Were there casinos below?

No, there were never any casinos.

I thought there was a casino under the Callejón.

There could have been, said the barber happily. There was a barbershop, a shoe store, a bowling alley, pool tables . . .

I think there are some places where people get together to play cards, said Yolanda.

The tubby man, who was a foreman, shrugged and said: There are tunnels all through here, and also on Juárez and Reforma. It's like a labyrinth.

As the fan slowly rotated along the edge of the mirror, they talked happily about the old days *when they were all killing each other.*

Around '46 a lot of this was burned, said the barber. Slowly he reached up to turn on the auxiliary ceiling fan. The first of these buildings caught on fire, in '45 or '46, a lot of Chinese died. The second fire, nobody was inside. That was in '91. That second fire was so big that they came from Calexico and El Centro to put it out. And by the way, it seems to me that there used to be a tunnel under the Hotel Imperial. There used to be a cantina . . .

There still is, but not underneath, said the fat man.

Were there ever any opium dens? I asked.

The barber said: I worked in the Hotel Cecil for six years. I started in '49 as a waiter. Then I became a manager of the laundry department. When I was up there washing clothes, I saw the Chinese people smoking opium. There was a basketball court, and under there were six or seven Chinese men with a big pipe, passing it around. The pipe was as long as my arm!

Another old man had come in to get his hair cut, and he said: Yeah, I was there then, too. They were up all night smoking and gambling. They were playing *baraja* for a lot of money. That happened in the tunnels. I am seventy-six, and I was born here.

Were there prostitutes in the tunnels?

No, that was above.

Did anyone live in the tunnels?

Over in this part, in the Chinesca, sure.

Can we see the place where the water is? I asked.

A woman named Inocencia has the key. I never had the key.

We thanked the barber and wished him good business. As he was saying goodbye to us, he remarked, very sadly: There really aren't any businesses here anymore. It's all boutiques. All the Americans come here to buy medicines.

And I knew that he would have loved to go back in time, even just for a day, to wander in the tunnels when they were crammed with life, glamour, commerce, and vice.

My First Tunnel

Near the Hotel Capri there was a certain clothing business owned
by an elderly Mexican who knew Yolanda quite well. Behind the
counter, next to the water closet, there was a metal door, which the
man unlocked, inviting us into a concrete room, where clothes
hung on a line. The man lifted up a trapdoor, and I saw stairs.
Yolanda had her flashlight, and Terrie, my translator, was carrying
the other flashlight, which we had bought an hour earlier for just
this occasion. Smiling, the man stood aside.

Yolanda wanted me to go first, because she was afraid of the
rats, so I did, and she came after me into that sweltering darkness,
gamely half-smiling with her pale, sweat-drenched shirt unbuttoned almost to the breast and her head high and sweat shining on
her cheekbones and sparkling in her short gray hair and her kind
proud eyes alertly seeking just as the straight white beam of her
flashlight did, cutting through the darkness like a knife. Terrie's
flashlight was very steady. Where were we? The humidity was almost incredible. Dirt and darkness, flaring pillars composed my
immediate impression. Lumber heaps leaped up as pale as bone
piles under those twin beams of battery-powered light. I saw no
rats. How stifling it was! Graffiti'd beams ran overhead, higher
than I would have expected but still in arm's reach, and wire hangers with flaring underparts hung like the skeletal outlines of head-
less women. I glimpsed the folding X-frames of something, a table, and a metal wheel of protruding spokes. Beneath the heavy
rectangular archways, the tunnel went on and on. Quite evidently
it was much vaster than the store above it, even allowing for
the fact that everything is always larger in darkness. Somewhere
ahead of us, skeletal perspective-lines approached one another
palely within the ceiling darkness; the place where they lost themselves seemed to be a hundred feet away and was probably ten. I
thought I could see a squarish passage. The floor was littered with
trash and broken chairs and empty cardboard boxes. Here gaped
an open safe. I picked my way as carefully as I could; for all I
knew, ahead of me there might be an uncovered well that would

lead straight to death in cheesy black currents of the Río Nuevo, which, thank God, I couldn't smell at the moment. Yolanda and Terrie were out of sight; they were in other worlds; I could see only one or the other of their flashlight beams. I felt almost alone. Chamber after chamber went on, connected by squarish archways. A palish blotch on the black wall gazed at me; my mind was beginning its usual game of dreaming up faces. Drumming and music came down to me from somewhere up above. The old Mexican who owned the place had said that he thought there had been a casino down here, and when I heard that music I could almost imagine it.

It might well be that the quality of the tunnels that haunted so many of us was quite simply their *goneness*. When I imagine them, my ignorance allows them to be what they will. Before we knew how hot the surface of Venus is, we used to be able to write beautiful science fiction stories of swamps and green-skinned Venusians. I could almost see myself descending the stairs into this place in the years when the electric lights still worked. Sometime between the first and second fires it might have been perfect down here. Having smoked opium in Thailand, I could imagine that one of these chambers might have had mats on the floor where I could have lain, watching the opium smoke rise sweetly from my pipe between inhalations. And from Thailand I also remembered Chinese men in black trousers, shiny black shoes, and white dress shirts; at an open-to-the-street restaurant in Chinatown, with stainless-steel tables and white tile walls, we were all drinking delicious sweet chrysanthemum juice the color of urine, and the handsomest man of all leaned on his elbow and gazed dreamily over his crossed fingers. Was this how the Chinese would have dressed when they went underground to drink, gamble, and womanize in Mexicali? Or would they have possessed nothing but the rough cotton clothes of the *braceros*?

There might have been a piano player here as there had been at Cecil Chin's, and when he paused to take a drink of Mexicali Beer, I would have heard all around me the lovely bone-clicks of mah-jongg. One hot summer day in the Chinese city of Nan-ning, I wandered through a park of lotus leaves and exotic flowers to a pagoda where ancient women sat, drowsily, happily playing mah-jongg amidst the scent of flowers, and that excellent sound of clicking tiles enchanted me; I was far from home, but that long slow summer afternoon with the mah-jongg sounds brought me back to my own continent and specifically to Mexicali, whose summer tranquillity never ends.

I remember a lady who smiled when she was dancing naked, a sweet smile of black eyes and glowing white teeth; she seemed so hopeful, so enthusiastic, so "sincere," if that word makes any sense between two strangers, and she was smiling right at me! She held my hand; that's right, she held my hand all the way to the hotel; I kissed her plump red lips and sucked on them as much as I wanted; she kissed me back. *Caliente!* the men in the street said approvingly. Afterward we walked hand in hand back to the dance hall, and all the men applauded. She was Mexican, not Chinese, and the place where she'd rented me her illusion of love lay several blocks beyond the edge of the Chinesca; all the same, it was she whom I now thought of in that tunnel whose revelry had turned to lumber and broken chairs; those click-clacking mah-jongg tiles in Nan-ning, the laughter and preposterously exaggerated moans of that prostitute, the sensations of opium intoxication in Thailand — these were the buried treasures that my flashlight beam sought in the Chinese tunnels of Mexicali, my memories, my happy dissipations, let's say my youth. No wonder I'd wanted to believe Leonardo the "tour guide"! Waiting for nothing in the hot thick night, with the ducklike quacking of a radio coming from one of the tin walls of that alley, that evil sand-paved alley overlooking Condominios Montealbán, I was already a citizen of this darkness; I was a spider luxuriously centered in the silk web of my own fantasies.

The Tunnel Letters

Next came the Restaurant Victoria, a tranquil paradise of coolness and reliably bland food (the Dong Cheng was better) where the waitresses were the only ones who hurried; the customers, who were mostly Mexican, lived out the hours with their sombreros or baseball caps on, lingering over their rice; here I had tried and failed on several prior occasions to find out if there might be any tunnels in the neighborhood. But it was just as my father always said, *it's not what you know, it's who you know,* and I knew Yolanda, who happened to be here, and who knew Miguel, the Chinese owner, a slender youngish man with jet-black hair who'd come here from Canton two decades before. He led us through the restaurant — white ceiling, white incandescent lights, white tables, at one of which a fat old lady and a young girl, both Chinese, sat slowly eating while the television emitted music that was sad and dramatic and patriotically Mexican. The white walls gave way to pinkish bathroomlike tiles as we passed beneath the rapidly whirling white fans and admired from afar the Chinese-captioned painting of the red sun floating on a turquoise sea — and through the swinging doors he led us, straight into the kitchen, where the Mexican cook and the Chinese dishwasher goggled at us; turning right, we came into a long narrow courtyard and entered a detached two-story building with what appeared to be an ancestral shrine just within the entrance. To the right, next to a shopping cart full of stale burned bread and a hand mill to grind the bread to flour for gravy, wide stairs descended.

This tunnel was less dark, uncluttered, and more self-contained. Indeed, it disappointed me at first; it appeared to be little more than a concrete cellar. Then I noticed that a five-socketed chandelier crouched on the ceiling like a potbellied spider, four of its sockets encased in ornate floral doughnuts, the fifth a bare metal bell. The ceiling itself comprised fancy-edged blocks like parquet flooring. But some blocks were stained or charred and some were moldy and some were entirely missing, leaving rectangles of darkness peering down from behind the rafters. It was a wide chamber that could have held many people, especially if they'd lived together like cigarettes. What had they done here? Had they gambled or simply banqueted? Had this place been an opium den? A tub held old Chinese porcelain bowls with floral designs. Then there were several dark and empty side-chambers.

The Victoria was in Miguel's estimation sixty years old, maybe eighty. Since we were in the heart of the Chinesca, this tunnel would have possibly already been here but so what, and how could I possibly speculate anyhow? On my second visit to this tunnel I saw a few more traces of fire, and I also found what might or might not have been a trapdoor in the concrete floor of the first chamber; it would not budge. In the dark room beneath some beds was a stack of bedframes. *Muchas prostitutas!* suggested one of my guides.

At the extreme end of the farthest room, another passageway had been bricked up. I asked Miguel how much it would cost me to have that obstruction broken down and then sealed up again when I had seen whatever there was to see. Smiling, he replied that there was no need for that; all I had to do was ask the pastor of the Sinai Christian Center down the street to let me into *his* tunnel.

When we turned back to the middle chamber we saw a desk, and we approached it without any great expectations since it was not so many steps away from the entrance to this place; all we had to do was turn around and we could see the supernaturally bright daylight of Mexicali burning down into the stairwell. I remember that a spiderweb as wide as a hammock hung on the wall; I remember how dismally humid it was in that place; I could almost believe Mr. Auyón, who'd claimed that of course the Chinese never lived underground, because that would have been too uncomfortable. In other words, I couldn't help but assume this desk to be a counterpart of the first tunnel's Sentry model 1230 safe, which sat upon the skeleton of a table that might once have had a glass top, lording it over broken beams and pipe lengths. Dust and filth speckled the top of the safe; behind rose a partly charred concrete wall. The door gaped open. Inside was nothing but dirt.

But as it turned out, under the Restaurant Victoria, in that rolltop desk with a writing surface of wood slats now beginning to warp away from one another just enough to let the darkness in between them, lay a hoard of letters, some of them rat-gnawed, all of them smelly, moldy, and spiderwebbed. Yolanda Ogás was standing against the wall whose pale sea-waves of stains were as fanciful as the serpent plumes of painted Chinese dragons; Miguel bent over the desk, fingering the old letters that had been crammed into blackened drawers for who knows how long. The darkness was hot, wet, and slightly rotten. Then he rose and turned away with indifference.

Miguel was a nice man, and he gave me permission to borrow the letters. When I chatted with him upstairs, in the richly glowing shade of the Restaurant Victoria, looking out through the lingerie-translucent curtains and the double glass doors with the red ideograms on them, the white rectangles of the street walls, and dried-blood-colored gratings of other Chinese businesses, the world one-third occluded by angle-parked cars and trucks, I found that he didn't want to talk, because he'd been here for only twenty years, which, he reminded me, *wasn't long enough to voice an opinion.* He referred us to the Chinese Association. There were actually either twenty-six or twenty-eight of those, but he meant the Chinese Association whose head was a certain Mr. Auyón.

The tunnel letters brought to life the time when there was light in the partly stripped chandelier, when that ceiling whose fanciness has long since been gutted into occasional waffle-pits of darkness was still whole, when the stacked tables were still laid out for reading, drinking, arguing, and gambling, a time before the walls were stained and the ceiling squares dangled down like laundry on the line. Here is one, an undated message from a wife in China to her husband in Mexico; perhaps he brought it downstairs to ask his Tong brothers what he could possibly do:

> *Everything goes well at home, except that my father-in-law cannot understand why there is no letter from you. Father-in-law questioned money sent via Hong Kong via Rong-Shi, and Rong-Shi denied receiving money. We borrowed money from neighbors. Father-in-law is not in good health. Please send money home. Also, when you send money home, do not send money via Rong-Shi, but addressed to . . .*

> *Thinking of you. The way I miss you is heavy and long; however, the paper is too short to carry the feelings.*

Days of Ivory

I've never really heard about the tunnels. The tunnels don't exist.
Meanwhile, I kept going into tunnels. Half a dozen times I had the
experience of descending below a Mexican-owned boutique or
pharmacy, asking the owner where another tunnel might be, getting referred to this or that shop a door or three away, going to this
or that shop's proprietor, and being told: There are no tunnels
here. Sometimes they'd say: There is a tunnel but I don't have a
key. The boss has the key. How long are you here until? Tuesday?
Well, the boss will be in San Diego until Tuesday. One lady assured me that the tunnels were a myth; another said that her establishment's tunnel was being rented out as a storage space and
she didn't have the key; a third, who'd operated her business in the
Chinesca for twenty-two years, assured me that there had never
been any tunnels in the Chinesca. Of course, with every passing
year the tunnels did come that much closer to a state of nonexis-
tence. Restaurant Nineteen, one of the oldest in Mexicali, was
abandoned half a decade ago and in the early summer of 2003
had already been for three months reincarnated as a pool hall,
with blue-felted billiard tables imported from Belgium. The Mexican owner, who wore blue to match his tables, was actually less
interested in billiards than in carambola, which employs only
three balls. He'd bought the building outright from the Chinese.
He'd remodeled extensively and knew that there had never been
any tunnels. I asked if I could visit his basement, but he didn't
hear me. I asked again but he still didn't hear me. Yolanda Ogás,
Beatriz Limón, and José Lopez from Jalisco were there; we each
ordered a Clamato juice with real clams in it, and when he
brought me the bill (I was the gringo; I always paid) it came to
thirty-five dollars. He had one young Chinese customer who came
to play; perhaps through him I could reach his father. The big fire?
Yes, everyone still talked about that. He believed that it had happened in 1985; that had been when *those Chinese came running
everywhere;* he didn't know where they'd run from. He couldn't care
less about the past, except in one respect: he sighed for the days
when cue balls were still made out of real ivory.

Dear Ging Gei. In response to your letter, we understand your situation. I asked Bak Gei to go to Wong Gei for the money Bak Gei had asked for to lend his friend for medical bills since Wong Gei owes your brother Bak Sei money. If you do not know who Wong Gei is, please go to Chung Wei for further clarification. — 1924

Creation Myths

Do you want to know how they started? Clare Ng told me how she and her daughter Ros went down to Condominios Montealbán as I had asked them to do, trying to find tunnels or at least to ask about tunnels, and she told it like this: *It was nighttime, and it was that big apartment down there, and we saw some Chinese woman who was fetching water for the vegetables down there, and in the beginning she was scared to talk. The husband has been there for ten years and she has been there only for three years. I asked how do you like it, and she said just since my husband is here I like it; that is the only reason. The daughter does not speak Spanish yet. So we were there, and they opened their hearts. They told us it was many many years ago, and too hot. These Chinese people cannot take the heat, so they decide to live underground in the tunnel. There was a big fire, and everything was burned. They don't live there anymore, but they still keep some things there. They say there's still a casino down there. Maybe it is kind of secret.*

That was one version. But since Chinese tunnels are involved, no version is definitive. When I asked Steve Leung where the tunnels had come from, he first advised me to meet a certain Professor Auyón, then, when I continued to question him, he said that "mainly they was made by the Mexicans, actually." The Mexicans had made the tunnels. Mr. Leung said the Mexicans had copied the Chinese, who dug tunnels to smuggle their people across the border, and made tunnels for smuggling drugs. Mr. Leung said that the Chinese at one time had casinos underground but that they were closed because of pressure from the Mexican government. *It is still a corrupt government, definitely, but it is more elegant now; it used to be you didn't need much connection as long as you got the money. Now you need the connection too.*

Women on Black Velvet

I remember tunnels that pretended to be cellars, and real cellars, and other tunnels of various sorts. I remember a plywood door partially ajar with two blood-dark ideograms painted on it, a hasp, a slender padlock. I remember cylindrical holes in the floor with locking hatch covers; these were the old Chinese safes. I remember how the palings of one tunnel wall resembled bamboo poles packed together, and around the top of them ran a stained metal collar. Then over a gap hung a torn ceiling, with strings and wires dangling down. The floor was a forest of paint buckets, toilets without tanks, cardboard, and upended chairs.

Late in the evening the sun caught the orangeness on the backward Restaurant Victoria lettering on the white window curtains, and the pleats of the curtains began sweating yellow and gold. A man on a crutch slowly hobbled out, and a boy held the door for him. For a long time I could see him creeping along outside, with backward Chinese lettering superimposed across his journey. The girls were already working across the street in the doorway of the Hotel Nuevo Pacifico; I counted six of them. Señor Daniel Avila, who'd worked at a certain supermarket for forty years and now owned a butcher shop, said that his son had once clerked at the Pacifico and that he had found tunnels but was never allowed to go inside them.

In your opinion, what is down there? I asked him.

He laughed and said: Secrets.

He took me down into his snow-white cellar tunnels, which had once been Chinese tunnels, and assured me that in a tunnel that had once connected with the tunnels under the supermarket and perhaps still did, there had been a cantina with paintings of naked women on black velvet; he knew for a fact that the paintings were still there, though he wasn't sure what condition they might be in. He was positive that the Chinese still lived underground just across the street. He couldn't say exactly where their tunnel was, because they entered at night *like rats*.

In that wonderfully Mexican way he had, he made everything

seem possible; any time now I was going to descend through the floor of a pharmacy or watch-repair store and hear piano music; I'd smell opium; I'd hear laughter and the click of mah-jongg tiles.

He knew a woman who trusted him and who could help me, but the next time I saw him he was more doubtful, and the time after that he was in a hurry to go to the cemetery for the Day of the Dead.

A Chinese Lived and Died Here

To the supermarket that Daniel Avila had mentioned there sometimes came a Mexican caretaker who requested that I not use his name. He had worked long and faithfully for the Chinese owner, who had recently died and whose memory he adored. The children did not care to operate it anymore, and goods sat decaying on the shelves. Really it was no supermarket anymore but the shell of a supermarket. His job was to air the place out. He proudly said: This is one of the first stores that the Chinese opened in Mexicali.

After some persuasion the Mexican took me inside and through the double red curtains to the back, past an elevator cage (one of the first elevators in Mexicali, he announced loyally), and then we went downstairs into a white corridor. He said to me: This passageway originally went all the way to the cathedral on Reforma.

Aboveground it would have been a good fifteen-minute walk to that cathedral.

With his hand on his hip, thinking for a while amidst the humming electric whine of the lights, he finally said that the last time any Chinese had lived down here was in 1975.

Why did they stay in the tunnels?

They didn't have their papers, so they hid here. Around 1970 was the big fire. A lot of them came out, *with long beards!* I saw them. All old people! Many went back to China.

He pointed down into a cylindrical hole like many that I had seen in other tunnels, and he said: The Chinese didn't keep their money in the bank but in the wall. Here you would have had a safe, but it is full of water.

The tunnel went on and on, wide and humid, with salt-white stains on the walls. Huge beams spanned the ceiling. It was very well made.

Pointing to a square tunnel that went upward into darkness, he said: An emergency exit. This is how they came out during the fire.

I asked him why robbers and gangsters didn't live down here. He said it was because Mexicans are kind of timid. They think there are ghosts here. I have been working with the Chinese since I was twenty-seven. Now I am sixty. I myself believe in ghosts.

We reentered one of the middle chambers. The floor was stained white. The Mexican said the Chinese had slept in rows on small wooden beds. I asked if I could see one of the tunnels where they slept. All that has disappeared, he said. Then he took me upstairs to the boss's office.

The fire started with a man who sold tamales, the Mexican was saying. It burned right down to here, and he pointed off the edge of the roof. This whole street was cantinas back in 1955. There was a lot of conflict, delinquency, prostitution. It was like an old cowboy town, he said longingly.

I asked him again to show me the cantina where the velvet paintings are. And so he took me to the street behind the supermarket, in an alley I should say, a narrow dark place that smelled of the Río Nuevo and of birds, and on the far side of this there was a wall in which was set a white grating; when the Mexican unlocked this, the recess within was square, and within that stood another door. He had to go back to the supermarket to find the right key ring for that one. Laughingly he said: The Chinese have a lot of doors and a lot of keys.

This was all a cantina, he added with a sudden sadness. Pedro Infante sang here. Like Frank Sinatra.

He unlocked the inner door and pulled it open, a task that took most of his strength. Here at street level ran a very dark high-ceilinged space that seemed to have been gutted or perhaps was never finished; there were many wooden pallets, and he explained that illegal things had been stored here. What kind of illegal things? I wanted to know. Oh, butter and rice, he said hastily.

Dark stairs led down into black water; that was the cantina where the black-velvet paintings were. He said that it would take three weeks to pump it out, and he wasn't sure about the price. Three weeks later I was back, and he said that the pump had broken; he stood frowning with folded arms and said that the old Chino who would have shown me more had refused; I could tell that he wanted me to go away and never come back. But that was three weeks later; right now we still had an everlasting friendship ahead of us, and so after the flashlight finished glimmering on the stinking black tunnel in the cantina of the velvet paintings, he took me up a crazy flight of wooden steps through the darkness to a concrete cell with three windows that looked down into that chamber of illegal butter and rice.

A Chinese lived and died here, he said.

There had been a stove, he told me, but the stove was gone. The dresser was still there. The bed was gone.

It was a ghastly, lonely place.

He was silent for a while. The place was so hot and humid that it was difficult to breathe. The Mexican said slowly: Our race is like Italians. We like to party. But they are very strange. Look down, and you can see that tunnel; it's full of water . . .

Where does it go?

They say that that one also goes to the cathedral, but I don't know.

We descended the stairs, happy to get out of that eerie place, and we went back out to the street, and he locked the inner door and the outer door. In the doorway of the abandoned supermarket he said: When I started working here, fifteen or twenty people lived below.

You mean, where you first took me?

Yes. They never left.

He pointed to another building and said: When the fire came, this is where the Chinese came out, the old ones with the beards . . .

Once Upon a Time in the Chinesca

Once upon a time in the Chinesca I peered in through the closed cracked window of the store that sold sombreros; there was supposed to be a tunnel underneath, but the owner had assured Yolanda and me that he'd never heard of anything like that. I looked in and everything was dim; how had I advanced my knowledge of tunnels? Now it was already six-thirty, and a few steps from me the fat lady was locking the white-painted, dirt-tinted gates of a roofed alley for the night. Sweet dreams to the store that sold communion dresses! A pleasant rest to the barbershop! There went the white number ninety-nine bus, crowded with standees; a man wheeled a dolly load of boxes down the gray sidewalk; a female radio voice was babbling cheerily from a store, and beneath that Mexican *carnicería,* which was very old, there presumably lay secrets dormant or active.

There was the old, low Restaurant Dong Cheng (Comida China Mexicana), where from time to time for half a dozen years now I've dropped in to get a beer or a half-order of fried rice, which was always as comfortingly large as a fat lady's breast. No matter how hungry I was, it was inexhaustible. Then a white fence stretched across a vacant lot, a palm tree behind; there was a parking lot, more Chinese restaurants, the Hotel Nuevo Pacifico, which is famed for its beautiful whores, many of whom are Chinese or half-Chinese; this was the Chinesca.

Once upon a time, in a certain street whose name I have already mentioned, not far from the sign where it said BILLARES and JAG-UAR and unsurprisingly near to the ironwork letters that spelled out CHEE HOW OAK TIN, there was a gate, and a Mexican woman pointed to it and said to me: All the Chinese go there.

Do you think I can go inside?

They won't let you.

Why?

She shrugged. Who knows? A lot of Chinese come out of there to work. At night they come back here. Everybody says they live underground.

We were nearly at the basketball court, which was also the volleyball court that Yolanda had told me was the place beneath which the Chinese supposedly lived.

Every day that I passed by, I glanced at the CHEE HOW OAK TIN gate, but it was always closed until one morning in November when it wasn't; nakedly interpreter-less, I went in, and there was a Mexican standing in the courtyard. I gave him twenty dollars and said to him: *Por favor, señor, dónde está un subterráneo?* He laughed at me. He could speak English perfectly well. He told me not to tell anyone his name or where the tunnel was, but he could let me know that it was less than three doors from there. And it wasn't even a real *subterráneo*, only a *sótano*, a cellar, on whose floor a man in a blanket was sleeping; he was old and Chinese and might have been drunk; he did have a beard, though not as long as in the Mexicans' stories; a bag of clothes lay beside him; perhaps I should have photographed him, but it didn't seem very nice to steal a picture of a sleeping man. It all happened in a moment. Now I knew at least that people still slept in the tunnels; the myths were true; there remained secrets and subterranean passages, just as there used to be once upon a time in the Chinesca.

The Red Handprints

Smiling a little grimly or more probably just anxiously, the Mexican girl held the candle jar out before her. From an oval decal on the side of this light, the Virgin of Guadalupe protected her. Although her family had owned the boutique overhead for several years, she had never dared to go down here, because of her fear of ghosts. Behind her, the other girl struck a match; a whitish-yellow glob of light suddenly hurt my eyes. I looked up and glimpsed a faraway ceiling's parallel beams, which might have been wood or concrete. Then the match went out. I went down and down. Suddenly the flashlight picked out something shiny-black: water. I thought then that it might be impossible to explore that tunnel, that the water might be ten feet deep or more. When I was in high school in Indiana, I'd once gone spelunking with some friends in a cave that required several hundred feet of belly-crawl with our noses almost in the mud and the backs of our heads grazing against rock; sometimes when it rained, fools like us were trapped and drowned. As I peered down into that Chinese tunnel, the feelings that I had had in that cave came back to me. And yet when I'd reached the bottom step and the flashlight split the darkness a trifle deeper, I could already see pale islands of dryness. Moreover, the floor appeared to be flat. So I stepped down into the wetness, and it came nowhere near the top of my shoe. Another step and another; that black water could have been a hundred miles deep the way it looked, but so far it wasn't. As always, my concern was that there might be a deep pit I couldn't see. I remembered helping a man from the Hudson's Bay Company drag a boat across weak sea-ice, which broke under me without warning; that was how I took my first swim in the Arctic Ocean. This memory proved as inapplicable as the first. With pettish, trifling steps I made my way, and presently so did the others. Soon the flashlight picked out the end of the pool; aside from a snake of darkness that narrowed and dwindled like the Colorado River, the rest of that tunnel was dry.

We were under Avenida Reforma. The two dark-haired *meji-canas* said they believed that Chinese had lived in this wide, high-ceilinged chamber. Always that pair stayed close together, often forming a right angle as they gazed or tried to gaze at something, usually close to the wall, whose blocks rewarded their candle's nourishment with paleness. Behind the stairs were three more huge rooms. At the end of the farthest, diagonal bars blocked us from the darkness's continuation.

The two *mejicanas* said that they thought this tunnel went all the way to the Restaurant Victoria, which would have been several city blocks from here. Shuffling with my careful old man's steps, I came across a mysterious square well of black water that might have been one foot deep or a hundred. Had I been a drainage engineer, I might have known what it was. Instead, I thought of Edgar Allan Poe.

The older girl, whose name was Karina, shyly said she'd heard that at one time people tried to kill the Chinese, so they came down here and hid. The other girl had already begun to feel nervous and declined to tell me her name.

Each concrete pillar in every niche had many shelves of dark spiderwebs. Receding rectangular arches of paleness made me feel as if I were inside some monster's rib cage. Perhaps everything was reinforced so well on account of earthquakes.

In the large chamber immediately under the stairs, we discovered an odd cabinet that was really a thick hollow wooden beam subdivided into shelves and compartments, with empty darkness above and below its dust — no, it actually had three sides, which went from floor to ceiling; it was simply that some of the back's slats had been pried off; on the back, in a niche whose ceiling was pegboard, someone had taped three pictures of space shuttles beside an image of the Virgin of Guadalupe, who presided with clasped hands and almost-closed eyes over the two plastic flowers that her admirer had also taped to that wall; and then below the cabinet the Chinese tunnel went on to its barren bricked-up end.

The nameless woman had already gone almost to the top of the stairs, and my flashlight caught the impossibly white cylinders of her ankles almost out of sight, while Karina, holding the candle, stood sideways on two steps, gazing at me with her dark eyes. Her wet sandal-prints on the stairs were almost as dark as her eyes. I remember her standing there and looking at me, looking at the darkness I remained in, and I will always wonder what she was thinking. Then she ascended the stairs and was gone.

I returned to that framework of bars from floor to ceiling; the tunnel kept going, but only rats and water could get through. Then I searched the niche behind the stairs.

On one whitewashed wall the flashlight suddenly picked out human handprints made in red; at first I thought it might be blood, but an experiment made with the rusty water on the floor proved that these handprints were part of a far less sinister game. Dashiell Hammett never wrote this.

The question of how vast the tunnels had been and still were preoccupied me. Old photographs seem to tell us how far they could have extended: In 1925, for instance, when Mexicali finally got its Chinese consulate, Avenida Reforma resembled a long, wide, well-ploughed field of dirt, with little square wooden houses going up behind a rail fence; Avenida Madero was much the same. How could there have been any subterranean passages here? But evidently these views must have been taken far from the heart of things, perhaps even as far as the future cathedral on Reforma; for here's a vista of the *edificio ubicado* on Reforma at Azueta *en zona "la chinesca," circa 1920:* A sign for the Mexicali Cabaret, pricked out in lightbulbs or wires, rises into the dirty-white sky above a two-story corner block of solid brick, fronted by squarish-arched arcades. Why wouldn't there have been Chinese tunnels there? Here's Chinese New Year, 1921: Two young boys, uniformed like soldiers or policemen, clasp hands atop a great float upon whose faded legend I can just barely make out the word CHINA; flowers, perhaps made of paper, bestrew the scene; behind them comes another float like a tall rectangular sail; an automobile's round blank eyes shine beneath it; a crowd of Chinese men and boys, their faces washed out by sun and time, gaze at us; everything is frozen, grainy, blurry, lost. Where are they? I don't know. And however many tunnels I ultimately entered, I would never be able to learn how many more remained. I tried to shine my feeble light as deep down into the past as I could, but I couldn't even see the bottom step of the tunnel's entrance.

LAUREN WEEDMAN

■

Diary of a Journal Reader

FROM *Swivel*

FRIDAY 9:05 A.M. I shaved my lady mustache (ladystache) off with my roommate's gay razor (it's a gay razor because it's his razor and he's gay) and now I have man-stubble on my upper lip. Then to make it just a tiny bit sexier I broke out where I shaved. So now I have an acne mustache. I should have left it alone. Like I do with the beard. The Korean ladies at the nail place were right. "You too much hair. You do mustache and arms and chin and back and neck. Please. Too much hair, lady-man."

Sunday 10:00 A.M. I keep telling my new sexy boyfriend how disgusting I feel. I give him all the reasons why. It's like when I used to stand and grab big handfuls of fat and show my ex-husband how gross I was. Then I'd cry and sob in the shower that I was too fat to live. I'd make jokes at parties about how I felt like a giant mattress that my ex would lie on. He'd just lie there on "mama" and I'd flip him over when he got tired of lying on his stomach. I'd also throw in a few jokes about trying to trick him into oral sex by pouring Jameson all over my crotch or getting a giant arrow tattooed on my stomach pointing down. Then we'd go home and I'd stand there — the monstrous mustachioed mattress — shaming him for not having sex with me.

I've learned some very hard lessons from the divorce. But I'm different now. I'm loving my new boyfriend, well. Better than I've ever loved someone before. I don't want to fuck this one up because he is the man of my dreams. I don't want to lose him.

Sunday 3:45 P.M. I read my new boyfriend's journal. He keeps this journal of fears and resentments that he writes in all the time. Whenever he grabs that gray notebook and stomps off to the couch I know that he's got some fears and resentments . . . perhaps about the joke I just made about being really good at blow jobs at the gym. I'm always telling him he doesn't get my sense of humor and he's always telling me it would help if my jokes were actually funny, not just ways of telling him how everyone — dogs, women, and children — wants to have sex with me the minute I'm not with him.

Anyway, all I had to do was look at his journal and I would get this huge adrenaline rush, because I was sure it was full of entries like "I have fear I'm gonna keep fucking that girl in my yoga class" or "I have fear that Lauren will keep getting fatter and I can't break up with her because she'll be devastated to learn that she really is too fat for me" or "I have fear that I'm dating Lauren because she is like a man and what I really want is a man."

I was on fire when I opened the journal, all shaky with reading something so personal. But it was a really good thing that I read it — there was something about his ex-girlfriend, and now I know not to fall too much in love with him. I know that he's still in love with someone else so I know not to trust him. That's good. Taking care of the old Laurita.

Monday 6:30 P.M. I have this technique where I'll confess to someone how horribly I'm acting and they laugh at what a mess I am and we shake our heads at my antics and it's OK — it becomes just a quirky story. So I told Gay Jon that I read J's journal and he was grossed out. He shamed me. He reminded me how I destroyed my last relationship. Then he berated his boyfriend for not caring enough about him to read his journals.

Wednesday 12:00 P.M. I've been taking hits off the journal. That fucking gray journal. My crack pipe. If I'm not feeling right or if I feel off, I open it up and read one quick thing and immediately I'm taken away. It alters me. I act like I suddenly have these amazing insights into him based on what I read in the journal. So, if I read "I have fear that I don't connect with Lauren very well," I wait a few minutes and then casually tell him, "I feel so connected to you." It's a dream come true: direct access to his thoughts. What he's really thinking. I know when he says, "You look nice tonight," I can run to the journal and read "I have fear that I keep trying to please women and tell them what they want to hear."

Friday 11:20 P.M. We were fighting about something tonight and while he was out of the room I grabbed the pipe for a quick hit. I was hoping to read what I sometimes find — a nice pick-me-up like "I have fear that I'm not worthy of Lauren." Or better yet, "I have fear that I love Lauren more than she loves me." Something that lets me know I have him right where I want him. But instead I read something like "I have fear that I will act on my sexual fantasy about. . . ." I tried to recover before he came in the room but I didn't have enough time. As soon as I saw him I said, "This is so fucking insane. I don't know how to love anyone. I can't do this."

Saturday 1:45 P.M. This morning he wrote, "I have fear that Lauren tries to create drama out of nothing." I keep waiting for the day it says, "I have fear that Lauren is reading my journal." I had a little plastic Barbie journal when I was in third grade where I'd write about what the cats did and what I ate that day. (Nothing has changed.) I remember finding "Jamie was here" written on one of the pages in my neighbor's scratchy handwriting. I was so mad I told his mother on him.

Maybe I should write "Hi, J" on one of the pages. Or "I have fear that Lauren is psychotic."

Sunday 3:00 P.M. Nobody is on your side when you tell them you've been reading your boyfriend's journal. I keep telling different people, hoping that I'll find the one person who will be casual about it. I should go to the prison and tell a child molester.

*

Tuesday 1:00 A.M. I told J I read his journal. It was hilarious! We laughed and laughed. He thought it was cute and grungy and sexy. And then we made love on the torn-out journal pages — the ones that read, "I have fear that I can't handle being in a relationship with Lauren." I wanted to make love on the "I have fear that Lauren is too needy" pages. But I wasn't really in a position to get demanding. Actually, I was so fucking scared. I figured it was the deal breaker.

Like when my ex-husband peed in the bed and I got so mad I slapped myself in the face. I thought it was going to be the deal breaker. Peeing in the bed is bad but he was drunk and asleep and dreaming about peeing into a toilet and the next thing he knew . . . But I was awake and sober when I hit myself. It was sexy when Betty Blue ran naked and crazy through the streets and poked her eyes out. But I'm not French. I'm a Hoosier. When Hoosiers hit themselves it looks trashy.

I am thrilled to report the reading of the journal was not a deal breaker. It turns out this boyfriend is not an easy one to shock. I thought about throwing in a quick upper cut to my chin and maybe shitting my pants just to prove I wasn't going to easily scare him away, but I didn't. He was more concerned about what I read. He wanted to make sure that I didn't have any unanswered questions or hidden resentments that were going to come out during some drunken Baja trip.

Wednesday 10:30 A.M. Now J has seen my "asshole" so to speak. In a fluorescent-lit room. I hate my real self being revealed. I like it better in the first few months of the relationship where I just lie. I never care where we go eat: "I don't care about that kinda stuff. Whatever you're into is fine." I'm just a giant yes-man. My ex-husband thought I loved video games, whiskey, hearing about his exes, and chewing tobacco.

And after I showed him my unbleached asshole (my friend Mary in New York called me one time to tell me that Lara Flynn Boyle bleached her asshole — lies), all he said was, "You know what, I appreciate you telling me so much because now I feel like you've set the bar for honesty. You telling me this means a lot to me. It makes me trust you more, believe it or not." I believe him.

Wednesday 10:45 A.M. But. What if he reads this and starts to wonder why I told him I only read his journal once? (When it fell off the bed in the earthquake. Open to a certain page. I didn't mean to read it but I was thrown from the bed and my face landed right on it. And in shaking my head side to side as I yelled, "No! No! Not J's private journal!" I accidentally moved my eyes across a few lines.) I'll just explain to him how I'm adopted and wasn't held for the first eight days of my life. And if that doesn't work, I'll tell him what I tell the ladies who wax my mustache: It's hormones.

CONTRIBUTORS' NOTES

Daniel Alarcón's fiction has been published in *The New Yorker, Virginia Quarterly, Glimmer Train*, and elsewhere. He is the recipient of a Whiting Foundation Award, and his first collection of stories, *War by Candlelight*, was published by HarperCollins in April 2005.

Jessica Anthony grew up in upstate New York. Her short fiction has appeared in *McSweeney's, CutBank, New American Writing, Mid-American Review, Painted Bride Quarterly*, and elsewhere. She won *McSweeney's* Amanda Davis Highwire Fiction Award, the Summer Literary Seminars fiction contest to St. Petersburg, Russia, and also appears this fall in *Best New American Voices 2006*. Recently she was awarded a residency at the Millay Colony in Austerlitz, New York, to complete her first novel.

Aimee Bender is the author of three books, the most recent being the story collection *Willful Creatures*. Her short fiction has been published in *Granta, GQ, Harper's Magazine, The Paris Review*, and other publications, and she teaches creative writing at USC.
   ▪ I made up this story based on a great painting called *Tiger Mending* by Amy Cutler, which shows pretty much exactly the scene in the story where they are mending the tigers. So that image is all hers. She paints wondrous, evocative images of women in unexpected places, sometimes with chairs on their heads.

Ryan Boudinot's story "The Littlest Hitler" appeared in *The Best American Nonrequired Reading 2003* and has since been picked up by *The Longwood Reader,* sixth edition, a college textbook. In other words, the story is now required reading. His work has also appeared in *Stumbling and Raging: More Politically Inspired Fiction, McSweeney's, Black Book, The Future Dictionary of America, Bullfight Review, Post Road, Hobart,* and elsewhere.

Dan Chaon lives and works in Cleveland. The selection included here is an early, alternative draft of a chapter that eventually became part of his novel, *You Remind Me of Me,* published by Ballantine Books in 2004.

Amber Dermont's work has most recently appeared in *The Georgia Review, The Gettysburg Review, Open City, Tin House,* and *Zoetrope: All-Story,* and has been anthologized in *Best New American Voices 2006.* She has served as the faculty fiction writer-in-residence at Rice University and is currently the James T. and Ella Rather Kirk Visiting Assistant Professor of Creative Writing at Agnes Scott College in Decatur, Georgia.

■ The best and worst thing about living in Texas is that you can hop in your Toyota Corolla, drive for twelve hours, and still be in Texas. During an endless road trip to the hill country, I made a detour to the LBJ Ranch to get my presidential fix. On my visit I noticed a mother and her adolescent son traveling together. The chubby teenaged boy wore a Bad Religion concert T-shirt, red, white, and blue Converse All-Stars, and a baseball cap with the letter *X* embroidered on the front. The mother ignored her son as he continuously hummed and waved a miniature American flag on a stick. Though he appears nowhere in the story, this strange child was my muse. While writing "Lyndon," I kept thinking about this boy and asking myself what it really means to be American, to be a part of a family that's no longer whole, and to have a deep appreciation for history at a time when history itself seems unable to justify its own historical importance.

Stephanie Dickinson has lived in Iowa, Texas, and Louisiana, and currently resides in New York City. Her fiction has appeared in *Cream City Review, Nimrod, Briar Cliff Review, Inkwell, Water Stone Review, Mudfish,* and *Feminist Studies,* among other publications. Along with Rob Cook, she coedits the literary journal *Skidrow Penthouse.* Her first novel, *Half Girl,* will be published this year by Spuyten Duyvil.

■ The story began as a series of lyrical images, a reaction to my studying the "Red Summer" of 1919, when a wave of lynching and race murders broke out in the United States. This bloodletting coming on the heels of WWI and the great influenza pandemic suggests that African Americans were made into sacrificial scapegoats. I assumed that most victims were male and in my first draft my protagonist was too.

Later, I visited the Without Sanctuary Web site where collector James Allen has gathered photographs of lynchings and found the 1911 sepia postcard of Laura Nelson hanging from a bridge. The sight of her and her bare feet and their utter vulnerability inspired me to write the story from Ciz's point of view. Although this seems to be the moment of the memoir, I believe in the revelatory power of fiction to recreate, to cross time and space and give voice to the silent.

A freelance journalist who was based in Baghdad from April 2003 through September 2004, **Tish Durkin** has written about Iraq for publications including *Rolling Stone, The Atlantic Monthly,* the *New York Observer,* and *National Journal.* Previously, she was an opinion columnist for *National Journal* and a political writer for the *New York Observer.* She now lives with her husband in Madrid, Spain.

Stephen Elliott is the author of four novels, including *Happy Baby,* and the political memoir *Looking Forward To It: Or How I Learned To Stop Worrying and Love the American Electoral Process.* He is also the editor of *Stumbling and Raging,* an anthology of politically inspired fiction benefiting progressive congressional candidates, to be released in January 2006.

Al Franken is an Emmy Award–winning television writer and producer, Grammy-winning comedian, radio host, and best-selling author of *Rush Limbaugh Is a Big Fat Idiot and Other Observations; Why Not Me?; Oh, the Things I Know!;* and *I'm Good Enough, I'm Smart Enough, and Doggone It, People Like Me!*

Jeff Gordinier has written for a variety of magazines, including *Details, Esquire, Entertainment Weekly,* and *Fortune.* Nobody is quite sure how to pronounce his last name.

Kate Krautkramer's work has appeared in *The Seattle Review, The High Plains Literary Review, The North American Review, Colorado Review, Fiction and Creative Nonfiction,* and *National Geographic.* Krautkramer's work has also been heard on National Public Radio's Morning Edition. She teaches writing at South Routt Elementary School in Yampa, Colorado.

▪ Because I was afraid I would remember nothing of my feelings in pregnancy, I had a great urgency to finish this piece before the child was born. There was almost righteous clarity for me while I was writing this piece, but it was coupled with the natural tenderness of pregnancy. People would ask what I was working on, and I would say, *Oh, you know, a little piece about gutting fish and childbirth and roadkill,* as if these topics naturally meshed for everyone.

Also this essay addresses probably my favorite problem in writing and in life — the issue of being a human being and also being an animal; sometimes those things seem the same and other times, usually because of culture, they are utterly incompatible.

Jhumpa Lahiri was born in London and grew up in Rhode Island. She graduated with a B.A. in English literature from Barnard College and an M.A. and Ph.D. from Boston University. Her debut collection, *Interpreter of Maladies,* received the Pulitzer Prize in 1999, and her latest novel, *The Namesake,* has been published to wide critical acclaim.

Rattawut Lapcharoensap earned an M.F.A. in creative writing from the University of Michigan, and his honors include the David TK Wong Fellowship, the Avery Jules Hopwood Award, and the Andrea Beauchamp Prize. His stories have appeared and are upcoming in *Granta, Glimmer Train, Zoetrope: All-Story,* and *Best New American Voices* 2006.

Molly McNett lives on a farm in Northern Illinois with her husband, son, daughter, and dog. Her stories have appeared in *The New England Review, Black Warrior Review, The Missouri Review,* and *Other Voices.*

Anders Nilsen is a curator and cook, and is the author of *Dogs and Water* (Drawn and Quarterly) and the series *Big Questions,* as well as a contributor to *Kramers Ergot* and *Mome.* He lives and works in Chicago, Illinois.

George Saunders is the author of two short-story collections (*Civilwarland in Bad Decline* and *Pastoralia*), a children's book (*The Very Persistent Gappers of Frip*), and a political fable (*The Brief and Frightening Reign of Phil*). His screenplay for *Civilwarland* is in development with Ben Stiller's company, Red Hour Films. Saunders teaches in the creative writing program at Syracuse University.

Joe Sayers is a cartoonist who lives and works in Berkeley, California. He started drawing comics when he was very young but stopped for nearly fifteen years while under the mistaken impression that there were more important things to do in life. Currently, he self-publishes mini-comics, paints, and draws a weekly comic strip called *Thingpart.*

J. David Stevens teaches creative writing at the University of Richmond in Virginia. His latest book, *The Death of the Short Story and Other Stories* (in which "The Joke" appears), recently won the Ohio State University Prize in Fiction and will be published in 2006. Because he has an irrational fear of never again publishing a story worth mentioning, he would like to take this chance to thank a few people for their ongoing contributions to his life and career: Janet, Lindsey, and Zachary; Mom, Dad, and Mark; Mike Czyzniejewski and all the folks at MAR; and fellow writer Gabriel Welsch, from whom he shamelessly stole the idea for the story anthologized here.

Jonathan Tel's stories have appeared in *Open City, Granta,* and *The New Yorker.* He is writing a novel. He is looking for an agent and publisher. He divides his time between New York, London, and Jerusalem. He flies frequently.

Douglas Trevor's fiction has appeared in *The Paris Review, Glimmer Train, The New England Review, Epoch, The Ontario Review,* and other publications. His first collection of short stories, *The Thin Tear in the Fabric of Space,* received the 2005 Iowa Short Fiction Award. He is currently at work on a novel set in Boston, and lives with his wife and son in Iowa City, where he is an associate professor of English at the University of Iowa.

William T. Vollmann's *Europe Central* was published by Viking in 2005. His newest books, *Poor People* and a work about the astronomer Copernicus, to be published by HarperCollins and Norton/James Atlas Books respectively, are forthcoming in 2006.

Lauren Weedman
- Note to readers:

I was careful to protect the identity of my boyfriend in this story — calling him "J" instead of "Jeff." Which is his actual name. I'm fairly certain that he won't mind that I just said his name. He's not home right now for me to ask him, so, I have to trust my instinct on this one. The same instinct that told me to stop reading his journal. And I would like to share that I have stopped. Not that anyone besides "J" (Jeff) would really care. Well, his family would care. And all my friends who don't trust me anymore. They might care.

I weaned myself off by reading a few of his e-mails — but they weren't that interesting. I get my fix these days by reading message boards that argue about how "lame all the VH1 comediennes are" and reading reviews of my plays. It's not the same — but it's all I have.

NOTABLE
NONREQUIRED READING
OF 2004

DAVID BARRINGER
  The Poll, *Hobart*
T. C. BOYLE
  Almost Shooting an Elephant, *Zoetrope*
AL BURIAN
  Burn Collector (zine)
BLAKE BUTLER
  Deposition of a Paperback Beating, *Pindeldyboz*
ROBERT OLEN BUTLER
  Severence, *Tin House*

LILLI CARRÉ
  Tales of Woodsman Pete (zine)
DANIEL CHAMBERLIN
  A Long, Slow and Grueling Thing, *Arthur*

RANDALL DEVALLANCE
  The, *eyeshot.net*
MARK DOWIE
  Gods and Monsters, *Mother Jones*

RANDA JARRAR
  You Are a Fourteen-year-old Arab Chick Who Just Moved to Texas,
    eyeshot.net

ARYN KYLE
  Company of Strangers, *Alaska Quarterly*

MICHAEL LARKIN
  From Shock and Awe to Shucks, *Kitchen Sink*
BIRGIT LARSSEN
  Red, *Harvard Review*

BRYAN MEALER
  In the Valley of the Gun, *Harper's Magazine*
JOE MENO
  A Trip to Greek Mythology Camp, *Gulf Coast Review*
KEVIN MOFFETT
  FunWorld, *The Believer*
RICK MOODY
  The Free Library, *Ploughshares*

ZADIE SMITH
  Hanwell in Hell, *The New Yorker*
ERIC SPITZNAGEL
  The Day the Aliens Brought Pancakes, *Monkeybicycle*

DEB OLIN UNFERTH
  Juan the Cell Phone Man, *Noon*

ROB WALKER
  The Hidden (in Plain Sight) Persuaders, *Times Magazine*
GREGORY WHITEHEAD
  On One Lost Hair, *Cabinet*

THE B·E·S·T AMERICAN SERIES®

THE BEST AMERICAN SHORT STORIES® 2005

Michael Chabon, guest editor, Katrina Kenison, series editor. "Story for story, readers can't beat the *Best American Short Stories* series" (*Chicago Tribune*). This year's most beloved short fiction anthology is edited by the Pulitzer Prize–winning novelist Michael Chabon and features stories by Tom Perrotta, Alice Munro, Edward P. Jones, Joyce Carol Oates, and Thomas McGuane, among others.

0-618-42705-8 PA $14.00 / 0-618-42349-4 CL $27.50

THE BEST AMERICAN ESSAYS® 2005

Susan Orlean, guest editor, Robert Atwan, series editor. Since 1986, *The Best American Essays* has gathered the best nonfiction writing of the year and established itself as the premier anthology of its kind. Edited by the best-selling writer Susan Orlean, this year's volume features writing by Roger Angell, Jonathan Franzen, David Sedaris, Andrea Barrett, and others.

0-618-35713-0 PA $14.00 / 0-618-35712-2 CL $27.50

THE BEST AMERICAN MYSTERY STORIES™ 2005

Joyce Carol Oates, guest editor, Otto Penzler, series editor. This perennially popular anthology is sure to appeal to crime fiction fans of every variety. This year's volume is edited by the National Book Award winner Joyce Carol Oates and offers stories by Scott Turow, Dennis Lehane, Louise Erdrich, George V. Higgins, and others.

0-618-51745-6 PA $14.00 / 0-618-51744-8 CL $27.50

THE BEST AMERICAN SPORTS WRITING™ 2005

Mike Lupica, guest editor, Glenn Stout, series editor. "An ongoing centerpiece for all sports collections" (*Booklist*), this series has garnered wide acclaim for its extraordinary sports writing and topnotch editors. Mike Lupica, the *New York Daily News* columnist and best-selling author, continues that tradition with pieces by Michael Lewis, Gary Smith, Bill Plaschke, Pat Jordan, L. Jon Wertheim, and others.

0-618-47020-4 PA $14.00 / 0-618-47019-0 CL $27.50

THE BEST AMERICAN TRAVEL WRITING 2005

Jamaica Kincaid, guest editor, Jason Wilson, series editor. Edited by the renowned novelist and travel writer Jamaica Kincaid, *The Best American Travel Writing 2005* captures the traveler's wandering spirit and ever-present quest for adventure. Giving new life to armchair journeys this year are Tom Bissell, Ian Frazier, Simon Winchester, John McPhee, and many others.

0-618-36952-X PA $14.00 / 0-618-36951-1 CL $27.50

THE B·E·S·T AMERICAN SERIES®

THE BEST AMERICAN SCIENCE AND NATURE WRITING 2005

Jonathan Weiner, guest editor, Tim Folger, series editor. This year's edition presents another "eclectic, provocative collection" (*Entertainment Weekly*). Edited by Jonathan Weiner, the author of *The Beak of the Finch* and *Time, Love, Memory*, it features work by Oliver Sacks, Natalie Angier, Malcolm Gladwell, Sherwin B. Nuland, and others.

0-618-27343-3 PA $14.00 / 0-618-27341-7 CL $27.50

THE BEST AMERICAN RECIPES 2005–2006

Edited by Fran McCullough and Molly Stevens. "Give this book to any cook who is looking for the newest, latest recipes and the stories behind them" (*Chicago Tribune*). Offering the very best of what America is cooking, as well as the latest trends, time-saving tips, and techniques, this year's edition includes a foreword by celebrated chef Mario Batali.

0-618-57478-6 CL $26.00

THE BEST AMERICAN NONREQUIRED READING 2005

Edited by Dave Eggers, Introduction by Beck. In this genre-busting volume, best-selling author Dave Eggers draws the finest, most interesting, and least expected fiction, nonfiction, humor, alternative comics, and more from publications large, small, and on-line. With an introduction by the Grammy Award–winning musician Beck, this year's volume features writing by Jhumpa Lahiri, George Saunders, Aimee Bender, Stephen Elliott, and others.

0-618-57048-9 PA $14.00 / 0-618-57047-0 CL $27.50

THE BEST AMERICAN SPIRITUAL WRITING 2005

Edited by Philip Zaleski, Introduction by Barry Lopez. Featuring an introduction by the National Book Award winner Barry Lopez, *The Best American Spiritual Writing 2005* brings the year's finest writing about faith and spirituality to all readers. This year's volume gathers pieces from diverse faiths and denominations and includes writing by Natalie Goldberg, Harvey Cox, W. S. Merwin, Patricia Hampl, and others.

0-618-58643-1 PA $14.00 / 0-618-58642-3 CL $27.50

HOUGHTON MIFFLIN COMPANY www.houghtonmifflinbooks.com